THE BRAID

READ WHAT THE CRITICS SAY ABOUT
IAN MACMILLAN

Village of a Million Spirits
"One of the best books of the year"

—*L.A. Times*

". . . a new benchmark in Holocaust literature"

—*Publishers Weekly*

". . . thoroughly convincing, ruthlessly absorbing...stands as a testament to the proposition that a well-chosen word is worth a thousand pictures"

—*Jerusalem Post*

"Incredibly powerful historical fiction"

—*Chicago Tribune*

"a shivery, heart-stunning piece of work"

—*Newsday*

"The impact of *Village of a Million Spirits* is so forceful that it negates the question such a fictionalization of the Holocaust raises: Why turn to art to dramatize an already intensely dramatic factual event? Eloquently, MacMillan shows that the truth we can absolutely, factually know . . . is not the whole story . . . to understand completely, we must go beyond all this to the rest of the story, to the truth . . . the only way to get at that truth is to imagine it. And the only way to imagine it is through art."

—*New York Times Book Review*

The Red Wind
"*Red Wind* is a saga in the very best sense of the word"

—*The Honolulu Advertiser*

Squid Eye
"Here's a book that brings you eye to eye with life in Hawai'i—not the flowery, painted-over stuff but the real nitty-gritty"

—*The Honolulu Advertiser*

OTHER BOOKS BY
IAN MACMILLAN

Light and Power
University of Missouri Press, 1980

Blakely's Ark
Berkeley/Putnam, 1981

Proud Monster
North Point Press, 1987

Orbit of Darkness
Harcourt, Brace, Jovanovich, 1991

Exiles from Time
Anoai Press, 1998

The Red Wind
Mutual Publishing, 1998

Village of a Million Spirits: A Novel of the Treblinka Uprising
Steerforth Press and Penguin Books, 2000

Squid Eye
Anoai Press, 1999

Ullambana
Anoai Press, 2002

STORIES IN COLLECTIONS

"The Red House," *Prize Stories: The O. Henry Awards*, 1997.
"from *Proud Monster*," *Best American Short Stories*, 1982.
"The Unknown Soldier Passes," *Pushcart Prize: Best of the Small Presses*, 1978-79.
"Sacrifice," *Best of TriQuarterly*, 1982.
"The Rock," *A Hawai'i Anthology*, 1997.
"Liar Liar," *The Quietest Singing*
(anthology of writing from Hawai'i, UH Press).

THE BRAID

Ian MacMillan

MUTUAL PUBLISHING

ISBN 1-56647-721-2

Library of Congress Catalog Card Number: 2005921843

Cover Design by Sachi Goodwin
Design by Emily R. Lee
Author photo by Susan Bates

First Printing May 2005
1 2 3 4 5 6 7 8 9

Mutual Publishing, LLC
1215 Center Street, Suite 210
Honolulu, Hawai'i 96816
Ph: 808-732-1709
Fax: 808-734-4094
email: mutual@mutualpublishing.com
www.mutualpublishing.com

Printed in Australia

For Susan, Julia and Ben, Laura and Rick

I

Leaning down into the odor of burning sap, he looked into the furnace firebox and blew on the embers until a weak, yellow flame licked up around a blackened piece of hemlock that he had once carved into the shape of a sitting figure, and then he felt the faint warmth radiating on his face. Never burn hemlock, he thought, it puts creosote in the chimney, but then you had to burn something. He stood up, briefly dizzy, and looked at a strip of dry duct tape hanging down under the faint, white stain of its own glue on the pipe. Back when it was below zero outside, he had burned gnarled blocks of wood that a couple of years earlier he had carved into the likenesses of turtles, crouching Indians, ducks, wild boars. This sitting figure was the last. Next would be the furniture, then maybe some books. Words would burn too, he thought, and then he cocked his ears, thinking he'd heard her call his name.

This was his plan: he would wait until his mother fell asleep and then walk the three or four miles to town to the 7-Eleven, and there he would try to negotiate with Phil Watson for a bottle, explaining in some credible way how he would pay him back. Or he could run in and steal a bottle, first maybe setting a fire in the dumpster behind the store with some newspaper. You'd be burning words too, he thought, and giggled at the idea. But they'd see him on the security videotape: Hey, that's that Branch kid.

He looked around in the gloom of the dirt-floored basement. Under the bulging stonewalls were chips of dry bark, and he had already burned the bigger ones and the old cow stanchion and a stall near the wide stairway that led out to the horizontal doors by the barn drive. That stall was last used probably fifty or seventy-five years ago, and the only person who might be angry about burning it would be his father, but he had been gone more than two months now and most likely would not be coming back.

His mother's condition had worsened, and he wondered if she would die while he was gone. He shook his head: No, you can't think that way. Just make sure to get the fire in the furnace banked up so she won't be cold. Lately, he'd had to drag a cart farther and farther away from the house to find wood. The chainsaw was broken, so he cut the wood with a bow saw. He burned rotted beech and maple leavings, dry branches from the trees they had cut last summer, and, after that, his carvings.

The angle of the light coming in through the little basement windows told him that it was around four, or four thirty, and the cup of scotch in the bottle in the kitchen was all that was left.

He blew on the fire, this time so long and hard that his head reeled with pressure and he felt his heartbeat in his eyes. He rose, putting his hand on the lukewarm furnace for support, and stepped through the dirt and woodchips to the window. He put his hand up into the weak light. Like every year for the past three years, everybody would think spring was just about here when they'd get another heavy snow.

The feeling of need agitated his flesh, and he hovered between bounding up the stairs to gulp the scotch down or studiously putting it off, saying to himself, you don't need that. They all said that he didn't need it, that someone his age should not be ruined by the abuse of this substance.

He went up the steep, worn steps and into the living room. Silhouetted in one of the windows was the small Christmas tree he had cut in December, brown now and skeletal, the balls on the branches glinting dully in the faint light. He stood on the faded Oriental rug and looked at the hallway that led to the kitchen, then at the little hallway at the front of the house that led to his mother's room.

"Adrian?" she called.

He went to her room, and smelled urine. His mother was sitting up, her hands folded on her stomach, her head a little to the side. She was too weak to hold it up very long. Her hair, black with strands of gray running through it, was draped over the pillow and on her shoulders. Despite the wan, bloodless look of her face, her skin was still dark, bluish half-circles under her eyes.

"Come sit here," she said.

He looked at the wooden chair next to the bed. "I gotta get wood," he said. "Gonna get cold tonight." He looked out the window. He could tell she wanted to have one of those warmhearted discussions about him, and he was through with them. "Half an hour of daylight left, so we gotta get wood."

"I remembered what I saw on TV," she said. "They said that dyslexics were tested with a special pair of glasses that . . ." She closed her eyes, appearing to doze off, and he was ready to go look for the wood when she whispered, "Don't leave."

He stood there. The sheets were dirty. The last time he had offered to wash them, she had said that they were fine the way they were. He understood that she was telling him that he would wash those sheets no more. We have to wash the sheets, he had said, and she had cried and told him again that they had taken everything inside her that had made her a woman. It had embarrassed him as it had embarrassed her, his helping her move up the bed and then wiping her and removing the dirty, sodden sheet, putting another one on, until they had run out of sheets and he'd tried washing them in the tub out back, holding his breath against the heavy, salty smell of urine and feces.

"Do you know how to braid hair?" she asked.

"No."

She began to cry. Not loud. It was only a change in expression, a movement in her chin, and she reached up and touched the corners of her eyes. "I'm not home," she said.

"Yes you are."

"Adrian," she said. She had slid down in the bed and now tried to pull herself up. He stepped to the bed and, holding his breath so that she would not smell the scotch on it, slid his hand behind the pillow and pushed her up, and then she slid her lower body up toward the head of the bed, supporting herself with her fists. The warm, heavy smell of the urine wafted up at him. She pulled the sheet up over her chest. He pulled the blanket over her lower body. "I want you to braid my hair," she said.

"Okay, so what do I do?" he asked, trying to control the irritation in his voice.

"Turn me a little so my back is to you."

Again, he slid his hand behind her back, and with his other hand held her by the bony elbow, and lifted. He was startled at how light she was, and easing her around so that the thick, black hair faced him, he thought, my God, how could she have lost that much weight?

"Separate it into three equal parts," she said.

Through the dirty pajama top, he could see that her shoulders were emaciated, and he couldn't figure out how he hadn't noticed it when he was helping her clean herself. Down below, her stomach and hips had seemed almost bloated, and he understood that the metastasized ovarian cancer had spread there, feeding on the rest of her body until she almost appeared skeletal.

"Light the lantern," she said.

He went to the lantern on the nightstand, pushed the lever that raised the glass chimney, and lit a match, the salty blast of sulfur briefly stinging his nose. He touched the flame to the wick, which shot up a smoky, trembling flame that went still when he lowered the chimney. A weak, orange light formed a vague circle around them, sending the rest of the room into a gloomy half-darkness. Had the electric company known of his mother's condition, he was sure they would have ignored the unpaid bill and turned the lights back on. But they didn't know. Nobody knew except the hospital people in Cooperstown, and they had done no more than send pamphlets on hospice care and bills that could never be paid. "Okay," he said, sitting down on the chair next to the bed. He picked up the heavy, black hair and worked his fingers through it, but it was tangled.

"Could you brush it first?" Her voice was soft and plaintive, as if they were involved in some strange, secret pleasure.

He grabbed the brush off the nightstand and began to pull it through her hair. "Careful," she said.

"Sorry." He placed his hand on the hard dome of her head and slowly pulled the brush down. Her hair was so long that he had to pull the brush away past his side.

She lurched forward a little, and her hand went to her stomach. "Oh," she said softly, and remained tense for five seconds. Then she relaxed, breathing deeply.

"Did you take a pill?" he asked.

"An hour ago. It's all right."

He picked up the brown bottle and saw six or seven inside. He had to get it refilled.

"Okay," he said, putting the bottle down on the little nightstand. "Three even parts." He tried separating the hair, but quickly became agitated. He couldn't stand it anymore. "Look, I gotta go to the outhouse a minute. I'll be right back."

He walked quickly through the living room and into the kitchen. Knowing she'd never get to the kitchen, he'd put the bottle right on the table, in plain sight. He unscrewed the aluminum cap and tipped the bottle up, allowing a good quantity of the scotch to fill his mouth. Then he held it there, savoring the vapor going up his nose, and swallowed. The hot liquid coursed down his throat, and within seconds a luscious, almost electric warmth spread throughout his body. He took a deep breath, and then blew it out. Leaning over the sink, he opened the tap and ran a stream of water into his mouth, which he swished around and spat out. When he straightened up and looked back at the table, squinting in the advancing darkness, he saw that the bottle was nearly empty. Against the counter was his rifle, an Enfield .303 his father had bought him when he was fourteen. He stared at it, at the familiar shape of the stock and the black, heavy steel of its works.

He went back to his mother's room. She was breathing deeply again. "You all right?" he asked, returning to the chair next to the bed.

"Yes."

He separated her hair into three equal parts. "I know how to do this," he said. "Over," and he pulled the left handful across, and passed the right handful under. "No," he said. "Wait, I got it." He passed the left handful over the middle section, and then grabbed the right one.

"I can smell it on your breath," she said.

"Smell what?" The heat raced into his face, but rather than feel ashamed he felt angry.

"Keep it tight," she said.

He pulled the sections a little tighter. Then he glanced at the hall. The little charge he had in him now wasn't enough. It was almost worse when you only had a little and wanted more, worse than not having any at all. By the time he was fifteen, he had discovered that it was best to have either a full load or none of it at all.

The braid looked good so far. He was seven twists down, and it was as thick as one of those ropes used to tie ships to docks. Thick as a baseball bat almost.

"I'm nineteen," he said. "I can have a nip now and then if I want. No big deal."

Holding her hair, he leaned around in the dim orange light to look at her. Her eyes were closed, the shadow of her profile projected on the wall sharp and stretched out, his own shadow above hers black and shroudlike, sweeping into the ceiling and resembling some high-shouldered bird of prey. Every movement he made was matched by the shadow in a sweeping exaggeration. He shuddered, thinking that most likely she would be dead one of these days, would disappear into some long sweeping oblivion where there was no thought or memory or pain. The strange ticklish sensation he had while imagining that oblivion, a comfortable suspension like near-sleep, a quiet breathless soaring dream, frightened him and at the same time haunted him with a strange, perverted attraction. The Enfield was leaning in the dark about thirty feet away. Others had their ways of doing it. He had his.

In the wind leaking into the house from outside, he smelled the flat, metallic odor of snow. Through the gray rectangles of the two windows facing north, he could see it flakes settling on the ground at a slight angle.

"I would like to know you're really all right," she said.

"I am," he said, crossing the sections of hair. Tightly braided, the foot-and-a-half length had an oily sheen in the light from the lantern. "I'm fine," he said.

"I want you to go back there."

With the bright, colorful lucidity of a movie, a picture formed in his mind: his father rising from a log and turning the chainsaw off, leaving the two of them standing in the hollow, ticking silence, the smell of exhaust and oil fading, the leaves above almost neon in their brightness, and the ground dappled with sunlight. "You'd look from somewhere and see the ocean," his father said, "and you knew that behind you was ocean too." He'd looked around at the trees and kicked at the pile of bright shavings sweeping down from the stump of the maple he had just cut down. "Them people don't even know it. She didn't even know it. Like I had to tell her, 'You know, the world is bigger than this,' but she'd get that goddam dopey happy look like she couldn't understand what bein' stuck on an island meant." He kicked again at the shavings. "Paradise," he said. "Fuck that. It ain't a place for people like us."

No. Adrian wasn't going anywhere. He would do what they had always done: cut pulpwood and pile it by the road for Jim Ainsley to come and collect. Barter with Ainsley as he had done a week ago: Pick me up a couple bottles too, okay, Jim?

"It really doesn't mean anything to me," he said. He leaned closer, holding the hair to the light. The three sections, braided together, had been reduced to the thickness of a broomstick.

She tensed again, moaned softly, her hand on her stomach, and then tipped back. He held her up with one hand, the three sections of hair gathered in the other.

He felt a long shudder in her back. Then she relaxed. "Oh," she said. "Oh my."

"You can turn and lie back down now," he said. "Do you want another pill?"

"After you finish."

He helped her slide over against the pillow.

"Just a couple more," he said.

She raised her pale, bony hand and waved it at the table. "Band," she said. "Rubber band."

He squinted. The thick, red rubber band was there by a pad and pen and two wadded-up tissues. He picked it up and looped it around the thin end of the braid until it was a hard knot; the little bits of hair at the end fanned out like a splayed paintbrush.

"You were born there," she said, taking the braid and holding it against her chest. "I want you to go."

"I will, I swear." But he'd already seen it. It was a quarter of the way around the world. He looked again at the hallway. "Wait," he said. "I'll get water."

He made his way to the kitchen, moving his feet slowly, his hands out to feel the walls, the doorframe. He didn't want to use the kerosene lamp in the kitchen yet. They had less than a gallon of fuel left. He slid his hand over the table until he felt the bottle, unscrewed the cap, feeling the familiar brittle grating of aluminum on glass, and brought the bottle to his lips, his hand shaking. The mouth of the bottle hit one of his lower teeth hard, and he ran his tongue over the tooth, the first one on the right side, and felt the sharp edge of a broken off corner. The piece of tooth was under his tongue, and he brought it up and spat it away, heard it ping off the stove. "Shit," he said. He drained the rest of the scotch, filling his cheeks till they ballooned, and then swallowed, waiting as the heat radiated outward. Then, his eyes adjusting to the dark so that he could see the white enameled stove and the bottle, he felt a familiar bleak devastation. Now he would have to go to the 7-Eleven. Or there was the other choice. It leaned against the counter, smelling of oil and spent gunpowder. Once, he had studied a picture of the human skull, cut away to expose the interior, and he speculated on what would happen if he put the muzzle in his mouth. The path the bullet would take would send it through what was called the medulla, shutting him off like a light. Quick and sure. If all that was ahead of you was a pointless silence, a condition of hopeless want, then this exit was a choice.

He went to the sink and filled a glass with water, swished some in his mouth and spat it out.

Running his tongue over the chipped tooth, he went to her room. She lay propped up, and the braid in a curve on her chest, the end of it in her hands. He tiptoed to the nightstand and placed the glass of water next to the pill bottle. Then he went to turn the lantern down.

"Leave it," she said and then pointed. Hanging on the wall across the room was the thin disk of a beech log he had cut when he was fifteen, the darker wood in the middle shaped like a butterfly, eyes and feelers and all. "I like to look at that," she said. "Why don't you make those anymore?"

"Kid stuff," he said. "No use in it."

She looked down at the braid, then at him. "You haven't seen the car?" she asked.

"No, he won't come back."

"I need to know that you don't have any plans to go to where he is. With those—"

"No, no chance. That white race stuff doesn't interest me. He's up there playin' guns with them, plannin' the revolution."

"And you didn't let him do that tattoo thing."

"No," Adrian said. His father had tried to convince him to get a swastika tattooed on his back. This'll show them where you're at, he had said. You're young enough that you'll go right up the ladder. But Adrian had conned him: Wouldn't it be better for me to have no tattoos so I can like hide my allegiance? You know, like a militia spy? Why tip your hand? And his father had thought this over and said, You're a smart boy—but for that readin' shit.

In his room upstairs there was a history textbook from eighth grade, one a teacher had told him he could keep. There were other textbooks too. He hated the word text, especially the sound of it. It was a four-letter word, vicious and brief, lethal in its sibilant directness. In that history book, on the first page of the chapter on Europe, there was a bloodstain. His father had said, Read those words, and he'd said, I can't, I tol' you. I look at the word, and something happens. I go blank. He could smell the anger in the room. Wait, he'd said, it says Europe! It says Europe! And his father had said, No, European, and grabbed the back of Adrian's head and slammed his face down on the page so hard that blood leaked from his nose. Read, goddammit, or I'll beat the shit outta you.

"Adrian, go to the kitchen," she said. "Take the lantern. In the cupboard by the sink, on the top shelf, there's a coffee can. I want you to get it."

He took the lantern and walked through the living room, the yellow light sweeping and dancing on the walls, the flame pulsing large and then small with his rhythm of his walking. He slid a chair over to the counter, set the lantern down, and got up on the chair. He felt cans, empty jars, and then the coffee can. Down in the lamplight, he opened it. Seeds, envelopes with pictures of corn and beans. He walked back into her room and set the lantern down. "Here it is," he said.

"Underneath," she said in a soft, hoarse voice, meaning that she had been crying.

He wormed his fingers past the seeds and felt a wad—money, he knew by the dense feel of it. He began to shake as he pulled it out, sending seed packets to the floor. "Ma?" He picked up the packets and stuffed them back in the can.

"It's eleven hundred dollars, mostly twenties," she said. "It took years."

"But Ma," he said. He stared at the wad of bills, a little piece of paper in it, bound in a red rubber band like the one on her braid.

"I'm not home," she said. "You can go for me." He made a calculation: fourteen dollars for the big bottle with the handle, three days' worth almost, times fifty-five twenties, plus six left over for each twenty making three hundred thirty dollars, which bought another twenty-three bottles for a total of seventy-eight. Two hundred thirty-four days: two-thirds of a year's worth.

"I wanted to take you back," she said, "but it never seemed enough for two. And he did things there that . . . He wouldn't tell me anything, but I was afraid." She paused. "It doesn't matter anymore. You were just little then. There's an address on that piece of paper: a lady friend from the old days who'll help you. I want you to stop and see her. Mildred Vierra. Her address . . ."

Did what? Adrian was thinking. He remembered his father sitting by the window in their apartment, looking worried every time a car came into the parking lot, and then getting up to check on something in a dresser drawer. Adrian had gone to the drawer and looked in when his father was in the bathroom. Under a shirt was a pistol: a blue-black revolver with a short barrel. But his father had always had guns. It didn't mean anything. Besides, it was so long ago. Who cared about those days anymore?

He could make it to the 7-Eleven in less than an hour and be back in less than two. He squeezed the wad and felt a brittle crackling. The bills were dry and old.

She turned away, pulling into a pain. "Oh," she said in that weak, surprised way, as if the pain was always worse than she had anticipated. "Adrian, give me one of the pills. Hurry."

His hands shook. He could barely get the lid off, and as he held the pill, and then the water glass, to her lips, he had to concentrate to keep from shaking so wildly that he would miss.

"Thank you," she said. She moaned again. "I need to rest now."

"I'll be right here," he said. He pulled the blanket up over her chest. "I'll go get wood." Resting her hands on the blanket, she held the braid on her chest and closed her eyes.

He shook badly. He went to the kitchen and drew out his matches. He lit one and flipped the bill corners under his thumb. In the glare of yellow light, he pulled two out from behind the slip of paper and dropped the dead match. He ran his now-irritated tongue over the chipped tooth and felt his way to the chair, then stood on it. Reaching over jars and cans, he put the wad of bills in the corner behind them. Then he felt around the table and found his jacket where it hung on the back of a chair.

He ran for a while, out toward the property line, then walked, and then ran again. Two hundred yards further sat John

Moore's trailer, a faint light in the small windows. Moore's four dogs barked, pulling at their chains. "Shut up" Adrian called. When he was little, those dogs had terrified him, but he had made friends with them a long time ago, and he frequently ran across them loose on the road. Past Moore's trailer, he settled into a fast walk. The thin layer of snow on the dirt road squeaked under his shoes. When the image of her waking up invaded his mind, he started jogging again, approaching the hill that descended to the little town. He reached the point where it started down, and scanned the countryside, and saw only one other house light, a mile away at the Richardsons' place, just visible through the thin snowfall. There had been other houses when he was younger, but now they were piles of dry, rotted clapboard and planking and rusted bedsprings on stone foundations, stained enamel pots and cans littering the brushy yards. There was also a house on his family's property, or what he had once assumed was their property. Set back in some trees off the road, it was in the process of falling apart. When he was thirteen, fourteen, fifteen, he had spent time working on it with old hand tools, fixing the floor and walls, scrounging around in the town for any material that would cover holes in the walls or roof. He had thought of it as his house, improved it enough that he could imagine a real house, and then learned that the property was rented. "Don't we own this?" he had asked his father. "Own it?" he said. "Shit no. Whatever gave you that idea?"

When the town appeared through the bare, scraggly trees, seeming to bounce with the rhythm of his walking, his mouth began to water. He needed only to find a patsy to get the stuff for him, and as he walked, he watched for headlight shafts on the other incoming roads. There were no cars parked at the 7-Eleven, so he walked to the dumpster and waited.

Within two minutes, Cliff Parker's truck coasted into the parking lot, leaving two darker lines in the snow.

"Hey Cliff," he called, "I need to pick up a couple big Douglas Glens."

Parker snorted. "Old man tyin' one on?"

"Yup, an' you know what I get if he doesn't get his load on."

Parker shifted a baseball cap on his head and said, "So how's your ma?"

"She's not bad," Adrian said. "Kinda plannin' to take a trip actually. My dad's gone sometimes, here sometimes." He waved his hand at the road. "Thinkin' a movin' actually, up Utica maybe. Better medical care too." He stopped. The more elaborate the con, the more holes it would have in it. "Can you help me?" He drew out the two twenties.

"Now Phil in there's gonna take me for a boozer," Parker said. "No offense intended."

"Could say you're havin' a party."

"Then I'd hafta invite the guy."

"True," Adrian said. "Hey, tell him you're stockin' up for the next six months. Tasted this Douglas Glen stuff and wanna stock up 'fore it's bought out."

"Douglas Glen?" Parker laughed. "Stuff's about as tasty as horse piss." He stared at Adrian thoughtfully, and then threw his hands up. "Okay, okay," he said. "Two?"

While Parker was inside the store Adrian considered his lie about his father and realized how stupid it was. He had to cover it somehow. A few minutes passed, and no Parker. Adrian began to sigh, to grind his teeth. "C'mon," he said. "What the hell takes so long?"

Finally Parker came out, carrying a white plastic bag stretched on the bottom by the two bottles, and a smaller bag. "Here you go, stud," Parker said.

"Thanks," Adrian said, feeling a rush of excitement when he felt the weight of the bag. "Listen, my dad would just as soon you didn't say anything to anybody about his bein' here. He got into a little trouble up Utica, so if you phoned or anything, he'd be—"

"Hey, no sweat," Parker said. "How 'bout you? You stayin' outta trouble?"

"Hey, I'm through with juvie court and youth correction school and all that."

"Oops," Parker said, digging in his jacket pocket. "Here's your change."

"Hey, thanks." Adrian took the bills and coins and stuffed them in his pocket. Parker got in his truck and pulled out, leaving another set of parallel lines in the parking lot and road.

Adrian stepped behind the dumpster and put the bag down, drew out one bottle and squinted in the dim, reflected light of the store window at the paper around the bottleneck. He ran his thumbnail in the gap, breaking the paper. He unwound the cap and, careful not to chip another tooth, took a long, hot swig, the scotch fresh and strong.

Then he walked, the bag heavy in his hand, the plastic handle stretching and digging into his fingers. When he thought of his mother, he picked up his pace. It'd been an hour at least, and he pumped his legs hard, imagining her waking up and calling him. The scotch made him feel dense and complete, and he walked with a vigorous, resolute strength. Scotch made the world a comfortable place, especially when it was a world without text, and everything was stark and lucid and beautiful: trees and rocks and animals and water. Cops and counselors and judges had lectured him on addictions, but they just didn't know that for him what dulled reality, as they claimed, really clarified it and gave it beauty and meaning.

Every hundred yards or so he shifted the bag from one hand to the other, and on flat stretches he jogged, the light snowflakes melting on his face. The only time he slowed down was when he squinted into the woods in the direction of the old house he had worked on. He knew exactly how he had left it: half of the windows redone with new caulk, more than half of the floor refinished, and some of his own woodcarvings on old chairs and mounted on walls.

Ahead, he saw the faint rectangle of dull yellow light from his mother's bedroom, then the black silhouette of the house against the falling snow. He would scrounge up some wood and get the house warm, then sit up and polish off a third of one of the Glens.

She was still asleep. The urine smell in the room had gone flat and acrid. He went to the kitchen and lit the lantern, adjusted the flame so that the room was bathed in soft orange light, and set the two Glens on the table. Then he went outside, walking behind the woodshed. The answer was there: his father's sawhorse. Within fifteen minutes, he had it reduced to a pile of foot-and-a-half sections of two-by-six planks. He took one armload down into the cellar and teepeed it up around the chunk of slowly burning hemlock, blew on it until fresh yellow flames licked at the wood, and closed the heavy cast-iron door.

He sat in the kitchen. One thousand and what? Seventy-two dollars give or take. There was only food and the electric bill and the rent, assuming that the owner cared about getting it. He wasn't sure, but he thought that hey hadn't paid in almost two months. Otherwise, it was free money, and he wasn't going anywhere. He ran his tongue over the chipped tooth, the little irritated patch stinging. He was staying here because this was a world without the written word. The deer didn't care.

In high school, he had developed an elaborate con to hide his reading problem. He'd lost a year when he was a freshman, and the shame of that made him want to dig in and make it. He had tried, but trying made him so nervous that the dyslexia was aggravated. Letter combinations would leave him airy and blank. The letters would intensify and then become cryptic markings, as if written in some other alphabet, their stark shapes nothing he had ever seen before. The teachers knew because they saw what he had managed to scrawl on tests and quizzes, but no one else did. Kids just figured he wasn't very smart. His mother helped him, writing the short papers he had to sometimes read to the class. She would read them to him, and he would commit them to memory and then copy them the best he could, and then in class he would throw the con in their faces. By the time he was fourteen, he sometimes did it half loaded and surrounded by a cloud of mint, which he used to cover the smell of the alcohol roiling hotly in his stomach. Adrian would go to school with a small, opaque, plastic squirt bottle in his pack, drinking from it when he needed to, then chewing a handful of Tic Tacs. His mother had all sorts of ideas about how to help him, but he told her not to worry. He'd be all right. He could memorize anything. And in his spare time, he would sprint off down the road and through the little patch of trees to work on his house.

Only once did his father bring up his reading problem in a positive way. When they were hunting one day he said, "You go into the service. I don't believe they'd care about your problem with words on paper." He'd looked down at the rifle leaning against the tree, then at a woodchuck oozing blood into dry, amber hay stubble, the body still twitching, although half of its skull was gone. "That was more'n a hundred yards. I never seen a kid your age can shoot like that."

"I got him clean." Like birds, squirrels, deer someday, he hoped. He was still giddy with the strange shock of joy he'd felt when the chuck had snapped with the impact of the bullet.

"You come back from the service, and these woods'll be yours," his father said. "They're yours to hunt and you're the boss here." He pushed the chuck with his boot, and the still body swayed heavily, like a bag of jelly. Adrian was fourteen at the time and had no clue that the ownership of the property was a scam his father had laid on him.

With his own scam, he knew that he might as well have been trying to manipulate a balloon through a bramble patch.

In the eleventh grade, he dictated to his mother a social-studies paper he thought up entitled "Things We Know But Don't Know We Know." It was an idea he was sure was his own. His theory was that all people have talents they are unaware of, and when he read his paper to the class, he tried to prove it with a simple demonstration. Holding the paper he had copied, that his mother had written and had read to him five times at home, he said that if you are walking at a normal gait on a flat surface, and see thirty-five feet ahead of you an object, or mark, on the ground, by fifteen or twenty feet you can know which foot will step on that object. This is not something you learn to do. It is something you know, and you need only invite your mind to say "right" or "left." This sense of distance, he said, has been forgotten because we depend too much on measurement.

He invited the teacher and the class out to the hall, put a strip of masking tape on the floor, and like a pitchman told them that he would walk down the hall and then call out "right," "left," or "straddle" by thirty feet, then close his eyes and keep walking. He did all this with good-natured confidence because he carried half a load and was chewing on the remnants of a mouthful of Tic Tacs. He tried five times, and five times he was right. A boy had him clap a baseball cap on his eyes at thirty feet, and he got it right again. The teacher appeared impressed. Other kids tried it, and one guy who played soccer explained that athletes have this instinct too.

When they were all back in the classroom, he explained that this instinct is inborn but unused.

A boy in the back, Ricky Entman, said, "So what good is all this? We got rulers, right?"

There were a few snickers. Adrian stared at Ricky Entman, a blank airiness sweeping over him.

"We like read the numbers, man," Ricky Entman said, "so why bother?"

The intensity of the light in the room changed, as if affected by the subtle inflection of the word read, and Adrian smiled at Ricky Entman and said, "Actually, we can deal with this outside, where I'll use my innate sense to beat the shit outta you and wipe that—"

"Adrian!" the teacher said. All the kids were sitting there with their mouths open, and with a strange, dizzy exhilaration, he turned to her and said, "Fuck you."

On the way to see the principal, he stopped at his locker and took a long squirt of scotch, and when he got to the office, he made sure to get close when he apologized so that he could blow the vapor of that scotch into the man's face. He knew he would be suspended. He sat and waited for the bus, drank more because the stupid fools hadn't thought to search his bag, and when Ricky Entman came out laughing and smiling with his buddies, Adrian walked up to him and knocked out three of his lower teeth, then beat him so badly that he had to go to the hospital. He did all this with a studious, inward-turning amazement, as if watching from the sidelines in awed fascination: Ricky's bloody teeth arranged in a triangle against the tan and gray of the worn bricks, the blood from his nose dripping in perfect, quarter-sized disks onto the bricks, the gasps and yelling. And then Adrian felt an exhilaration unlike anything before, an intensification of the feeling he had when he'd shot the woodchuck, as if he had taken some powerful drug.

He was sent to a group home in Utica called the Tallman House, an estate that had been converted into a facility for wayward children. It was a combination of elegant brick structures and a newer concrete building ringed with cyclone fencing that was topped with razor wire. He was placed in one of the brick buildings, which housed a dormitory room, three classrooms, and a small cafeteria.

One of the other boys there, who seemed far too young to have done much in his life, had shot his father to death. Adrian had developed a respect for this boy upon hearing about his crime, but at night in the dorm, he heard the boy weeping under his covers. Adrian lay there, staring into the blackness and thinking, We are all freaks. Other boys were drug addicts, runaways. The ones in the newer building, he heard, had committed acts of violence so bizarre and extreme that he could not believe it. One boy had killed and dismembered another. Another had taken out his father's eye in a fight. Another had gone berserk and opened fire on a herd of cows. He rarely saw these boys. When he did, he was amazed at the normalcy of their appearance.

In his own group was a pasty-faced boy who seemed to possess the mental perversity of those more seriously deranged boys, but not the will. His name was Mark Brough, and he attached himself to Adrian for reasons Adrian couldn't figure out. The boy followed him, sat with him when they ate, and began talking to him, but always in a whisper: I killed our cat by hanging it like you see people hanged on TV. I snipped the legs off a baby bird with a pair of wire cutters. Mark was so fascinated by mutilation and death that, when he was thirteen, he had started a scrapbook of pictures of dead bodies, men hanging, black-and-white photographs cut out of books and newspapers, old drawings of things like the original Count Dracula eating at a table over which hung people impaled on wooden pikes. "They called him Vlad the Impaler," he whispered to Adrian, and then he told Adrian an elaborate story about the Count. Mark's parents had taken the scrapbook away from him.

One night the boys were watching a TV program that included a videotape from Rwanda, watery and vague, of bodies lying around and men walking here and there, and in the left foreground, four men, two standing, and below them, one lying on the ground and having his face worked on by one of the standing men using a long-handled tool. There was another man sitting, and one of the standing men picked up a machete and raised it and brought it down as hard as he could on the sitting man's head. The man flopped backward, and the man with the machete brought it down twice more, with swings in which he snapped his wrist at precisely the moment the machete hit the man's face. Mark watched all this with his mouth open and then whispered to Adrian in that conspiratorial, secret way he had that he wanted to have that tape because you don't get to see people killed on film that much, except in old war stuff. He wanted that tape, he kept saying. Adrian was sickened by the tape, and frightened because what the man with the machete had done was what he himself would have done to Ricky Entman if he'd had a hatchet or a machete while he looked down at him.

One of the buildings housed wayward girls, whom Adrian would see during classes, most often in the auditorium, where the coed ones were held. Sometimes the counselors would arrange get-togethers where the kids could dance, listen to music, or watch movies. Leigh Donaldson was sixteen and had spent two years as a runaway and prostitute in Albany. She arrived the same week that Mark Brough left. Adrian had a hard time believing what he had heard about her because she was small and pale and looked like an anorexic preteen. A drug addict, she had scars on her wrists from a suicide attempt. One of the boys said she had bipolar disorder, which meant that she had huge, unpredictable mood swings.

The running of the group homes was lax enough that she had already put out for a couple of the boys, and Adrian had been shocked at that. The boys laughed and told him about her. She's a real slut, Ade. Your dick'll fall off. She'll eat you alive. All the girls here are like her. They took drugs and spread their legs before you even knew what it was about. But all this didn't make Adrian dislike Leigh. She was a freak just as he was, and sometimes she got this strange, wistful look on her face when he talked about the house he was rebuilding. He described how he had scraped the old paint off every molding and window frame, had cut glass from pieces he had found. He had repaired the roof using corrugated aluminum that he had dragged crosslots from the town dump, and had started to furnish it with stuff people had thrown away. When he talked to her this way, she had that look most of the time, but other times she was jumpy and short with him, as if she were anxious about some problem. For no apparent reason, she would even cry. Then, the next time he saw her, she would be upbeat and talkative, almost too excited.

He had known her about three weeks when she asked him straight out if he'd ever been laid, and when he told her he hadn't, she said, "We'll fix that." And so they did, under the large porch of her group home, on a spot of dirt against a foundation. They did it while she was supposed to be studying in her room. She made him use a condom, which she supplied, because, she said, she'd had an abortion and didn't want to go through that again. In the darkness under the porch, her skin was pale, almost phosphorescent. It didn't last very long that first time, but he ended up so taken with her that he began to dream of living with her in the restored house. The second time under the porch, Leigh watched him with a flat, detached stare as he whispered, Jesus, so that's what they all talk about. When they were done, she pulled out what she called her works, which she had gotten from a friend in town on free-out day: a hypodermic needle, a spoon, a lighter, and a plastic bag with powder in it. When he saw these things, he became almost faint with an awed conspiratorial giddiness. She was crazy, and she had more wild guts than anyone he'd ever met. With the spoon and lighter, she boiled the off-color powder, which looked like stale flour, drew the liquid into the needle, and injected herself in her pale, fragile-looking leg, behind the knee. He watched, amazed by the skill, the assurance, the quickness with which she did it, her leg raised up as she looked for a blue vein to poke, the thigh vibrating a little with the effort until she asked him to steady it for her. She found the vein and pushed the needle, which drew the skin in. It popped a little when the needle broke through, and her hand shaking, she slowly pushed the little red plunger so that he could see the other end of it, fuzzy and indistinct, moving past the little measuring marks in the plastic. When she was done, she buried the needle, spoon, and bag in the dry dirt and went into a moaning half-sleep, sitting against the foundation wall. He watched her, thinking, You wait until we're out of here. We'll go to the house and live there.

He wanted to tell the other boys that he had scored with Leigh, but decided not to out of respect for her. The plan to take her away with him preoccupied him every night. Staring at the dark ceiling with his fingers laced behind his head, he'd picture it. He would restore the well out front, and maybe eventually get electricity installed. He didn't care that she was a whore. Freaks stick together. They were kids who had fucked up, and that was what defined them. The world wanted nothing from them, so they wanted nothing from the world. They were the world's defective leftovers, wondering only whether or not hanging around was worth it. All of the kids at the home had heard of the ones with guts, who raised their middle fingers to that world and blew their brains out or OD'd in a glorious, impudent farewell.

Tallman's counselors discussed his dyslexia and what they called his agraphia, his inability to write. Adrian amiably agreed with everything they said, but eventually he proved to them that he could write. It just took time. He behaved well, believing that all he had to do was wait it out—wait out Leigh's sentence too—and they'd be out of there and in his house. At night, the soft glow of the lights of Utica filtered through a line of trees across the road, and he worked on his dream, revised it over and over.

One day the word of her suicide went through the house. She had cut herself again, this time with a razor she had found somewhere, and sat in a bathtub with her hands under the water, and that was how they found her. And for one strange moment after he fully understood what she had done, he thought, Goddam that took guts. She did it—she had the guts to do that.

He began to think of his soul as being in his trunk, next to his spine, and shaped like a tube. That tube grew into a black, malformed snake, and he thought he could feel it there, pulsing against his spine. He wondered about his responsibility for her death—if, somehow, his stoking her with that dream, and then doing what they did under the porch, had pushed her over the edge. He did not talk about it with anyone. As people said, inmates and counselors, she'd had a problem she ultimately could not deal with. Lying with his fingers laced behind his head, he stared at the ceiling and in his imagination revised the reality he feared was his doing. In those speculations, the two of them did go to the house and did finish it, and lived there until the end of their lives.

Then his father requested that Tallman let him out, so that he could come home and look after his mother, who was recovering from cancer. Tallman's response was to expel him, which he thought was fine. He didn't need any school. At home were a couple of medical books his mother had bought at thrift shops in Cooperstown. He tried reading them with a device he'd contrived at the group home: in two plastic cards that came in junk mail he found in the dumpster, he cut a two-inch-wide window and slipped in a strip of plastic that he could slide back and forth. He would lay the device on a word to isolate it then try to read it. If he stared the sharp, nonsensical hieroglyphics down, he could do it. Reading a page took forever, but it worked. He would mention to his father something he had read on nutrition or medical research, and his father would say, "Yeah yeah, that's interesting I guess."

Adrian began cultivating convictions about his own power to make her well by simply staring at her as she slept, focusing his eyes on her stomach and willing the cancer to reverse itself.

Then his father told him that his mother's condition was terminal, that she had left the hospital because she wanted to be at home when she died. Adrian didn't believe it. Nothing was a sure thing. A sudden turnaround was still possible. He asked his father about paying the bills for the operation she'd had, speculating on whether they'd have to sell the place. By then, he had gone back to restoring the old house. His father told him that they didn't own the property. They rented it. Adrian was hardened enough by then that when he went out to the old house, he laughed at the work he'd done, at the wood sculptures he'd made before going to the group home. Own it? Shit no. Whatever gave you that idea?

It became clear to Adrian that his father had wanted him back home because he himself wanted out, and in fact he left only a few weeks after Adrian returned, when the weather had started getting colder. In late fall, he returned, looking, Adrian thought, for some change in her condition. He walked around the place, staring at tools and car parts and stuff they had stored in the barn. Having found nothing in the house he could sell or take with him, he left. Twice more he returned, the last time to find that she spent more time in bed than out. With no reaction other than a pained expression, he headed for the car. He said he didn't want to disturb her if she was in bed. He was living with the militia men up north of Utica, on a farm he referred to as a compound. As the car headed down the road, Adrian yelled, "Fuck you!" and then he walked to the little village to buy her something for Christmas. Using the bit of cash he had saved from the spending money he received at Tallman, he went to the 7-Eleven and bought her a can of candied almonds, a set of picture postcards of classic New York State barns, and a bottle of multiple vitamins. So that she wouldn't feel bad, he got himself a bag of beef jerky, wrapping it as a present from her. On Christmas, he helped her to the living-room easy chair and they opened their presents and watched TV. His father had been gone long enough that they figured they'd never see him again.

He took another swig from the bottle. The fresh taste of it in his mouth warmed him, and he could feel his head reeling a little, and knew that he had had almost enough.

He slept in his clothes on the couch under a dirty army blanket. He could get up and drink a mouthful anytime he wanted, and the comfort of that caused him to drift off, until he sat bolt upright in the silence. It was black outside, maybe three or four o'clock. He listened. Had she made a noise? In his head there was an echo, as if he were recalling a sound that had awakened him. Then he heard her, that strange crooning sound she made, and he got up. He waited while his balance wavered and points of light swept across his eyes. Then he went into her room.

"Adrian?" she whispered, "I had a dream." The tiny flame in the lantern illuminated the room enough for him to make his way to the chair. He rested his hand on the mattress and then pulled it away quickly. Cold urine had seeped to the edge. He shuddered, wiping his hand down his pantleg.

"Tomorrow we'll clean this up and I'll turn it over," he said. "You want a pill?"

"No."

Heat flashed through him. He did not like the tone of her voice. There was no sound of hope or tomorrow in it.

"I don't want them to get my body," she said.

"Hey, let's not talk about stuff like that. I'll get a pill."

"No. I—" She seemed to tense, to be locked inside the pain. "I had a dream. I—" She rested her hand on his knee. "I was alone. I was floating in nowhere, and it was black most of the time. And then I saw fields, grass and mountains, cars, stretches of highway with stores and things along the sides, but I just kept floating and I was scared." She moved her hand up to her face. "I was scared."

"It's only a dream," he said.

"It was me. I was going to spend all of time scared. Adrian? Don't let them get my body."

"Don't talk like that," he said. "Wait. Lemme go outside a minute. Be right back."

He went out through the dark living room, then felt his way into the kitchen and reached through the blackness toward the image of the bottle. He felt it, took off the cap, and raised the the bottle to his lips. He took a long swallow, his hands shaking, and waited while it burned him. He hated it when she talked like that. He went outside into the frigid air and urinated in the thin snow, shivering. Then he went back to her room.

"Okay," he said. "Tomorrow we'll clean up a little, and I'll make something really good for you to eat. I don't know, I could go down to 7-Eleven and get one of those—"

"No. I want you to promise. I want you to bury me in the pine grove behind the barn."

He had played in that grove all his life. A windbreak for the barn, it had branches that were low and brittle. When he was little, he had hacked paths into the center with a hatchet. No, he couldn't do what she wanted. He was supposed to call someone when it happened, and that was what he would do.

"Get me the big scissors out of the drawer there," she said. "Then go get a piece of wire, that copper wire in the woodshed."

He struck a match in the shed, then cupped it in his hand while he walked along the dusty shelves, his shoes crunching in the woodchips on the dirt floor. The roll of wire was there next to cans of paint. Wire and scissors—what was she up to now?

He put the roll of wire on the little stand next to her bed.

"Turn the lantern up," she said.

"How do you feel?" He rolled the little knob on the lantern, and the room turned a dull orange, the wooden butterfly materializing on the wall.

"I'm past most of it," she said. "But could you give me some of your whiskey?"

"What whiskey?"

"Please."

In the kitchen he felt shame prickle his skin as he poured the scotch into her glass, going by feel. He put his finger in the glass and felt it a little less than half full, and took it back to her.

"I never was much of a drinker," she said. "Back home, we drank beer." She sipped the drink, then held the glass with both hands on her stomach. "I know you'll do it, because I'm making you promise. You'll bury me in the pine grove and then go to Albany, and they'll take care of connections and all that. Just don't lose the money. Mildred Vierra will help you settle yourself. She can even help with a job. Take the scissors and cut the braid off."

"Why?"

She sipped at the drink. "It makes me warm," she said. "Just cut the braid off. But before you do, wrap a piece of wire around it two or three times so it won't come apart."

He took a deep breath and picked up the roll of wire. "Can I cut this with the scissors?"

"Yes. I didn't know why I wanted you to braid my hair, and then it came to me in the dream."

He cut a foot-long piece of the wire. "You'll have to raise me," she said, handing him her glass. When he raised her to a sitting position, the ammoniac smell of the urine and a warm, dead fecal smell roiled out from the space behind her back. He held his breath and looped the wire around the braid at the back of her head, winding it around twice and leaving enough of the ends to twist. He pressed the twisted end downward, into her hair. "Cut it off," she said.

He slid the narrow, pointed blade into the thick base of the braid and began cutting. When he was done, he lifted the braid so that she could see it, and he was surprised at how heavy it was. He eased her down against the pillow, and she took the braid from him and stared at it.

"I want you to take this to a place there and bury it."

"Bury the braid? Why?"

"It wasn't a dream, it was a foretelling. It was how I'll be if—" She looked straight at him, and he became nervous again. "That's how I'll be if you don't."

"Aw c'mon," he said and then laughed. "Who's to say that this is gonna happen at all? I think if we just clean up in here and I get some good food in you, then maybe—"

"Adrian, I'm past that," she said in a near whisper. "There isn't much pain left. I'm glad that I still have my voice—my voice is all I am now. I'm scared of wandering over all that scenery or whatever it is, forever. That's why you have to bury the braid there. You've got to promise."

"Yeah, but—"

"No, listen. If you don't, I'll wander for eternity. Bury it with my people. Remember this. I know you will, because you remember everything. Mālaekahana."

The peculiar relaxed look on her face might be due to the scotch, he thought. "Okay, what's that?" he asked. It was just words. He wasn't going anywhere.

"It's a place, on O'ahu. When I was little, we used to go out to the beach there, and one day we girls were digging in the sand and found a human jawbone, and the lady, a scout leader, told us to put it back because the place was probably an old burial ground. I—" She stared at the braid. "Do you remember much of home?"

"No."

But that was a lie. He did remember—too much, in fact. When he was six or seven, the stories she told had fascinated him, but when he was a little older, they bored him. The whole history of kings, queens, blue water, all that shit. He hated it. She didn't understand that he had grown up here and had no interest in that old place. She told him how he was part this and part that. Once, in the woods, his father had stopped, turned the chainsaw off, and said, "Don't you never tell anybody at school that you got Chink blood, you hear? Say you got this blood or that blood, but don't you say anything about Chink blood."

"Say it," she said.

"Mālaekahana."

"I don't know how you can remember like that. Even pronouncing it."

He shrugged. He wasn't going anywhere.

"I feel all right now," she said. "I feel taken care of. And when you get there, you'll know it's your place too."

He pulled the covers up to her chin and placed the braid next to her on the bed. "You sleep," he said. "I'll be right out there."

He sat in the kitchen, thinking, Your place? His father had his opinions about that: "It's the mixin'," he had said. "Something dirty about it. Hell, in the Philippines I had any girl I wanted, young ones too. But that was sport. You get a little older, you'll see—but I got tricked, and I don't ever want you to tell nobody you got Chink blood. You can say you got this blood or that. Polynesian ain't that bad—hell, nobody really knows what it is. But Chink blood, no. Never tell anybody you got one goddam drop."

A day with a ready stock of booze was a good day. Early in the morning he towed the wooden cart to the back edge of the property by the state land, the bow saw bouncing around in the bed, and cut wood, dead maple mostly, and towed it back. That she hadn't eaten anything in almost two days worried him, so he decided he'd cook something up, maybe macaroni and cheese.

He checked on her every hour or so. And each time she was in that comalike sleep that he hated. He would watch until the blanket covering her chest moved a little as proof that she breathed. His hits on the bottle were one every hour or so, small ones because during daylight it was just too bright for more. Getting up a load at night was okay. At night, reality had a dark firmness that the booze collaborated with just right. Besides, when you had a steady source, you didn't need to drink too much of it. You conserved when you had plenty and you were extravagant when you had little.

Just as it took a long time for the sun to penetrate the overcast sky in the morning, daylight waned too early. It was after four when she woke up. He heated up a can of beef stew, ate half of it, and took a bowl to her, walking through the house now made warm by a fire crackling in the furnace. She was sitting half up, holding the braid across her stomach.

"Chow time," he said. "You can't keep goin' on without food."

She smiled at him. "You know what I miss? The TV. We could have been watching it every day. And not game shows either. I liked the education ones. So I watch the butterfly."

He looked at it. "Yeah," he said, "I liked those arty shows."

He spooned a little food to her lips, sauce with a couple of peas and a little chunk of potato. She swallowed, looking at him. He gave her another spoonful. And another. The urine and feces smell had gone flat and soily. He looked at the dark stain on the edge of the bed. "Look—"

"I want to sleep now," she said. "Funny, but it's all right now that you promised. I sleep all right now. I don't dream or anything. I feel taken care of."

"Okay." And he thought, No, I'm not going anywhere.

He sat in the kitchen and sipped at the bottle, careful not to have too much, which sometimes made the room spin when he tried to sleep. It made him feel whole and optimistic. With the little food she had eaten there would be a turn for the better, he thought. He'd try again in the morning.

At about eleven, he stretched out on the couch and covered himself with the army blanket. He went to sleep quickly. But sometime later he felt cold. The chill penetrated his flesh and seemed to make his organs cold, and he saw a tangible darkness sweeping past him as if he were floating. The dark snake in his trunk was moving, flexing, hurting the organs around it, leaving him rigid with fear. He sat up.

"Something's wrong," he whispered. He stood up and stumbled to her room, went to the stand and turned the little wheel of the lantern, bathing the room in the orange light. She was lying sideways, and the flat smell was there. "Ma?" he said. He put his hand on her bony shoulder, and it was cold. He turned her up on the pillow, but she resisted a little, and the resistance suggested the beginning of a horrible rigidity. Her eyes were partway open, crusted, the iris and pupil dull.

He went out of the room and down the hall to the kitchen, his heart pounding. He picked the bottle up and, running his tongue over the broken tooth, swallowed a mouthful. He went back to her room. "Maybe—" No. She was dead. The braid sat on the edge of the mattress. He experienced a jerky anxiety, staring at her. "My God," he whispered. "She died."

He went back to the living room and over to the phone. But nobody would be in any office now. He didn't know why he felt no more than a shaky panic and a peculiar sensation of relief. He didn't feel sad, he thought, because her agony was finally over.

And then he felt a fatigue so great that he sat at the kitchen table and put his head down on the backs of his hands. It was over. His mind filled with images of his mother when she was young, taking him out to the huckleberry patches by the swamp at the edge of their property, walking the dirt roads with him, taking him to the store in town—and, further back, beaches and water. And watching TV. And the way some people looked at her because of the slight darkness of her skin and the cut of her features. And now she was dead. He sat up and reached for the bottle. He thought as he drank that he had to call. He saw them coming up the bumpy dirt road, their vehicle swaying, saw them enter the bedroom and look at her, saying, Hmm, she's not all white is she? Maybe they would put her in some kind of bag. Clean her up first. Then they'd say, Hey, I saw women like this when I was in the service. Ain't all white, but—

He slept, and somewhere inside that oblivion he felt the snake move as if it were flexing, moving its eyeless head toward his heart, preparing to bite it, sliding in against membranes and bones. Then he was lying on his back, and his mother's face hovered above him, coming down slowly to kiss him on the lips, but her face had a leer on it and her breath smelt of urine. Fear paralyzed him, and he heard her whisper, "You promised." The face moved closer, the leer replaced by a look of contempt, and then he saw that her lips and eyes were stitched shut with large black sutures, and it was as if she were planning to tear her mouth open to bite him rather than kiss him. Her face touched his, and all the blood was sucked from his heart.

He opened his eyes to the blackness. He couldn't locate himself in time. He felt Leigh Donaldson's presence in the room, sensed her frail, death-white limbs. He leaned away from the table, and his hand hit the oily stock of the Enfield, and he pulled it toward him and held the stock-encased barrel. He gripped it just under the muzzle, his fingers around the bayonet seat, and experimentally rested his mouth on his thumb and forefinger encircling the muzzle, and with his tongue, touched the cold steel ring of the muzzle, the hole in the middle. The powerful metallic astringency of the taste made him jerk his head back.

"Adrian?"

He jumped up from the chair and then willed himself to slow down because of the darkness. He rested the rifle against the counter and made his way through the living room to the faint glow of her bedroom. But she was the way she had been.

He shuddered. It had been his imagination. He would go back to the kitchen and take another hit and sleep some more. But as he walked slowly, hands out in front, he sensed strange smoky shadows all around him, and the fear bored into his flesh with such force that he had to get out of the house. Standing by the woodshed in the night cold, he looked up for stars but saw only blackness—no horizon, no trees—only the faint suggestion of snow.

He lit the kerosene lantern in the kitchen and went back to the woodshed. He held the lamp out in his left hand while he tried to carry both the pickaxe and the shovel in his right. Heavy and awkward, they clacked against each other as he made his way past the barn and toward the pine grove, walking on a disk of yellow light that shifted on the snowy ground, a black shadow where he placed his feet. Dry and brittle, the pine branches scraped at his jacket, pulled at the pickaxe and shovel, and caught the sleeve of the arm that carried the lamp. In the little clearing in the grove was room enough, he decided, and he began by driving the blade of the pickaxe into the frozen ground. He broke out and levered up plates of dirt six inches thick and as big as chair seats. He had to hack through roots to loosen them completely.

He worked without knowing what time it was. No dawn suggested itself to tell him, and at one point, smelling himself because he had begun to sweat, he went back to the house and took a swig from the bottle. He stopped and waited for the awful feeling to come back, but it did not, and he knew that it had not come back because he was digging and would hide her body from them. They would not see her. They would not look at her while they cleaned her up and say, I seen women like this when I was in the service. Cancer was it? Boy, does it ever smell bad in here.

It was still dark when he decided the hole was deep enough. He would put her in there and cover her up, and then put the plates of dirt back like pieces from a puzzle. He'd scatter the leftover dirt to erase the spot. Nobody would ever be able to find her.

He wound the dirty sheet over her side and chest, and over her head, the hair sticking out on the sides and shorter on the back, and the smell billowed up at him, sharp and foul. He wormed his hands under her hip and side and lifted, felt a wad of fecal stuff with his right hand squishing and then wetting his hand through the sheet, and it was cold where her body joined the mattress, cold as meat from a refrigerator, and when he was standing straight, the sheet dangling to the floor, he was shocked at the lightness of her body. He cradled her with one arm and pulled the sheet up under so as to soak up the urine, which was now on his clothes, the smell leaking upward across his face so that he suddenly felt the urge to vomit. Standing there and holding her, he fought it off. Her head did not droop: it just stuck out, her neck stiff. He carried her into the dark living room, the sheet snagging on the Christmas tree and tipping it down against the television. Then he approached the narrow hall, and her head hit the edge of the opening with a flat thud. He slid her body along the hallway, and went out through the kitchen, using her feet to push the door open.

There was a hole in the sky through which stars shone. By the arrangement, he knew it was about four o'clock. He worked her through the pines and toward the glow of the lamp, the branches pulling at the sheet, scraping her face and head, scratching her feet. They snapped back in place once he got past. Then he struggled down to his knees and, as gently as he could, lowered her down into the three-foot-deep hole. He got up and went back to the house, gathered the rest of the bedding, and picked up the braid, carrying it all out to the hole. Standing there in the dim light, he could just see the shape of her body. He put the bedding into the hole, pushed it in around her sides and feet, and slid the pillow under her head. He held the braid over the hole.

He began to tremble, to breathe rapidly, that fright lancing him like needles, the sensation of organs bruising and of blood being sucked out of his heart. No. It had to be in— He had forgotten the name. Began with an H or N or something. He looked at the faint whiteness of the form in the hole, hidden below the illumination of the lantern. He put his hand up to shield his eyes from the glow, and the form intensified so that he could see her shape, the sheet stretched down from her head so that a quarter circle of a starburst of ridges appeared, fanning outward toward her shoulders, another where her hand stretched the fabric upward. He draped the braid over a branch and began shoveling dirt in the hole, the hard clods thumping on her.

When the hole was filled, the puzzle on top completed, he hurled heavy chunks of dirt in various directions, clods bouncing under the trees and out of the lamp's circle. Then he used the shovel to spread the pine needles and flatten the surface.

Back inside, he wrapped the braid in one of his T-shirts, coiling it around itself into a thick disk, and put it on the table. He filled a small duffel bag with everything he thought he would need, mostly clothes and shaving stuff and his toothbrush. He put the shirt-wrapped braid in the bag, on the side so that he could see the circle stretching the green canvas.

He rolled up the soggy mattress and carried it to the back door, sliding it through the narrow hall, and then he dragged it across the yard and threw it over the bank, where they had a little dump out of sight of the house. The snow would cover it, rain would later blend the stains, and eventually it would only be an old mattress on top of a rotted refrigerator, a broken bike, a pile of brittle shingles, broken jars, and sun-bleached plastic toys.

The bathtub in the bathroom had not worked in years, so he washed at the sink in the kitchen. Shivering in the dim lamplight, he dried with a dirty towel and looked at his clothes.

They were filthy, so he carried the lantern upstairs to his room to find his school clothes, which were only half dirty: jeans, a plaid shirt, fairly clean socks, and a light jacket that did not smell heavily of pinesap and gasoline. He hadn't been in his room in days because it was too cold. He paused after he dressed, then looked at the dim circles on the walls: other disks he had cut from logs, each with a darker shape in the middle, one a man, another a haunted-looking face of a woman, two more butterflies from the same log as the disk downstairs. He sat down on the bed. "Oh boy," he whispered. He took a deep breath and let it out.

He filled the squirt bottle, wrapped the full bottle of Douglas Glen inside his clothes, and then put it in the duffel bag. He poured what was left of the second bottle into a large peanut butter jar and put that in the bag. He rigged a belt and fanny pack in which he stashed all but a hundred dollars of the money, his state ID card, and the number and address of the lady, and fastened it around himself, under his jacket. He put the hundred dollars under the heel pad inside his right running shoe. When he paused to look around, he felt a strange panic because he had no idea how to do this. Nobody should see him go. It would be best to go crosslots to the hard road that went in the opposite direction of his school. A few miles away was the six-laner that led to Albany. He pulled the squirt bottle out, filled his mouth with scotch, and swallowed, the heat radiating into his flesh. The windows now showed the flat light of dawn.

II

When for the fourth time he felt the strange rising in his stomach that signified the plane's slowing down, he sat up and looked around. It was dark outside, and the woman sitting next to him was asleep under a thin blanket, her head on a pillow with a blue paper case. He wormed his hand into the end of the duffel bag he had jammed under the seat in front of him and pulled out the squirt bottle, half full of Douglas Glen. He took a mouthful from the plastic tube, the sting of it biting the tip of his tongue where it was scraped by the chipped tooth, and put the bottle back. The ticket had cost him nine hundred dollars, so he had less than two hundred left. He could hardly put what he had done into any linear recollection: Chicago, Denver, San Francisco, underground shuttles and moving walkways and soft voices coming from overhead speakers. The sap and gasoline smells of his dirty clothes wafted with increasing richness up to his face.

He reached down and felt the canvas side of the duffel bag for the circular lump created by the braid. The problem of remembering the name of the place his mother told him bothered him. An "H" word, he thought, and it seemed strange that she wanted the braid buried there. She was superstitious, and now he felt a wave of shame and frustration because he had bought into that superstition. The plane did another dip, making his stomach rise a little, and in the blackness outside the window, he saw nothing but the dim suggestions of clouds.

He figured he'd stay long enough to see what it was like, get rid of the braid, and go back home. His return date was open-ended, so he could stay as long as he liked. His sense of connection with the hills and fields where he had grown up was so built in that he had not realized how strong it was until he got on the first plane, and a horrible lump formed in his throat. As for the "H" place, he had the feeling it would pop into his mind as clearly as if she had said it to him a few seconds before.

The plane landed in rain. The lights he could see were from an industrial-looking area fronted by a strip of beach with what looked like waves breaking in tiny white lines. Next to it were warehouses and large oil or gas tanks through which a highway snaked, the white shafts of car lights coming out of the rain, and watery red dots going away. While the plane taxied toward the gates, the air warmed up a little and the odor from his jacket got stronger. He was dirty, but had no way of doing anything about it.

He filed out behind the same woman he had sat next to, followed other people through a series of doors, his body tipped with the weight of the duffel bag, and then they were outside, walking through a warm wind along a suspended walkway into another building, and down an escalator into a large and very cold, low-ceilinged room. A crowd of people had gathered around the stainless steel, oval-shaped conveyor belts that were turning. They chatted amiably, hugging each other and watching the bags as they came out. Skin colors were dark, faces oriental, mixed, some something else. He looked around and saw doors leading out into the night.

He made his way to those doors and outside into air that seemed too warm, sodden with humidity, and almost instantly his face flushed as if he would break out in a sweat. He sat on a low concrete wall, from which he watched people getting in cars, some of them wearing leis, and then the cars driving off toward a series of highway ramps. Out there it was raining, the rain white in the glow of streetlights. He could see nothing beyond the lights.

Then a man appeared coming from the direction of the ramps and carrying a suitcase in one hand and a half-full black trash bag in the other. He walked in a hunched, stumbling gait, his clothes wet, the thighs of his pant legs black with grime. The man's shirt was just as dirty, and his face was florid and anguished, barely aware of anything but the concrete at his feet. He had a sore on the side of his neck, a hole that glistened wetly in the dim light. People walked around him, and a security guard with a whistle looked briefly at him, then caught Adrian's gaze and shrugged. The man carrying the suitcase and trash bag went on his way, fecal stains marking the back of his pants. Adrian left the duffle bag on the planter and walked over to the guard. "What's with him?" he asked.

"Jus' one nodda homeless druggie," he said. He shrugged again. "No mo' notting fo' do."

Adrian nodded and went back to the concrete wall. He remembered the sound now, the pidgin. He wondered about the sore on the man's neck, if anything was being done for it. He shuddered at the thought. Where was the man going? In that direction there were only car lights and the rain coming down, illuminated by the streetlights next to the overhead ramp. He decided to go up to those ramps to look around. If they had lived in Honolulu, then he would find it. Then he saw that one of the green signs with white lettering up by the ramps had the name on it.

The rain had let up. The smells coming off his clothes were strong: wood smoke, gas and oil, and a rancidness that he associated with fear. He picked up the bag and made his way on a narrow walkway toward the ramps. Out where he could see at a distance, he scanned the landscape, and to his right he saw a flat galaxy of pole-mounted orange streetlights, and beyond that the winking of lights sweeping upward on mountainsides miles away. In that direction was Honolulu probably, but the way to it did not seem to involve the ramp he was on. H-1, the sign said. No, he would go back and cross the airport to the other side, following the direction of the man with the hole in his neck.

The crowd had thinned out by the time he got back to the concrete planter. He was hungry and felt sick. He stopped in a quiet area where there were more planters, pulled the squirt bottle out of the duffel bag, and took a long swallow. The warmth of the scotch radiating into his flesh made him sweat, but he now felt good enough to walk on. The duffel bag was weighted toward the front end because of the full bottle of Douglas Glen, and that reassured him. In ten minutes, he was past the other end of the long building and saw a way to get to a road that went under the elevated highway. He worked his way across a six-lane street to another corner with a traffic light, where the road ran under the elevated highway and the orange lights. Beyond them was a series of taller buildings, some with blinking blue lights on top, about three or four miles away. That would have to be Honolulu.

He could hear traffic on the highway above him. On the wet blacktop, a few cars and busses hissed past him. There was a sidewalk, so he set off, every fifty yards or so shifting the duffel from one hand to the other. On the other side of the road, two men walked. They stared at him too long, he thought, and he began to feel vulnerable and wary. He ran his free hand over the side of the duffel, checking for the coil of his mother's braid. The elevated highway swept off to his left, and he saw a cluster of buildings beyond a dimly lit area dense with what looked like warehouses. Some distance to his right was waterfront with elevated cranes.

He could hear rain drumming across a series of rooftops, and he looked around for something to get under. The elevated highway was too far behind him, and ahead there were only weeds and small bushes along the side of the road. So he pulled the collar of his jacket tight to his neck and stood there while the rain hissed along the road and drenched him, leaking through his clothes within seconds. In about a minute and a half, it passed, and then he heard it drumming on the warehouse rooftops to his right. He felt a chill that was clammy—a cold that in some ways was worse than the one at home.

But the cluster of buildings was closer now. He saw a guardrail and a damaged chain link fence and, past that, the end of a street that ran straight at the buildings, so he made his way over the rail and through the fence, then down a brushy, beer-can-littered bank to the blacktop, which had weeds growing out of cracks. The buildings on either side of the street were dark, and in the distance he saw the shadowy movement of people near a corner. Again he became wary. They could be seasoned versions of Mark Brough, might want to rob him and, as an afterthought, decide to cave his head in simply because it was there. He decided to wait.

Nearby was an electrical thing about the size of a telephone booth and enclosed by a chain-link fence. He walked to it and positioned himself on some weeds at the base of the fence. Immediately he felt himself drifting into a half-sleep, lulled by traffic humming in the distance. His mind pulled into itself and manufactured voices: his mother calling out his name, and Leigh Donaldson whispering, "That's so cool." Then, from farther back in the past, the snapping sound of his .22 when, during the winter, he wandered through the state reforestation land and shot chickadees, one after another, because they followed him from sapling to sapling, making their little sounds. He stood there laughing because they were so stupid, and then he shot them, their bodies falling into the snow, followed by feathers that settled slowly after them.

He snapped awake, sweating. His stomach pulsed with acidic pain, and his mouth and throat were dry. The cluster of buildings in the distance sat in a stillness that suggested deep night. The streetlights on the road that led toward the buildings threw circles of pale light on the blacktop. He shook his head and smoothed his filthy hair back, wondering why he would dream of chickadees. He calculated the time that had passed since his mother died: something like twenty-four hours. She was there in the hole, wrapped in the dirty sheet. Now he wondered about himself. He felt small and soiled and lost, not so much in terms of where, but in terms of what, if anything, was he now connected to. Maybe Leigh Donaldson had found herself in the same spot, and cutting her wrists turned out to be the easiest way to deal with it. He pictured her in the bathtub, picking the razor up and aiming the corner of it at the little stretch of wrist at the base of the thumb, where the pulse was. When she poked the razor in and saw the spurt of arterial blood, what did she think? Okay, it's just about over. It'll just be like sleep. Shuddering at the thought that he could have caused it, he stood up. He picked up the duffel bag and ran his hand over the side, feeling the circle of the braid, and made his way through the weeds and toward the road.

He passed stretches where stores were clustered, dark parking lots where car roofs glinted under streetlamps, then older-looking buildings with corrugated roofs and alleys crammed with garbage. At the edge of one building was a pool of dirty water covered with the faint iridescence of oil, toads hopping around a grocery cart, a kid's plastic car, and some rotted paint cans. In a mud bank next to the puddle was a pile of elliptical globes—coconuts—some with little branches, or fronds, growing out of them. Then the road stopped at a canal, or a huge culvert, and the way across it was a bridge to his left. The buildings loomed close, up a slight rise, and in the dark hollow under the cluster he could see warmer light, and an area that looked like some kind of park.

He kept walking to where the road divided into a large area of blacktop with various directional arrows. Beyond that was a park. He saw figures moving and the sharp blue light of a police car. The presence of the police car reassured him, so he made his way to the grass. On a bench sat a man hunched down in a coat, and behind him was a grocery cart crammed with white and black plastic bags full of stuff. Other men were sitting on benches, and some sat on the ground, leaning against trees.

A person about thirty yards away was pacing back and forth on the sidewalk. The movement and size suggested a woman, who had a light green backpack on one shoulder. She seemed agitated. She turned and walked partway down the sidewalk, headed in his direction, gesturing at the air before her and then angrily elbowing the backpack behind her, and when she got closer, he wondered if she were not quite right in the head. Insane people, regardless of gender, scared him. In Utica, he had seen homeless people with major screws loose, and though he was fascinated by them, he instinctively avoided them, as if their conditions might be infectious. He made wide berths around them as they ranted at cars going by or babbled to themselves.

He heard more rain and made his way to the overhang of a restroom building. Hunched down in a blue athletic jacket, the agitated woman walked in his direction. When she came within twenty feet of him, she stopped. “You normal or are you a creep?” she asked.

He shrugged. “Normal I guess. I’m not gonna do anything.”

“Ooo, haole boy,” she said, walking across the grass. The jeans she wore were fairly clean, and her running shoes and green backpack almost looked new. She stopped a few feet from him and looked around, then back at him. “I can smell you from here.”

He slid his bag along the concrete and moved over to give her more space. She got under the overhang just as the rain came down.

"So, you come from where?" she asked. "Frisco or Santa Cruz or some cool place like that?"

"New York."

"Times Square," she said. In the dim light he could see her features. She was not Caucasian.

"No, the New York that's sorta remote—upstate, woods, and all that. So where do you live?"

"Here," she said. "But I don't have TB or cancer or AIDS or herpes. Not even gingivitis."

"Oh."

"So how old are you? Sixteen? Got pissed off at your lawyer father because he wouldn't let you watch the Playboy channel? Didn't buy you a BMW?"

"Nineteen."

She looked at the street. "Fricken guy," she said. "He owes me money, says he'll blah blah right here." She looked at him again. "Like do you have anything in the bag? Even a cigarette?"

She seemed harmless enough. "I got a little booze."

"For real?"

He unzipped the bag and drew out the squirt bottle. "Scotch," he said. "Here, wan' a belt?"

"Sure nuff ah do," she said. "Wah, thank ya, Fred." She took the bottle and squirted a stream of scotch into her mouth, then smacked her lips and said, "Fred, that sho takes the edge off."

"It isn't Fred," he said. "It's Adrian."

"Adrian! What a cool name."

"It isn't so cool if you gotta walk around with it."

She shot another stream into her mouth, swallowed, and then grimaced a little. She pointed the squirt bottle at her chest. "So how about mine? Tenley."

"That sounds all right to me."

"One more belt," she said, and squirted more of the scotch into her mouth. Then she burped and said, "Ho, crude yah?" Now it was nearly empty, and he held his hand out. She gave him the bottle, and he squirted a stream into his mouth. The acidic roiling in his stomach felt awful.

"Where can you get something to eat around here?"

"Gotta wait," she said. "It's"—she pulled her jacket sleeve up and tipped her watch into the dim streetlight—"four thirty."

A car slowed down on the street, and she squinted at it. She turned to him and said, "Touch the bag and I'll have you neutered, 'kay?" He nodded and she ran through the rain toward the car. There appeared to be two men inside. She put her hands on the half-open window even before they could pull over. She was talking to them, her voice raised, and the two silhouettes in the car looked at her, one centered by the orange glint of a cigarette. When the car started to pull away, she walked with it, her hands still on the window. Then it took off, and she yelled, "Fuck you!" after it and raised her middle finger.

She walked slowly back to Adrian, her shoulders hunched. Her hair was wet and stringy, the expression on her face one of bitter devastation. It wasn't his business. He stooped to put the squirt bottle back into his duffel bag, but before he could, she called out, "One more, please."

He handed her the bottle. She was shaking a little as she raised it to her mouth. She held the bottle up to the dim light, and her hand shook as she did that. "Almost gone," she said.

"I got some more," he said, and realized that he shouldn't have said that.

"I don't feel good."

"There's like a ladies' room right—"

"No, I'm going to hold on to my toxins. Think of the waste if I got rid of them."

"Was that the guy who owed you money?"

"Yeah, and he had a real peculiar way of paying it back."

"What was that?"

"It's none of your business, but I'll tell you. The guy with him had the money, but they had a little clause in their offer. All I had to do was go with them and let them have their fun. This offer, however, didn't have any guarantees attached. For example, whether or not the stupid creep in the car with him has some grotesque affliction that might end up being *my* grotesque affliction. The terms of this agreement were not acceptable. Actually, a good friend of mine has been missing for almost a month now, and it was the same deal. She was picked up by two men, and her stuff was found by the road out that way." She pointed toward the airport. "Donna Leong."

"Okay."

"Her picture was in the paper. That was three weeks ago. Did you say you had more dakine?"

"Dakine?"

"You know, booze."

"Yeah, but it's actually a half a gallon and a small jar. Maybe your friend decided to leave."

"Jesus, you come loaded now, don't you, Fred?" Then she said, "Adrian? That's it—Adrian."

"Branch," he said. "My last name, I mean."

"Chong," she said. "And no, she wouldn't leave naked. Twenty. My age, I mean."

He wormed his hand into his bag, past the coiled braid and the Douglas Glen, and found the peanut-butter jar. He got it out, took the cap off, set it down, and undid the top of the squirt bottle, which she held for him.

"Fill that puppy up," she said.

Two-thirds of the way, he stopped, recapped the jar, and slid it carefully back into its clothes cave. "It's all I got, and I can't buy any more 'cause I'm not old enough."

"That's the least of our problems." She squirted a stream into her mouth and looked in the direction of the airport. "I'm worried that she's dead. I mean Donna." She shook her head, then seemed to brighten up. "So pardner, what brung you to these parts? That ole notion of paradise? Hula beauties an' stuff?"

"No, I was born here. Moved away when I was about seven or eight, I think."

"Hell, musta been some fucking-A prodigy. Pack by yourself too? I mean, you use a credit card? How, for example, would you be able to, say, sign a check? Wouldn't the lady at the counter like tell you, Sonny, you don't look old enough to have a bank account."

"My parents moved."

"After you did? What'd you do? Get there and then call them up? Mom, Dad, it's good here. I got a job, got a really cool two-bedroom. You can come now."

He reached out and took the bottle from her, then squirted a stream into his mouth.

She laughed. "Okay," she said. "Enough of this shit." She looked at her watch again. "I'm going to turn in." She looked around. "Upwind of you, of course. I think I'm a little drunk, but not that drunk, if you get my drift. I mean I get yours, big time." She sat down on the concrete next to the building and pulled the backpack alongside her, one arm through the straps. Then she pulled her feet under her, drew the top of her jacket up around her face, and hunched herself over.

He sat down a few feet away from her and put the duffel bag in his lap, then leaned over on it and turned his head a little to the side, trying to find a comfortable fit for his face. He found it in the hollow formed by the coil of his mother's braid.

III

He opened his eyes into a flat, cold light, heard the hiss of traffic on the street along the park. There was a large drool stain on the duffel bag, and he wiped his mouth. People crowded the sidewalks: old women carrying shopping bags, men in suits or bright shirts and pressed slacks, sharply dressed young women. The girl sat next to him in the same position she had put herself a few hours ago. His body felt raw, electrified with discomfort. He wormed his hand into the duffel bag, drew out the squirt bottle, and shot a stream of scotch into his mouth, waiting for the warmth to seep into his flesh. Tenley Chong, that was it. He looked at the top of her head, her hair parted down the middle, her knees under the blue jacket. This was the time for him to sneak away, but he wondered, What would she think when she woke up with him gone and wanted just one more squirt of the scotch?

At least he should let her know he was going. So he waited, watching the cars going by. In a few minutes, she moved, one leg extending a bit. Then the jacket slid down around her head, her eyes opening slowly. She stared blankly at the traffic and began to cry, her face down in the jacket. He cleared his throat to let her know he was there. She wiped her eyes, then stretched a little and looked at him. "Oh, it's you," she said. She wiped her eyes again. "Shit," she whispered. She opened her backpack and pulled out a rolled-up towel.

"Just thought you might want another squirt before I left."

"Sure," she said. "It'll get me off the ground."

He gave her the squirt bottle, and she tipped it to her mouth and shot a stream in. She swallowed it, grimacing, and handed the bottle back. "This, I believe, is an inadvisable lifestyle," she said. "Will you please excuse me while I go to the ladies' room and puke."

She was gone about five minutes and came back looking nauseated and red-eyed, wiping her face with the towel. He could see that she was darker skinned, like his mother.

"What a waste," she said. "One more, 'kay?"

He handed her the bottle, and she squirted a small mouthful in, swished it around, and swallowed it. Then she wiped the rolled-up towel down her face and took a deep breath. "But golly, you never get a second chance to make a first impression, and I think I've blown it."

"Well," he said, "me too. I smell."

She sniffed the air. "It's dormant now. Look." She stared off at the buildings. "I'm broke. You got enough for me to eat? I know a good plate-lunch place just up the street here."

"It's early."

"No, all-day plate lunches. I like the shrimp curry. For you, I recommend the teriyaki steak. Mini-plates. But plenny grinds." She put the towel back in her bag.

"Okay, I'll just use the men's room," he said. He decided to leave the bag and walked around to use the restroom, which turned out to be clean and well lit. He washed his face and hands and used the toilet, producing hardly anything and vaguely worried that he wasn't eating enough.

She had her backpack on and was standing when he returned, so he picked the duffel bag up. She pointed the way, up the street toward the big buildings. At the edge of the park, they waited in a drizzle for a traffic light to change, and he looked up the street. It was lined on each side by small shops, all in old, low-rise buildings. Elderly Asian women walked up and down the sidewalks carrying umbrellas and bags of groceries. Men stood in front of the stores, smoking cigarettes and talking, and almost all of them were Asian too. He had the feeling he had landed in a foreign country. Then, as he and Tenley Chong walked, he felt embarrassed because of the dirtiness of his clothes. On storefront windows he saw sharp, black and gold characters that looked like little houses or boxes or crosses, Chinese writing he guessed. Toward the top of the long block, Tenley turned to the right, and they stood before a little shop with pictures of plates of food taped to the window.

"I will now relieve you of a few bucks," she said, her hand out.

He put the bag down and took his wallet out. Inside were only twenties. He gave her one.

"Be back shortly," she said. She slung the pack over one shoulder and went inside.

He waited, watching her as she talked with the man behind the counter. Then she stood waiting, scanning a newspaper on one of the tables. Within three minutes, she came back out with a white plastic bag with two small styrofoam boxes inside. "We gotta get outta the rain," she said. She led him up the street into an area where some of the buildings were twenty or thirty floors high, the grounds around them elegant enough to make him feel even more out of place. He was relieved to see a homeless man pushing a grocery cart on the other side of the street. Tenley pointed at a bench under a tree. "Dis Fort Street Mall," she said.

"Okay." She still had his change, and he got ready to say something about it.

"We bums, junkies, and human wreckage like it. We like to in-your-face the people with the best clothes, to blob ourselves out on these benches as if to say 'Fuck you, this is a free country.' We enjoy being jobless, hooked on all kinds of toxic shit, hungry and dirty. It's a proclamation of our freedom and solidarity. We are cool." She sat down on the bench and shrugged the backpack off. "Donna and I sometimes dozed on this bench. I asked the guy in the store if there was any news about her. He didn't even know who I was talking about. Girls disappear. Who gives a shit?"

She patted the bench. "Here, pardner, setchaself down." Adrian sat down. She opened the plastic bag and pulled out a styrofoam box, sniffed, and said, "That's yours." She pulled the other out, sniffed, and said, "Mines."

He opened his. There were two thin pieces of meat, a ball of rice, and a ball of macaroni salad. Underneath was what looked like strings of cabbage. "Rice?"

"'Ass right, brah. Rice dakine. Staple."

"You talk three ways: Western, egghead, and that one my mother told me about—pidgin."

"Right." She ate some of her rice. "So ono dis," she said.

"Okay, so where does the egghead come from?"

"I was in college a year and a half, the University of Hawai'i. My mother sent me there."

"You quit?" He ate some of the meat. The sauce was good.

"My day life and my night life just didn't mesh. I had to choose one."

Down at the end of the street, he saw the top rigging of a ship. "Is the beach that way?" he asked, nodding in the ship's direction.

"Up that way," she said, pointing to her left.

"You know, my mother told me some names of places," he said. "Are there like a lot of places around here that go by those, uh, those language names? Hawaiian-language names?"

"Everything goes by Hawaiian-language names. Why?"

"Just wondering," he said. "I forgot a name, that's all."

She finished her food and closed the box, making it squeak. She stared toward the ship, her hand on her stomach. "Well, thank you. I believe I feel whole again, ready for a new day."

"Me too," he said. He thought of the change again. It had to be twelve dollars, at least—a half-gallon's worth. He ate the last of the macaroni salad and the strings of cabbage and closed the box. She took his, picked hers up, and went to the end of the bench and threw them in the trash, but kept the napkins, which she put in her bag. When she came back, she sat and looked at him.

"You got a look on your face there, pardner. Is this where we take our different trails?"

"I guess."

"You know," she said. "You don't seem like an asshole to me. I mean, most of the drifters who come through here are jerks." She shifted on the bench and dug into her jeans, snorted, and shook her head. "Your change," she said, and then added, "boy was that ever stupid."

"You can have it."

"You know what I'm going to do with it?" she asked. "I'm going to go see if I can buy a little off-white rock of some chem-lab toxic shit, and then I'm gonna put that rock in a pipe and smoke it. And if I don't have a pipe, I'll bust it up into a powder and use a straw. I'll be on top of the world, and then later I'll shit my guts out for a couple days."

"Everybody's hooked on something," he said.

"You got that right." Now she looked pensive and sad. "It's been a problem for me," she went on. "I can't get away from it. There's a lot of stuff that I am trying to get away from. Help is available. The problem is that I just said yes, and those who just say no and want me to say no can't get me to stop saying yes. Yes, yes, yes."

"I guess I did too." He nodded his head toward the duffel bag.

She smiled. "That's sweet," she said. "Alcohol."

The rain came back, blowing toward the ocean, and she said, "The crops are saved." They sat and watched it for a minute, and when it began to let up, she shook her head slowly and said, "Well, I fear that I am boring you, pardner." She put out her hand.

He laughed and shook it briefly. "No, but I know you got stuff to do," he said. He thought a moment. "Let's assume that although institutional help is available, but not your thing, as they say—"

"My God, that was well put. What skoo you wen'?"

"I quit when I was seventeen, but anyway, if I could be of any assistance . . ."

She looked at him, thinking. "I surmise that you're not just setting things up to get a little honey on your stinger, are you, pardner? You're serious."

"I guess so."

She looked in the direction of the ship and shook her head. "I'm a waste of time, pardner."

"I don't think so."

"How much money you got in your wallet there?"

"About eighty dollars."

"Okay, I'll see how much of that I can get by the end of the day without giving you anything in return. It's a kind of game."

"You can have it right now. I'll give you, say, half, so you can get yourself a bigger whatever you called that. Rock or whatever."

"Wouldn't you like to get a little something in return?"

He shrugged. "I guess not."

She stared at him. "Fuck you," she said flatly. "I don't want your fucking money."

"Sorry."

"All right," she said, standing up. "I'm off. Go someplace and get run over by a truck. I don't need your help." The agitation in her bearing scared him. She snatched her pack off the bench and hung it on her shoulder. He moved to the end, pulling the duffel bag behind him.

She raised her hands and waved them at him once, as if she were throwing him away, then turned and walked toward the ship. He felt sweat forming on his skin and waited for her to vanish around a corner. She stopped, looking at the ship, then turned around and came back. He stood up, grabbing the duffel bag. But as she approached, hunched in her jacket, she did not appear angry. The expression on her face was more a kind of doubtful anguish.

"I'm sorry," she said from twenty feet away. "Really, I just don't feel good today."

"Okay."

"The rain's stopped, so I'm gonna go over to Ala Moana Beach and sleep awhile."

"How far is that?"

"A mile, whatever." She looked tired and ragged. "C'mon," she said.

They walked past a huge building she identified as the federal building, and then crossed a six-lane street to walk by some dock warehouses. Then they walked past businesses, mostly car dealerships. On the ocean side they met the water again, this time a little harbor with fishing boats docked right near the road. The park was just beyond that, and they walked off the street, through a parking lot, and onto sand. He looked down at his running shoes. "Take 'em off, dude," she said, and pulled her own running shoes off. His socks were filthy, so he took them off quickly and jammed them inside the shoes and put them in the duffel bag. He would have to leave them in the bag because the money was in the right shoe.

"Jesus, pardner, you been on the trail a long time," she said.

The sight of the water made his heart beat faster. He did not expect it to be so blue, especially under an overcast sky. Where the waves broke far out, the foam was snow white.

"Get out your bathing suit," she said.

"Bathing suit? I don't have one. I can't swim that well."

"You're shitting me. You come out here and you can't swim?"

"I did a little, in like a lake, but I always sorta went down like a rock."

She found a spot she liked, pulled her towel out, and spread it crossways so that they could both sit on it. Then she started stripping off her clothes. He looked around, wondering. But she was wearing a green two-piece bathing suit underneath. While she jammed her clothes into her bag, he watched the movement of her body, surprised at how well built she was, rounded and strong looking.

"I saw you look," she said, standing up straight, her hands on her hips. "Juicy, yah?"

"I wasn't—"

"Yes you were. So here are my wares." She put her hands under her breasts and lifted them a little. "Nice jugs." Then she slid her hands down her sides. "Killer ass. Aren't I just what you haole boys come out here for?"

He looked around. "Is there a men's room here? I got shorts."

"I got a small backup towel. Just wrap it around yourself and change. I'll hold my nose."

She pulled the towel out of her bag, and he wrapped it around his waist, took off his shirt and undershirt, and then felt around in his bag for the shorts. When he found them, he stopped, stuck in a little fit of anxious modesty. Within ten seconds, he was wearing only the dull-blue shorts.

"Ooo, Patagonias," she said. Then she folded her arms, looking at him. "Pale as death," she said. "I mean that's haoleness full on. Look, pard, if we're gonna bunk together, you gotta get that trail dirt off. Foller me," she said, walking toward the water. He was afraid of how deep it might be. But twenty feet out, the water was only up to her knees. Then she fell back into it.

He was about to walk into the water when an oriental couple stopped and looked at her, and the woman, speaking in Japanese, gestured at her with a camera. The man, wearing tan pants pulled up too high and a white shirt, stood looking at her too, while his wife chattered, frequently bowing her head in quick jerks. They were both very pale and looked out of place. Tenley came out of the water, shrugged, and went toward the woman, who, still jerking her head quickly, motioned her over to the man. Tenley went to him and stood next to him, and he put his hand around her waist as the woman raised the camera and took a picture. Then they both bowed and left, Tenley staring after them as if she were still confused about what had just happened. Then her expression turned into one of thoughtful anger, and she looked as if she was thinking she had been tricked into doing something she hadn't wanted to do.

Adrian stepped into the water, surprised at how warm it felt. Tenley still stared in the direction of the couple.

"So what's the matter?" he asked.

She jerked her head, almost as if she had forgotten he was there. "No— Nothing. No problem," she said flatly. "Forget it. Lemme have some more dakine, then I'm gonna crash a while. You can use the other half of the towel."

Because of the crustiness of the salt on his skin, Adrian's sleep was warm and heavy. From time to time throughout the morning, he opened his eyes and looked around. He saw only old people, a few small kids, and swimmers going back and forth about a hundred feet from shore. The sound of the water breaking over the distant rocks lulled him to the point that he almost forgot where he was and who was next to him. Half-dreaming, he felt that something was vastly wrong, out of balance, as if he'd been swept into oblivion, a state of being without perception or feeling, where everything he had once been was gone. Blank nothingness. He thought that this was death, and the only reason he was able to feel it was that he had laid his head down on his mother's braid.

He sat up, shaking. His flesh felt raw with a wretched itching, and his mouth was dry and fuzzy. Gape-mouthed, he stared out at the ocean in a rapidly dawning shock. His mother was dead. She had lived, and now she was no longer alive. The familiar animation of her face as she talked was something he had assumed would always be there, and now it wasn't. He turned and put his hand on the circular lump made by the braid, and he thought, She is in a hole under three feet of soil. She will not come back.

He was so shaken by this that he could barely control his hands as he got the squirt bottle out. It was empty, so he pulled out the jar and emptied it into the squirt bottle. Then he shot a long stream of scotch into his mouth and worked on swallowing it without gagging or coughing. Keeping the promise she had him make, which had seemed so strange, now seemed as essential as feeding a baby or stoking a fire so that people wouldn't freeze. "H" or "K"—he couldn't get past those two letters.

He looked at Tenley Chong. She was sleeping on her stomach, turned so that she was facing him, and had her arms around her bag. She now seemed to him a frustrating distraction. He was supposed to be looking at Hawai'i, and he had looked only at her. It was true that she was not bad to look at, lying there like a seal, but she had distracted him from what he was there for.

She opened her eyes. "Howdy pardner," she said, then rolled up on her side. She yawned and wiped her eyes with the corner of her towel. "How 'bout a little o' the hair o' the dawg."

He hadn't realized that he was still holding the squirt bottle. He handed it to her, and she sat up and squeezed a stream into her mouth, then swallowed. "All right," she said, handing him the bottle, "a couple of things. One is this: were you serious when you said you'd give me forty bucks?"

"Yeah."

"Okay. I'll even wait until later to ask you for it." She stared at the ocean, then looked at the sky. "Two: you looked at me. I could see you looking, but I realized that you were just a hick from whatevers, so I let you go ahead and run your eyes over my ass and all that."

"Sorry."

"No, it's all very natural. Anyway, before you looked at me, you looked at the ocean, and, pardner, I've seen expressions before, but never one like that. What'd you do, kill somebody? I've never seen a look like that."

"My mother died."

"'Kay, I can understand that."

He studied her features, then looked down. He had not wondered before, but did now. She was not Chinese, although her name was Chong. She was probably a mix of some sort, as his mother had said many people in Hawai'i were. "Look," he said, "can I show you something?" She nodded, and he opened the bag and pulled out his mother's braid, wrapped in his shirt. When he opened the shirt, her face was filled with inquisitive wonder.

"My God," she whispered. She reached out hesitantly, as if to touch the tightly braided hair, thick as a mooring rope and shining in the flat light with a faint, oily sheen. But she did not touch it. "Why?" she whispered. "What happened?"

"She was sick. She had cancer." Adrian touched the braid. "She was sick a long time and I was taking care of her." Once he had said that, he found it easy to say the rest. He described how his father had left after he and his mother realized that she would not make it. He told her about the cold, how he had to scrounge for wood, and her request to braid her hair and then cut it off, about the money she had given him. "She wants— I mean, she wanted me to bury the braid here, in a place whose name I can't remember."

Now Tenley touched the braid, lightly, with her index finger. "So when did all this happen?"

"The night before last."

She leaned away. "Wait a minute. She died and you got on the plane?"

"I promised."

"But why would she want it buried here?"

"She was born here."

"So can't you just bury it somewhere, maybe in the woods or something?"

"She wanted the braid buried in a certain place. She said that if it wasn't, then she'd wander for eternity. She said she knew that from a dream."

Tenley stared at the braid. "I still don't see why—"

"She wants it put in a place near an old burial ground so that she can be with her people. Something like that."

Tenley moved away a little, staring at the braid. "That's Hawaiian hair, isn't it? She was part Hawaiian."

"Yeah."

"Oh no no no. I don't like this," she said, waving her hands before her. "I get a funny feeling about this. That's why you're here. Would you have come here if she hadn't made you promise?"

"No. I wanted to throw the braid in the hole with her, but I got this strange feeling."

"In the hole? You mean at the funeral?"

"There was no funeral," he said softly. "She asked me to not let them have her body."

Tenley stood up and backed off the towel. "She died and you buried her."

"She asked me to do it. I buried her in a pine grove. Nobody'll ever find her there. Never."

Tenley put her hand to her mouth, then crossed her arms and looked out at the ocean, at a family walking at the edge of the water, two small kids wheeling an inflated inner tube on the hard sand.

"I did it by myself," he said. "Nobody knows."

Tenley knelt down on the towel. Then she squinted up at Adrian, her eyes on his face, until he became embarrassed and looked away. "I think I can see it," she whispered. "It's the eyes. I can see the Hawaiian in your face."

"No, I'm really Caucasian—I mean basically."

"You don't understand," she said. She looked at the braid, and her expression fascinated him: it was awe, fear, and maybe sadness. She leaned closer and put the flat of her hand on the braid. "You have to remember the name," she said.

"So she wasn't just crazy, you think?"

"No, no way." She sat back. "You don't understand." Staring at him, she nodded slowly. "Your dad's a haole and your mom was Hawaiian."

"She was part Hawaiian—less than a quarter maybe. Her maiden name was Macklin. So I'm like less than an eighth maybe. That makes me Caucasian."

"Around here that doesn't matter. I'm Chong and a quarter, more or less."

"My dad said if I ever told anybody I had Chink blood, he'd beat the shit outta me."

"She was part Chinese?"

"Caucasian, Chinese, Hawaiian, and something else, I forget."

"Portagee maybe. And she lived all these years in one of those cold places?"

"It was my dad. He really hated this place here," he said, nodding at the water. "It pissed him off that America got all polluted by nonwhite people. I guess you would call him a racist."

"Hmm, I think I'd call him an asshole."

"Same smell."

She laughed, then stopped abruptly. Again she reached out and put her hand on the braid, then she touched the wire at the base of it. "You put this on here?"

"Yeah, she had me do it and then cut it off, and then a little later she died."

She put her hand under the braid and gently pulled it out of the shirt, keeping it circular, and then lifted it up and looked closely at it. "It's heavy," she whispered. She squinted at him. "Look, you can screw up one way or another, like I've screwed up. You can lose friends, all that. But you can't mess up with this." She shook her head slowly, staring at the braid. "You can't."

"It's just superstition. What would happen?"

"I don't know," she said. "If I knew, then it wouldn't be as bad. Around here we're all superstitious. And you can't remember the name?"

"That's the problem. I think the place started with an 'H' or maybe a 'K.'"

"That's three-quarters of the places here," she said, carefully sliding the braid back into the shirt. "I know people who could help, though."

"My mother gave me an address. There's this lady she wants me to talk to." He looked in his bag and found the slip of paper and showed it to her.

"Vierra's a common name," she said. "And Date is toward the mountains from Waikīkī, past a golf course. I can tell you how to get there."

"That'd help." She gave him the slip of paper, and he put it in his wallet.

"Okay. Just let me think about this." She got to her feet. "Look, I'm gonna go shower and put some clothes on. It's like three thirty now, and I've got a couple of things I gotta do."

Still holding his wallet, he took two twenties out. "Here, here's the forty bucks."

She took it and put it in her backpack. "I'll be back in a few minutes," she said. "Thanks." She picked up her backpack and walked toward a low building just inside the park. He took another squirt of scotch and put it in his bag. It was nearly empty. His hand on the braid, he watched her walk, and then he put the braid back into the pack and zipped it shut.

She came back carrying her bag in one hand and sandals in the other, and she was flanked by two men and two women. One of the men was tall and pale and wore sunglasses and a bright shirt with pictures of palm trees on it. The other man was shorter and dark. The women were young and pale and wore shorts and tops, one of them with a lot of gold jewelry on her wrists and neck. Tenley seemed agitated, as if she were trying to walk away from them while they tried to keep up with her. Adrian stood up.

"Look, there are people here," Tenley said.

"Ten," the tall man said with a kind of pleading slowness, "you look a little pale. How'd you get so pale? Gosh, where've you been?"

"There are people here," she said again. She came to the towel and put her bag down, then pulled at her wrinkled tank top. The tall man stopped and looked at Adrian.

"Just a friend," Tenley said.

"Hey, what's your name, sonny?"

"Adrian Branch."

The man screwed his face up.

"Branch?" he said. "What kind of a name is that?" The girls giggled. The dark man stood beside them with his arms folded.

"You're new here?" the tall man asked.

"Just coming back," Adrian said. "My mom grew up in Hawai'i. My father did construction here years ago."

"What's your father's name?"

"Ray."

"Look," Tenley said, "I—"

"Ten," the man said slowly, turning his attention back to her, "it's only a question of obligations. Wouldn't you say that, Art?"

"'Shright," the dark man said, staring at Adrian. He seemed to be staring too long. "'Ass dakine, one obligation, yah."

The tall man looked like a preppie, but Art looked lethal. He glanced from Tenley to Adrian and back with an expression of aggressive speculation. The girls, all-American types, ambled down the shore toward the water.

"We've got to talk," the tall man said to Tenley, adjusting his sunglasses. "Call me."

"I told you—"

"No no," he said, chuckling. "But hey, let's not spoil the day now."

The girl with all the gold had returned. "Hal," she groaned, "can we go?"

"So who are you?" Tenley asked the girl. "California, right? New meat from California?"

"Girls!" Hal said dramatically. "Let's not fight." Then he again addressed Adrian. "So Mr. Branch, what do you do?"

"I just got here, like I said."

"Welcome to our islands," he said. Then he repeated, "Branch . . . Branch." He looked at his watch and then at Tenley. "Later, Ten," he said to her. He and his friends walked away.

"So who's he?" Adrian whispered to Tenley. She didn't answer. She was fiddling in her bag, and her hands were shaking. She pulled out a little mirror and looked at her eyes.

"It's nothing," she said. "Forget it." She continued to root around in the bag. "I'm going that way," she said, pointing east. "Waikīkī. I'll meet you back here later. Just be right about here."

She picked up the backpack and a pair of sandals and walked barefoot down the beach. She didn't look back.

The sun did not come out, and the sky gradually dimmed. He sat on her towel and watched the waves break into white lines of foam. Then he sat and watched them in the fainter light of evening, and finally in darkness, a phosphorescence expanding and breaking up and then disappearing. The sound they made was monotonous but soothing. He was hungry and decided to find something to eat and come back and wait for her. But she would probably not return. Her interest in the braid was probably only a ploy to make him give her the forty dollars.

The blue light of a police car moved through the parking lot, and he sat still. Off in the distance he could see the movement of people on the beach. He remembered passing a shopping mall just before they'd turned into the beach. He opened the duffel bag and wormed his way past his rolled-up jacket and pulled out a shirt and smelled it. It still held faint remnants of the wood smoke smell from the house, tinged with oil and gasoline. He pictured the wood stove, the living room, the bedroom in which his mother had died, the barn. He pictured the unfinished house off the road, its window frames and sills so carefully restored, and he felt a flush of shame and something approaching self-hatred for having abandoned it. What would happen to it now? Eventually the rain would penetrate the unfinished parts of the roof and ruin all the work he had put into it. When he was thirteen, he had taken his mother to it, to show her what he was doing. She'd responded with that patronizing enthusiasm of adults, all the time unable to conceal a strange expression on her face—one he later realized meant that she knew he was being scammed.

He put the shirt on and got out his running shoes and socks. Then he made his way across the six-lane street and found a burger place on the road where the mall was located. He bought two cheeseburgers and fries and watched the people, and the jaunty, amiable expressions and gestures of the workers. The majority of them were of ethnicities different from his, and he remembered what his father had told him about this place, how dirty it was to have everybody mixed this way. But if all these people could exist together without any trouble, then maybe he was looking at the future of the rest of the world.

After getting a couple of strange looks from people sitting nearby, he felt uncomfortable enough to go back to the beach. There he took off his running shoes and dirty socks and waited, because he supposed he was obligated to wait. Every fifteen or twenty minutes, he heard the wail of sirens. There were no stars out, and from time to time, a light mist blew from behind him and over the beach. After his eyes had fully adjusted to the darkness, he again saw a faint, broken white line across thc horizon, its shape and size changing as the waves expanded and died.

He thought that he might have been sleeping when he first heard moaning. He stared into the blackness in the direction of the sound, felt behind him for his shoes and socks, and put them on. Then the moaning became coughing, and he concentrated on it until he was fairly certain it was Tenley Chong. Another blue police light moved across the parking lot. He remained still. By the time the light moved off behind the pavilion, the sounds had stopped. He got up slowly and moved toward where they'd seemed to be coming from. About fifty feet ahead, he saw a shape on the sand, and beside it something brighter. Her backpack.

As he approached, she crooned a little, a soft sound signifying wonder. Then he was standing above her. "Is that you?" he whispered.

She rolled up on her side and giggled. "I've fallen down and I can't get up," she said.

"Here," he said. He grabbed her wrists and lifted her up, and she draped her arms around his neck and fell against him. She smelled of vomit. She was warm and limp, and her forehead came down hard on his collarbone. She started to sing, "All I wanna do is have some fun, till the sun—"

"Let's go over to the towel," he said. He began to pull her along, but her feet wouldn't work, so he ended up with his arm around her side, half-carrying her. Surprised, he realized that, compact as she was, Tenley was heavier than his mother.

"Don't go over there," she said. "I left my fettuccini alfredo over there. I wanna cover it up." She continued singing, "—sun comes up over Sanna Monica Bouleva-ard." She giggled. "You wash your car on Tuesday while I drink my beer?" she asked.

"Yeah," he said. "I know that song."

When he got her to the towel, he meant to gently lower her onto it, but she went down like a sack of feed or a corpse. She giggled again and tried to sit up, but ended up lying on her back.

"Somethin' wasn't right with that shit," she said. Then she went still. He sat down beside her and after a while began to worry that she wasn't breathing. He put his ear to her mouth and felt the warm breath and the heat from her skin. He used the part of the towel she wasn't lying on to cover her, and then he laid out his jacket for himself.

He stayed awake because he thought it would be a good idea to. He sat looking into the blackness and listening to the traffic on the street fronting the beach park. An hour or so passed, and she briefly talked nonsense in her sleep, then rolled over and draped her arm over his lap.

Beyond a peninsula to his left, a soft orange-and-pink light appeared over the horizon, and then the light increased, pushing upward, and ahead of it the sky slowly turned into a clear, dark blue. He saw the clearer details of the breaking surf straight out from them, the trees on that peninsula, and right next to him, Tenley, hair draped over her face, a little drool glinting in the corner of her mouth. Her closed eyes looked puffy, partly because they were naturally so and partly because of whatever she had done the previous night. He had seen it before: kids who happily engaged in activities that made them pay the next day, never learning from it. He had done it himself, still was. He was nineteen, she was twenty. By this time, they should have figured out what to do about themselves, but then he had also seen adults, like his father, who went through their lives without ever getting the message. When he thought this way, the next thing he always wanted was another belt of scotch, and so he wormed his hand into the duffel bag.

By the time she had begun to stir, the sun was above the horizon. It cast its light obliquely over the beach, which was occupied by old folks walking, swimmers doing slow laps, and people surfing out on those waves that broke into dotted lines at the rocks. They were still in the shade, and Adrian shivered in the moist morning air.

Tenley sat up and put her face in her hands. "I can't do this anymore," she said. "I can't."

"What'd you do?"

"I got high." She rubbed her face with her hands, and then looked around, and at her watch. "Six thirty. You wanna eat? I got an idea."

"Yeah, I'm hungry."

She stood up and reeled a little. "Shit, I'm still seein' double. You still got any dakine?"

"Yeah," he said, then reached into the duffel bag and drew out the squirt bottle. She took it, squirted a short stream into her mouth, swished it around, and swallowed. "This is a good idea," she said, holding up the bottle. "How'd you figure this out?"

"I had to take it to school, and it was the only way. It was that an' peppermint candy."

"Cool," she said, and thought a moment. Then she cleared her throat. "Pard," she said, "I gotta ask ya. Got any money?"

He pulled off his right shoe and lifted the insole. "Hold your nose," he said.

"How you gonna give anybody those bills?" she asked. "Take them out and let them air, 'kay?"

He put the money in his shorts pocket.

"Let's break camp," she said. "I know a couple places, that way." She pointed in the direction of the peninsula. "I'm gonna go wash up."

"Yeah, me too," he said.

This time, when he left the men's room, he felt clean enough to imagine he was normal.

She talked as they walked along the harder sand near the shorewash, Adrian wearing his shorts and a T-shirt and Tenley wearing shorts and a tank top. "You're so haole," she said. "You talk well, I mean the words you use and all that. On top of that you've got Hawaiian blood." She stopped and stared directly into his face. "A little less pale and you can almost see it," she said. "It's the eyes." She was thinking, she told him, of working up a scam on her family, particularly her mother, who hated her for the mess she had made of her life.

"What'd you do?"

"It's a long involved thing that doesn't matter anymore, but last night I was thinking, I mean like about as far as anybody in my condition could think, yeah?" She had felt like shit, she told him, and ended up on the beach fronting the Moana Hotel. Staring out at the water all stoned and sad about everything, she had realized that she wanted to go home, which was a nice place a half a block from the beach in a place called Waimānalo, way that way, and she pointed. Not that she really could "go home" in the literal sense. Her room wasn't hers anymore. But there on the beach she'd been remembering all the stupid shit she had done, dropping out of college and all that, and it was almost like a whatchucall—revelation. She was considering this when a bum walked by, babbling to himself and filthy and stinking and half out of his mind. How can anybody be filthy when the nicest water in the world is a few feet away? But there he was, carrying his worthless trash in the most appropriate container for all he owned: a garbage bag. The man stopped and took a piss in the sand, then moved a few feet away and sat down and went to sleep, or started to, mumbling and coughing this deep, wet cough and sounding like he might not get up in the morning. "an' I was like all staring at him and I'm all, Jesus, there's me a couple of years from now, except that for girls it's probably worse." That's when, Tenley said, the idea of the scam came to her.

By the time she had gotten this far into the story, they were past the peninsula and moving through a parking lot toward a bridge over a wide canal, beyond which were hundreds of boats lined up in a harbor, and huge hotel buildings along the sand. They crossed the bridge and then went across a parking lot fronting the boats to another beach, and from this perspective he could see a line of buildings stretching for about two miles, then a gap and a cluster of more buildings under what he assumed was Diamond Head. In the bright morning sunlight, it looked clean, the buildings different bright colors, the sand a rich tan, the water a pastel blue. Next to the parking lot was a beach-encircled lake, or a lagoon, he supposed, and behind that a building with a huge tile mural of a rainbow. In the parking lot by the lagoon sat a white truck with a sign listing various dishes.

"Here, gimme one of those twenties," Tenley said.

He did, and she sniffed it and then, shrugging, went to the window. "Two manapua an' two spam bombs," she said, "an' one Aloha Maid juice—no, make dat two."

She returned with a white plastic bag in one hand, gave Adrian the change, and nodded at a picnic table under a tree at the edge of the lagoon.

He did not like the look of the food. The clear cellophane wrap held a squared-off block of gluey rice topped with a chunk of what he guessed was spam, and the rice was wrapped around the middle with some green stuff. "'Kaywait," she said, unwrapping it. "No sneer. Try um."

He shrugged and took a bite. "Whoa, this is good."

"See?" She opened her spam bomb and started eating. "The green stuff is seaweed."

He watched her as she ate and sipped the juice, wondering if he thought she was pretty. Initially, he'd felt he was in the presence of what his father would have called a darkie or a slope, saying that, for him, these women were for fun. Believe me, boy, a lot of 'em spread like that, he would have said, snapping his fingers. But don't ever get serious about one of them mixed-up part-this and part-that girls—there's something kinda unclean about that. The world wasn't made for people to get all fucked up that way. Adrian could have asked, But what about Mom? But he never did.

There wasn't any dominant ethnicity in Tenley, not that he could pinpoint. Was that Asian, the tilt of those eyes? The thickness of the flesh around them and the almond shape? Was that hair, which was not black but a deep reddish or copper brown, Caucasian or oriental hair? He finished his spam bomb and looked at the other thing on the table, a lump of dough the size of a half-flattened baseball. Tenley pulled the wrapper off it and took a couple of bites. Inside was what looked like raw meat.

"Dis manapua, filled wit' dakines." She looked into the red center of it. "Char siu pork, some egg, some other stuffs dat make it so ono. Try um."

It was good too.

When they were finished, she said, "'Kay, let's chase that with some of your dakine."

"We gotta get more. The bottle's low. There isn't that much dakine left."

"We can loiter by a liquor store," she said, holding out her hand. She took two long squirts.

"Now I know why the bottle's low," he said. He followed her with a medium squirt, swallowed, and then sat up, feeling a little better. "Okay, you can continue with your scam thing."

"'Kayden, so I want to go home, like to reestablish something with my family, or what's left of it. I mean, I was going to do great things. And I didn't. I fucked it up and now they hate me for it. My mother threw me out a year ago. She said she never wanted to see me again. So I thought, Fuck you, I don't want to see you either. I toughed it out, but at the same time I wondered why I cried every night when nobody was around to see me and ask why." She paused. "What are you good at?"

"I don't know. I used to do stuff with carving wood and carpentry and stuff."

He told her about the old house he had found on the property, how it was falling apart and how he'd discovered how well built it was, refined in its construction, with rounded beams supporting the floor in the basement, beams that still had birch bark and maple bark on them, and perfectly cut dowel plugs, and how every window had a beautiful frame. He told her about restoring the house to the way it was a hundred or a hundred fifty years ago. He told her that for a while it was all he'd really thought about, except girls, but when he thought of girls, he always imagined them in the context of that house. If there was a pretty girl in school, it would be him and her inside the house, maybe married or something like that. Tenley sat with her chin resting in the palm of her hand, her elbow on a green plank of the picnic table, and he noticed what happened to her eyes as he talked. They got this misty, distant look, as if she were envisioning the house, taking a brush and polish and working on some old door hinge, discovering that the hinge was brass, the surface like gold once it was fully polished.

"Did you finish the house?" she asked softly.

"No. My father finally said that the land wasn't ours. We were only renting. So it didn't matter what I did with the house. It was never going to be mine. There went the house."

She sighed. "Well, that's the way of the world." She shook her head.

A horrible heat raced through his flesh. Leigh Donaldson had gotten that same look when he'd told her about the house. He stared blankly at the table, wondering if the story was cursed, if all who heard him tell it would commit suicide.

"But it was just a house," he said.

"No, that's more than a house." She looked at the lagoon. "That's like your own security. You walk along a street, and there's like this buzz of doubt right to your bones, like a little space. You walk into your own yard and the space fills up."

"So anyway," he said, "the other thing I did was cut a couple trees to clear like a back yard, and I discovered this thing: you cut across a log and get like a pattern in the wood, like a butterfly or an animal or whatever. So you cut a thin disk to make like a round picture. You take a paintbrush and paint and you alter the pattern to make it look like whatever you want it to look like. I did that. My mother thought these disks were great, but I was afraid to take them to school because that was an art thing, and where I went to school, the boys thought of art as a faggy thing, if you know what I mean."

"You're an artist and carpenter," she said. "You're into cultural things."

"Okay. Actually, I did carve some other wood stuff too. Yeah, call me an artist."

"Say something cool about art."

"It's a rendering of an alternate vision. Nature informs us. We merely interpret."

"How did you come up with that?"

He shrugged. "Something I heard. It's the rendering of an aesthetic vision. Look at Brancusi's *Bird in Flight*."

"Jesus," she said. "Who's he?"

He shrugged. "An artist, I guess." He thought a moment, then said, "Contemporary art lacks visionary expansiveness. It is mired in the mundane."

"Pardner, can I register for the next class you teach?"

He pulled the squirt bottle out of the bag. "Here, have a snort. Oops." The bottle was almost empty again. He pulled the big Glen out and refilled it. "Here you go."

When she wiped her hand across her mouth and gave the bottle back to him, she put the flat of her hand on the green plank and said, "You and I are engaged."

He screwed his face up at her. "Why?"

"I want to go home. See, there are all sorts of perks in being part of a family. Then there's my friends at school. I go up there with you, and you talk so haole, they'll say, 'She's finally cleaned up her act.'" She scowled at the table. "It's more than that even. It's—" She waved her hand around. "I don't know."

"No," he said. "So you're what? Wayward. You had a few problems. I don't see why you can't just go home. I mean, what could you have done that would make it that serious?"

Her stare was level, as if he had challenged her. The look made him remember the mall and how she had flipped out on him. "Well," he said, "I guess you got your reasons."

Her expression became flippant. "You're interested in the sleazy details," she said. "Okay, I was employed in a disreputable profession for a few months. Hal from yesterday, you know, that guy, was my—supervisor."

He thought, Okay, hooker, whore, whatever.

"That's prostitute," she said. "You shocked?"

"No, I guess not."

She looked flatly at him. "You're not as 'Aw shucks' as I thought," she said.

He shrugged. "So you wanted out."

"Yeah, but the look on your face, it's like, Aw jeez, I guess it's time for me to get out of this business. Yawn. Today is the first day of the rest of my life."

"I wasn't saying that. I don't know the circumstances."

"I had a bad meth habit," she said. "This shit produces a high where you think you own the world. You don't even have to sleep. Don't you have that where you come from?"

"No, it's bad, low-level bumpkin stuff. A little cocaine maybe, but only the cool ones know how to get it. Up there it's grass, sniffing glue, junk like that. Bush league. I never took anything else but grass, and it made me freak out so that I thought everyone was laughing at me."

"Pakalolo paranoia," she said.

He didn't know what that was. He was about to ask when she said, "Think of it. I met these cool people in Waikīkī, got these suggestions from people that I talk to this guy Hal. It meant a steady supply. What would I hafta do? Well, when I heard about that, I was all, Oh my, I can't do that, but I knew what it would mean if I had a supply. You'd do a lot for a supply. I had boyfriends in high school, and like sex wasn't any big deal and all. So I went to talk to Hal at his apartment, a very expensive one. There were two other girls there, mainland ones, from Portland or someplace. We were sitting there drinking Merlot, and he was like giving us this philosophical lecture. 'Ladies,' he said"—Tenley laughed then and shook her head—"'no woman should ever do it for nothing. In my perfect world it would be major international commerce, a sexual utopia where this act would have a going rate and be reported in the news along with the Dow and the long bond yield, so that men would never again take for granted what they are getting.' Blah blah blah, like that. Actually one time he was a graduate student who taught classes, UC something. He was impressive. And then alone with me, he said in this intense but soft voice, 'Tenley, it is you they come here for. You are Hawai'i, you are the girl on the travel-brochure cover. For a hundred years it has been your face, your body, your aura that they've dreamed of.' Jesus, did he ever talk a good game. Anyway, he had a little underground catalogue with pictures of us, real ones, even high-school yearbook pictures in there, and he had ways of showing this to clients. The clients were mostly older, mostly Japanese—like from Japan, I mean—and we did it in nice apartments or hotel rooms, only a couple times a week, for big money. The clients were paranoid about AIDS and other stuffs like that. We made like two thousand dollars, split sixty-forty: sixty for Hal and forty for us. Yeah, yeah, I know, seems unfair, but Hal had to do all the coordinating and stuff. He'd watch us closely. 'Tenley, you need to keep up your tan, keep your weight up too. Good heft and a rich complexion are important. They like the contrast of the rich darkness of skin and then the paleness of what's kept out of the sun, if you know what I mean. That is what they pay so much for, that sudden paleness punctuated by a little this and that, in the semi-darkness of a room. They pay big bucks to get to finally uncover that prize, that center of a lifelong dream.' It was all very clean. So far from the short-skirted meat that walks Waikīkī and gets reamed ten times a night for chump change. This was high class. We dressed almost like missionaries. But I quit. Forevah."

"Why? I mean, what—"

She snorted and looked at the table. "Okay. I might as well finish it then. One time he set up a meeting in a hotel with two brothers, Japanese businessmen I guess. I told him I didn't like the idea, didn't want to be the baloney in a sandwich or any of that, and he said, 'Ten, I almost doubled the fee, it's a good one for you, good money. They're okay, I swear.' So I went up there, a little apprehensive as you might imagine. I was whispering to myself, 'I am Hawai'i,' over and over. Well—" Tenley stopped there and sighed, staring at the green planks. "I'll shorten it for you. One of them was at it while the other was standing above with a camcorder—you know, like the tourists carry? I was partly watching this and producing routine little gasps and moans and saying 'yes' in a strained voice, and the guy with the camera got closer and closer, filming the thing, way close, I guess making sure all the time that the focus was correct and his hand was steady holding the camera, and he was so concentrated on what he was doing that I could watch, you know. I would say yes, and then I was all, What the hell is he doing? He leaned way down, his brother slowed down, and I could see saliva on this guy's lower lip, like a drop of it still hanging, catching the light and all, this little sort of jewel jiggling there, and then it dropped from his lip and fell on the inside of my thigh. I felt it hit, then felt it run a little while he kept on filming. I felt nothing else. When we were done,

I went to the bathroom and washed the spot, but the little patch of skin where it hit sort of burned. It almost felt like the skin swelled in a little circle. When I got out of there, I ran away, keeping the money minus the down payment. Fifteen hundred dollars total. I didn't even go back to my apartment because I figured Hal and Art would be there. When I did get a chance to sneak back, I took only stuff I could carry, you know, like in a bag. And for days I thought something was on my leg. Even now I feel this irritation on that spot. This was more than a month ago. I still owe Hal the money, but I spent it." She stared at Adrian, thinking. "You wanna escape now, don't you? Now you do."

"No."

She gestured at the duffel bag. He pulled the squirt bottle out and gave it to her, and she took a long swig. "I quit," she said, wiping her mouth. "I won't do that anymore."

"So Hal's mad."

"He can't do anything. It's like I violated a contract is all."

The scotch had begun to calm her. She turned sideways on the bench and looked out at the lagoon, where kids were playing in the water and people had beach chairs and towels set out on the sand. It was strange, but the more repulsed he was by her story, the more fascinating she became. It seemed to him that he had known her a long time. He watched her as she stared at the people, her gaze drifting up the side of a huge hotel, along the multiple railed porches where people sat, some of the sliding doors of the rooms open so that curtains drifted out. Then she got up and walked toward the water. He could see her wiping her eyes. He became embarrassed, wondering what he was supposed to do about that. None of this was his business. Added to that was the obvious question: why him? He heard the voice in his mind, saying, Oh no you don't. Don't get into another thing with a girl like that. Don't feed the snake.

He got up and approached her, feeling awkward. She was still watching the people around the lagoon. When she finally turned, she had on her face a look of such pensive anguish that he wondered what else was wrong. "I messed up my life and I want it back," she whispered. "I just need a little help."

"Okay, I'll help you," he said. "Waimānalo. That was it, right?"

She explained things as they made their way along the beach: the huge hotels, the long outrigger canoes, the Hawaiian music whose sounds leaked out from classy beachfront lounges crowded with tables protected from rain and sun by colorful umbrellas. He was mesmerized by the people lying on towels, the smell of suntan lotion in the air, the bright bathing suits and tanned flesh of the girls. He told her that she was a good tour guide.

The beach led to an opening on the street, and along that section with no buildings there were covered park benches with men sitting around playing chess, then a huge park. The long stretch of beach fronting the park was lined by trees Tenley identified as ironwoods. Date Street was up that road, she told him, pointing at a tree-lined street that began at what looked like a zoo. In the park there were men with shopping carts and plastic trash bags full of stuff, and people flying kites. He was the perfect tourist, she said, because of his dopey gape-mouthed look. At one point he remembered something from way back in his past, something about the parched flanks of Diamond Head seen from the perspective of the park. "I think we used to go to a beach around here, but it wasn't an open one."

"How old were you?"

"Around seven."

"And you remember that?"

"Yeah, it was a shorter beach, and I remember water coming up through these little hollow coral heads, like little rounded-off caves. And behind us was a huge house. I remember a rusty chain link fence where we used to hang our towels and looking back at a veranda or something."

She thought. "Maybe it's Tong's. That's right at the end of the park."

"Can we go there?"

From time to time he studied her as she talked or pointed things out. She had said she would do anything to get her life back, and he wondered what "anything" was. He knew right away that the thought was rotten, sleazy, and foul. He found her powerfully attractive now, and it wasn't just the cover-girl exoticism of her looks. It was something else, as if he'd known her much longer than a day and a half.

He saw the house from the street and knew that it was the one. They went through a little park, which he did not remember, but when they came to a concrete wall and jumped the foot and a half down into fine greenish-brown sand, the memory came back clearly. His father had fished right over there, and his mother had sat on a towel about here. There was the break in the line of rock along the shorewash. "This is it," he said. "I spent a lot of time here."

They sat, and each downed a long squirt from the bottle, then stared at the ocean, where whitewater broke over the reefs.

"How much money you got?" she asked.

"Eighty, give or take."

She squinted at him, assessing his appearance. "We gotta get you some clothes. An' cut a little hair and shave off the fuzz." She giggled, touching his cheek. "You really nineteen?"

The gesture made him tense. She had her arms around her knees, and he looked at her feet with their stubby little toes, then her legs and her shoulder, the soft shape of her breast. If all she had said about her "job" were true, then how could he ever be anything but another man who wanted her in that way? No, the two of them were simply involved in a scam that would help her out, and sex had nothing to do with it. She was probably turned off to it anyway.

She fiddled in her backpack and drew out a Swiss knife, opened the little scissors, and looked up at his head. "Take your shirt off." He did, and she said, "Ho, getting a little color." She sat close to him, her breath in his face, smelling of spam tinged with scotch. He looked at her throat and then at the wide V of collarbones and, beneath that, the brown top of her chest. She snipped and then with her heel dug a little hole in the sand. She dropped a lock of brown hair in the hole, snipped again, and dropped in more hair. He stared at the hair in the hole, and when she had snipped the fourth lock off his head, she stared into it, too.

He said, "Ma . . . It was Ma, then something else. It started with an 'M.'"

"Makapu'u."

"No."

Reaching up to cut more hair, she pushed his head down, so that he was looking at her half-spread legs. She sat sideways, one folded leg leaning against his thigh. He felt an erection coming on and quickly shifted his legs to give it room. As she cut, her thigh moved, swaying out, then in, the little crease down there closing and then opening. One breast slid up his arm, then down, and he watched the flesh swell. He held his breath, then let it out, and held it again.

"I'm only cutting your hair," she said. "I not giving you bolo head, you know."

"Okay," he said. "Bolo head is bald head, right?"

"Uh huh," she said vaguely, snipping more. Now he stared directly at a wide, pale armpit centered by a small dark patch of stubble that held flecks of white deodorant, one droplet of sweat inching down from it. Her shoulder moved, tensing as the muscles under the skin slid forward and back. "'Kaywait," she said. She pushed at his shoulder so that he would move around and put his back to her, then she snipped more, and after a while turned him so that he faced the house, which seemed abandoned, its windows boarded over.

"I remember this house. Why did they close it?"

"City probably bought it," she said. "They tear them down and make mini-parks of the land."

She worked her way around to the front of his head again, and he stared again at her throat, the heartbeat visible in her neck. Again, she pushed his head down and he watched the subtle movements of hips and thighs, her heel pressed against the inside of her buttock, her toes braced against his thigh. He could barely stand it, and the breast that moved against his left arm did what the other one had done on his right, the flesh surging upward as it slid down his arm. When he peeked at her face, he saw her wet tongue clenched firmly between the white teeth, the tip moving up and down. She bit down on her tongue a little each time she snipped, her chin puckering.

"There," she said, letting out a breath. She sat back, closed up the Swiss knife and put it away, and looked at his head. "Not bad. Get rid of the fuzz, and you're a natural." She smiled at him.

"Eighty bucks won't buy much in the way of clothes, and what about dakine?"

"Brah, Salvation Army. Dakine we can work out. Right now, though, I'm going for a swim. There's a shower up there." She pointed at the little park, where two men were leaning on a pipe rail on the rock wall ten feet above the ocean. She glanced back at the water. "It sort of cleans you." Then she looked at his duffel bag. "Funny, that scotch takes the edge off. You don't jones so bad over the heavier stuff." She reached in her bag for a second towel and her green bathing suit. In an expert series of movements under the towel, elbows and knees and fists punching this way and that, she put her suit on and jammed her tank top, underpants, and shorts into the bag.

"Jesus," he said. "That was amazing."

She got up and went down toward the water, then turned, and in a flash he understood why he was so attracted to her physically, why she had been such a commodity to that guy Hal. "You coming?" she asked. He stood up and brushed hair off his back then watched her wade into the water. The feeling of her closeness when she cut his hair stayed with him. He had been seeing her in terms that bypassed time and baggage and his past and hers. He had looked at her with eyes ten million years old in an innocent reveling in physical proximity that was and was not sexual at the same time, an amazed and lucid perception of moving flesh and skin, blood inside veins, all in a cloud of aromas erupting in microscopic emanations from that flesh.

"Remember," she said, "seawater is dense, so you float bettah. No worry. Come on in."

He asked if he could interrupt the Salvation Army trip to check the lady's address on Date Street. She'd had enough of walking, so she could hang at the zoo while he went. Up past the golf course, she said, and pointed. "An' you can leave your bag here." He checked the slip of paper again: 2210, it said in his mother's handwriting. Apartment 14.

He felt sleepy as he walked, and the heat made him sweat. Date Street was lined on both sides by low-rise buildings. The Vierra one was a seedy-looking place with the smells of cooking and sounds of kids coming from it. Number fourteen was on the ground level, the door in amongst a line of other doors shaded by porches jutting out from the second story. The chance that any lady named Vierra would still be here seemed remote to him, but he felt he had to try anyway, if only because she might help with the place name he had forgotten.

A middle-aged man with no shirt on opened the door. He was dark, pot-bellied and unshaven. Caucasian, Adrian thought. "Yah?" he said.

"Is a Mildred Vierra here?"

"Whatchu want?"

He introduced himself, said that his mother had been a friend, that his father had worked construction here, and that Mrs. Vierra would recognize the name.

"She's sick," the man said, "but I recognize da name. Knew him, yeah." He looked at Adrian. "She cannot talk now, sick that's why. Whea you goin' be?"

"Well, it's a house near the beach in some place. Wai—Waima-something."

"Waimānalo."

"That's it. I just wanted to tell her that my mother died, and she gave me this address."

"I mention it to her when she gets bettah," he said. Then he raised his eyebrows as if inviting Adrian to leave.

"Hey, thanks," Adrian said.

They took the bus to the Salvation Army store. It was on a street he thought he recognized, near where he had left the elevated highway and gone down the road the night he arrived. He described his visit to Mrs. Vierra's apartment to Tenley, and she said, "So is one dead en' den."

"I figured it would be. But it's done, so I don't have to think about it anymore."

When they were inside the store, she turned to Adrian. "What size your waist?" she asked.

"Thirty-two."

"'Kay, we look fo' jeans firs'. Ho," she said, looking at a pair, "dis nice. Try um on." She pointed at a booth with a curtain hanging over the opening.

Within an hour he had a pair of pants, two aloha shirts, a tank top with a picture of a fish on the back, swimming trunks, socks, and black tennis shoes. Tenley bought shorts for herself.

On the way out, she stopped by a bin and said, "Lemme have your ol' jeans an' da pilau shirt."

He dug them out along with another shirt, which made her sigh and look up. She checked the pockets and put them in the bin. "Now we hang out at one liquor store and take care of dakine."

The liquor store was in a seedy-looking spot near downtown Honolulu. They waited on a sidewalk under the wooden roof of an empty store until the right sort of man came walking by. "Sir," Tenley said, and he stopped. He was a local man, Chinese or Japanese, with flashy clothes and sunglasses and slicked hair. "You do us one favah?" she asked. "Go buy one bottle scotch, one half gallon o' whatevahs, da cheapes' inside?"

"Eh, how you know I not one cop?"

"Cops aren't good dressers," she said. She held out a twenty-dollar bill.

The man laughed. "Half gallon? I check um out fo you."

The bus that took them back ran through the city, then along the beach road, past the place they had spent the previous night, and into the center of Waikīkī, which Adrian had not yet seen. It was dense and bright: tourists all over the place, huge hotels with stretch limousines parked at opulent entryways, expensive shops with brass fittings on doors, and in the center of it all a jungly-looking place that glittered with various wares, especially jewelry. "International Market Place," she said, pointing at it. "The park where we were is ahead, remember? We passed by here just down there on the beach."

Sitting on the bus and looking at all the buildings and people suddenly made him tired, and he wondered what they were going to do about a place to sleep. Everything took on a two-dimensional flatness, and sounds were sharp and at the same time hollow, as if he had made his way into a fast-paced animated dream. At one stop she elbowed him and they got off. They were again near the zoo and the large park. "We'll go into the park an' sleep a little," she said. "Then, I don't know. We—" She looked around. "We'll work that out laters."

He more or less fell on the towel she laid out, and after a while opened his eyes to a patch of watery sunlight moving back and forth on her cheek. She was facing him with her knees drawn up, her other cheek in the palm of her hand. He looked around. People flew kites, cooked in the late-afternoon sun. The patch of sunlight moved over her cheek, then over her closed eyes, the eyebrows two black lines like bird's wings.

When she shook him awake, it was nearly dark, the sky to the west pink and partly filled with tall cumulous clouds glowing orange at their tops. He was covered with bugs. Ants, he guessed, and he worked at slapping them off his arms and legs. Tenley was doing the same. She seemed agitated at first, but once she seemed satisfied that the ants were off, she held out her hand to him. "What?" he said.

"Dakine. Now." With her other hand, she reached behind her back and picked up flowers strung in a circle. "Found this in the can over there," she said. She picked a couple of browner-looking flowers off the string and held it up in the faint light.

He got out the squirt bottle and handed it to her. She took a long stream, swallowed, and then did it again. When he reached out to take the bottle, she held up her hand and took a third stream. "I don't care," she said. "Whatever it takes. I gotta calm down."

"You'll pass out."

"Not a bad idea, passing out," she said, handing him the bottle. He took one stream himself, and then put it away.

"What's that for?" he asked, nodding toward the string of flowers.

"Somebody's lei," she said. "I had an idea."

"You gonna go over there again tonight?"

"Don't do that," she said. "I'm not doing that anymore. No way. We need to eat, then find a better place to sleep. Here," and she gestured around at the park, "there are creeps at night. I was thinking of that other beach we went to." She held the lei up to put over his head.

"I'm not wearin' that," he said as he pulled away.

"Oh come on," she said. "It doesn't make you gay, you know. It's just something people do here." She placed it over his head. The flowers produced a powerful, sweet aroma.

She seemed equally agitated as they ate, this time at a burger place a block and a half away from one corner of the park. She sat there jouncing her leg and thinking, watching people walk in and out of the little place. He sat there embarrassed because he wore the lei, but nobody seemed to notice. When she looked at him, her expression of agitation did not change, and he realized what it was: denied scotch, he would do the same, and he knew the squirming irritation, the wanting that dominated everything else.

"I still have money," he said. "I mean if you—"

She shook her head and stared at him. "You'd give your last nickel wouldn't you? Why?"

"If you need it—"

"That's not help. Money we need, but not for that. I need to rip off a purse."

"Count me out," he said. "That stuff scares me. I mean, how would you do it?"

"Something I did once. We gotta put our good clothes on."

"I'm not doin' anything like that."

"Okay, then *I'll* put my good clothes on."

They changed in the park, he into black pants and an aloha shirt with tropical flowers on it, in full color, and she into a skirt, heels, and a nice-looking silk blouse. As for the lei, he was to continue wearing it. "Okay," she said, looking into a little mirror tipped so that it caught a streetlight, "just make believe we belong where we're going. I'll show you how dumb people can be." She snapped the compact shut. "Shit, I could set up a table on the street and sell fat-free carrots." She looked at her watch. "Eight fifteen. Just about right. Gimme your bag."

"What for?"

"We just store them here, and come back for them when we're done." It was simple. Hide them in one of the trashcans. The cans were the galvanized steel type, with plastic bags put in and stretched over the top edge. You pulled the trash bag partway out, left your stuff underneath, and put the bag back. All you had to do was zip them up tight so that the centipedes wouldn't get in.

"Centipedes? What's that?"

"Big, this long," and she held up both hands. A half a foot? The cans had holes in the bottom and they would crawl in. Nobody in his right mind would look for valuables in a trashcan.

He followed her, but he worried about the bag. The braid was now in a trashcan, and each step took him farther away from it. Tenley walked quickly, with an agitated determination that kept her from talking. They went across the street by the zoo and into Waikīkī. About three blocks in she stopped and looked into the entryway of a large hotel.

"This is a banquet for some huge state workers' credit union, 'kay?" she said. "Usually it would be earlier, but this one starts late for some reason. I saw the sign before. By now there'll be three hundred people in a line getting food at a buffet and a whole bunch of empty tables with pocketbooks and stuffs under, 'kay? Da comedian is telling jokes. You get in line. I'm gonna go running around with the lei," and she reached up and grabbed it. He bowed his head, and she held it up and shook it. "'Kay, this looks good. We'll be out in forty-five seconds."

"What if somebody asks me anything?"

"Just say you're here with ah . . . da Freitas family, over there, and then you point, 'kay?"

"Don't you hafta have a ticket?"

"Yah, but when the comedian gets going, an' everybody inside—" She stopped and looked at her watch. "Cannot talk anymore. Let's go."

She led him through the lobby to the elevators. In the elevator light, he could see sweat on her forehead, the eyes roaming with a look of frightened but gleeful anticipation.

Off the huge carpeted foyer of the banquet room was a large porch where people stood smoking, and in the foreground a desk with a woman sitting at it with her back to them. Tenley studied the scene for ten seconds. A voice on a microphone came across the room, the man telling the jokes. When the man began singing, the woman at the desk moved a few feet toward the wide doorway of the banquet room, and Tenley whispered, "Follow me," and they walked across the plush carpet to the crowd of people smoking outside on the porch. She led him through, holding the lei out in front of her. People stepped aside to give them room. At the other end they stood before an open door. Inside, there were lines of people moving along buffet tables, and in the middle of the room, empty tables set up around the stage, on which a man dressed as a woman sang a song in pidgin, the laughter almost drowning him out.

"Go in straight first," she said, "then go stand in line."

He did so, feeling both ridiculous and frightened. When he got in line, he saw Tenley walk in with the lei draped over her wrist, looking around anxiously at the people. Then she waved and called across the hall, "Hi, Auntie!" She went straight to a table, and sat down and put the lei on the top, then reached under, looked up and then gestured at him with a doubtful shrug. No one looked at her. Then she waved her hands as if saying forget it, and sat down again. She reached under the table again and did something, then got up and headed back toward the porch where everyone was smoking. Adrian caught a cue from her, a jerk of the head, and followed, and they made their way back to where they had entered the hall. The woman who was supposed to be sitting at the table stood a few feet away, listening to the singing.

On the elevator Tenley was shaking badly, clutching her purse to her chest. "Jesus," she said, "I can't do that anymore. Oh Jesus."

Two blocks away from the hotel she finally looked. "Eighty-two dollars."

They went back to the park, and now she walked more slowly. She did not talk. The look of distance on her face told him that getting high was on her mind, nothing else. And he thought, It's not my business. A junkie is a junkie. He had talked to one of the older kids at the group home about Leigh Donaldson, and the kid told him that girls like that used sex, stole, would sell their mothers to get their dope. He'd said, "If she stood there looking at you and next to you some drugs, and someone said, 'You can have the dope, but I'll have to torture this guy to death if you take it,' she would put her finger in her mouth and look at you and say, 'I'm sorry.'"

Their bags were still under the trash bag. He took them out and carefully checked them for bugs, and gave Tenley hers. Her face was a flat gray in the moonlight, and she was sweating.

"So you goin'?" he asked.

She said nothing. He shrugged, and felt the side of the bag to make sure that the braid was still there. When he looked up at her again, she was staring at him. Then she swung her bag at him. "Stop asking!" she yelled.

"Hey," he said, jumping back. She moved toward him and swung the bag again, then threw it to the side and came straight at him, punching, swinging her hands at the air before his face, making strained squeaking sounds. He backed away, holding the bag. She swung again and lost her balance a little. She lunged and caught his wrist, and put both hands on it and pulled, kicking at him. In the moonlight the look of rage on her sweat-slicked face frightened him, and he tensed his arm, fearing that she would bite his hand if she could get it to her mouth. He dropped the bag and moved away from it, still keeping his arm rigid while she held onto it with both hands. When she tried to kick again he pulled hard, breaking her grip and turning her, so that he was behind her. He wrapped his free arm around her chest and held her against his own. He felt the trembling of her body and heard the rapid breathing, the cold, slick flesh of the top of her back wetting his shirt. Then she relaxed.

He held on tightly for another five seconds, then slowly loosened his grip.

"I'm cold," she said.

"Okay."

"We can sleep on that little beach by the house."

They sat on a towel partway hidden in a bush with pulpy leaves, and she held her fists under her chin and drew her legs up, and leaned against him, shivering. Then she began opening and closing her knees, in and out, in and out. He put his arm over her shoulder, and she pumped her knees. From time to time she drew herself further into a trembling ball, and he sat with his arm around her shoulders and looked out at the waves that broke over the reef, then beyond at the dim distinction between the water and the sky, and above that a dome of stars that reminded him of the night sky seen from the front yard of his house in New York. The moon, a bright, phosphorescent three-quarter circle unnaturally sharp in its definition, slid behind thin clouds that swept to the southwest. The blinking lights of airplanes preceded the distant roar of their approach, or departure, but otherwise the only other sound was the water breaking over the reef.

Tenley finally stopped rocking her knees, and Adrian slept a while, his chin on his knee and his arm still around her shoulders. When he jerked awake, the moon had moved a few degrees, an hour or two's worth, he thought. But something bothered him. It wasn't Tenley and it wasn't the idea of bugs, or anyone in the empty house behind them. Then he looked to his left and saw the orange glint of lit cigarettes, and around those orange glints the shapes of men. He remained still.

"Can smell um," a voice said. "Pussy. I smell um, brah. What? Get chance you tink?"

"Hui!" another voice said softly. "She all used up, or can we have some too?"

Then Tenley stiffened under his arm.

"Brah," the first voice called, "you like share wit' us ah? We frien's ah?"

"'Ass right," a third voice said. "We learn um skoo."

Adrian felt around in the sand for rocks, tried to remember what he had in his bag.

One of the orange points shot into the air and did a strange pinwheel down into the sand.

"Fuck off," Tenley called.

"What, you get rags?"

"Fuck off." She reached for her bag. "I got Mace here, assholes," she called.

"Ooo!" one voice said. "I all dakine now, I shakeen in my fricken boots."

One of the orange points floated down and ended in a thump, one of the figures landing in the sand. Then another jumped down from the wall.

"You got Mace?" Adrian whispered.

"No."

"Okay, let's get up and walk," he said. They pulled up the towel and shook it off, and walked through the fine, heavy sand toward the opposite end of the beach, where a palm tree grew horizontally out over a wall, curved, and then went straight up, its fronds black against a bright cloud. Adrian glanced behind as he walked, but he couldn't see anything. He stooped down and felt around, but found no rocks. His hands shook absurdly and he felt his heart beating in his face. He angled toward the slippery, rounded rock formation along the water's edge and felt in the sand again, and found a rock, baseball sized and heavy.

He sensed movement behind him, and turned. If they came too close he would throw the rock right at a face.

"I sneef um good now," a voice said.

"I have a rock," Adrian said.

"Haole? Dat one haole boy? Sistah, you do dakine wit' one haole boy?"

Then one of the figures flashed past them, astonishingly fast, and Adrian didn't have time to even raise the rock. "Ho, fuckah missed," the voice said from the other side.

"I didn't throw it," Adrian said.

"Well den t'row um. I waiteen."

He held the rock tightly in his hand, and walked in the direction of the one who had run past. Tenley walked beside him, her upper arm against him, their bags bouncing into each other. He felt movement behind him and sidestepped Tenley a little way up the beach and turned just as a second figure hurtled past, punching him on the shoulder as he did. Tenley screamed.

He was trying to focus on a figure to throw the rock at when a beam of powerful light swept over the sand from above them, illuminating one of the men, who immediately covered his eyes.

"Get off the beach!" a voice called, and Adrian squinted at a porch about halfway up an apartment building at the end of the beach, above the right-angle palm tree. "The cops are on the way!" the voice called. "Time to move on, trash!"

The two men who had run past them went back toward the wall, one of them saying, "We get you, sistah," as he passed. "We come back an' take turns on you, sistah, whoah, haole fuckah."

Now the spotlight was on Adrian and Tenley. "Time to move on, trash!" the voice called again. "The cops are pulling in right now. Bye-bye, losers. Move on. I can smell you from here." Tenley squinted up into the light. She whispered to Adrian, "Let's go this way." As they walked toward the bent tree, the circle of light followed them. Tenley shaded her eyes and looked back. "This is a public beach!" she called to the man on the porch.

"Bye-bye, trash!" the voice called.

Adrian dropped the rock in the sand. They climbed up on a narrow seawall and went over the trunk of the bent tree, and then they crept along, holding on to a chain link fence and then a rock wall to offset the weight of their bags. They turned into a right-of-way that led to a street. "What now?" he asked.

"We'll go back to Kap'iolani Park," she said. "But let's wait. Those guys are still around."

They waited for five minutes, looking out at the little street and then back at the right-of-way. Then they went out to the little street, quickly turned onto a smaller side street, and returned to the park.

IV

He opened his eyes to a woman jogging past, a key ring on her hip jingling with each step. One slat of the bench had bruised the middle of his back. His right foot was asleep, and Tenley's head was in his lap. She was rolled into a ball under the towel, and his arm was also under the towel, his hand lying on the soft swell of flesh on the side of her breast. Her face rested on his shorts, right where an erection was making its painful slide into a more comfortable position, and he tried to will it away, but it wouldn't go. He sat still, not moving his hand, and looked around. Then he looked down at a pink ear, hair tucked behind it and draped over his right pocket, and a fine sideburn that made its way past the bottom of the ear, the hairs ending in a soft point. She seemed to be in an extremely sound sleep. He leaned forward a bit and looked at her smooth cheek, the closed eye with the black eyelashes fanned gently in a perfect line. The face might have been that of a child sleeping, healthy and innocent, and he wondered how her skin could be that smooth after all she had done to herself, how her body could have the appearance of strength and smooth, healthy roundness. Inside the sleeve of her shirt, he saw the side of her breast under the loosened bathing suit top, the skin lighter than her shoulder. And the head in his lap, the body under his arm, seemed to pulse, to emanate a hot glow of vitality. He felt as if he were looking into and through her, held in an awed fascination by the slick three-dimensionality of her, and a shudder, a low-level electricity, raced through his flesh. He didn't think he had ever looked at another human being this way, except his mother when she was dying. When he'd stared at her so hard as she slept, it had felt as if he could focus like a laser on her cancer and kill it. But Tenley was not dying. She was alive, breathing, bone and muscle and viscera and membranes and veins all covered with smooth, thick skin. The pinnacle of evolution, yet it all amounted to incredible, baffling waste. She could be on the cover of a magazine, he thought, but for the individuality that sidestepped the usual cover-girl beauty. Maybe her face was too wide or the nose not the right shape or the forehead too high, but given a choice between a cover girl and Tenley, he'd pick Tenley. The speculation was pointless anyway. What would she want with him, beyond the use she could make of him now?

When she finally opened her eyes and moved her mouth, trying to deal with the foul taste, it was six thirty or seven. She sat up, groaned, and moved her head back and forth, getting rid of a stiff neck, then arched her back so that the strong muscles flexed. Squinting at him, she said, "We go my mom's house today. You hafta shave."

He remembered that his razor was dull. He had a thin-enough beard that he didn't use it much, and the sparse fuzz on his chin and upper lip and cheeks—fine hair interspersed with thick, heavier hairs—was a quarter inch long. Then he remembered something his mother had read to him years ago. "You got a lighter?" he asked, "and a mirror?"

She produced both: a little compact and a red lighter. In whatever his mother had read, men shaved with candles. He flicked the lighter, quickly swept the flame under his chin, and smelled the acrid odor of burning hair. "This is something my mother read to me from a book."

"Jesus," she whispered. She watched as he swept the flame around his cheek, along the side of his jaw, all the time holding the mirror out so that he could see how close he was coming to his skin. "What about your lip?"

"Just don't breathe in?" he said. Before he started his upper lip, she grabbed his wrist.

"Leave that on," she said, her face close to his. Mixed with the smell of the burning hair was that of her breath: a rich, salty mixture of sleep-glued saliva and old alcohol. She looked at the bag. "Get out dakine."

They took one long stream each. "No more," she said. "We gotta be sharp."

He looked into the mirror, and seeing his own eyes made him unsure. "I gotta tell you something," he said. "I can't really read."

"Not," she said.

"It's called dyslexia. I have agraphia, too, which is the inability to write. Some words on a page just sort of turn my brain off, like a malfunctioning computer or something." He ran his hands over his face, aware of a slight, rashy burn. "Certain combinations of letters, like t and h together, or that o-u-g-h thing. I developed a way of reading using a piece of thin plastic with an opening about an inch long and only a quarter inch high. I would lay it on a page to isolate the word, then try to read it. I have the card in my wallet."

"But how can you talk the way you do? You sound like you went to college."

"If you can't depend on words on a page, you have to depend on your memory. I used to sit up with my mother and watch TV when she was sick: PBS shows about history and all that."

"You mean that art thing you mentioned yesterday, or whenever it was? Was it yesterday?"

"I think so. I don't know who Brancusi is. I hear it, remember it, then repeat it. Simple."

She stared at him, her mouth open a little. "I've known you only two days? No, it's—" She nodded slowly. "Two days," she said. She looked at him in a way that made him suddenly feel embarrassed and shy. Then he felt tense and defensive. So open an expression seemed too familiar, somehow invasive.

They would dress casually, he in shorts and an aloha shirt and she in shorts and a tank top. They crossed the street into the park, and walked toward the pavilion, where they washed up and changed.

They got on a yellow-and-white bus that left the line of tall buildings and went over the hill that began at the end of the park, the flanks of Diamond Head above them to the left. As the bus moved through neighborhoods with large, opulent houses, she talked.

'Kay, we're engaged—we met right here, when you came out to do your art. What art? You're going to look into art which is part of Hawaiian culture, 'kay? But what do I say? Well, you're the one who comes up with these things. What do you say? Well, I say I'm interested in a kind of resurrection of these images and practices that move the ancient into the current and functional. Cool, she said. That's cool. And I'm oriented toward nature as informer, he said, so that I yield to its information. He laughed. That's PBS about two years ago.

The bus passed through the neighborhoods and turned up toward a highway, and he saw green, cloud-topped mountains in the distance. In the morning sunlight, they were five or six different hues of green, depending, he supposed, on what trees he was looking at. Some hues were pale, but in the folded-in valleys and nearly vertical chasms, the green became black. After a while, the bus went up a hill and came down in an unpopulated area where the ocean appeared very deep right at the shoreline, blasting white froth against outcroppings of reddish, brown, and black rock.

"Pretty yah?" she said.

"Uh huh."

The sound of the engine lulled him, and then she started talking again. "My mother won't speak to me," she said. "My sort-of stepfather is John Murai, a nice Japanese guy she got involved with after my faddah lef' fo' Vegas, like when I was thirteen. My parents rent da house from John, and my gran'parents live in the little cottage out back. My fadda leaves. John gets a divorce and moves in with my mother. My only odda sibling is my sistah, an' she married to one air-force guy. Dey live Texas now, no get keikis. You know what 'keikis' means?"

"Yeah, my mother used that word."

"So anyway, my grandmother is dead . . ." Tenley paused and looked at the ocean. "I loved her, I mean more than myself almost. My granfaddah's really a great guy, but not as with it as he used to be. When I tell my mother that you're part Hawaiian, I'll say you're a third."

"But I'm not. I don't know what I am."

"No mattahs, you should be a third because my mother is, plus Chinese and half-haole. She's very involved in movements, sovereignty for Hawaiians, culture stuffs, alladat. Once she was an entertainer in Waikīkī, hula dancing and stuffs li'dat. Then in like the late eighties she had this revelation where she decided to reclaim her heritage, so she dumped that career and started demonstrating for sovereignty and whatnot. Actually, a lot of people had this revelation in the eighties, not just here. Like Native Americans and so on."

"But what about being half-haole?" he asked. "If she's half-haole and only a third Hawaiian, how—"

"No no," Tenley said. "You don't understand. Here, you *choose* your ethnicity. This is stuff that's taught at the University, 'kay? All you need is two platelets of Hawaiian blood and you can be Hawaiian. If you don't have any Hawaiian blood, that makes you second or third class. If you're all haole, you're on the bottom. It's haoles that colonized this place, and haoles gotta pay—it's guilt by racial association. You stole the kingdom, blah blah. It doesn't matter if you were born yesterday. This is like heavy University talk—that's where this all comes from."

"That's crazy," he said. "My mother said this was like the future world where everybody lived in . . . whatever. Harmony. I mean, the way you talk—"

"All I'm saying is that people think what they think, but at the University, this is what you learn. I tell you one story," she said. "This goes back to way before this University stuff, 'kay? Picture me when I'm twelve an' thirteen 'kay? My favorite sport is paddling. Dis where six girls get in a canoe forty feet long and race. It's a big sport here . . ."

He was fascinated by Tenley as she talked, sitting there next to him, close so that he could hear her voice over the motor. She had her hands folded in her lap, and the bouncing and swaying of the bus made her jounce slightly. He watched her face, the unselfconscious earnestness of her as she talked, the straps of her bathing suit just above the neck of the tank top she wore depressing the flesh inside her shoulders so that when the bus swayed the straps dimpled the flesh a little more, then a little less.

"So I have really good frien's, other girls, mostly haoles. There's Brenda Emory, there's Amy Roberts, there's Serena Fernandez, an' others, 'kay? There are like eight kids, and six get to go out onna canoe at regattas. Da ones who sit da beach yell an' scream an' cheer 'cause nex' week they'll get inna canoe and other girls cheer onna beach. We're like all twelve and thirteen, really good, have a good coach, and the firs' season, we get three gold medals, two silver, and get one silver at the state races Ke'ehi Lagoon. Second season da same, 'kay? But at the end da secon' season, da kids' coach has to quit and my mother takes over. By this time she is up to her chin in this new political stuff. She sees how things are, so she brings in kids from da neighborhood, some cousins I don't even know, kids of friends of hers, all girls wit' Hawaiian blood. Nice girls, but they have hardly any experience in paddling canoes, and it's hard, paddling canoes. She puts them in the canoe and me in the canoe, but all my bes' frien's sit da beach. We lose. We come in sixth, eighth, last, whatevahs. I get so pissed, I say, Ma, put Brenda dem inna canoe, an' she says, I got in the canoe who should be in the canoe, and I'm like, Ma! We lose alla time, an' she's like, Don't bother me with this, and then I'm all, Look, it makes no sense, blah blah blah. I go to my frien's. Already they're looking at me like, Hmm, you're in the canoe and we no mo' inna canoe. What's up wit' dat? I'm all, Look, I'll talk to my mom. So I talk to her. I'm all, Look Ma, what's the sense in losing when you can win? And she's all, Don't bother me with this. And I'm like, Ma, this is dumb! We lose alla time."

The bus went up a rise, past parched grasses on both sides of the road and a single mountainous outcropping. "Makapu'u Point," she said.

"Makapu'u. Maka . . . Maka . . ." He shook his head. "No."

"'Kay, so I nevah get it. Finally I get mad and I'm all, You one shitty coach, you dumb, an' she finally gets mad and yells, This is our sport! This is not their sport! I yell back, Dey my frien's! An' she's all like fuming and wild-looking and yells back, This is our sport! So I finally get what she's saying an' I say, So that makes you a Nazi, that makes you a . . . a . . . an' I can't think of the word. She slapped me, like hard, and told me to get out of her sight. But that's only part of it. I mean, there was other stuff too, later. I gotta tell you about that—the University and all that."

The bus went over the top of another hill. She stopped talking, and he looked out the window. "Jesus," he said, "this is beautiful," and she said, "Well, duh." The shoreline ran miles off into a misty distance, with what looked like an island far away, two larger islands right underneath them as the bus curved high above a beach. In the rows of waves he could see heads bobbing. Surf crashed on the sand. He figured out that the different, lucid blues of the water represented different depths. Farther off was a series of black rock outcroppings, and he leaned forward and squinted down at the bright geography. Something about the landscape was familiar, and then he remembered that his mother had brought him there, to tidepools where he went around with a little net and looked for tiny fish to catch and put in a bucket until she and he got ready to leave. Then he would pour the fish back into the pools. The memory carried with it a sensation of a calm serenity. Of the times here that he could remember, this was one of the better ones: when his father was off doing whatever he did, and his mother brought him out here with a packed lunch and his toys.

"My mother brought me to that place down there," he said. "I'm sure of it."

"That's called Makapu'u too, but the beach by those rocks has another name. Kau something . . . Kaupō, I think. My house is up the road another couple miles. Or my mother's house, that is."

The bus coasted down the incline. Tenley had a strange expression on her face, and Adrian thought he knew what it meant. She was looking at the place she thought of as home.

"What if they want me to read something?" he asked.

"They won't. Why would they?"

She pulled the little compact out of her bag, looked at her face in it, put it away, and turned to him. "Well," she said, "let's just see, okay?"

There was a long park, and beyond it on the ocean side was a cluster of houses. Tenley stood up as they approached a bus stop. They got off, and she led him down one of the streets to a small, older-looking house surrounded by a chain-link fence. At the end of the street, he saw a path that led to the ocean. Tenley stopped by the fence. The gate was open, and she nodded to

Adrian to follow her. When she knocked, an Asian man opened the door. "Ten!" he said. "How you doin'?"

"Fine," she said. "John, this is Adrian. Adrian, this is John Murai." The man put out his hand, and Adrian shook it. He saw a woman inside—Tenley's mother, he thought—who was looking toward them.

"Hi Mom!" Tenley called.

She came to the door. "Well, you should have called," she said. She stayed in the doorway, nodding suspiciously while Tenley introduced Adrian. She was attractive. A little heavy, but with a familiar look to her face—something, he thought, like his mother's.

"Mom," Tenley said, "Adrian is my fiancé."

"Oh really?" she said. "Well."

"We just wanted to come and tell you guys. Where's Grampa?"

"At the beach. Fishing as usual." She turned to Adrian. "So what do you do?"

He shrugged. "Well, actually I'm an artist—not painting. Wood sculpture."

"Are you at the University?"

"Well," he said, nodding thoughtfully, beginning to feel a little buzz of anxiety at the lie, "an artist I know in New York recommended against any institutional education. I apprenticed to him, and he believes that colleges and classes foster too much uniformity." He thought he should stop there, but the expression on the woman's face seemed to invite him to go on. "He believes that contemporary art is mired in the mundane. He wants art to be pushed back to being real work or real visionary creation. I mean, what modern artist has the strength to do The Pieta?"

"That makes sense," John said.

"So what do you plan to do here?" Tenley's mother asked. "I mean with your art?"

"He's part Hawaiian," Tenley said.

"I'm interested in studying native imagery," Adrian said, embarrassed by Tenley's declaration. "But more from the nature side out." What the hell did that mean? he wondered. "I mean— What I mean is that my mentor in New York believes that nature informs and the artist interprets. It's not really as esoteric as it sounds, though."

"Interesting," Tenley's mother said.

The sun was getting hot on his shoulders, but they stood there clustered around the front door. Tenley looked into the darkness of the house, then at her mother. She waited, but what was supposed to happen wasn't, and Adrian could see it in the anxious look on John's face. Tenley's mother was not going to invite them in.

"Well," Tenley said, looking toward the ocean, "maybe we'll go see Grampa at the beach. Would you like to do that, hon?" she asked Adrian.

"Yeah, let's do that," he said, a little taken aback by the 'hon,' but feeling relieved to be getting away. He turned to John and Tenley's mother and said, "Nice to meet you."

Walking away, he saw Tenley wiping her eyes. "God, I hate her fucking guts," she whispered. "She didn't even ask when we were getting married."

He paused a second. It was as if Tenley were buying into the scam. "But you know," he said, "as time goes on, maybe she'll come around."

"She'll hate me for the rest of her life, so my response is to hate her for the rest of mine."

"Did the art story make sense? I guess all you gotta do is say you're one."

"You had me believing it," she said.

The beach was wide and lined with trees, the sand a heavy dark tan. To the left, he saw a pine grove. To the right, the beach swept away in a gentle arc, the line of sand describing a bay, in the middle of which small waves broke. Tenley looked first toward the woods, then toward the two islands out from that place she called Kau-something. Squinting, she said, "Oh, I see him, down there."

Adrian saw him then: a man sitting on the beach, shirtless and wearing a hat with a wide brim. He saw the thin line of a fishing rod, its curve changing slightly every few seconds, the line being pulled gently and randomly by the water. Tenley removed her shirt and shorts so that she was wearing only the green bathing suit. "You too," she said to Adrian. He took off his shirt and shoes and put them in his bag.

They approached the seated figure. He was old and had very dark skin, heavily creased, and appeared to be sleeping. Tenley turned to Adrian, her finger to her lips, and tiptoed up behind the old man and put her hands over his eyes. He reached up to grab her wrist, and she walked around to his side and sat down and hugged him. Then she waved Adrian over.

"Dis Grandad, name Jacob Chong," she said. "Dis Adrian. He my fiancé."

"Howzit," Jacob said. His voice squeaked, as if the air that carried it had wheezed through a crack. "Le' me look you," he said to Tenley, and she stood up in front of him. "I knew you come," he said. He struggled to sit up straighter. "Tutu come to me inna night fo' talk," he went on. "She say, da girl come back wit' some nice young man, an' I say when, an' she say soon. She look young too, you know."

"Grampa, what happened to your voice?"

"Ooh, voice go away so fas' you know. But Tutu look young when she come to me, an' you know? You look like her. I say, how come you young and know about dakine? An' she say, Babooze, I dead awready—ma-ke. What difference anyway?" Jacob looked at his fishing rod, the bell on it swaying in the breeze. "She say you come an' now you come. When da wedding?"

"We haven't decided the date yet," she said. Then she sat down and said to Adrian, "Show him."

The braid, Adrian thought, and unzipped the bag. He put his hand under the braid and pulled the shirt off gently. Meanwhile, Tenley described where and when Adrian's mother had died and explained the request she had made. Adrian held the coiled braid before the old man. Jacob stared at it, then picked it up carefully and held it in his hands. Tenley's eyes were fixed on his.

"Dis mana," he said. "Bones an' fingernails an' hair mana. Teet mana. I can feel um."

"Everything would be all right if Adrian could remember the name of the place, but he can't," Tenley said.

"Dis mana. So you come allaway heah fo' put dis wheah she like you put um?"

"Yes."

"You good boy," he said. "But mus' get dat name back and put da braid wheah she want."

"'H' or 'K,'" Adrian said. "A name that started with those letters, or maybe 'M.'"

"I feel life in dis hair," the old man said. "Mus' get da name."

Adrian supposed that because this old man had taken it seriously, he himself had finally been relieved of feeling stupid or superstitious, and he felt the doubt wash off him like dirt. As he watched the old man holding the braid with a wary reverence, and Tenley kneeling in the sand and staring intently at him, Adrian felt the shadow of a fact settle on him like a mist, and he was struck by a revelation: his mother's having made him promise to come out here was more than it seemed. This was something she had known would happen.

The idea stayed with him. When Jacob handed back the braid, Adrian took it, wrapped it carefully, and put it in the bag, and Tenley sat down next to the old man and held his forearm in her lap and talked to him. Adrian got up and wandered down the beach, walking on the firm, wet sand above the shorebreak. After a while, Tenley joined him. "Let's go in," she said. "Get your bathing suit and put your wallet in the bag." He used the towel-around-the-hips method to change then put his wallet away.

Tenley took his hand.

"What's this?" he asked.

"Shh. We're engaged, so act like it," she said, then added, "hon."

They waded into the water up to their waists, then up to their chests. She was right about the buoyancy. He could tell that if he drew his feet up, he would float. She dove away, stayed under for a few seconds, and then he saw the shimmering brown shape of her, the rippling, dreamlike splotch of green of her bathing suit, moving toward him. He felt her arms around his buttocks, and her body sliding up his, and was startled at the sensation. She emerged blinking, her face streaming with water and her hair straight back from her forehead. She put her arms around his waist, and her stomach against his, warmer than the water, and he stood there holding his breath, amazed at the sensation of her flesh against his. Then she moved away and turned to look back at her grandfather.

"He looks so old," she said, "and alone."

"He thinks the braid is important."

"It is," she said.

Adrian thought, Two days? That was all he'd known her? It seemed impossible. When she had slept with her head in his lap and he had studied her so closely, it was as if she were someone he had known for years, the familiarity of her flesh, the proximity of their bodies as natural as breath. But now, standing in the water, he knew he was scamming himself. We're engaged. Act like it. At the group home he'd been told to stay away from Leigh Donaldson because junkie-hookers might as well have had brain damage, a selfishness that nothing could penetrate. She'll sell you for one good high, they said. When the time came, Tenley would no longer have any use for him and that would be that. He could fool himself into believing that his help would result in something good, but despite his help, his mother was dead and Leigh Donaldson was dead. Tenley was next, he supposed, even though his help had brought her back to her family. Having listened to the old man, he now hated the idea that they were deceiving him. He waved his hands through the water and thought of how he'd felt when the old man was holding the braid, and the strange shadow of its meaning was both there and somehow hidden, like the name he could not remember.

The bell on the fishing rod jangled as three teenaged boys came down to the beach from the right-of-way Adrian and Tenley had used. When Tenley saw them, she waved, and then she waded toward her grandfather, who was limping down the beach to grab the fishing rod, which was bent into a quarter-circle. Jacob began reeling the fish in, and the boys walked over to him and stood by his side. The line's angle off the water opened as the fish got closer. Adrian made his way to the beach.

The fish was bright silver and about six inches long and its eye a deep black, its forehead high and rounded down to its mouth. "Pāpio," the old man said.

"Eh, Gramps," one of the boys said, "you still get um."

Jacob worked the hook out of the fish's mouth and then said in that high, strained voice, "I no want you now. Come back to me in six mont's, 'kay?" He threw the fish back in, and in a single sun-reflecting flash, it was gone. He went back to his toolbox to get more bait.

The boys went to Tenley, each one kissing her on the cheek. She introduced them to Adrian, explaining that they were second cousins: the grandchildren of Jacob's sister, who had died some time ago. Walter Martin, Junior Martin, and Billy Chang—all of whom were very dark and appeared more Hawaiian than Chinese or Caucasian—were visiting from the Big Island. They responded with howzits and nods to Adrian's pleased-to-meet-you, and then Tenley told them that she was engaged to Adrian. A flurry of questions followed. When? Where? We invited too, yah? No, no date yet, but we're working on it, she told them. We let you know an' you can come up fo' wedding. Adrian's an artist, and he wants to get himself settled here first. Artist, ah? What you do, what kine pitchas? Wood sculpture, he told them.

They all sat on the sand, the rod before them, the little currents and wind making it bend slightly, the bell swaying. The cousins were interested in Adrian because, although he was born here, he talked haole. Junior Martin asked him straight out, fo' real? But den you talk da full-on haole talk. Wha's up wit' dat? Yeah, my father worked here until, let's see, thirteen years ago. Yeah? His name Branch too? Yeah, Ray Branch. He did all kinds of jobs and then we moved to upstate New York, where I got my haole accent.

Watching Tenley now, he understood why she had said she wanted to get her life back. She was completely relaxed and comfortable as she sat in the sand and talked with her cousins about their girlfriends, families, and so on. And the occasional thoughtful look at her grandfather, the simple familial concern she showed, seemed natural too. It was family, and nearby was a house that she would belong in if she had not fucked up her life.

After a while Adrian began to get hungry, and he felt a burn on his skin. He saw Tenley's knee jounce and a look of anxiety cross her face. The cousins chatted on, Jacob dozed, and Adrian's eyes drifted to the duffel bag.

An hour later, the boys said, Goodbye, yah, we come nex' mont', ah? Tell Jacob we say bye, 'kay? No like bodda him. Then they left, and Tenley went to the bag. She got the squirt bottle out, took a long stream, swallowed, and then took another long one. She finished with a sigh of relief. She handed the bottle to Adrian, who took two long squirts.

"Isn't there a 7-Eleven or something back there?" he asked. "I can walk over and get food."

"Yeah, get spam musubi an' whatevahs. I stay here an' watch Gramps, 'kay?"

Adrian put his shirt on and went out the right-of-way past Tenley's house and toward the two-lane highway. The cluster of small buildings was back the way the bus had come, and as he walked, he looked around at the houses. Some were dilapidated, but had mowed lawns, boats in driveways, people out doing things. The town sat on a plain surrounded by gray and green mountains that to the west formed an almost vertical wall. Cut into the wall were dark-green, water-eroded crevices lined up like curtain folds, and topped with clouds resembling an extended wad of cotton that someone had placed there. All the people Adrian saw were dark, and one or another of the men would stop what he was doing to look at him briefly and nod or say, "Eh," or "Howzit?" He walked past what appeared to be a dead chicken, flattened into the pavement so that it was no more than a splat of broken feathers, one standing up and fluttering in the breeze. There was a sparse but steady stream of traffic going both ways, a few tour buses among the vehicles.

Going back to the beach, he carried a plastic bag with five spam bombs, a six-pack of the Aloha Maid juice Tenley had bought in town, and four granola bars.

Tenley sat next to her grandfather, talking to him. Once, she laughed and put her head on his dark shoulder. Adrian stopped in the shade of a tree. They were the only people on this stretch of beach. He felt separated and alone. Now that she was back with her family, the ruse of him being her fiancé had probably run its course. What would she say? Oh, Adrian's going back to town—gotta set up his art thing. But that was all right, he figured. If he could leave this situation as it was now, then he could go away with the belief that he had left her better than he had found her.

He took his shirt off and walked out on the sand, feeling the burn on his shoulders and face. Tenley saw him, and her eyes drifted down to the bag. "Ho, spam bombs, I hope. Gramps, you like?"

Jacob nodded, smiling. Adrian handed Tenley the plastic bag. She knelt and undid the clear wrap from a spam bomb. The backs of her thighs were covered with perfect elliptical patches of sand. She gave the bomb to Jacob, then grabbed one for herself. Unwrapping it, she looked at Adrian. "What?" she asked.

"Nothin'. I just wondered if you had sunscreen."

"Oh, pua Adrian! You one lobstah." She fiddled in her bag and pulled out a green plastic bottle. "Put some Boofrog on you. Turn around."

She worked fast, rubbing it in, and he wondered if her speed had something to do with the junkie's unpredictable manias and the time of day. She turned him around, poured goop into the palm of her hand and swept it across his forehead, the hand holding the bottle shaking a little.

Jacob had caught no more fish. The rod still stood, the bell swaying in the breeze. Tenley leaned over to him and said something. Then she turned back to Adrian and nodded in the direction of the trees. They walked together, and in the shade, he felt a little better. Underfoot was a bed of long, soft pine like needles and little cones with sharp points. The breeze was cool.

"'Kay," she said, "I see the look on your face. Time to go, right?" She stood with her arms folded. "I know. Dis da boonies." She glanced back at Jacob Chong. "But he wants us to stay over in his little house. I can't really believe it. I mean, I almost cried when he asked me. I can tell him you had to go somewhere to ask about a studio or a shop or something—"

"No, that's okay."

"For real? I mean this is my thing. I gotta tell him about our scam, but I don't wanna do that yet." She squinted at Adrian. "You don't want to go to Waikīkī and party?"

"I never thought about it."

They made their way to Jacob's cottage by walking into the empty driveway and along the side of the house. Tenley sighed and whispered, "Thank God." Her mother was out. The cottage was tiny and in need of repair, one corner on the street side three or four inches lower than it should have been, its footing sunk in the sandy soil. It had a front door and a window, a small, cramped room in which sat Jacob Chong's bed, chair and table, and a tiny bathroom with a worn-linoleum floor and circular brown stains on the ceiling. In the back corner, a hot plate encrusted with grease sat on a shelf under the window, which had louvers. There was no room in the place to "stay over."

Jacob sat down in an easy chair with grime-blackened arms, the ends split open and blooming with browned stuffing. "Cool eensai," he wheezed. Tenley looked at Adrian.

"I think there's room in back," she said.

"Oh yah," Jacob said, "you go in back an' check um out."

Adrian followed Tenley out the front door and along the short wall of the cottage. Attached to the back of the cottage, under the branches of a large tree, was a pitched corrugated roof supported by two four-by-fours spanned by a large mesh hammock. Beyond the roofed space was brush, rotted palm fronds, and the remains of a fence bordering a vacant lot with a flat, concrete house foundation in the middle. To one side of the roofed area, a single pipe rose six feet out of the ground, crooked at the end like a cane, its showerhead pointing at a heavy wooden pallet sitting on mud and tufts of grass. A strong breeze knifed through the space between the Chong property and the house next door. Tenley stared at the hammock, her index finger on her chin. "Well," she said, "we'll have to work this out later."

Adrian saw a workbench against the back wall of the old cottage. Above it, tools hung on nails, and up high, suspended from other nails, was a bow saw. "Well, lookee here," he said, pointing. "My principal tool."

"For what?"

"I find old logs and cut thin disks from them and look for pictures inside."

"Did you tell me that?" she asked. "You told me that, right?"

"That's the 'interpretation of nature' thing. It's based on something real, even though it's probably dumb. Anybody can do it."

Jacob came around the corner carrying a chrome-and-vinyl chair, the chrome browned with rust and the red plastic repaired with mismatched red tape, grime stuck in the glue around the edges. He put it down and sat on it. "So, you can figgah how fo' sleep in dat, ah? No can fool around 'cause make da roof squeak." Then he laughed in a sustained, airy squeak.

"Grandad, you kolohe o' man!"

"Go mahket an' buy one tray laulau, lomi salmon, an' poi. We cook um up an' talk story ah?"

"What's laulau?" Adrian asked. "Poi I know."

"Pork and fish or chicken wrapped in taro leaves and baked," Tenley said. The old man struggled to get his wallet out of his back pocket. "No," she said. "We buy."

"Not. My treat," he said, producing a ten-dollar bill.

Adrian went out to the road and, following Tenley's directions, turned right. He walked past the old houses toward store that was the first in a line of buildings at the edge of the grove. A tree-lined road ran straight toward a lone mountain in the distance. To his left was a large field where horses were kept in fenced stalls in the shade of the bordering trees.

The ten wasn't enough, so he added a couple of dollars of his own and made his way back. Tenley's mother's car was parked in the driveway. He walked down the driveway and past the house, then heard an angry voice that made him stop.

"—you didn't ask me first, hah?"

"Mom—" He heard a soft screech and then the groan of the roof. Someone was rocking on the hammock.

"You were not to come here. You were not to try to contact me. We made that clear."

"I came to see Grandaddy." Then the squeak and groan.

"It so happens, then, that you came here. So we have a problem."

"Dat yoah house," the old man wheezed. "Dis mines. Go eensai yoah house den."

"And who's the guy, hah? 'Contemporary art is mired in blah blah'—sure. And he's part—"

"Oh my," Tenley said dryly, "he could be a white male. Perish the thought."

"Fucking trash-mouth little bitch."

"Shaddap," Jacob said.

"You shut up. This is my house."

"Dat yoah house. Dis mines."

"Who has the deed? You?"

Silence. Then the squeaking began again.

John Murai appeared at the corner of the cottage, saw Adrian, and held his shoulders up in a shrug, his hands out. Adrian went past him and into the shaded area behind the cottage, where Tenley sat on the hammock, her feet close enough to the ground that she could push the hammock with her toes—a slow swing producing the soft squeak and groan. Her mother stood with her arms folded, her eyes on Adrian.

He had had enough experience with this kind of tension to know that it was better to go about his business without changing his expression, so he handed the bag to Jacob, who nodded and struggled up out of his chair, then hobbled around to the other side of the cottage. They heard the sound of a pot grating in a sink, then water running. They listened while water drummed in the bottom of the pot. When it stopped, Tenley looked at Adrian and patted the hammock, and he sat next to her. She put her arm around his waist and pushed with her toe. John looked on warily, his eyes moving from one person to another.

Tenley's mother unfolded her arms and said, "Of course, we shouldn't argue like this in the presence of a guest, now should we?"

"No, Mom, we shouldn't," Tenley whispered.

"Well," her mother said, "I suppose, then, that I'll go to my house."

She left, followed by John, and in a few seconds a door slammed.

Tenley let go of his waist and growled, rubbing her face.

"I guess I have a hard time getting it," Adrian said.

"I'll tell you about it later. Shit, it's not even her house. Jacob's my father's father, so he's allowed to stay because he has no place else to go. It's John house, but he doesn't own it—his ex-wife does. He stays here only because she lets him. It's complicated. But I'll tell you the rest later."

Jacob announced that he was going to sleep—you guys can use da batchroom whenevahs, jus' be one a my dreams. Tenley sat on the hammock and Adrian stood on the hard dirt, the faint light from Jacob's back window illuminating her oversized T-shirt, the white mesh of the hammock, and the wood pallet under the shower. The breeze between the houses now had a wet chill in it, and the idea of sitting all night on the dirt, against the wall of the old cottage, was not appealing. There were piles of rotted palm fronds and other weeds just beyond the tree, and the odor coming from them was funky and damp.

"So I had one boyfriend firs' year of college, 'kay? A sorta sorta boyfriend?"

"Yeah?"

"Like I told you, years ago my mom got tired of being a hula dancer in Waikīkī, all that stuff, and she wanted to finish her education. She went to college with me, and first I thought, Ho, dis good fun, me an' my mom at college, even though I was hanging out with the wrong people already and she knew it. I thought maybe because we went together, I'd find the right people to hang with. I take some courses, freshman writing and so on, and she takes courses too, one taught by some big-deal guy from the mainland, this part-black guy who tells his class that Hawai'i is still a colony, that all white people have to take responsibility for this colonialism. Around this time, I meet Michael, and he's a junior from Minnesota, and we sort of, you know . . . So anyway, I think my mom is falling for this professor from the mainland, and when we talk at home, right over there," she said, pointing, "she says all this stuff about 'people of color' and white people and how this and that happened, and how this professor guy said his job is to come here and teach us about something right in our midst we don't know about. It's right, of course—the way the monarchy was overthrown was bad—but I felt a little weird about how she was taking it all so . . . what's the word? Literally, that's it. Like the people who overthrew the monarchy were sitting there in the class and walking past you at Safeway." She pointed at the duffel bag sitting against the back wall of the house, and Adrian went to it and drew out the squirt bottle. After they each took a stream, she said, "I think my mother maybe even sleeps with this professor guy, I don't know, and meantime my boyfriend and me are getting more and more serious.

"Second semester, I even sit with him in one of his classes. It's a literature course, where the teacher, this Asian-American lady, says that white people can't understand the plight of people of color, and my boyfriend says right off, I think I can, and she says, No you can't because you're white. All the kids in class are cringing because the rule, you see, is that you can't disagree with the teacher. You come from a position of power and privilege, she says. All the other white kids in the class agree. He sits there and says, I disagree, like that. Says, I can make this course an inquiry into whether or not I can understand. The lady tries to convince him to drop the course, and he says, No, I want to understand. I try to convince him to just go along with it like everybody else. You want a good grade, an' the other white students are all agreeing, right? All you need to do is agree. The students are okay and the class is actually a lot of fun, and the subject is really interesting, but there's always this feeling that the lady's running down the white people in the class as if they were responsible, right? Michael has this really sarcastic sense of humor, so one day, they had a skit assignment, where people go up and do a short thing illustrating colonial stuff, yeah? Two guys go up and do a job interview, showing racism, like that. So Michael's turn comes. He brings a pink plastic baseball bat—you know, a little kid's toy—and he goes to the front and says, Hi, I'm Michael, from Minnesota. Can I come in? and he pauses like he's listening, and then nods and hits himself on the head with the bat hard, *bong, bong, bong*, maybe fifteen times. The class is howling, and he stops, pulls his pant leg up, looks at his skin, and goes, Oh my, and hits himself on the head fifteen more times. Then he says, Thank you, and sits down. They were screaming with laughter, even the teacher, but she had this look on her face, like, You sarcastic son of a bitch.

"But that's just school, 'kay? It's fun, the information is cool and all. But my mom gets too wrapped up in it, I think. At home she tells me, you should get rid of that guy. Who? I say. You know who. Oh come on, I say, this is just ideas, Mom. You're not supposed to look at the people like *they're* guilty. Why not? she says. I start after a while to get sarcastic. Pua Michael, he no get color, he a person of no color, and my Mom gets more and more pissed at me. So you insult me every time you open your mouth? she asks. No, I no insult you, Mom, I insult the idea that you fall for this professor guy's shit, and she says, What shit? What shit do I fall for? You're damn right I fall for that shit. Because I want to see it turned around. My culture has been made into a whore for a hundred years, and I want it to stop, I want the white pimps to lay off and allow us to reclaim our heritage. But Mom, Michael didn't do anything to you. He grew up in a foster home. His younger brother died in a farm accident, his sister is sick, he worked his ass off to come out here. Isn't this supposed to be just like theoretical? So she says, Don't buy that shit that he didn't do anything to you or me. It's in his blood, it's part of a tradition hundreds of years old, and they still come out here sniffing around for one kind of opportunity or another. Oh, I say, you want to kick him outta da canoe, ah? She stares at me for a long time. I have no more to say about this, she finally says, only one thing: stop spreading your legs for that piece of shit. Oh? I'll stop if you stop spreading your legs for that asshole at school. She stares at me again. I mean, like the look of hatred in her eyes is amazing. I pity you, she finally says. Don't think your blond stud doesn't look in the mirror and say, Yeah, I came out here looking for a sweetie with a flower behind her ear and a sarong, and I found one almost like she came off the goddam tourist brochure, and lucky me, I'm sticking it to the little Polynesian beauty and it feels great—not that I want her for anything else. And I'm all surprised like and I say, Am I Polynesian now? When did we decide that? Finally she said something to me that I can't remember but made me so mad that I said, Mom, I always thought you were beautiful, but this guy has made you ugly. And you're stupid too. Michael didn't overthrow the monarchy and he didn't keep slaves. He's got more to complain about than you. But it's like, he's blond and available, right? I mean, if the real enemies are dead, then go ahead and find new ones. Make new enemies. That's what the University is for, right?"

"Now I get some of it," Adrian said.

"I don't think it can be repaired—ever."

In the darkness, she was now a compact elliptical ball, her arms around her knees. "So what about John?" Adrian asked. "How much Hawaiian is he?"

"He's Japanese. Funny that when it comes to sex, you can be less discriminating." She was now moving on the hammock, worming her arms under the T-shirt. She passed the bathing suit top out of her sleeve and put the strap in the mesh so that it swung with the hammock. "When I was fourteen or whatever, she got rid of the white girls in the canoe—my best friends. Then when she went to college, she had it all, what? Validated for her. I'm sure she was excited about that. See, you don't learn this in the neighborhood and you don't learn it in high school. And it's really funny: you grow up and learn to accept everybody, you know, stop taking sides against one group or another—you know, haoles or Japanese or whatever—and then you go to the University and it's adolescence all over again. That's how Michael put it. He called it adolescence, and then he said, But at the University it's called 'theory'." She paused, then snorted. "Michael had to leave around that time because his sister was sick and he had to help her with her kids. He wanted me to go with him. I didn't wanna go to Minnesota. Maybe I was just his sorta girlfriend, I don't know. But that's over. End of story. Except that after he left, a friend of mine convinced me to take a hit on a glass pipe right down there on the beach. Fifteen seconds, that's all it took. I was sad about Michael, and then in fifteen seconds I felt stronger and happier than I ever had. When it wore off, I wanted more."

He had begun to shiver a little. His eyes drifted from one dark patch of ground to another, then to the pallet.

"You like stan' dea all night? I won't bite you."

In the middle of the night, he woke up, aware of the body pressed hard against his own, the back rounded because she had drawn her knees up, and he worked slowly at getting himself into a comfortable position so that they would not be spine to spine. The only one that was comfortable was one he worried might send the wrong message. He was so tired that he did it anyway, and if she was aware of it, he couldn't tell. Her back was now cupped by his chest and stomach, and the problem of where to put his hands was solved when he tipped away a little and let one arm slide up on his top side, the forearm across his own lower back. He could smell her hair, shoulder, and neck. From time to time, she would twitch, then squirm, pushing her back into his chest, her buttocks into his upper thighs, and this caused an erection he had to concentrate to get rid of.

In the house in the woods, he saw her sitting in a shaft of yellow sunlight on a spool chair he had repaired, one he had found in a back room. The chair's spools had been broken and scattered around on the floor. He had carefully sanded each one, then drilled holes into the ends of the broken pieces and inserted nails that had their heads clipped off, first dipping them in glue. Then he had fit the parts together so that the ragged points and valleys of the break melted into each other. He varathaned each spool, then put it into the carefully sanded chair. Tenley sat on the chair in her bathing suit and watched him while he sanded the delicate frame moldings of a window. Snow fell outside, but she was not cold. She sat in the shaft of light, points of golden dust swirling around her. She watched as he climbed up and repaired the roof. Then he went and started a fire in the old black stove while she watched. He looked at her sitting in the chair he had repaired, her body brown and compact and vibrant with the electric glow of life. In a room in the back his mother sat, looking out a window. Tenley went into the room to sit with her, and they talked. With the sounds of their voices in the background, he studied a doorframe. The wood was covered with layers of paint—green, then white, then pink—and it was scarred, but underneath, it was beautiful, its grain like overlapping waves in a shorebreak.

The clouds he saw through the leaves of the tree were a faint pink. There was no wind, and Tenley was facing him, her head above his, her hot thigh over his side, her shirt pulled up almost to her neck so that he gazed blearily in the semidarkness at a large dark nipple, three hairs around it. The outlying tissue melted into the pale skin that surrounded it—a perfect rounded shape. Her fists were up under her chin, and in the faint light he saw one outstretched leg and then the other, flung over his side and crisscrossed with marks from the strings of the hammock. A white crust of dried drool formed little parentheses at the corners of her mouth, and the tiny fans of her eyelashes twitched. He could see the faint pulsing of her heart in her neck, and the heat of her body radiated against his chest and stomach. He wanted to shift because parts of him were numb. Then she squirmed, pushing her leg down, and pulled herself around so that her back was to him again, making the roof squeak and groan a little. Now he stared at the back of her neck and the side of her face. The back of her neck sprouted fine, long hairs. He thought, I am in a hammock with a junkie-whore, and then he frowned. I am in a hammock with the most mysterious and amazing of things: a human being with billions of cells, enzymes and oils and organs and capacities that are limitless. I am not in a hammock with a human being being eaten by the billions of worms of cancer, being shut down, swelling and seething with death expanding over organs and extending its claim with a lewd, insistent compulsion over the life that is left. That heart had stopped. It finally understood that it was sending its blood into death, and it gave up. While this heart, encased in this cage of ribs, beats despite all that has happened to it.

"Mālaekahana," he whispered. "Mālaekahana." He was not surprised. It had to come to him sooner or later. The voice that had spoken it had stopped only days ago, and it seemed as if the sound had taken those days to reach him.

But the relief of knowing was cut off by the sensation of something wet on his stomach, a cold wetness, which at first he couldn't identify. And when he could, he was mortified. He'd had a wet dream. The clouds had turned from faint pink to pinkish yellow, and he could see off the end of the hammock a light-blue sky.

He tried to think of how to extricate himself, his body tense, the half-numb arm across the rib cage with its fingers through the mesh of the hammock. "Mālaekahana." Okay, now he could finish this up and leave. He got himself free, then gently pulled her shirt down so that she would be covered. He tried to get out of the hammock without making the roof squeak. Once on his feet, he went to the shower and turned the spigot handle, mounted down low on the pipe, and let the tubular jet of water run down over his shoulders and into his shorts so that, shivering miserably, he could wash off the evidence of the dream.

He stood in the sunlight, waiting for his shorts to dry. Tenley slept on, from time to time moving so that the roof squeaked slightly. A light went on inside the cottage, and he heard Jacob scrape a pot onto a hot-plate element, then cough.

Tenley's eyes opened, and she stared at Adrian. Then she stretched out and pointed at the duffel bag. He pulled out the squirt bottle, and peered inside at the big bottle, which was down to a third. He handed her the squirt bottle, and she drank a long stream without sitting up. She burped and sat up. Then she looked at the crisscross marks on her arms and legs. "Turn around," she said to Adrian. He did, and she said, "Ho, you one person of color."

He turned to face her again. "It's Mālaekahana," he said.

She nodded. "You even pronounced it right. Most people say 'Molly-kahana,' and you said 'Mah-lae-kahana.' Did your mother know the language?"

"Some. Back in New York when I was little, I even recited a paragraph in a class, part of one of those 'My Heritage' things. What is this place? I mean, is it around here?"

"It's up the windward coast. I'll tell Grampa Jacob." She thought a moment. "So you'll bury the braid and what? Go home?" She laughed softly. "Our game's run its course, huh pard?" He tried to make some sense of the look on her face.

"I don't know," he said.

"Be that as it may," she said, getting out of the hammock, "I gotta pee."

He heard her talking to Jacob in the cottage. Her questions were answered by a high, wheezing voice speaking words he could not make out.

She came back carrying two Pop-Tarts that dripped butter into the dirt. "Here you go," she said, handing him one. "He can borrow a car and we'll go out today. He thinks it's important. He wants to see it done."

The car Jacob borrowed was a decrepit Datsun pick-up with large bondo spots all around the roof, each of which was ringed with rust and fissures. The seat was covered with brittle plastic, cracked from the sun and erupting with browned rubber foam. Jacob drove, his long-handled shovel bouncing in the bed. Tenley sat in the cab between him and Adrian, her bag at her feet and the full squirt bottle inside, and pointed things out to Adrian, who held the shirt-wrapped braid on his lap. That mountain is Olomana, and up there is the Pali tunnel. Sure, I remember that. Is it windy up there? Yup, you can lean way into it. That's where Kamehameha pushed one of the last armies off when he unified the islands.

When they went past a town called Kailua and toward another called Kāne'ohe, Jacob began talking, mostly to

Tenley. "When she wen' die, I los' interes', you know." Tenley put her arm around the old man's shoulders. "I figgah, well, 'ass it den. I guess I do um too. I mean, what use I got anyways? Yoah sistah, she marry one go-get-um guy an' she say, Nah nah nah, we no wan' keikis, too much trouble, so I tink, Well, no point waiteen fo' dem, ah? Besides, they gone mainlan' now."

"She'll come around," Tenley said.

"She tell yoah maddah, What use fo' bring keikis into one worl' li'dis. By da way, how come yoah maddah such a fricken bitch about dis? All I get is stink face from her. Wahine drive me nuts."

"That might be my fault."

"But why she geev up on you, ah?" They waited at the light, the cab of the truck vibrating from the low idle of the engine. "So den las' night, I lay on my bed an' heah dakine squeak-squeak from da roof—" Tenley laughed. "Nah," Jacob said. "I not, whatchucall, implyin' any stuffs li'dat."

He started up when the light changed, then turned left toward more mountains. Adrian remembered nothing of this area and didn't care. He was cringing with shame because the old man had bought their scam. It was cruel, and he blamed Tenley for it. But the expression on her face was blissful. She was reveling in the closeness to her grandfather, her arm draped over the back of his seat.

"So I lyeen deah, an I happy," he said. "Firs' time in long long long time I happy."

Tenley patted his knee, then looked at Adrian, and he saw that she felt as ashamed as he did, if not more.

They drove past small stands of papaya trees arranged in rows, some topped and the stumps covered with coffee cans, then past lower areas where the roadsides were choked with brush and vines. Here and there, a rusting refrigerator or stove sat in a ditch. After a while, they passed more beach, a park with a cone-shaped island to the right, and beautiful mountains looming above. "Chinaman's Hat," Adrian said.

"You remember that?" Tenley asked.

"Yeah." The thin beach stretched off into the distance, only ten or fifteen feet wide in places, so that the water sloshed against rocks at the road's edge. Jacob drove in silence for a few miles and then said, "You can stay long as you like. My house 'ass why. Leas' da little one. John's wife sick but. We no can know what goin' happen because she owns da house."

Okay, Adrian thought, so he would say he had to go over to Honolulu and Tenley could stay, and after a while, they could break up.

Jacob pulled off onto a dirt road that led to a parking lot set in among tall trees. He carried the shovel, and when they walked out of the trees and stood on the beach in the strong breeze that came off the ocean, he turned to Adrian. "I figgah bes' fo' put um high onna beach an' deep inna sand, maybe up neah one tree, so nevah have chance fo' wattah erosion, li'dat to wash um out."

"Okay," Adrian said. He looked around. There weren't many people there, just a couple sitting on a towel about a hundred feet away and some kids in the water.

"Many bones heah," Jacob said. "Bones undah us."

Adrian looked back at the trees. "Maybe up there, behind that big tree?"

He walked to a spot between two strong roots that vanished into the sand four or five feet from a tree trunk. He took the shovel from Jacob, and in the V formed by the roots he began to dig, piling the sand near the hole. He dug until the hole was about two feet deep, and when he started bringing up sand that had reddish, wet soil in it, he stopped. "Okay," he said, "right here."

He had thought it would be no big deal to simply drop the braid in and cover it up, but when he removed it from the T-shirt and held it over the hole, he stopped. The familiarity of her hair, the wire that had kept it intact, the fact that he had slept with his face against it—all this made him unable to let go of it. The bottom of the hole glistened with moisture, and Jacob and Tenley were watching. He tried to put it down, but could not.

"Adrian," Tenley said. "We go over there. You take your time."

They moved away, and the breeze pushed long pine needles into the hole. He stared at the braid. He had to do it. This was what he had come here for. Rather than dropping the braid, he carefully eased it down into the hole, not letting it touch the sides, and then turned it so that it lay flat. "There you go, Ma," he whispered. "And thanks." He stood up, grabbed the shovel, and pushed the sand back into the hole. Then he brushed the excess sand off the roots and looked around. No one had seen him. The braid was safe.

He took a deep breath and let it out slowly. Now that it was done, he didn't know what to think. Tenley sat nearby on the sand, but her grandfather was not with her. Adrian scanned the beach and saw him strolling on the wet, hard sand just above the shorewash, his slippers in one hand. With her chin on her knees and her arms around her legs, she gazed at the old man, and Adrian thought that barring something unforeseen, she would be all right. About himself, he didn't know. He felt a bleak nothingness, because with the burial of the braid, he had finished the only thing he was alive for. And now he was nothing.

He walked to Tenley, and once there, he looked back at the tree. "Well," he said, "that's taken care of. I guess I won't forget that tree either."

"Me too" she said. "It's a good place." She gestured at her grandfather. "I wonder what he's thinking," she said. "Maybe something about my grandmother. They came out here in the old days. I did too, camping and stuff like that. Girl Scouts." She stood up, wiped the sand off her bathing-suit bottom, and snorted softly. "It was a bad idea," she said. "I mean, of all the things I've done, this feels like the absolute worst, leading him on like that. I feel like there're only two things you can do about something like this." She turned to Adrian, took a deep breath, and said, "Pard, I wanna ask you one thing, and you can take it any way you want, 'kay?"

"Sure."

"We go back an' you can do whatever. Take the bus back to Waikīkī, pick up where you left off. I mean, you don't owe me anything, but I owe you. Without you, I wouldn't be here." She held her hands up and shrugged. "Okay, okay," she said. "I don't mean to bore you." She sighed. "Oh boy," she said, looking in the old man's direction. He was a dark speck on the beach. "I'm scared."

"Okay."

"When I said I wanted to quit stuff, I thought I meant it. Now I know for sure that I do." She looked back at the tree. "It's a good place," she said.

Adrian waited, but she said nothing more. He went to her left side and bobbed his head around into her line of vision. "Well?" he said. "You were gonna ask me one time, you said."

"I wanna keep going with this. It's either leave, or keep going."

"What? You mean with the scam?"

"Yeah. I wonder if there's some way you could play it out. It would mean everything to me."

"Play it out how?"

"It means that I want a baby."

Adrian cleared his throat. "Lemme get this straight. You— No, that's crazy."

She shook her head. "My God, you should see the look on your face."

He felt as if all the blood had drained from his head. She was out of her mind, that was it. He laughed. "Come on, that's crazy."

She looked again at her grandfather. "I am standing on bones. We're right next to being dead, like him," she said, nodding in Jacob's direction. "It's strange, being right next to being dead."

He understood. "I know the feeling," he said. "I've known it for a while."

"Jacob said it," she said. "We are standing on bones. Hell, everywhere you go here, you're standing on bones. I want a baby, and I don't want just anybody's baby. I want yours." She stared past him. She opened her mouth to speak, but didn't.

"That makes it a strange scam," he said.

"You heard him. He's thinking about my grandmother, and he's happy and it's my fault. I shouldn't have done this, but it's too late now. My sister won't put out so I will. I'll give him a reason to stay alive. It'll blow my mother's wires, and I don't know what she'll do with her hatred when—" She paused, frowning. "I mean, I could do this with plenty of people, but you feel—like, comfortable to me. The world is full of creeps, and you're not one of them."

He didn't know what she meant by "comfortable." A chair might be comfortable.

"Listen," he said, "I don't know about this. I mean, how do we— How—"

"We'll go to a hospital and get a sperm sample," she said, nodding thoughtfully. "Then we'll take the sample and we'll freeze it? Then a gynecologist will do an artificial insemination."

He nodded, thinking that she had to be joking.

"You should see the look on your face. There is an easier way, of course. You're a guy, one who, I assume, likes girls, and I'm a girl." She frowned at the sand. "No," she said. "It was just an idea. It's okay." She nodded at the tiny, dark figure walking on the sand, now moving toward them. Adrian felt the flush in his face receding. "You should have known my grandmother," Tenley went on. "She was sick a long time, and I would stay with her when I could. My grandfather worked back then, for a nursery. Really low pay and all that, but he liked it."

As the figure of Tenley's grandfather came closer, she walked down the beach to meet him. "No way," Adrian whispered. "Not a chance." He walked back up the beach to the tree where he had buried the braid, put on his slippers, and picked up the shovel. He leaned against the tree, the palm of his hand on the rough bark, and stared at the sand covering the hole. The breeze had smoothed it out, and the wind had blown leaves over it.

Jacob helped them with the scotch. He went to a liquor store in Kailua, and while he was there, Tenley told Adrian that if he intended to say, they'd have to do something about the back part of the cottage, maybe put in a floor and walls or something. That way, they would be out of sight of Tenley's mother, who would be so pissed that it would make Tenley's month.

The road back to Waimānalo went through several neighborhoods. Wondering where they would get wood to enclose the back, Adrian looked at house after house. He turned to Tenley. "Some people have palm trees in their yards, and some people don't."

She looked at him as if he had told the first half of a joke. "Okay," she said. "That is certainly true. Used to be a lot more around town, but I guess people don't like them because of the rubbish."

"When they're babies, what do they look like?"

"The people?" she said. "No, of course not. You're talking about a tree. It's a coconut with a couple of little fronds sticking out. Why?"

"I saw some. Back toward the airport."

"They're all over the place. In ditches, dumps. Why do you ask?"

"Just an idea. What do palm trees mean? I mean to people."

"Well, the Hawaiian word is *niu*. The original Polynesians brought them here. In school, I think the teacher said that the coconuts probably didn't float here because they won't remain viable after about four months in salt water."

"What else? Anything?"

"Oh Jesus," she said. "You asking me to remember alladat?" She frowned at the windshield. "The palm tree provided food and drink," she said. "The trunk and leaves had all-kine uses. On some Pacific islands, life was not possible without the niu. It wasn't as important in Hawai'i, but people used it. You get the milk inside, oil from the copra, which is the white stuffs inside, you use husk fiber to make cordage for tying, especially in canoes—the rigging an' li'dat. Coconuts were used as offerings to the gods, leaves were woven into baskets, mats, platters. The meat cream was mashed into taro, sweet potato, breadfruit. It's called 'The Tree of Life.' An' le's see, its life-span is like a man's life span, so one planted when you're born will last your lifetime."

"Okay," Adrian said. "That'll be enough. Just a scam to make a little money. When does Jacob have to return the truck?"

She turned and spoke to Jacob, then turned back. "Whenevahs. Da o' guy almos' blin', 'ass why. He say bring um back tomorrow."

Now the agitated bouncing of Adrian's knee was not for another stream of scotch. The Tree of Life: how a yard could not have a palm tree in it now baffled him.

After they got back and had a couple of long streams from the squirt bottle, he had Tenley negotiate with Jacob for the use of the truck, and then he asked Jacob where he might find some of the sprouted coconuts. The old man gave directions to Hīhīmanu Street. Tenley watched with a skeptical squint, but went along because there was nothing else to do. It was around three by then, Adrian figured. "Okay," he said to Tenley, "let's go. I don't have a license."

She sighed and looked up at the sky. "I got one," she said.

Hīhīmanu Street ran off the shoreline road and inland into neighborhoods, then past what looked like nurseries and farms.

In the ditches, there was some debris, but it took them a half-mile before he saw the first pile of coconuts beside the road. Rotten-looking, they were submerged in filthy black water over which flies hovered. He found three sprouted ones, the sprouts between eight and sixteen inches long. One even had the beginning fan of a leaf. Farther down the road, lying next to a rusted refrigerator, there was some wood planking. "Stop here," he said. He got out. They were tongue and groove, the ends apparently eaten by something.

"Termites," she said.

He pulled at the wood and saw some of it was firm and undamaged.

"It's no good," she called to him in irritated voice. He ignored her and started throwing the damaged pieces of wood into the bed of the truck. Back inside the cab, he looked at his hands, which were filthy. "This is stupid," she said. "What the hell you gonna do with that?"

"Some of it's still good," he said. "Let's find more coconuts."

They drove past farms and stretches of brush. Here and there, he found sprouted coconuts. By the time Tenley had had enough, he had eleven of them in the bed of the truck, plus some chunks of four-by-four, the tongue-and-groove boards, two odd pieces of pressure-treated three-quarter–inch plywood, and some damaged two-by-sixes. "Okay, let's go back and change," he said.

"For what?"

He opened his mouth to explain, and then stopped. "Can we try this once?" he asked. "Just one time, and if it doesn't work, no problem."

"Okay," she said uncertainly, "you're the boss." She was about to pull away from a ditch when he spotted a brown clipboard in the weeds.

They went out again. He had Tenley carry the clipboard and a pen she got out of her bag. The paper was a flyer for a Kailua gas station offering a cheap oil change. The back was blank. They parked the truck at the beginning of a neighborhood that looked new, right off the highway at Kailua. He did not want people seeing the truck. He picked up three of the cleaner sprouted coconuts, ones he had washed under the shower at home, and carried them by their thin, tough necks in his right hand. At the first house, he took a deep breath and said, "Okay, here goes," and went and knocked on the door. A man opened it, looked him over, and said, "We busy," then closed the door. At the next house, it was, No, we get alla pawtagee sausage we can handle.

"What's with portagee sausage?" he asked Tenley.

With a tired laugh, she explained that kids always sold Portuguese sausage for their fundraising for soccer an' stuffs li'dat.

The third house. A woman answered the door, and she looked receptive to whatever he had to say. Tenley stood behind him, holding the clipboard. He cleared his throat.

He held up the sprouted coconut. "This is a baby palm tree—"

"I know that," the woman said.

"—and the Hawaiian word for it is *niu.*"

"I know that too."

"Sprouted coconuts like these were brought by the Polynesians hundreds of years ago, because the tree was of great value to them. It provided food, a nutritious liquid, copra. It provided the makings of cord for their canoes and for lashing their houses together. The leaves were used for making baskets and mats. Coconuts were used as offerings to the gods. Its life-span is that of a human being's life-span, which is interesting by itself. This tree was referred to as The Tree of Life."

The woman nodded. "I think I knew all of that too. What is your point?"

"I want to plant this tree in your yard and charge you ten dollars. I know that you can find these along the roadside and do it yourself, and the reason I'm here is to do this for you."

"What? Is this some kind of fundraising thing?"

"No. I am here trying to remind people of the importance of something they pass by rotting in a ditch. If you look closely at this, you know that because a coconut can't remain viable floating in salt water for more than about four months"—he paused, staring at it because he was afraid he was losing his train of thought—"this one here, the one I'm holding in my hand, has to be directly descended from the coconuts brought here by Polynesians a thousand years ago. This is a direct descendant of one of those trees, maybe one of the first ones. This is a living thing with a past—even its own genealogy, if you will. I am doing this out of respect for something crucial to the culture that flourished here, and I don't like to see them lying in ditches."

The woman stared at him, then at the coconut. She thought for a long moment, her finger to her lips. "Ten dollars?" she said. "Well, that's not too bad. Let's find a spot for it."

"If you don't mind," he said, "we'll record your address and I'll come by, and if I see it's dead, I'll replace it." He turned to Tenley, and the woman named the street and number for her.

Ninety dollars. Each sale came with a refinement of the speech. If a tree lives about as long as a human being, then it makes sense that its genealogy resembles that of a human. This little sprout has in it all the natural information that a baby might have, all the potential to grow fifty, sixty feet high and bear thousands of coconuts in its lifetime. Do you have little children here? Because if you do, don't let your kids play under it. Planting this tree will provide a sort of parallel that you'll be aware of all your life—and one of your kids will become aware too. And all you need to do to make that parallel complete is to use the coconuts from time to time.

Tenley was so fatigued that she kept drifting back behind him. When they got to the truck, she walked to the driver's side and then stopped. She looked inside the bed and saw two of the sprouted coconuts left, the smallest, and she reached down and touched one. Then she got in the truck, but didn't start it. She sat staring out the window at the twilight and thinking. "It's not a scam," she said.

"What? This?"

"You remembered everything I said, and added the history thing. I never thought of that."

"I didn't think of it until I was standing there. But it's true."

"All that was off the top of your head."

"Yeah. There's the scam."

"It's not a scam."

When they got back to Waimānalo, they parked out on the road rather than in the driveway, and Adrian unloaded the wood and carried it back behind the cottage. Tenley's mother's car was there. Jacob had a little pot of rice and what Tenley called teri chicken ready for them. The neighbor lady, Mrs. Matsuura, had passed the chicken dish over the hedge. Too much 'ass why. She passed food over the hedge to Jacob three or four times a week, Tenley explained. She had been a good friend of Tutu's. An' see the old lemon tree there? It looked scraggly, and the trunk and branches were black. Jacob passes lemons to Mrs. Matsuura when we get them. The big tree, right there, shading the area around the pitched-roof addition, is a banyan.

After they ate, Tenley washed the few dishes and Jacob went to bed. Long day 'ass why, and he wanted to go fishing early in the morning.

Adrian found himself looking around again, for a place to sleep. He could take some of the wood he had piled in the weeds, and make a platform to sleep on.

She was so tired, she said, that she was going to sleep right then and there. She took a long stream of scotch, then he did too. She put on her oversized T-shirt and took her bathing suit top off. "You can come join me whenevers," she said.

"Actually, I want to make a platform out of some of that wood," he said.

She sat there, reached with her toe, and moved the hammock a little. "Whatevahs," she said softly. She sat there staring at him, the hammock making the faint squeak in the roof. "It's dark," she said. "Get real. We can worry about the platform tomorrow."

The awkwardness he felt was overcome by his own fatigue. He went over to the hammock, took off his shirt, and climbed in, careful not to make the roof squeak again. Back to back, they lay there, Adrian trying to figure out a comfortable position. He was aware that Tenley was not sleeping. He could feel her moving her feet, squirming with that agitation he had seen before. Then he felt her turning, her back sliding against his, and the roof squeaked and then shuddered slightly until she was on her back. "Shit," she said.

"I can try making the platform," he said, sitting up.

"I have a problem," she said. "A big problem. I shot my big mouth off. I—" She sighed and groaned at the same time. "I told you too much. That's my problem."

"You didn't tell me any more or less than you'd tell a friend, right?"

"You've been a good friend," she said. The feet squirmed again, and he waited for her to speak. Something moved in the brush where the wood was piled, maybe a frog. "I shot my big mouth off," she said, "and blew my chances. I told you everything."

"That's all right."

She turned more toward him. He let himself up on his side, and she moved in and against him, and then slid her leg up over his hip and rested it above the bone. "I shot my mouth off and ruined it."

He was caught in an almost breathless suspension. Her face was right there before his, and he couldn't think of anything to say. When he did speak, he said, "You didn't ruin anything."

"I didn't?"

"No, this is today. That was something else. It—" His mind stopped there. He was still tense, one arm behind him, the other under him and blocked from movement by her lower body, as if trussed up in rope. She didn't move for a few seconds. He could feel her thinking. Then she moved, and in the darkness he saw the shirt shrink as it moved up and then off, her shoulder hitting his chin so that his teeth clacked together. She moved toward him again, and he felt her, the two points touching his chest, then the expansion of two circles of hot flesh as she slowly pressed herself against him, the heat of her body almost astonishing against his chest, which he realized was cold, like refrigerated meat. And then she was fully against him, her arm gripped around his shoulders. He could feel her heartbeat in his chest, and it was so fast that it seemed her heart might stop, or explode.

"Do something with your hand," she whispered.

He rested his hand on her hot side, then ran it down over her buttock and along the thigh over his side, still amazed by the heat of her flesh against his. He wormed his hand between his side and her stomach and down inside the bathing suit bottom over coarse hair, and then felt the space there along with a moist heat, the fleshy lips and the bottoms of her buttocks. She was wet there, and he drew his hand out a little, making her shudder, as if he had hurt her. "Sorry," he whispered. "Sorry, I—"

"No, touch me. Touch me where you want. Take them off." She pulled at her bathing suit bottom, but it was too awkward. He pulled his hand out and held her still because the roof was squeaking. Then they both heard a cough, and the sound of Jacob moving inside the cottage. "Shh," Tenley said. They waited through the sound of urination in the toilet, then the padding of feet back to the little cot, then the sound of the springs. Then she was struggling again, her legs away from his, and the leg came back. "I want to seal this," she whispered.

"But the—"

"We don't have to move. I just want this sealed and I don't want to go backing away from it. I'm scared of what could happen. I want it sealed now. I mean right now."

She fumbled at his shorts, undid the button, then pulled at it so that the zipper opened, and pushed at his shorts until he pushed her hands away and pulled them off. As she drew her hand up from fighting with the shorts, she ran across the erection and whispered, "Oh," in a strange, high-pitched whisper, and then flung her leg over his hip as before. With the cool breeze moving over his bare flesh, he felt frightened and vulnerable, as if lights would suddenly come on, but the fear vanished in the sliding movement of her body. She rose up a little, her breasts moving in the darkness. He felt the contact down there, hair sliding on his lower abdomen and the head parting flesh. In a long, careful movement of her body downward, he was engulfed in a rich, liquefied constriction that felt almost scalding. The immersion was stopped only by bone on bone, and an abrasive scratching. She slid her arms around his neck and pulled him to her chest while he placed his hands on her back. "Oh Jesus," she whispered.

He felt it happening, slowly, the powerful release on the way, and said, "Look, it's gonna happen and I don't—" She gripped him more tightly, thrusting her hips back and forth, grinding against him. He felt the heat of her body, the smell that had risen around his face, the powerful sensation of being inside a woman who pulsed with a raw, frightening energy. He felt it coming and thought that it was a mistake to allow this to happen, but then he reveled in the simple fact that it was all too late. He exploded in a series of pulses that robbed him of breath. Tenley bucked, making the roof shudder, and a funny, squealing sound escaped her mouth. She whispered, "I felt that happen. I felt it." Then she relaxed, and for a few moments they lay still, breathing evenly, and then he felt himself slide out of her.

The air on him was cold, and he became aware that both of them were covered with a sheen of sweat. The roof made a soft eep-eep as the hammock swung forward and then back.

"Oh shit," she said. She giggled, sounding free of any tension. He thought he should probably feel shame or guilt, but didn't.

"I'll get my towels," she said. She slipped off the hammock, making it swing, then turned on the water, and he watched her phantomlike figure moving her hands around on her thighs and between her legs. Then she ran to her bag and pulled out a towel and dried herself. The water was still on, splattering loudly on the pallet. He got off the hammock and showered, surprised that the water was not as cold as he thought it would be. He rinsed his lower body. A towel came flying through the air, and he caught it and dried himself.

He put his underpants, shorts, and T-shirt back on. They got themselves back into the hammock, Tenley facing him with her fists under her chin. He drew the large towel over their upper bodies. He wrapped his arm around her shoulders, and she pulled into a ball in the hollow formed by his chest and stomach.

"I want to know what you're thinking," she whispered. "I don't mean, Gee that was great, let's do it again, you're so cool, blah blah. I need to know what you're thinking."

"It's hard to say."

"Say it anyway. I want to know why this happened." She was silent a moment. "Because I think that if you hadn't been there at A'ala Park that night, I would have gone with those two creeps. But you were there. Why? That was a week—"

"Four days ago?"

"Not," she said. "But maybe you're right. Say what you're thinking."

He took a breath. "It's like those disks I used to make. At first the pattern makes no sense, but then I look again and I see the man, or the butterfly, or whatever."

"'Kay."

"When we were in the park that first night, I felt like I knew something about you. I was staring at your face while you slept, you know, with your head in my lap."

"Really?"

"Yeah, and I saw right through you, I think. I saw miles of veins, I saw bones, organs and tissue and skin and a brain and eyes and stuff, and I was amazed, because I was looking at life. A beating heart. Stuff like that. When I was fourteen or fifteen, I used to take my rifle out in the winter and shoot these little birds called chickadees. They were so dumb that they'd follow me through the woods, going from tree to tree, really close up, these pretty gray-and-white birds with black caps on their heads making their peeping sounds, and I'd aim, pull the trigger, and there would be this puff of feathers and what was left of the chickadee would land in the snow with little droplets of blood around, and I could smell that metallic smell of blood in the air, mixed with the gunpowder smell, and I'd wait, and more chickadees would come around, and I'd aim and shoot again, laughing all the time because they were so stupid. Then one day, when I went out to do this, I aimed, and the bird jammed one of its feet into its feathers and stood there on one foot, and I couldn't shoot it. The bird sat there like it was glad to see me and all, and I stared at it and it ruffled its feathers and peeped and looked all sort of happy that I was there, this bird standing on its tiny dark toothpick leg. I saw its life. That tiny leg, the little toes wrapped around the branch. And I never shot them again. I fed them old birdseed we had in the woodshed.

"My mother was sick, and it was clear that she wouldn't get better. And I could see her that way, too, the life inside her, but all going wrong. So when you were lying there, I looked at you, down into your shirt, yeah, because I wanted to see all I could. But it was at least partly because you're strong and healthy and I was amazed. So I looked, and I guess I would have looked other places if I could have. It was like a geography I wanted to see. Same thing when you were cutting my hair. It didn't have that much to do with sex either."

"So it doesn't matter to you?" she asked. "I shot my mouth off about all the things I've done, and it doesn't bother you?"

"That's what I'm saying. All I know is what I see. I see life. Nothing else matters." He stopped, thinking he shouldn't say more, but went on anyway. "I don't want anything bad to happen. Ever. I'll do anything you say. I'll think of you like a religious person thinks of a cathedral. Oh Jesus, that is stupid—right out of a bad movie." He didn't want to mention Leigh Donaldson, but knew that he should. "I was involved with a girl once, a teenage prostitute at a group home, a place I'll have to describe to you sometime. Anyway, she had tracks, little blue scars, over every usable vein on her body. She was like sixteen. After I was with her twice, she committed suicide. She was a corpse, though, before she even cut her wrists. Somebody told me she had bipolar disorder."

"That's sad."

"And I buried my mother's braid today. I did that today, and it's over."

"I think you buried your mother today—at least that's the way Grampa Jacob sees it."

It was warmer now under the towel. Tenley stretched her legs out and slid one up over his hip. "You've had too much death," she said, grabbing his wrist and putting his hand on her stomach. "A cathedral, huh? So you want to explore, and what—pray?" She laughed. "Corny, but you know, I like that. Maybe what we need is a little corn."

"Oh well," he said, embarrassed. He tried to pull his hand away, but she held it there.

"And I'll never look at a palm tree the same way again," she said.

V

He woke up before she did and checked the wood he'd left in the weeds. Then he paced the space off. It was about thirteen wide and twelve deep, which was one hundred fifty-six square feet. You could live in that space, he thought. The roof was good, the dirt firm, and the height from dirt to leading edge was still about eight feet, pitched up to around ten. You needed nine footings, he figured. He had to go to the bathroom badly, but didn't want to disturb Jacob.

The shower was outside, so they could make a wall around it to the wall of the enclosure. And there should be two windows, one on the ocean side and one on the back, assuming that the wind would come from the water.

When he walked past the hammock again, he stopped and looked down at Tenley, and then he felt a flash of fear and anxiety about the whole thing. She lay with her knees drawn up, her fists between her thighs, the towel partly covering her head. Part of her stomach was visible, little hairs there reflecting the morning light that came through the trees in faint amber needles. He recalled the previous evening and affirmed to himself what was happening: he was hers, sort of, and she was his, sort of. The fright he felt at the idea made him sweat.

He heard Jacob's toilet flush and went around to the front of the cottage to knock on the door. It was open, and Jacob was sitting at his small table. "Eh, howzit?" he said.

"Hello. Can I use the bathroom? And do you have like a razor I could borrow?"

"Eh, in heah or da bushes, you pick um. Razah right by da mirra inside."

Adrian shaved, then went back out, rubbing his face because Jacob's razor was as dull as his own. Jacob was no longer sitting at the table. Adrian heard voices coming from the driveway by the house, one of them Tenley's mother's.

"—make this a habit. Stopping by is one thing, crashing is another." This was followed by the slam of a car door, then the sound of pebbles raining against the insides of fenders.

He waited for Jacob to appear, but he did not. A shadow moved across a light inside the big house, and he assumed that John was still there. Adrian went back to the hammock. Tenley was up now, holding the squirt bottle to her mouth, and as she drank, her eyes shifted, watching Adrian. He felt nervous in her presence. "Was that my mother?" she asked.

"Yeah. She's pissed about us being here."

"Well, fuck her," she said. "I love to piss her off." She ran her hands through her hair and then shook it.

"What if you tried not to piss her off?" Adrian asked. "With my father, when he said that America was meant for white people, I agreed with him even though I knew it was horseshit. Call it a scam."

She looked as if she didn't accept the suggestion. He still felt nervous and strange. Walking over to where the wood was piled, he said, "Anyway, I gotta start this thing, buy some footings and stuff."

He looked down at the wood and noticed that, deep in the brush behind it, was a large, blackened tree stump. Then he felt her behind him. When he turned, she wore an odd expression. She slid her arms around his waist and pulled herself close. "I acted too much like a whore, didn't I?" she whispered. "Last night. The things you said. That was the scotch talking last night, wasn't it?"

"No, I—"

She pulled herself closer and pulled at his arms until they were around her.

"I meant every word of it," he said.

"Really?"

They heard Jacob moving around in the cottage. Tenley let go. "I wanna cook something," she said.

After she went inside, he turned again to the brush. The huge stump looked as if it had been burned. He took a closer look. Maybe he could make footings with parts of it. He tried rocking it, and it lifted on one side and toppled over. He lifted the stump from the back, upending it a couple times until it was in the cleared area. It consisted of two trunks joined in a black knob the size of a motor block. The whole thing looked like a three-foot-high mushroom with two stems. The ends of the trunks were sawed off straight. He looked at the bow saw hanging on the back wall of the cottage. Maybe he could—

He saw John coming back toward the cottage and carrying a cell phone. "Ten?" he called. His arm went out, then came back without the phone. Then, seeing Adrian, he waved and ambled back in his direction. They stood in an awkward silence. Finally John said, "This afternoon a group is coming over for a cookout. I guess you can tell that Ten and her mother don't really get along."

"We don't have to be here," Adrian said.

"Tenley's mother thinks it would be all right for her to be here, and you too. She just called and said it's okay. Though she's still not happy about the—" He looked at the hammock. "About the arrangements."

"Okay."

"This is a Hawaiian group, a cultural and political group called Ku I Ka Ni'o. That means something like 'to reach the high point.'"

"Okay. Ku I Ka Ni'o."

John looked at him. "For someone from the mainland, you pronounce it well."

"My mother taught me a lot about things here."

John looked at the stump. "That's from a monkey pod tree a couple houses away. Jacob saved it to make a table or something. He never did, so we were going to take it to the dump, but never got around to it."

"—black bag?" Tenley said. She had come out of the cottage and was now standing at the corner, the phone to her ear. "I don't know anything about it. I had a key, but I don't now. None of the girls would have seen me because I wasn't there, I was—" She listened. "No, someone's trying to lay the blame on me." The expression on her face was not one of anger, but a pleading defensiveness. "I'm not lying. Who told you that?" Then she saw that her voice was carrying to where Adrian and John stood. She walked down the driveway.

"There'll be fifteen or twenty people here," John said. "Tell Tenley, okay?" He turned to leave as she was walking back. She passed the phone to him and joined Adrian in the shade. "One of those California bitches stole something from Hal and is trying to lay it on me."

"What'd she steal?"

"A black bag. I don't know anything about it. He kept saying, 'We've got to settle this matter of the black bag.' That's how he talks, real smooth and all, but I hope it wasn't a bag of money or a bag of crystal. That would be serious."

She looked at the stump.

"Oh, this," Adrian said. "Yeah, I was thinking of making footings. Anyway, John said that there's a group coming today called Ku I Ka Ni'o. That means 'to reach the high point.' He said your mother invited us, too."

Tenley looked suspicious. "What's she up to?"

"Nothing maybe. Just try to be nice to her and see what happens."

Adrian counted nineteen people, including Tenley's mother and John. All appeared well educated, and he became increasingly nervous when they were introduced as doctors, artists, professors, businessmen. Adrian and Tenley wore their good Salvation Army clothes. They circulated among the guests, Adrian shaking hands with men or being hugged by women—all because he had been introduced by Tenley's mother as her daughter's fiancé. The scam had been too successful. He overheard two girls talking to Tenley. "When you do um?" one asked, and Tenley said, "We haven't decided yet," to which the girl responded, "He cute, ah? Why wait?" The other girl advised, "No let um get away." It was like a ratchet, clicking farther and farther down its own bizarre illusion. Adrian watched Tenley and caught her mother watching her, too, a thoughtful, wondering look on her face.

One of the guests, a guy in his midtwenties named Anson Martin, who had been introduced as an artist, ended up near Adrian again and again as he circulated. That Martin might want to talk about art scared him. He tried to figure out what to say should he be asked serious questions. He knew that the bullshit he'd said about taking a look at Brancusi's *Bird in Flight* wouldn't be the answer. Tenley's mother might buy the lie, but not someone who knew about art.

He and Tenley went back to the cottage to get some scotch, Tenley saying that she still couldn't figure out what her mother was up to. But she really liked all the people there. She took a stream, then Adrian took one. Soon after they put the bottle away, Anson Martin and Tenley's mother appeared around the corner of the cottage. "Anson's interested in what kinds of projects you're into," Tenley's mother said brightly. There was no malice in her voice. Martin rested his eyes on the stump.

Adrian shrugged, his face warming. "Yeah," he said, "it's just an idea," and he tried to come up with an explanation of what he wanted to do with the stump. "I was going to do it this way," he said. Stepping over to it, he felt the horrible airy blankness in his mind expand, so he circled the stump, trying to control his panic. "It's a hand," he said, pointing at the cube shape sitting on the two thick trunks. "And this smaller trunk is the top of the shaft of a paddle. This thicker trunk is a wrist, this part a fist gripping the paddle handle."

Martin circled the stump. "What about checking?"

"Well, I douse it with wood protector, and the fact that it's been burned might help."

"I see it," Martin said. "I can see it."

Tenley was looking too. "You mean one of those rounded paddle handles?" she asked.

"That depends on the wood," Adrian said. "But there's little difference between a tubular handle top and a rounded one. You know, the ones that fit the hand."

"Oh yeah yeah yeah," Martin said, "I know: the ones that sweep up from a neck."

"Yeah, and this isn't shaped right for the old pole handles, the ones without the T top, because there's no protrusion here for the end of the handle."

"I'd do the rounded handle because of the Y-shaped downward sweep of it," Martin said. "That'd be cool. It could end up in a bank building."

"So do you think Ku I Ka Ni'o might buy it from me?" Adrian asked, and then he laughed.

Where had it come from, Tenley asked him later, the business of remembering the name of the club and pronouncing it perfectly? And the hand thing, too, the idea for the design? She picked up a forkful of macaroni salad and put it in her mouth while Adrian sawed with a plastic knife at some teriyaki beef. He said, I got the hand idea as it came out of my mouth—it was that close. There was this blank, and then I said it. But what about the handle of the paddle without the T top? Tenley asked. How did you know that in the old days they didn't have T tops? Well, it was probably a picture my mother showed me. Not to mention that if you don't have a T top, it might look like some guy doing you-know-what. Hahahaha. My God, she said, I bought it all. My mother bought it all. Anson is no fool either. I heard him talking with someone else later about this thing you're doing. Know what he said? He said, And the guy's only twenty. Hell, Adrian said, I could have said it was a forklift or a huge screwed-up Siamese-twin mushroom. I didn't have a clue what to do but now I have to do what I said.

He ate more of the beef, then some macaroni salad. "Well," he said, "I guess I'm stuck. If I fuck it up, I'll call it abstract art, okay?"

She laughed, grabbed his knee, and shook it. "You're the one who could sell the fat-free carrots." She left her hand there, still smiling at him. That smile made his face warm again, and he stared down at his food. She withdrew her hand and went on eating, and he looked up at the sky, which was darkening now that the sun was going down.

In order not to have the imprint of the hammock mesh all over her legs and arms, Tenley put a reed beach mat in the hammock. She slipped the oversized T-shirt on, pulled the bathing-suit top off, and eased herself up on it and sat.

"I keep wondering about Hal," she said. "I mean, how serious he is about a threat."

"What about the police?"

"No, that *would* be serious."

All he could see of her now was the white shirt and the dark, phantom shapes of limbs. He could hear the faint ticking and groaning sound of the roof and could smell the ocean in the light breeze that moved over him. He took three steps toward the white shape, holding one hand out until it touched the rope suspending the hammock, and it was taut, as hard as a thin stick of wood.

"Sit here," she whispered. He let himself down on the hammock. She put her arm around his lower back and said, "You're a genius at fooling people. I can see that now, but I wonder if that's what you're doing with me."

"No."

"I mean any number of guys would go along with this just for a little you-know-what. Even if you are, don't let me in on it, 'kay?"

"I'm not. The . . ." He couldn't put the right words to it. "The body contact doesn't lie. So if you're fooling me, you know, selling me the fat-free carrot, then sell me the carrot."

"I wonder if everything is a scam," she said. "I wonder if my mother is scamming me. I can't figure out why she's actually been, well, nice almost, at least today. And Hal. Is the black bag just a scam to get me over there? I don't know."

"Maybe your mother's not up to anything."

"I learned a long time ago that most people are into the scam. A counselor in intermediate school called me in because I was swearing and wearing a short skirt, so I sit in his office and he tells me that this behavior is not acceptable in his school. All the while, I see his eyes go down between my legs, and he's got this look of being almost out of control. If there'd been nobody around he'd dive right over his desk."

She shifted and then settled herself against him. "It's the only comfortable way for me," she whispered. She slid her leg over his side, and the heat of her flesh raced into his. She fumbled at his shorts, undoing the button, and he heard the zipper opening. "Maybe I'm not as tired as I thought," she said. "Let's just get these outta the way." She rolled over on him a little, chest on chest and stomach on stomach, her head right next to his. He put his hands on her back and ran them down over her buttocks and to her thighs, and folded her legs up until he felt their warmth on his sides. Then he felt where her thighs curved into her buttocks, and the hair, and centered himself there as she pushed herself down on it so that it sunk all the way into that liquid heat, and then she straight-armed herself up, with him watching, teeth clenched, because surely Jacob Chong would not be able to sleep through this.

He snapped awake before dawn. They had fallen asleep before showering, and she lay half on top of him. He worked her shirt down over her buttocks and then tucked the tail under her. He was sure they could be seen from the street beyond the vacant lot. It was just getting light enough that he could make out the tree stump sitting on its cut-off trunks. A fist with a paddle handle. He had to make good on the scam, but at the same time thought it would be just as important to get the hammock space enclosed. First, one long stream from the squirt bottle. But he changed his mind: scotch made him sweat too much. Not drinking produced a familiar feeling, a dim sadness, a sense of a dully frustrating separation from what he sometimes thought he lived for. He lifted the part of the duffel bag the big bottle was in and assured himself that it was more than half full. Then he pulled his shorts and underpants off, turned on the shower, took a deep breath, and let the cold water fall on his head.

By the time it was light enough to see clearly, he was sawing at the stump, making a plane that would define the knuckles and first joints of the four fingers gripping the paddle handle. He made the cut at an angle, the illusion of the hand on the inside. He cut with the bow saw across the plane, got seven or eight inches under the little hill he was removing, and then broke the waste off. The wood looked rich, but there were black, ant-filled fissures here and there.

"Is it any good?"

He turned. Tenley was sitting up, dangling her legs over the edge of the hammock.

"Fulla these little holes," he said. "Maybe I can fake people out by turning this weakness into a strength. I'll make the thing anyway, and if you can see through it, then it's . . . what? Experimental."

She laughed. "I got a paddle in the back-porch room. I'll go get it. Go bat'room first." She went around the corner of the cottage, the shirttail he had stretched down to cover her down over the backs of her legs.

"You're bored," he said sometime later, rising up from the saw with sweat dripping down his face.

"No I'm not," she said, pushing herself on the hammock so that the roof groaned. Jacob was moving around in his kitchen. "Ooo, I smell Pop-Tarts," Tenley said. He went back to sawing planes off the tree stump, every minute or so stepping to the paddle sitting in a crack between two boards in the pallet and gripping it. He would stare at his knuckles, the veins on the back of his hand, the veins in his wrist, the cords on the inside of his wrist, the way the flesh of his thumb and forefinger and that webbing in between puckered when he gripped the handle. He studied the thumbnail, the creases in his fingers and how far they went up around, the depth of the spaces between each finger, the lump of muscle behind the webbing between his thumb and finger. He turned his hand to study the lump of muscle on the little-finger side, the four creases at the first joint of the finger. Tenley watched all of this silently, her head turning as he went back and forth. From time to time, she giggled. Once he stopped, stood up, and looked at her. "What?" he asked. "Nothing," she said, then giggled again. He worked with the same sustained fury he had repaired and varathaned a door for the old house in New York or polished a brass keyhole plate and the hinges. There had been only two things in the world: himself and a door. Now there were only three things: himself and a tree stump and Tenley Chong, her toe in the dirt under the hammock. That figure whose geography he had blindly explored the previous night, that altar he prayed at. Or in? He felt an erection forming. No, he said to himself, don't think about that. Don't think about the hot blood moving through those veins, those damp armpits with their little patches of stubble, and those breasts settling on his chest, that subtle swipe of an eyelash tickling his cheek.

"What's the matter?" she asked.

"Huh?"

"You're standing there with the saw staring at the wood, and you're not doing anything."

"Sorry, I was thinking." He sawed three times, then stopped. "About you. Thinking about last night. Geography and religion."

She giggled. "You're a real Marco Polo, a genuine Saint What's-his-name."

He pulled another section of wood off. "Shit," he said. "Look at that. Another hole."

"Ignore it."

It was a good saw. The wood was dry enough inside that the saw didn't bind. He had feared that carrying out the scam would be impossible because you can't just make a fist out of a block of wood. But he really saw the fist now, the planes of its form. He wondered how it was that more people didn't do stuff like this. It was easy as long as you were willing to put the sweat into it, and he knew that when it came time to file and sand, he would work on it the same way he had worked on the house in the woods, with a focus almost imbecilic in its totality.

"I see it," Tenley said. "Here, have another Pop-Tart."

He went over to her, wiped his hands on his shorts, and took the Pop-Tart. He ate it in three bites and returned to the saw. "The knuckle of the thumb," she said. "Is that too big?" He went and got the paddle, gripped it, and then held it up for her to see. "No, I guess not," she said.

Jacob came around the corner and looked at the stump, then at Adrian. "Eh, you look hot. You disappeah too much li'dat. Go beach an' cool off."

Adrian practiced swimming while Tenley watched, standing in water up to her chest, from time to time jumping up and down when the waves moved her. It seemed strange that there was no one else on the beach, except some figures down toward the rocky point with a small lighthouse on its flank. If it were not for the lighthouse and those figures, it could have been a thousand years ago.

The image of his mother came to him again, then the image of the cold body in the hole. It was only six days ago, or seven. "Somethin's wrong with me," he said. "I mean, my mother died only a few days ago, and I don't feel bad. I feel like I should, but I don't."

"What would she want you to do?"

"What I'm doing." He ran his hands around in the water. "She grew up here. I remember a lot of it, but I hated the idea of coming because I was tied to the house and the woods in New York. Now, that place doesn't mean anything. And she's there in the pine grove."

"No, she isn't."

"But I left her body there. It's illegal, you know. I used to have this vision, or dream maybe, of a black snake that lives inside me. It runs up and down right next to my spine, snaking past organs and so on, my heart beating and denting the snake's side each time it beats. The snake is fed by all the bad things I ever did. When Leigh Donaldson committed suicide, it almost doubled in size. And it's still sitting there, and I was afraid it was getting even fatter."

"Jesus," she whispered, "I don't think I like that."

"It's stupid."

"No, but there aren't any snakes here."

He had known that, he thought, yet the information caused a little zap of a half-recognition, and then it vanished. No snakes here. Again he was convinced that his mother knew something that he didn't.

Jacob had sandpaper, files, scoop-nosed and flat chisels, their shafts rusty and handles cracked, old handsaws of various sizes down to little ones that folded into plastic handles. In the late morning, Adrian looked at the hammock, which swung slightly, but incessantly, so that the squeaking of the roof became a sound as natural as the wind in the leaves, Tenley's toe having created a little trench in the dirt. It was time to work on the room.

"I wonder if we can borrow the truck again," he said. "I gotta get more wood."

"'Kay, I ask Jacob."

Not only did Jacob have the truck, but he also had a neighbor right up the street with a pile of half-rotted wood, old louver frames, pieces of redwood, four-by-fours, and pieces of plywood. He wanted the stuff out of his yard because it housed rats' nests. As Adrian and Jacob loaded it into the bed of the truck, gray rats scampered off into some weeds behind the man's house. Adrian found a little nest made of reeds, cigarette wrappers, and pieces of trash, inside of which were six tiny pink bullets, their eyes not yet open: hairless baby rats. He lifted them, nest and all, and carried them to the brush. There he found a good spot to put them down, knowing that they wouldn't survive but, should the mother rat come back, giving them the chance anyway. Then as they continued loading, he looked back again and again at the spot, thinking he should go and check. Jacob thought he was crazy. "'Ass rats you know," he wheezed. "Step on um. What, you some kine religious fanatic o' what?"

Then Adrian borrowed a hammer from Jacob's friend and pulled nails out of all the boards, set them on a brick, and hammered them straight. "You buy nails, brah," Jacob said. "What, you so pake dat you use o' ones?" "We need nails, here are nails," Adrian said. Jacob looked down at them, some rusted, some coated with tan stuff from the termite damage. "Yah, whatevahs," he said.

The pieces of plywood were three-quarter-inch industrial grade, but were not in square pieces. Behind the cottage he began laying out the irregular pieces to form the floor. Tenley got the idea and started turning pieces over, staring at the arrangement as if it were a puzzle. The plank wood was old six-inch-wide tongue and groove—good wood once he cut the termite-eaten sections off with Jacob's crosscut saw. The rust on the metal blade gradually vanished, revealing the dull silver sheen. Jacob sat on his kitchen chair and commented as Adrian worked. How da hell you tink you make one wall wit' pieces dat shawt? Well, you go up about four feet, then across with one of the four-by-fours. Then you take more short pieces and continue up to that four-by-six supporting the roof, leaving a hole for a window. If the four-by-four isn't long enough, and he looked, which it isn't, then you support it with another four-by-four, see? Nail a block of two-by-four to the cottage wall and rest the end of the four-by-four on that. It isn't weight-supporting necessarily, but the T and G is strong. Then Adrian went to the shower and drank four gulps of water.

'Kayden, what about dis? Jacob asked, pointing at the strange puzzle-like arrangement of plywood pieces, Tenley still turning some over, looking for better fits. Here's what we do, Adrian said. I'm gonna arrange these old four-by-six pieces along the joining of these pieces of ply, then cut the ply straight for the outer edges. You nuts? Why we no jus' go buy um, ah? You ack like you gotta use every little bit. No, not really. Once the floor is done, you won't notice it, and I'll cover it with something.

Lauhala, Tenley said. Adrian took four more gulps of water.

Whatevahs, Jacob said, but den you cannot put um onna dirt. Yeah, that's true. I need footings of some kind. Eh, I get heavy-duty hollow-tile stoffs piled up oddasai da cottage. You like see? Sure. When Adrian did see them, he wasn't sure. Then he picked one up. Jesus, this weighs about forty or fifty pounds. It'll work fine. 'Kayden, what we standeen heah fo'? But you carry um. I break my back try fo' lif' da buggahs.

So you start by making a square, a hollow-tile footing under each corner, and nail the short boards together. Then, where the short boards meet, put down another hollow-tile brick. Join the four-by-sixes with nails, and shoot out another two-by-six, placing a tile brick under where it ends. Simple. Jacob watched skeptically until Adrian laid down the first section of plywood and nailed it in place. Be able to store a Sherman Tank on this, he said. 'Kay, 'kay, whatevahs. Soon Tenley could sit on the hammock with both feet flat on the floor. Walls? Simple. Just start by nailing the T and G into the outside of the two-by-sixes that form the perimeter of the foundation. Okay, now you make sure that the pieces form one level line. By the way, where do you want this oceanside window? Oh, Tenley said, I guess right about there, and she pointed. Good, so we'll leave a space, but how wide? Hey, Jacob, can you hand me that louver frame? Eh, wheah you put da doah? Oops, I forgot. You no like open dakine out to da weeds an' you no like open um an' climb ovah one pile bricks, ah? Oops, you're right. How about we put it here by the cottage wall. That way—

"I can get to the bathroom without climbing over the house," Tenley said.

"Akamai, da girl," Jacob said.

"We'll find a door. I'll sand it down and make it look like the door to the . . ." He snapped his fingers. "The . . . What is it? That Castle?"

"Iolani Palace," Tenley said.

"Don't you ever get tired?"

Adrian stopped at the sound of the alien voice and stood up straight, then wiped his face with his dirty hand. Tenley's mother stood there. Tenley's eyes went to her, then to Adrian, then to Jacob.

"No, I just figured I ought to get this done," Adrian said. "The sculpture has to be housed somewhere—I mean, if it's okay for me to put it in here, once I get to the fine sanding."

There was curiosity on Tenley's mother's face, and for a moment Adrian was struck by how pretty she was. With her thick, black hair and clear, dark skin, she must have been absolutely beautiful when she was Tenley's age. "I can see the fist easily," she said, "but the thing is full of holes. What do you do? Fill the holes?"

He looked at it. Because his mind had been racing all day, it raced now, and he did not feel the panic he had anticipated at being asked about it. He tried to think of something to say. After a few seconds, he opened his mouth and said, "The hand and the paddle are damaged, you know, eroded by time, by pests and so on, but they're still there. I want the hand to look strong even though it has gaps, holes and so on." He stopped. "It's like the grip is strong despite the passage of time."

"I get it," she said. Then she said, "Ten, can I talk to you out here?"

Tenley got out of the hammock and padded barefoot across the floor. She looked once at Adrian with a weary fatalism and followed her mother out and around the cottage.

Adrian and Jacob worked on. "So den, you gonna put paint on um too? I get um, junk cans but. We see, we open um up an' check um out."

"Okay. Hey, let me know if there's anything you'd like me to install while we're doing this, okay?"

"How 'bout one wahine?"

"Haha, yeah."

Through the little kitchen window, Adrian heard sniffling, then the sound of Tenley crying. "I'll go check," he said to

Jacob, who nodded, looking angrily in the direction of the bigger house.

Adrian tiptoed around. "You okay?"

Tenley was wiping her eyes. "She wants us to stay. She invited us to dinner," she said. Then she pulled herself against him, her head on his chest. "I don't understand it."

He felt a flash of heat. Now Tenley's mother had bought the scam, and it didn't make sense.

"I don't either," he said. "Maybe we should own up to the whole thing. You can't just—"

She looked up at him. "Could we wait?"

Tenley's mother and John placed the plates of food on a table—teriyaki chicken, teriyaki beef, macaroni and other salads, most of it leftovers from the party the previous evening—and then ate in the living room on a couch, two easy chairs, and, for Adrian, a folding chair. At the outset, the conversation made Adrian tense because it was initiated by Tenley's mother and seemed aimed at him. Ten said you were born here. Yeah, Kap'iolani Hospital. And your mother was from here? Yeah, she met my father after he got out of the service. He worked construction, and she was like a secretary. And what was her maiden name? Rose Macklin. Or Loke Macklin. Her mother was Hawaiian and Caucasian and Chinese, I think, but I don't know her mother's maiden name. She apparently died a long time ago, and my mother was an only child, so I don't really have any relatives here.

John got up and went to the window. Then he turned and shook his head. "Same stupid car: a Honda with tinted windows. A tan one."

"Somebody trying to find some house to buy drugs," Tenley's mother said.

"Once yesterday, again today," John said.

And Tenley stole a glance at Adrian, seeming to say, Hal, that son of a bitch just won't let go.

"Tenley mentioned that your mother died recently. I'm sorry."

Adrian nodded. He knew where this was leading, and he had to manufacture something right then or it wouldn't work. "Yeah, three weeks and two days ago. She wanted me to come out here, so after the funeral I did. I met Tenley right away, at the beach. We talked a lot, and she helped me reorient myself to Hawai'i, especially with figuring out how I might continue my art projects here." He nodded at his food. "It happened, you know, the way you see it in movies sometimes: people meet and get struck by each other. I asked her in Kap'iolani Park, actually—when was it?" he asked, looking at Tenley.

"Uh—" She nervously snapped her fingers a couple times.

"Two weeks and— No, just two weeks ago." He ate some macaroni salad, accidentally biting the plastic fork hard enough to make one of the tines crack off. He placed it on the edge of his paper plate. He was in trouble now. What had he done during the two weeks since he'd met her, or the week before that? The question was obviously coming, so he worked on an answer in the little silence that followed.

"So have you seen much since you got here?"

"I had this idea that I could come here and camp," he said. "Probably something my mother told me. So I tried it, but ended up like one of those homeless people you see. I didn't have enough money for a hotel room, so looked around for a place."

"Then he stayed with us," Tenley said.

"'Us'?" her mother asked.

"The girls I was rooming with in Makiki. He slept on the couch."

Adrian groaned. "Talk about uncomfortable," he said. "But it worked out okay."

He could see Tenley working the story over as she ate, going over all the holes there might be in it. "The first day I was here,

I tried to find the kahuna rocks, you know, the healing stones of Waikīkī, but that place is so confusing—"

"Kūhiō Beach," Tenley's mother said, "by the surfboard racks."

"I was way down the other end, at Ala Moana Beach." It was odd. He hadn't thought of those rocks in years. "My mother went to them from time to time."

They ate in silence for a minute, Adrian flushing because he had constructed so elaborate a lie that he was convinced it was bound to fail.

"It must have been hard to come here so soon after your mother died," Tenley's mother said.

"Yeah, but she wanted me to, so I thought I should."

The conversation turned after that. "Those people who came last night," Tenley's mother said, "are activists for sovereignty and various other rights issues for Hawaiians. The artist you talked to—he's not so much an activist as a sort of practitioner and defender of the old ways. His art turns out to be political in that it condemns haole hegemony through its imagery. He's got this great one, made of a tub full of dirty water with a sort of rock-wall foundation, a broken poi pounder on the bottom of the tub next to some American coins, and then on top a floating hamburger wrapper, a Coke can, a plastic model of an aircraft carrier, and some other stuff. He calls it My Hawai'i. Do you know about these issues? I mean, did your mother tell you about them?"

"I grew up on stories about the overthrow," Adrian said, "and about the Hawaiian kings and queens, but my mother wasn't political." He wondered, What was hegemony? The nervousness crept in again because of that word. Tenley's mother was intelligent, and it made him feel vulnerable.

"Are you political?" she asked.

There had to be some other answer than yes, because he was being too agreeable. "Well, no," he said, "because an artist remains separate from all that. An artist is necessarily an enemy of the state, of any state. It's all in the interests of preserving an uncorrupted consciousness." He wasn't that sure of what he was saying because it was straight out of a TV show he and his mother had watched. Tenley's mother looked surprised, as did Tenley. Then he realized that he had in effect just trashed Anson Martin. But he was committed to what he was saying, so he went on. "An artist sees into things too deeply to be affected by a movement or a cause, like too involved looking into things." Now the expression on Tenley's face was so unsure, or cautionary, that he looked back at her mother. "I mean, that's what I've come to realize. An artist looks at the precise geography of all things with a searching eye." He had heard that on TV, too. Or half of it, making the other half his. But it made sense.

"My God," she said. "You're not exactly patronizing, are you?"

He shrugged. It was good, her sarcasm, because now he was not just an obliging fool who agreed with everything she said. He was now believable, and it made him feel secure, as he had once felt secure standing in front of a class with a piece of paper and reciting, without a flaw, what his mother had recited to him.

"I no unnastan' anyting you say," Jacob said. "Eh, but dat okay. You know how fo' nail stuffs togeddah, so you okay in my book."

"It sounds like speechmaking," Adrian said, "but I don't mean it to. And it doesn't mean to me that the U.S. government doesn't owe Hawaiians their sovereignty either. My mother told me that when they overthrew the monarchy, they auctioned off all the queen's furniture and then planned to tear the palace down. The arrogance of that is incredible. I may be an enemy of the state or whatever, like I said, and I may be nonpolitical and so on, but only an idiot wouldn't be angered by that."

They got not only a couple of chairs and a small side table, but also Tenley's bunk bed from her room—sheets and all. The room was used for storage, right up to the ceiling—Tenley's mother's and sister's stuff, and John's stuff—so they would be unable to use it. That's fine, Tenley told her mother. Adrian can sleep on the hammock, no problem. John gave them an extension cord, a power strip, and a little lamp so they could see at night.

Standing in the nearly completed room, they each took two long squirts of scotch. Tenley was amazed by what had happened. Her mother had walked them back to the room at about ten, after everything had been set up, and had given Tenley a long hug and a motherly kiss. "I actually sat there kind of remembering when you and I met, and how you asked me to marry you at the park." She went and sat down on her bunk bed, pushed the heels of her hands into the mattress.

"We gotta remember all that."

"You did ask me at the park," she said. "In your own way, looking in my ear or something, with your searching eye, scanning the precise geography of whatevahs."

He shook his head wearily. "Jesus, I'd just about run outta gas before all that enemy-of-the-state shit started. 'The uncorrupted consciousness'—I think it's just the sound of the words that makes me remember them." He tried to comprehend the totality of what was going on. "I'm wearing a mask," he said. "You know how it is—how, after a while, your face changes to fit the mask?"

"Yeah, I know."

"I mean, I guess I always wore it. When my father told me that his goal was to work for a white America, I agreed with him. What else could I do? If I hadn't, he'd've just beaten the shit outta me. And if I wasn't here, then I might be back there with a swastika tattoo on my back, standing under a Nazi flag with my father proudly looking on."

"So what now?"

"I wanna buy varathane and a wire brush for the fist and paddle, for the black stuff inside. It has to be shiny—you know, finished. I gotta find some way of making the art convincing." He stopped. How could it have carried itself this far? "I think I also wanna figure out how to lay it all on the line."

"Yeah, but I'm afraid of spilling the beans. She'll kick me out, or us. But it's not your problem. And if you want out, that's okay. You can bail when you need to. I've gotten what I wanted."

He couldn't think of why he would hang on with this, considering that he had gotten what he had wanted, to bury the braid. "No," he said, "I have nothing, nobody. There isn't any use for me. I mean, all anybody ever said was don't fuck up. And I say, so what do I do? They say 'do?' What do you do? Beats me. Just don't fuck up."

"Well, you aren't," Tenley said. Then she looked worried. "And I gotta call Hal. This business of sending his idiots around to threaten me like this is dumb."

"Why would you think that the car had something to do with him?"

"It did," she said. "You can't just walk away like I did. It comes back to bite you." She pulled the sheet back. "I got so tired watching you all day with the saw and hammer that I'm really outta gas," she said. "I'll get over against the wall. Just jump in when you want."

She went out the door hole and around the side of the cottage to go to the bathroom.

He went to the bathroom next, and when he got back, she was where she said she would be, fast asleep and wrapped in the sheet, having left a reasonably large space for him. He carefully slid onto the bunk bed, and within five minutes felt himself begin to swoon.

Cold before dawn, he felt around for the sheet. The breeze almost felt like something from New York. Tenley was wrapped too tightly in the sheet for him to pull it over himself. He stayed as he was and drifted to sleep again. He felt the snake later, worming, the tubular shape surging inward toward the softer organs, pushing against them so that his breath became light and shallow in his throat. The fat shape surged upward with a sluggish persistence, sliding along slick membranes toward the softer space between his lungs, next to his heart. He remained still because the sheet-wrapped corpse of his mother lay next to him, and he had yet to do something about her. He turned his head to look at her, and saw her face, eyes, nostrils, and mouth closed and sewn shut with large, black stitches. Under the eye stitches, the protruding lumps of retinas were moving, and the nostrils were flexing because she could not breathe with them sewn shut. Then Leigh Donaldson floated across the room, her small, puckered rose of a mouth in a half-open, searching desire for him. She lifted her skirt and floated one pale leg over his midsection, the little scars on her arms and legs becoming squirming dotted lines that moved on her skin like speckled snakes.

The faint light of dawn defined the window holes while his mind figured out where he was. He felt the ticklish fading of the dream, and rolled his head sideways to see Tenley wrapped in the sheet. He tried pulling part of it from her, and enough came free to cover his upper body. He slid himself under and smelled the warm, sweet air coming from her. In the dim light, he could just make out her body. He tried to see the bathing-suit bottom but could not, so he reached out and settled his hand on where he thought it would be, but it was not there. She said she was out of gas, but did it mean that she liked sleeping with nothing on as a matter of course? Well, maybe it did make sense. He carefully slid his hand over her side to her lower back. She shifted, but didn't awaken.

When the light coming through the window hole turned a bright yellow, the entire block illuminated her upper body, the rich skin of her shoulder, the paler skin of her breasts squashed between her upper arms, one nipple slightly depressing the skin inside her upper arm so that, with each deep breath, it rolled slightly into the flesh. It was probably the light that made her open her eyes and look directly into his.

"Hey," he whispered.

"Could you take a towel and cover that?" she asked, squinting at the window.

He got up and found a towel, and hung it over the hole, securing it by jamming the edge in two places between unnailed T-and-G boards. When he went back to the little bed, she was holding the sheet up. "Leave them on the floor," she whispered, nodding at his shorts. He sat down and took them off, and she pulled him over her.

"Kukui-nut oil," Jacob wheezed.

"Okay, where do we get that? I know it's candle nut. My mother talked about that."

Jacob pointed up toward the mountains. "See da light-color trees up dea? 'Ass kukui tree. We go up an' colleck dem, den I show you." Adrian looked at the deep vertical furrows in the mountains, some of which held clusters of trees with pale-green leaves.

"I think you crush the meat and put it in something and squeeze the oil through," Tenley said. She sat on the corner of the shower pallet. He looked at her and experienced a little flash of amazement. Twice they'd done it in the warm, filtered light coming through the towel hung over the window hole.

With his arms straight, hands on the mattress making large, star-shaped creases in the sheet, he'd looked down at her, and her eyes were closed so that he could look down and watch himself disappear again and again under that sparse-haired mound at the base of the V formed by her thighs. He shook his head and tried to concentrate.

Afterward, he got up and went back to the crude, squared-off fist, the pole coming out the bottom far too thick. It seemed simple enough: just keep looking at veins, creases, the bulge of muscles in the hand, and transfer them to the wood. Anybody could do it. The question was why.

He worked an hour on the fist. Wait wait, she said, why you leaving da raised line? Because it's a vein, he said. Then he turned back to the little room, fitting the louvered window frames in place and putting the biggest one on the back wall. High up, she said, because I no wan' people watching us exploring and praying or whatevahs. Then it was some paint on the inside—the outside could wait—because the brighter it was inside, the easier it would be to read. For you to read, you mean, he said.

Some oiliness on the boards showed through. "Hafta put another coat on," he said.

"Looks good to me." She pulled the squirt bottle out and took a short stream.

"Looks like shit until I get another coat on."

"Did you paint your house in the woods? The one you were working on?"

He stopped, visualizing it. "Yeah, it was like two months from being really nice."

"Your arm looks tired. I'll paint." She took the brush.

He watched her. "I don't understand it," he said, "what we're doing."

"I told you I wanted a baby. It won't get in your way." She went on painting. "I'm as serious about it as I was when I first got the idea. I can't read what you think. There are things I would never say to people, or to you, and I assume that you're the same way. So I have what's left, and that's getting pregnant."

"These fumes are making me dizzy," he said. "Let's go to the beach for a while."

All right, if she still suspected him of having other motives, then he would do something to end those suspicions. He practiced swimming. As he did so, he thought about his problem. He'd come here to bury the braid and he'd done so. Now it was over. If the world offered nothing more than a strange, businesslike silence, no reason whatever for doing anything at all, then the problem of the scam could be solved. Just get out of it. But Tenley was in the way. He could not put into words the reaction he had to her, that even if he had met her in the woods in upstate New York, he would still have dreamed of taking her to the house and then establishing a ring of protection around it. It embarrassed him to think that she might know the degree of his attraction to her. He was sure that she only needed him for putting out, as she called it, for her grandfather and her mother. That she "loved him" was no doubt her own scam. He wasn't egotistical enough to think that she really did.

He stood up in the water, blew snot out of his nose, and then walked toward her with a dreamlike slowness through the water's resistance. When he got within five feet, he cleared his throat. She looked at him, almost in alarm. "What's wrong?" she asked.

"Uh," he said. He couldn't find the words. "I—" He looked away. How was one supposed to do this? "I want to ask you a question," he said.

"Okay."

"Are we gonna get married then? I mean, if that's what you want, then let's do it."

She opened her mouth to speak, then looked away toward her house. Then she looked back at him, drew breath to speak again. "What are you up to?"

"Nothing. You ask me what I wanna do. Go back to Waikīkī, go back to America." He frowned. "This is America. What do you call it? The mainland. Well, I don't wanna do that." He was getting cold standing in the water. She saw him shivering and moved through the water to him.

"You are serious," she said.

Jacob had a caulking gun that Adrian used around both window frames, drawing it carefully in the seams, then wetting his index finger and following the line so that it produced a soft, rounded joining. Now they had only to install the strips of glass inside the little clips, and the windows would be done. Tenley sat on the bed and watched. The whole idea of actually getting married had tripped her up, because it had started out as no more than a vengeful whim. It involved too much, he guessed. He didn't really know what it meant for him. After all, there really was nothing the world wanted him to do, no obligation or purpose that he could remember all the way back to when he first started to think. It was just a vast, random series of images and noises that meant nothing, and he guessed that his talking marriage was a way of thumbing his nose at the world.

"I get it," he said. "Getting married is too much for you."

"No, it isn't."

"Having a baby for the hell of it was okay, but having—"

Something hit the wall of Jacob's cottage with a loud bang and knocked the bow saw off one of its nails. It slid down and swung back and forth, softly scraping the wall until it stopped. Tenley looked up, then around at the floor. "Jesus," she said. Adrian looked out the window at the vacant lot. Through a tall hedge, he could see the glint of a car driving away and turning the corner. There were no kids around.

"Somebody threw something," he said. He went and hung the saw back on its nails.

"What? You mean like a slingshot?"

He went outside and made his way into the brush and rotted palm fronds, toward the rusted back fence of the yard, and pushed himself through the brush to where he could see the vacant lot. But there was nothing.

Back inside the room he said, "Nobody there. Kids probably."

"I heard a snapping sound, then a *ping* when it hit. From outside, I mean. Or a pop."

He stepped to the wall and pulled the bow saw off its nails and held it to the light from the window hole. One part of the rusted tubular steel handle had a silvered dent in it, like a dimple. "Look at this." He pointed at the dent. "That looks like it's from a bullet."

"Not," she said. Then she touched the dent. On one side of the dimple there was a gray stain. Lead. "No, I—" She looked out the window hole.

"That looks like a dent made by like a .22 slug. Do kids around here have stuff like that?"

"Kids, no. Crooks, plenty," she said. Then she got a calculating look, staring at the brush out the window hole. "Unless Hal—"

"Could he be that pissed off? I was standing in the window hole." His skin prickled. If it was a bullet, then it had to have gone right past his head, which was now suddenly full of a number of fleeting images of people being shot in the head from World War II documentaries and a recent one in color from China: a row of men being shot by soldiers in the backs of their necks so that they toppled forward on their faces. "Uh, something's not right here," he said.

Again her eyes darted around. "Jesus," she said, "I wonder if we should call the police. I wonder what was in the black bag."

He looked out the window hole again and then turned to her. Her eyes continued to scan the walls, floor, bed. "Look," he said, "I'm gonna go outside to that lot and take another look, okay?"

He made his way to the back fence, which was bent down in places, so he could straddle a low spot and step into the vacant lot. He walked across it, passing sturdy clumps of high grass that scratched his legs. There were oxidized beer cans and pieces of cardboard and paper that had rotted onto the pebbles and roots. There was a rusted grocery cart, red plastic near the handle faded to a light pink. He stepped out to the street and looked back at the cottage. Over the fence was the window hole, a rectangle that appeared white because the wall on which the saw hung was white, and he pictured his upper body in that hole and realized that the distance was such that nobody in his right mind would try to scare someone by deliberately missing him. Again his flesh prickled, and he whispered, "You almost died."

But then he himself had placed the muzzle of a rifle in his mouth only a few days ago, and it occurred to him now that he had chickened out over eleven hundred dollars. The symmetry of it frightened him. His scalp prickled and he was afraid, wondering if whoever pulled the trigger might be aiming again. He walked quickly across the parched lot and to the fence, returning to the room. Once there, he avoided the window hole and sat on the bed. "I don't like this," he said. "Maybe you should call Hal."

"No, he'll think I'm recording it or something. I have to go see him. Where's dakine?"

He pulled the scotch out of the bag, and she took a squirt. He did too. "Funny," she said, "I don't need as much as I did just a few days ago."

"Me either."

The best time to talk to Hal, she said, was around four or five in the afternoon, after the various pieces of meat sleeping in his pad got up. She and Adrian would take the bus, then go up to his place and knock on the door. It was a big, airy place with a large lanai, and there wouldn't be any hanky-panky or violence because all you would have to do was scream and all the rich neighbors would be on the phone calling 911. Hal was fastidious about his place, so nobody would try to gag you or do anything that would mess up his precious oriental rugs or his expensive glass tables. The various whores would be sitting around drinking martinis and eating microwaved breakfasts, chatting about makeup and movies and clothes. Tenley would try to convince him that she knew nothing about the black bag. If there was a lot of money in it, or some colossal rock, the bimbo who'd taken it was already on the mainland, sticking her ass out in some cold, rainy street in Portland or Seattle, pissed off at herself for leaving paradise.

"I'll go with you," he said.

"It would help, because I'm a little scared," she said. "Put on good clothes."

They took the bus to Kailua, down through the center of the small town and then up toward the mountains on a series of steep switchbacks toward the Pali Lookout, which she pointed out when they were under it. On the mountainside, an old highway was suspended like a curving shelf on old concrete pillars.

After that she sat there chewing a fingernail and staring pensively at the seat in front of her. He decided not to talk. He looked out the window down at a golf course hundreds of feet below the highway. Then they went into a tunnel. He remembered that too: the short tunnel followed by a longer one, which let out in a heavily wooded area with mountains on both sides and deep clefts, some of which showed the pale lines of waterfalls.

He saw the cluster of buildings in the distance. "We made a circle," he said.

"Yeah, right down there is where we met."

The bus went down and through the middle of the city, and they got off at the Diamond Head end of Waikīkī, right near Hal's building. It was across from the zoo. When they were in the glitzy-looking foyer, Tenley looked at herself in a large mirror. "Okay," she said, "I look more like a college student than a slut." She wore her good jeans and a kind of high-end tank top. They got off the elevator on the twelfth floor, and Tenley cleared her throat and pulled a little compact out of her purse and peered at her face in the mirror. "If anyone asks, you know the routine."

"Look at Brancusi's *Bird in Flight*."

She pressed the brass button and waited. The door opened to Hal's face, which went from surprise to false joy to good-humored reproach. "Ten," he said softly.

"I want to talk to you," she said.

"Good!" he said. "My, and you brought— Was it Andrew?"

"Adrian," Tenley said.

"Right right right," he said. "Please, come on in. I'm on the phone right now, but you can socialize with my friends here," and he swept his hand behind him. Tenley and Adrian went inside. The place was large and had black-leather overstuffed furniture and a big-screen TV, beyond which was a large lanai. The doors to the lanai were open, so drapes wafted in the breeze until Hal closed the front door. The floors were covered with expensive-looking oriental rugs, and the walls with Japanese or Chinese paintings, some in triple frames, depicting angular tree branches with flowers on the ends and birds sitting in the middle. It took Adrian a full five seconds to realize that in the living room there were two girls, sitting on a couch, and that they were not the ones he'd met before.

Hal leaned against the wall in a hallway beyond the living room and talked on the phone while Tenley looked around. She said "Hi," to the girls, who nodded at her. One had a strange look on her face, a kind of gleeful outrage, as if she wanted to say something to Tenley or to Adrian. Tenley snorted and folded her arms, and then looked over their heads out to the ocean.

"You new?" the girl with the strange expression asked.

"No, just a friend," Tenley said.

"A friend?" the girl said, drawing the word out as if she could not believe what she had heard. She asked the other girl, "Does Hal have friends?" Both girls were blonde, and Adrian thought they were nearly beautiful, but for a hard edge. It was probably because they were a little older, maybe in their late twenties or early thirties. "Well," the girl went on, "I'm so stoked to find out that Hal has a friend. That's so cute."

"You'll get over it," Tenley said.

"Will I?" she said brightly.

"Fuck you," Tenley said. The girl uttered a theatrical gasp. Adrian cleared his throat.

The girl who had not spoken yet cleared her throat, too. "Kids," she said, "be nice."

"Do you have a hanky?" the first girl asked. "I think I might weep."

"Keep the hanky and wipe yourself off when you get reamed tonight," Tenley said.

Both girls laughed. "Oh my," the first one said, "we're being scolded." The girl ran her knuckle under her eye, her lower lip coming out in a childish pout. "Mommy said to save it for my husband," she said in a squeaky voice, "and I gave it away."

"Diane," the other girl said soothingly, "don't cry. Can't you see she's reformed? She's a convert, and you know they're the worst kind."

"Yeah," Tenley said, "all for nice clothes and some dope."

The first girl looked Tenley up and down, then Adrian. She giggled. "Looks to me like you sure have been saving it, because—" She laughed heartily. "Because that stuff looks like Goodwill."

"Salvation Army," Tenley said.

"I love Salvation Army," the girl went on. "They have my clothes from a month ago. In fact, those jeans look like they might be mine."

"No," Tenley said, "I always give the crotch a sniff before buying. They can't be yours."

The girl laughed again.

Hal came in from the hall. "So, I see you folks have made each other's acquaintance? Excellent." Then he turned to Tenley. "To what do I owe the pleasure of this surprise visit?"

"Can we talk alone?" Tenley asked.

"Of course!" he said, clapping his hands. "Let's see . . . maybe the lanai." He ushered them out through the sliding glass doors and then closed them, giving them some privacy.

"Sit down," Hal said. Adrian looked over the railing at the ocean, the foreground to the left blocked by a shorter building that was very close. Hovering there in the bright sunlight, it looked as if its wall of bright windows and lanais were levitating in the air.

"I'll stand," Tenley said. "I'll make this short. I don't know anything about any black bag. I don't have any key to this place. You should ask one of those girls in there about it."

"Ah yes, the matter of the black bag," Hal said. "I've almost gotten over it."

"What was in it?"

"Cash. I was holding it for the slow deposit. You know, always under ten thou."

"Do you think I'd be sleeping on the fucking beach if I had money? Get real."

"Okay, okay," he said. "You still owe some, though."

"I'll work on paying it when I can. I can't now. So tell your friends or whoever is doing this to leave us alone."

"I don't know what you're talking about," Hal said, frowning.

"Driving past my mother's house, and then that business this morning. That was a bullet that came through our window, and Adrian was standing right there. I want it stopped."

"What bullet? Are you crazy?"

"Listen, we both know you're lying. Just stop it."

Hal looked at her, then at Adrian, thinking. He stared at the ocean and then whispered, "Jesus."

"Jesus what?"

"It's not you," Hal said, and then he turned and looked at Adrian. "It's you."

"What does that mean?" Adrian asked.

"Somebody might be after you."

"Why?" Tenley asked.

Hal thought again. "It's gotta be," he said. "Remember Art?"

"Your 'bodyguard'?"

"He told me something that day on the beach. Something about a guy named Branch. Not Adrian, though. Someone else."

"My father," Adrian said. "Ray."

"Yeah, Ray. Art's a murder fan, you know, keeps up on them, likes to talk about them, like the senator that time, and what? That labor leader? And this one he remembered because it was famous for a while. Sometime ago, it seems, your father was in business with some people from Kalihi, or Pearl City. And two brothers from that outfit were done away with, execution style, and set on fire in a cane field out in the uplands somewhere. Your father supposedly did it, but he wasn't ever charged. And there was a third brother, too. Art couldn't remember the names. He kept snapping his fingers and saying, 'Shit, what was the name?'"

"I was a kid," Adrian said. "Why would anybody be interested in me?"

Hal stared at him, as did Tenley. "When did this happen?" she asked.

"Art didn't say. I mean, it didn't mean anything to me. Ancient history."

Adrian stared at the levitating wall of windows and lanais. When he shifted his position, it moved against the background of dark-blue ocean. His mind filled with images of his father back then, sitting by the apartment window and watching cars come and go. Was he capable of murder? Adrian didn't believe it. And the idea that someone would want to kill Adrian seemed to him too old-fashioned, too backward, to make sense. Like something in an old Mafia film.

"I had nothing to do with it," he said.

"You need to understand Hawai'i," Hal said. "People have long memories here, and a kind of smoldering desire for vengeance runs underneath things. It doesn't matter that you had nothing to do with it. It matters only that you're connected by blood to the person who did. If I were you, I'd get out of town. Not for a while either. For good."

"Why would this place be different from any other?" Adrian asked.

"Because of its size," Hal said. "Unlike the mainland, everything that happens here, happens nearby. Even the monarchy was overthrown just down the road a piece. Nobody can escape it. Every rip-off, every murder. The original culture of this place put vengeance very high on the priority list."

"That's professor talk," Tenley said.

"Be that as it may," he said, "what chance is there for vengeance if your father had killed two people in, say, Vegas or L.A.?" He raised his eyebrows. "A lot less, because the culprit might be gone, be a thousand miles away. Here it's someone you could run into at Ala Moana."

"Maybe it was just a stray bullet," Tenley said. "Kids fooling with a gun."

"Maybe," Hal said. "But if I were you, I'd be careful. About the black bag? Forget it, Ten. You've got problems enough."

"Well," Tenley said. "Thanks. I guess we should be going."

They made it past the two girls without any further exchange and then took the elevator down, Adrian thinking that if it really was this third brother who was after him, he was in trouble. And how had they found him?

Once on the street, Tenley said, "Let's go sit on a bench over there."

They waited for the light to change, watching stretch limos and tour buses go by, then crossed to the ocean side in a crowd of tourists. They headed for a series of covered tables, at which people sat playing board games, and found a bench in a corner and sat down.

"We've got to go up to the University and look through microfilms of old newspapers," Tenley said. "When did you say you and your folks left here?"

"I think it was 1987."

"Do you think your folks left because of what your father supposedly did?"

"I don't know. I remember him sitting by the window, worried about something and watching for cars. He had a gun, too. A pistol. We left around that time."

"It's funny. Here we were in this whole scam thing, all that stuff, exploring and praying or whatever, and then the fist and paddle and my mother and all, and now this just flattens it. I mean if it's really true that this guy is after you, what do you do? Leave?"

"I know. It's not your problem, it's mine. No, I don't leave."

Adrian stared at the ocean, at the widening white lines of surf and at the surfers. In the shallow water, kids played inside a protective wall over which the waves sloshed.

"'Kay," Tenley said, "we go University tomorrow. Right now we go get something to eat, maybe at the Subway up the block there," she said, pointing behind them.

"Imagine 'at," Adrian said, "me at a university."

Inside their room, the light coming in the window hole faded as the sun dropped behind the mountains. They stayed out of clear sight of the road on the other side of the vacant lot. "You see anything?" she whispered.

"No," he whispered back. Then he said in a normal voice, "Why are we whispering?"

"I don't know," she whispered, and then she giggled.

"This is stupid," he said. He went to the window. The fading light was gradually being replaced by the faint glow of a streetlight. "Here I am," he said out the window. "Fire away."

He remembered himself with his rifle, exploding woodchucks and the feeling he always had: a strange, giddy expectation just before he pulled the trigger, and then the rush when whatever he shot at got hit. Did the person who pulled the trigger, aiming at him, feel the same anticipation?

He could not sleep. He lay on his back, his fingers laced under and cupping the back of his skull, and stared at the faint square of light of the window hole. He tensed with every toad-generated swish of dead leaves outside, with every sound of a car moving along the street beyond the vacant lot. From time to time, Tenley turned in her sleep and banged her knee into his hip, but he continued staring at the window hole because if he fell asleep, then someone could simply lean in and pull the trigger, sending out a small slug that would enter his skull and shut him off like a light.

At some point in that heavy darkness, with the irritating sound of a mosquito hovering around his face, he slept. He woke up seeing pink light in the window hole, his scalp prickling because he had slept and made himself vulnerable. Only one thought came to him: finish the fist and paddle handle. If there was any reason beyond Tenley to try to prevent a piece of lead from hitting his head, it was the fist and paddle handle.

He was filing the hand when Tenley got up. Up early too, Jacob came around to look at the room. "Glass pieces," he said. "I fine um fo' you."

"Most people have them under their houses," Tenley said. "How about that old guy you borrow the truck from?"

"Yah," Jacob said. "Fujimura. I check um out."

Adrian tried to ignore them and went on filing, looking at his own fist, and filing again. Then he went into the room and got Tenley's paddle and stood there in the morning sun studying the way his fist gripped the paddle. Stretched skin, cords on the backs of the hand crossed by veins.

"This looks really good," Tenley said.

He looked at it and stood up. "Anybody can do this," he said.

"I couldn't do it."

"Yes, you could. All human beings can do this."

"Buggah's pupule," Jacob whispered. "Wheah da hell you fine him?"

The University was in full swing. A lot of Tenley's friends still went there, and she wanted to see if she could run into some of them and introduce Adrian. "I don't know about that," he said. C'mon, she said. When you can talk as good as Hal and remember stuffs like Adrian did, how could there be a problem? There was, and it was called dyslexia, he told her. She waved her hands at him as if waving off flies, then said that dyslexia would make him cool, just as all sorts of, whatchucall, challenges, made people cool. I'd bet, she told him, that there are students with dyslexia, and the Kōkua program—What's that? he asked. Kōkua means "help." 'Kay, so da Kōkua Program would help you out. Yeah, but I never graduated from high school. No, no, she said. We're just talking theoretical, 'kay? You mean "hypothetical." 'Kay, whatevahs.

He rose up from the hand and looked out across the vacant lot. A car went by, and he waited, almost as if to present a clean target, but nothing happened. He looked again at the hand, and now, with its veins and creases and stretched skin, it was beginning to convince him. He did not want to go to any university. The whole business of looking up stuff from nineteen eighty whatever-the-fuck it was now seemed to just get in the way.

But they went anyway. The bus that ran through Kailua went over the mountain and through downtown, where they changed to a bus that went east and pulled to a stop under some trees growing alongside a low building built on the edge of some kind of cliff. The law school, Tenley said, and beyond that was a round building with a dome that she identified as the arena where the college basketball team played. Two or three miles away was the line of tall hotel buildings that made up Waikīkī and ended at Diamond Head on the left.

She said, "Come on, we go library and look up ol' newspapers on microfilm. I know how."

He had his reading card in his wallet and realized he had not shown it to her yet. He took it out and handed it to her. She studied, pulling the little strip out and pushing it back. "You put this on a word and then what?"

"Then it's isolated. I look at it and sound it out, recognize it, and so on."

"But what happens when you just read?"

"I start, but then certain letter combinations turn my brain off. It's like . . . let's say the letters *g*, *h*, and *t*, appear together. I should recognize it and just read on, but I can't. Then what happens is you start to fear reading, and you end up hating it. Can't read when you're cornered, you know, standing in front of a class. So you memorize what you have to say and then hold the paper up and recite, the words just nothing but a gray blur on the white page. You don't even look at it. If you're caught off guard, you start coughing, knock a chair over, anything to get out of it. I memorized a lot." He looked ahead at the lines on the sidewalk and said, "I'll show you something. All human beings are born with talents they aren't aware of. All human beings are born geniuses without the plug in." He explained to her the right foot–left foot thing and urged her to try it, to discover her latent genius.

"'Kay, so plug me in," she said.

Lines that would fall between her footsteps confused her, so he said that she could just say "middle" to indicate that her foot would not hit the line. She got it on the third try. "It works," she said.

"See? What'd I tell you?"

"Library right heah," she said, pointing at a low building with tinted windows. Bulletin boards stood out in front, crowded with flyers, and students passed by or sat on the little benches by the boards, reading or picking at food in styrofoam boxes. Tenley looked around for her friends, shrugged, and turned to the library door.

She led him to the reference section at the back of a large lobby. At its center was a counter, and next to that a row of computers at which sat students staring into blue screens. The reference she was looking for was a five-volume register of newspaper reports from the late sixties to the midnineties.

She set these books on one of the tables and flipped through them, looking for the heading "Homicide." She found plenty of entries, man charged with knife slaying of daughter, gang beats sailor to death, woman throws infant from high-rise. Among these headlines were various stories of indictments, releases, convictions. "This'll take a while," she whispered.

Watching her move her finger down the columns, he began to get impatient, so he drew out his reading card and grabbed one of the other volumes. He found the word "Milk," and under that, the words: "Dairy," "cows," "face." Then came one that made his head reel until he got the *ght* part: "slaughter." "Unless," "milkers," and "found" followed. Dairy cows face slaughter unless milkers found? "Hey," he said, "what do you make of this?"

"Shh."

Okay. He closed the book and put his card away. Would you slaughter dairy cows because you couldn't find someone to milk them? It seemed absurd. He wondered about the old house in the woods. What would the headline for it be? House to be demolished because no one can be found to live in it?

Girls dressed in jeans and floppy shirts, and guys in shorts and slippers walked past. In an alcove off to the side, two students were kissing, the guy's hand on the girl's hip.

"Bingo," Tenley said. "Name is Montross. Two brothers found dead in cane field. Now we gotta go check microfilms."

She walked up to a microfilm machine, pulled a strange sort of negative thing from a sleeve, put it into a slot, and then brought the words up, faint and ethereal looking, on the screen. Because he was to her side, the words bled into each other and vanished for him. "'Kay," she said. "A jogger found blah blah blah. Wait, here it is." She took a piece of paper and a pen from her purse. "Ke'ali'i Junior Montross, thirty, an' Vincent Montross, twenty-four. Both shot in the back of the head and set on fire." She read more and then turned to him. "No suspects, so we gotta go on to da nex' day until we get dakine. Autopsy, so on." She turned a wheel, squinted at the screen, and kept reading.

How any of this could be connected to his father was still something Adrian resisted. His father did not seem capable of it, despite his tough talk and his capacity for violence. Murder was something no one should be capable of, yet there were plenty of murders. And there, over in that alcove, sat two kids kissing, in fact now getting out of hand, considering what the guy was doing with his hand. He thought of that oddly filtered image he had seen on TV back in New York, of a man picking up a machete and bringing it down with all the force he could muster on the head of another man, and the look of awe on Mark Brough's face.

"Oh Jesus," Tenley said. "Autopsy showed that the younger one, Vincent, was alive when he was set on fire, cause his lungs was fulla remnants of smoke an' still had accelerant of some kind, like lighter fluid, in his mouth. So he burn him first an' den shoot him."

Adrian looked away, trying to imagine it. If the accelerant was in the guy's mouth, that meant that whoever did it had squirted the stuff in his face and then set him on fire. Could it have been a botched murder in which the killer squirted the fluid on the guy as a last resort? If you were going to kill two people and then burn their bodies, why would you burn the person first and then shoot him? The cruelty of it was worse than a machete blow to the head.

"Gotta look more," she said. "Cause get nothing about anybody being questioned." She turned back to the machine. The two lovers in the alcove were now sitting with their heads bowed over books, the girl speaking to the guy and thumping her index finger on the page.

Tenley squinted into the machine, then turned the little wheel. Adrian sat and watched the students. After another ten minutes, she said, "Ho, says two men arrested, one named Chan Gouveia an' odda named Raymond Branch, business associates. Says dat bot' released inna same day."

"Uh oh."

"The release," she said, switching back into formal English, "is because the police had nothing to charge them with. You know, there are murders here where the police know who did it but can't pin it on the guys. Fairly common, actually."

"Still doesn't mean he did it."

"'Kay, so now we find out what happened to Chan Gouveia."

She went back to the machine. Adrian felt a sudden, fidgety desire to get back to the fist and paddle.

"Oops," she said. "This is like months later. Some guy named Burden Vierra picked up in the Montross case. Let go the same day. Says he was an associate of the Montrosses and Raymond Branch."

"Hey, that's the name my mother gave me: Mildred Vierra. But didn't you tell me it was a common name?"

"Nope, this is too close. And it looks like they all were 'associated' in something."

"You know," he said, picturing his mother that night, "she did pause before saying the name. She was talking about what my father might have done." He now pictured the man at the Date Street apartment. "So that's how they know I'm here, I guess. I think I told the guy about where I'd be."

On the way back on the bus, he got an idea: he would figure out where this Montross family lived and call them up. He would explain that his father was dead, that he'd died under horrible circumstances, maybe that he had had a hunting accident in which he shot himself, in the groin, and then bled in the snow and froze to death. He told Tenley, who sat with her chin on her fist and looked out the window at the scenery as they moved through the afternoon traffic.

"They'll never believe it," she said. "It's too clean, or maybe too much poetic justice?"

"They've had too much bad stuff happen." He thought this over. "Both of our families have. I can say that I was the one who found him, the frozen body partly eaten by stray dogs—"

"That's going overboard."

"Okay, frozen body with the frozen blood matting his clothes down around his groin, the rifle a couple feet away, evidence that he had been alive for a while, maybe a cigarette butt or two?"

"That makes him too tough. Make it a cell phone with a dead battery."

"Okay. Actually, that's good. The cell phone with the dead battery."

"God, what a way to die."

When they got back to Waimānalo, Tenley could tell that something was wrong at the house, even from the driveway. John's shadow flashed back and forth across the kitchen window, and they heard voices, not arguing, but speaking with an intensity that signified something was wrong. She checked to see that Jacob was in back and found him sitting at his table and reading the newspaper. She rejoined Adrian in the driveway.

"I know my mother's voice," she said. The shadow flashed across the window. The discussion moved off into another room. "It's about the house," she said. "John's ex is sick, and apparently when she dies, the house automatically goes to their two kids. And they're rotten kids." She stared at the house. "Wait here."

"I'll go work on the fist."

She came around the corner of the room just as sweat had begun to bead on his forehead. He'd been facing the vacant lot and waiting for cars. None came by. He turned and said, "Is everything all right?"

"John's ex died. They're very likely going to kick us out. Let's dakine."

In the little room, she took a long squirt of scotch, and then he did, too. She sat at the table, folded her legs up, and put her arms around her knees.

"So what now?" he asked. "What about Jacob?"

"They don't give a shit about him, or us, or anybody. It's money. They'll either live here, one or both of them, or they'll sell the house. We're talking four hundred thousand dollars."

"Really?"

"That's what houses cost here. A few years ago, it was worse. Five hundred, even more."

It seemed hard to believe. Four hundred thousand was almost a half a million dollars.

"It's the real-estate boom," she said. "People make a lot of money off property."

Just after sundown, a car pulled into the driveway, its headlight beams illuminating the brush behind the room. "It's them," Tenley said.

The conference took place in the driveway. Adrian and Tenley stood off to the side and watched. John stood with his arms folded, Tenley's mother behind him, while two well-dressed young people, a guy and a girl, leaned against the car. Their faces were a dull orange from the light of the single bulb above the front door. "—because we need it, and now," the young guy said.

"Wouldn't it be more proper to wait until she's in the ground?" Tenley's mother asked sarcastically. "By the way, that's a nice car. Is it a Lexus?"

"We've had her cremated. Yes, it's a Lexus."

"I see," Tenley's mother said. "And so you figured that moving in couldn't wait."

"I'm sorry you feel that way," the guy said. "Dad, look, we need it now."

"Why?"

"Do you know what rent is in Makiki? I pay fourteen hundred a month."

"So where do we go?" John asked.

There was a silence. The sister looked at the brother, then said, "That's not our problem. That's your problem. Look, you were supposed to be out months ago. We already told you that."

Tenley and Adrian walked into the dim light. "Hi Ten," the girl said flatly.

"Yeah," Tenley said.

The girl looked at Adrian with disgust. "And—"

"Adrian Branch," Tenley said. "My fiancé."

The word startled Adrian. He had forgotten. Fiancé. The girl looked at him as if he were some fascinating lower form of life.

"So how long do we have?" John asked. "I mean, we have some time to move, right?"

"No," his son said. "I think it would be better for us if you could go now. Like it was supposed to be done a long time ago."

"So do we put our stuff on the street?" Tenley's mother asked. "We've got roomfuls of stuff in there. Should we have a big garage sale?"

"I'm sorry you feel that way."

"The way I feel is one thing," she said. "The way you act is another. You probably called each other every day, like, 'Hey, she's almost gone, we're almost there.' Goddam pilau little shits."

Adrian turned to ask what it meant, but Tenley said, "Shh."

"Ex-kay-use-me," the girl said. "What do you have to do with this? I mean, who the fuck are you? You're not any part of my family that I know. Fuck you."

"Fuck you too," Tenley's mother said.

"Hey," Tenley said to the girl, "you like to go out there on the street, you stupid cunt? I'll kick your ass to kingdom come."

"Uh . . ." Adrian said.

"Shut up," Tenley said. Then she turned back to the girl. "You fucking little slut. You like beef wit' me? I kill you. I'll rub your face in your own shit."

The girl sighed at the sky. "I got a cell phone here—" And she reached down into her bag.

"Go ahead," Tenley said. "By the time they get here, your face'll be on the street."

"And who's the slut by the way?" the girl asked sweetly. "The last I heard—"

"Fuck you," Tenley's mother said.

John cleared his throat. "This is getting us nowhere."

"Look," his son said. "We have legal title to this property, have had it for a while. Mom has now died. So now we take it over. It's as simple as that."

"Yeah," Tenley said, snorting. "It's simple all right, since you can afford a Lexus."

"It's just a car. I don't know why you're acting this way."

"I'm acting this way because my grandfather has no place to stay. But you don't care, do you? And your stupid bimbo of a sister—"

"He's not our problem," the guy said.

The girl grunted, then whispered to her brother.

"Say it out loud, you cheap bitch," Tenley said. "Fucking chicken. Tell me out loud."

Her mother laughed. "Ten," she said, "stop it already. Let it go."

The sister held her middle finger up in Tenley's direction. Tenley snorted and said, "Yeah, asshole—that's the only sex you'll ever get."

"Ho, cute yah?" the girl said to her brother.

A pained expression on his face, the guy said, "I'm sorry. I don't want to cause trouble—"

"Then maybe you shouldn't," Tenley said. "How about that?"

"—but we need it now."

Adrian had not noticed until then that a car was moving slowly along the road fronting the house. He backed up a little, then slipped into the shadows, moving along the side of Jacob's cottage to look over the fence. But the car was gone.

When he got back to the driveway John's children were in their car. The son said something out the window to his father, and they slowly backed out.

And what would Tenley's family do now? No one had any good ideas. Storage was out of the question because they didn't have enough money. What would five people do with no place to live? No, the beach wasn't on the list. And what about Jacob? Adrian tried to tune in on this conversation, but his eyes kept drifting off to the street.

Later that night, while Adrian and Tenley were in their room, they heard sounds coming from the house. Something was up, she told him. Not only did John and her mother have to move out, but it became apparent that there was trouble between the two of them. It made Adrian jumpy. Every thump or raised voice made him look quickly out the back window hole, searching the vacant lot for shapes, the hulking shadows of people coming for him.

"What's up?" Tenley asked.

"It's just that car I saw. Went by while you guys were arguing."

"For real?" She stared out the window hole. "Maybe taking off is a good idea then. You wanna get an apartment? After all, I gotta get a job. We'll do okay." She reached for the squirt bottle.

"What about Jacob? Somebody has to take care of him."

"He can come with us."

A car moved along the street that dead-ended the vacant lot. Adrian watched, holding his breath, until it went past.

The later it got, the more he wanted to sleep, but he was afraid to. Tenley suggested they sleep in shifts. She could stay awake, she said, because she had to think about what to do next anyway. So he finally slept, aware that sometimes she was sitting there next to him on the bed. Waking up at one point, he saw her silhouette at the little table. She had her chin on the palm of her hand and was staring obliquely at the window hole. "Okay, your turn," he said. He sat up and put his feet on the plywood floor. "What time is it?"

"Three thirty," she said. "I'm tired." She crawled onto the bed and pulled the sheet over herself. He went to the table and sat, then looked out the window hole at the reflections of streetlights making things on distant rooftops glint. Eventually, he dozed off, and awakened when the sky out the window hole had turned a faint pink.

In the morning they went to talk to Jacob. Yes, he had been tinkeen' about dis too. He get one idea. Richahd Fujimura, da o' man I borrow truck from, lives in one rotten, beat-up house a few blocks dat way, neah Sherwood Fores'—

"Which is?" Adrian asked.

"The woods there toward Kailua," Tenley said.

Right, Jacob went on, an' Fujimura nice o' man, might let us stay his house until we figgah out what fo' do, 'kay? Ten's maddah? No way she accep' da liveen conditions wit' termite damage every windowsill, but den, she might stay a few days until she an' John figga what fo' do, ah? Me, I so fah gone dat I no need place fo' live aftah while, ah? No, Tenley said, no talk li'dat! But den, Jacob went on, Fujimura so beat up himself dat he might be gone t'ree, foah days, whodahell knows? Ho, we all getteen to be o' futs, ah? Fujimura, his wife rent da place many yeahs, anna landlawd, one haole guy who like teah da place down, let him stay—keeps da o' house occupied an' all li'dat.

"That's nice of the guy," Adrian said. "He lets him stay just because?"

"Yah. Someteen about tearin' house down, cos' money fo' build new one."

Jacob would talk with him. Tenley suggested that she and Adrian go along, and Jacob liked the idea, so dat Fujimura get fo' meet his grandattah and dakine, her fiancé. Tenley then wondered if her mother should come, but Jacob rejected the idea. Tenley's mother was capable of making such stink face at stuffs she no like, dat da o' man feel shame.

The house seemed larger than a single-story tract one because of its height, the ceilings maybe ten feet from what Adrian could tell by looking in through the windows. Sunken on its posts, the house drooped at the oceanside front and back corners, badly off plumb. It had louvers missing from windows, had bulges in the walls, a badly damaged roof, clapboard siding that had fallen off and uncovered split, termite-eaten tongue-and-groove walls. The roof ended front and back with damaged wooden air vents through which Adrian could see the dim shapes of upside-down Vs, fanned slightly, of supporting roof beams. The yard was well kept up, though, with potted orchids along the fences, old citrus trees in back, and a lawn cut very short, almost like a golfing green. While Jacob was inside talking to Fujimura, he and Tenley stood outside. He looked at the yard, then at the dilapidated structure, and then in through one window at a bedroom ceiling. "It's got a wooden-slat ceiling, like thin wainscoting," he said. "This is an old house."

"I'll say," Tenley said. "I'm not sure I want to stay here. The place'll fall down if we move in."

The two old men went outside, and Jacob introduced Adrian and Tenley to Fujimura, who had age spots on his face, a sparse stubble of hair, and bony little hands that still appeared strong. He wore very thick glasses, each lens centered by a tiny eye.

"He like us all stay," Jacob said, "leas' until da ownah fine out. Den . . ."

"Well," Adrian said, thinking that he should say something nice about the place, "it sure is beautiful with all the flowers and stuff. Does the owner come around much?"

"Nah," the old man said. "Keep two kayaks inna garage deah. Come Sunday morning fo' take kayak out, but oddawise I no see um. Or maybe Sattahday. Sometime he come Sattahday fo' take kayak out, but he jus' say hello, how you doin', everyteeng heah all right? and stuffs li'dat."

"Nice guy," Jacob said. "Sunday we move out, so get at leas' six days, ah?"

Adrian nodded. The house tickled his imagination, and he wondered more about this landlord. But he decided not to ask. In any case, the problem of where to stay the day after tomorrow was solved. And it would get him away from that window hole.

Later in the day, Tenley reported to Adrian the latest developments. John was moving to Las Vegas now that he was being thrown out by his own kids. He wanted Tenley's mother go with him, but she refused. Okay, if that's the way you want it, and so on. "They're breaking up," Tenley said. "Why do I feel like I'm responsible?"

"You're not," Adrian said, glancing again out through the window hole. A telephone company truck passed by. Not likely that anybody in a truck like that would be aiming a rifle at him. "This is their thing. But I've got an idea, a scam, something about the roof of Fujimura's house. I want to know about this landlord."

Tenley went to talk to Jacob. Adrian pulled the scotch out of his bag and saw that it was getting low. They had to refuel. But the squirt bottle was still half full. He took a long stream and swallowed, feeling the warmth spread into his flesh. It was not as comfortable here as in New York because when the warmth spread through your body, you ended up sweating.

Through the wall, he heard Jacob wheezing out the answers to Tenley's questions. Yah, the landlord was rich, owned mo' den one house, and maybe dis only one investment. In any case, the guy was in his forties maybe, and retired military. Bought property heah befo' da boom, so his hobby is buying houses and renting um. Plenny peoples who had money fo' buy property back den so fricken rich now, no mo' notting fo do but count money. And what about other stuff? Was the guy married or anything like that? Dunno. Nice guy, but.

Adrian tried to explain his idea to Tenley when she came back. "This isn't coconuts or fat-free carrots," he said, "but that house looks old. It's a classic house. If I owned a place like that, I'd have two options. Tear it down and spend fifty thousand dollars building a new one—"

"Fifty? Hundred fifty you mean."

"Yeah, even that. I'd have that option, or I could restore a historic house. Houses like that will never be built again. It's a wealthy person's beach, uh . . . cottage, that's it. It has that expansive feel. The moldings, ceiling boards, and the like are cut in a manner almost impossible to replace. That wood is—"

She stared at him. Then her eyebrows went up. "Is?"

"Milled," Adrian said. "That's it. Milled out of some hardwood that nobody would use today because it's much too expensive. They'd use sheetrock, and they'd have low ceilings to save money. Wealthy people with beach cottages didn't need to save money."

"It won't work," Tenley said.

"There's an elegance of a bygone era in that house. I would guess that under that crappy floor there's hardwood that would be easy to restore until it would gleam with the dark brilliance of a pool of oil."

"Jesus."

"The walls have been painted over numerous times. Do you know what is under that paint? What kind of wood? Tearing this house down would be like demolishing a Colonial or Federal desk because of a little damage to its veneer. Why is it that contemporary architecture is mired in this mundane cookie-cutter mentality? Look at Brancusi's *Bird in Flight*."

Tenley was laughing. "I believed it until you came up with that shit. What's a 'Federal desk'?"

"No clue. It was just an idea."

He was sweating a little. The wind had died off, so the sun slanting through the window hole heated up the room. "Thinking makes me sweat," he said.

"Sweat can be sexy," she said. "I got some too." She ran her hand along her thigh.

Instantly, Adrian's mind was full of images: dark, suntanned skin changing into pale skin, smooth skin, and then hair, creases, flesh that in his imagination dented slightly from the subtle pressure of his fingers. Uh oh. Was she really serious about this? Somebody would surely appear at the door opening.

He looked at the window hole. "I think it's worth a try," he said. She got an excited, mischievous look on her face. "No, not that," he said. "Isn't Sunday the day after tomorrow?"

"Bummers," she said. "But yeah."

"And the guy's coming to take out a kayak or something?"

"Yeah."

"In order to make this work, I need words. Where's the nearest library?"

Because they didn't have the truck, they walked the five blocks of Laumilo Street to Fujimura's house, then past it. Adrian studied the house from the street as they walked by.

"Hey, we didn't bring dakine," Tenley said.

"We can dakine when we get back," he said, looking over his shoulder at the house. He felt a flash of fear about being separated from the squirt bottle. They walked out to the highway that ran toward Kailua and then walked along a polo field, the road lined with ironwoods. They came to a grade school, which, she explained, also had a public library.

Inside, he tried to explain to her while keeping his voice down to a near whisper that he needed something about the way roofs are made, the size of their beams and so forth. I don't need words like "dado" or "flange" or "flap joint." What's that? she asked, and he said, No, I just made that one up. I just need the basic stuff. Okay, I go look, she said. They found the section on home improvement, but it had Sunset books on how to build decks and furniture. No, that won't do. She stooped and looked in a lower corner at some beat-up books, older ones, and found one on steel, one on water runoff, one on timber engineering, one on—

"What's timber engineering?"

She pulled the book out from the shelf. "'Modern Timber Engineering,'" she read. She opened it to a random page filled with bizarre-looking formulas with parentheses, letters, and numbers. "It says, 'Allowable unit loads: For short columns, where l slash d ratio of an individual member—'"

"Nah, that's no good," Adrian said.

She flipped to another section and found something else. "Trusses," she whispered.

"Wait, what is a truss? That rings a bell."

"'Kay, it says, 'Some of the usual types of timber trusses are illustrated in figure 38. The introduction of timber connectors into the United States in 1933 made possible more efficient utilization of timber in truss design. Prior to this time, larger sections were necessary in order to secure sound joints and only forty percent to sixty percent of the working stress capacity of the members could be utilized—'"

"But what is a truss? What's figure 38?"

As soon as she turned the page, he saw it. "House roofs!" she said.

He put his finger on the little pictures. "Okay, 'King Post,' 'Fan.' What's this one?"

"'Scissors,'" she whispered.

"That's one of those words I can't make out," he whispered. "What's this one here?"

"Six Panel Pratt," she said. "And Six Panel Howe. Here's one called Fink, and then Belgian."

"It's Six Panel Pratt," he said. "That's Fujimura's house. Now I got it. It's a Six Panel Pratt truss, uh, system, built before 1933, before timber connectors. Pratt sounds better than Howe."

"But is it?"

"I don't know. He's not gonna go up there and count Pratts. I mean panels. You've gotta read a bunch of stuff from this book to me."

She feigned dizziness and looked at the ceiling. "Are you kidding?"

So she read in a whisper while he listened: "'Kay, 'Classification of Structural Lumber: Knots, slope of grain, checks and shake vary in their effect on the strength of lumber according to the type of loading to which the piece is subjected. The effect of seasoning varies with the size of the timbers. Consequently, the efficient use of lumber requires the classification of timbers according to size and use.' Then there's blah blah, other stuffs, but, hey wait. It says, 'Structural lumber requires more precision in grading than the other classifications.

All four sides of every piece must be examined for size and location of knots. Compliance with the density requirement, limitation on shakes and checks, slope of grain and other characteristics which are related to strength and soundness must be determined. The Grading Rules are very exacting and seem complicated, but to a competent lumber inspector, the process of grading is not difficult.' Hey, this is cool. I thought a board was a board."

"That's good," he said. "I mean, 'slope of grain,' 'density requirement.' That's good stuff."

She skipped over the confusing parts with formulas and then went on: "'Kay, 'Drift pins are round or square steel pins without threads, usually driven into pre-bored holes about one-eighth less in diameter than the pin.' Then, 'The allowable load in withdrawal should be about one-fifth of the' blah blah. And, 'in which P is the ultimate load per lineal inch of penetration, G is the specific gravity of the wood, and D is the diameter of the drift pin in inches,' Ooo, dis kinky."

"Read about trusses again."

"I was hoping you say dat. Dat da hottes' section. No can control myself when I read about trusses. I mean, 'Determine the loading,' an' 'Compute the stresses in the members.' What, you get only one? I like read dis paht: 'Size of Member.'"

He had her reread three sections to him while he listened, whispering some of the words to himself. Finally she said, "So, how's your hard drive?"

"Hey, I got sixty megathings, you know, lineal drift pins. Like my head is full of them."

Walking back along Laumilo Street, they saw Mr. Fujimura's truck coming their way swaying badly, its front end riding high. The two heads inside were those of Jacob and Tenley's mother.

Jacob pulled to a stop as they converged. "Mr. Fujimura's garage has a dirt floor," Tenley's mother said.

"So?" Tenley said. "Put stuffs on one blue tarp."

"This is so unnecessary. What happens when the owner sees all this stuff in his garage?"

"I talk to Fujimura," Jacob said. "He say nah nah nah, no worry."

"I'm forty-four years old. I can't do this."

"So what?" Jacob said. "I seventy-six. I can do um."

"You don't understand." She leaned toward Tenley and Adrian. "I have to go to work Monday. I mean, it's only a temp job, but—" She flopped back in her seat and waved her hands at the windshield. "Forget it, drive on."

Tenley and Adrian watched the old truck labor down the road toward Fujimura's. When they got to their house, John was busy loading another truck. A man Tenley recognized was helping him. "Billy," she said, "howzit?"

"Eh Ten," he said. "Heah fo' help da homeless."

John groaned and went inside for another box. Tenley pointed at Adrian and said, "'Ass my fiancé, Adrian Branch." The man what he was doing and walked to Adrian and shook his hand. "Howzit?" he said.

"Pleased to meet you," Adrian said.

When John came back out, he stared skeptically at the box he carried. "What the hell I need with this I don't know. Storage costs money."

Tenley hesitated, then said, "I think Mom should go with you."

He put the box in the bed of the truck, shook his head, and flexed his fingers. "I tried to convince her, but she's not gonna do it." He looked at his watch. "I'm hungry," he said. "I gonna get a sub sandwich. You want anything?" he asked the man helping him.

"Nah," he said.

"I like go with you," Tenley said.

Back in their room, Adrian again stared out the window hole, thinking about the car. In a while, Tenley returned with more scotch.

Maybe sleeping in shifts was unnecessary, she said. After all, Friday night the creeps who might want to kill him would most likely want to take their girlfriends to clubs and li'dat. And now that with John's help Tenley had brought in a supply of dakine, and they had only one more night in their little room, they might as well fo'get da creeps and jus' have fun. She looked out through the window hole. It was dusk, and John had left with Billy.

"I don't know about carrying on with this scam," Adrian said. "I wonder if we should go ahead and spill the beans. I mean, what are they going to think when I talk to the owner of Fujimura's house?"

She stared at him. "No. Don't tell yet. Besides, can't an artist also be a house restorer too?"

"This is ridiculous." Sitting there, he wondered what would have happened to him if he had never met her. Not much of any use, probably. She sat on the bed in a little ball with her arms wrapped around her folded legs.

"I ought to be happy that she got kicked out," she said, "but I'm not. I mean, what's up with that? But hey, let's see about eating."

Jacob had already planned dinner. At the door to the bigger house, he held a white plastic bag out to Tenley's mother, who looked down at it. Then she and Jacob walked to the cottage.

"Eh, you keeds," he said, holding out another bag. "Chicken katsu."

"Chicken katsu give me da runs," Tenley said. "Get lots paper da batchroom?"

They crowded into Jacob's little kitchen. There were only two chairs, so Tenley and Adrian ate standing up, balancing the red sauce in the open tops of their Styrofoam containers.

"Why the rush?" Tenley's mother asked. "I mean, we can stay tonight and tomorrow night. John's already moved most of his stuff out."

"Let's get out of here tomorrow," Tenley said.

"But what do I do?" her mother asked. "I go to work on Monday. I'll be in Mr. Fujimura's way. He has only one bathroom and—"

"Fujimura all excited we coming," Jacob said. "He try fo' poo one picnic table outta da garage so we can sit ahsai. He run up an down da hall inna house talkeen to himself, 'Ho, we put Mrs. Chong in heah, we put Jacob in heah, an' put da keeds inna big back room.' I say, 'Look, we only stay couple days, ah?' He say, 'Why? What, you tink I like liveen alone all dis time?'"

"What about your friends?" Tenley asked. "Could any of them help you out? They seem really nice."

"No," her mother said. "I don't even want them to know. These are University people. I know it's what we talk about sometimes, you know, homelessness, but it's so embarrassing that it's ridiculous. I mean, I'm forty-four. How did this happen?"

They ate now in silence. Adrian ran the list of words through his mind again: *six panel Pratt*, *truss*, *grading*, *density requirement*, *slope of grain*, *drift pin*, *load*, *timber connecters*. It wasn't enough, and he didn't have time to go back and have it read to him again.

They decided that it would be a good idea to be off the property the next day and get the whole thing over with. Adrian was glad because he could not see himself sleeping in shifts anymore, and he speculated on the kind of security Fujimura's house had. Tenley's mother went back to the big house, and Jacob started to fall asleep in his chair.

"He'll wake up later, den go bed," Tenley whispered. "I go talk to my mom, be in laters."

While Adrian waited in their room, he listened for any sounds outside, but all he could hear was surf in the distance and, closer in, the sounds of cars gunning here and there, the *dweep*! *dweep*! of alarm devices, and laughter about a block away. Again the air seemed sodden and heavy, and at certain moments when no human sounds came through the hole, there was that surf sound and the rustle of toads and lizards in the brush pile behind the room.

He took off his shirt and lay on the bed with his fingers laced under his head. His mind swam with *drift pin*, *density requirement*, *trusses*. Then a drifting wooziness swept over him, and he began to manufacture imagery that had no time: his mother sitting in the sand at the beach, his mother lying in bed with the braid lying across her chest, him at thirteen staring at a dry-rotted windowsill, birds chirping outside in the hush of the woods, his father saying, "Just squeeze slowly an' keep the sights on the can," going to school near the ocean, the kids around him all with black hair, a fishnet with a little yellow-and-black-striped fish writhing in the mesh as he lowered it into the water so that it could swim. Then, he was aware of walking through some arid landscape with rubble at his feet: oxidized beer cans, faded plastic toys, rusted hypodermic needles, rotted clothes webbed over rocks, and beyond that, fossils embedded in stone, dotted lines of tails and necks, leg and paw bones dusted and parching in the harsh sunlight. He was wandering in the vast empire of death, past pyramid-shaped mounds of human skulls and the dry litter of pelvic and spinal bones. When he found a place to lie down, he felt a jostling, out-of-balance feeling that made his breath halt. Then he felt hot flesh slide along his chest, and when he put his hands out, they fell on a long, smooth back, then buttocks, and he felt hair settling on his face, then breath.

"Someteen inna way down heah," she whispered.

It amazed him. He could hear her, he could hear air moving in lungs, blood pounding through arteries, and, he thought, even eyes blinking. He moved to struggle with his shorts while she raised herself up. When they were off, she lay back down on him and the contact was complete.

When he woke up, it was light outside and the window hole appeared benign. She was rolled up into a compact ball, her fists under her chin and her hair draped over her face. She breathed into the little hollow of warmth between them.

VI

After they had unloaded the last of the stuff from the other house, including the fist and paddle and Tenley's bunk bed, Mr. Fujimura led them around, showing Jacob one room, Tenley's mother another, and then Tenley and Adrian a larger room attached to the back of the house but one stair step lower. This room had higher windows against which scraped the thin outer branches of what Tenley identified as a mango tree. The floor was littered with old fertilizer bags, small cement pots stacked against the walls, and a rusted motor block by a back door that opened to a rickety set of stairs that went down into weeds. They went back out into the living room where Mr. Fujimura had his couch, chair, TV set, and pictures of his wife and, Adrian guessed, his kids and grandkids. Through the window, Adrian saw a black Jeep Cherokee pull into the dirt driveway. A man got out wearing surf shorts, a tank top, and shades. He had graying light-brown hair and a florid complexion, and he was strong looking and businesslike. He opened the back of the Jeep and took out a two-wheeled cart, probably something to take the kayak down to the beach. The personalized license plate on the Jeep read "Carter."

"I go out say hello," Mr. Fujimura said.

Tenley's mother looked out the window at the man, sneering. Jacob sat down on Mr. Fujimura's couch.

Adrian and Tenley watched as Mr. Fujimura talked to the man, who nodded as he reached into the Jeep and pulled out a small, white plastic bottle of sunscreen. He squirted the liquid on his hands, then wiped it on his face, arms, and legs.

"This is a bad idea," Adrian whispered. "He looks too smart. He'll never buy it."

"Buy what?" Tenley's mother asked.

Tenley went to her and whispered something, and Tenley's mother gave Adrian a bemused look.

The man was out of sight now, dragging the cart down the side of the house. Within a minute he reappeared, pulling the carted kayak by the nose, the wheels bumping on the stones in the driveway so that the paddle danced in the sitting well. He went out to the street and walked toward the beach.

Fujimura came back in. "He say, Eh, no problem. Yoah house, he tol' me."

Tenley's mother heaved a sigh. "Well," she said. "At least one good thing happened. This gives me a chance to look for an apartment without brushing my teeth at a park shower."

"Mom," Tenley asked, "you wanna go for a swim? I mean after General What's-his-name is out on the water?"

Go for a swim, she seemed to be thinking. "Well, sure," she said. "I'll get my suit on."

Adrian carried parts of Tenley's bunk bed around the back and then worked his way through the mango branches to the stairway. Tenley had swept the floor of the room, so grit and sand and little pieces of rubbish ended up in the weeds at the bottom of the precarious set of stairs. The motor block was still there. Adrian speculated on the amount of damage the block would do to the stairs when he rolled it out. Stepping carefully into the room, he got the squirt bottle from the duffel bag, took a long stream, and thought about the man who owned the house. He went outside and around toward the front. The man's Jeep was still there. As Adrian walked back, he saw that the concrete footings of the house were tipped and sunken. He got down on his haunches to look underneath at the rafters holding the floor up. They were set about eighteen inches apart and were two-by-tens, old ones that were not cut to the same dimensions as modern wood. The beams looked like they were too close together. He could see floorboards that had holes in them and piles of termite droppings in the dry sand under the house.

When he stood up, he felt dizzy for a second, and felt a long shudder pass over him, making him sweat. The discomfort waned slowly. He leaned against the house and thought of the snake. It was the scam, that was it. He felt a hot flash of self-hatred. The feeling was rotten enough that he wanted to go back for more scotch, but rejected the idea because he wanted to be sharp if he approached the owner about the house.

As Adrian was dropping the mattress on the bunk bed, he saw the man through the dirty window. Once again, the paddle danced in the sitting well as he towed the kayak. Tenley and her mother had returned from the beach, too, and were out in the living room, talking with Jacob and Mr. Fujimura. Adrian decided that it would be best to intercept the man at the garage door.

He took a deep breath and went down the steps. The man was wheeling the kayak into place, next to a bigger blue one, and turned when Adrian cleared his throat.

"Frank Carter," he said, sticking his hand out.

Adrian shook the man's hand. "Adrian Branch. Just wanted to thank you for letting the folks stay with Mr. Fujimura. The loss of their house was kind of a shock to them."

Frank Carter hoisted the end of the kayak up and pulled the little cart out from under it, then rolled the cart toward his Jeep. Adrian stayed in the shade of the garage, deciding that it was stupid to try to scam the guy. He just didn't look the type.

Carter stepped back into the shade. "Hot," he said.

"Yeah."

"So the two ladies are Jacob's what? Daughter-in-law and granddaughter?"

"Yeah. I'm Tenley's friend. Tenley's the granddaughter."

"And her mother's name is Denise, right?"

"Yeah, I think so."

"Very attractive," he said. "I mean both of them."

Carter's red complexion and his stocky, no-nonsense strength made Adrian feel awkward and a little wary.

"Welp," the man said, "nice talking to you, even if I did most of it."

"Something occurred to me when I looked at this house," Adrian said. "I understand that you were considering demolishing it."

The man snorted. "Obvious innit?"

"No," Adrian said. Carter squinted. "The house has some interesting features. High ceilings, close to ten feet it looks like."

"True."

"There's an elegance about it that—"

"An elegance?" Carter said, screwing his face up.

"I know. I'm not making myself clear. I was looking at the house and saw that it could be restored rather than demolished. It's an old-style house with a six-panel Pratt truss system, without modern timber connectors, which means that it was built before 1933. Underneath, it has two-by-tens spaced about eighteen inches apart and a hardwood floor."

"Pratt?"

"Upside-down V, but leaning outward rather than just up and down, unlike the Howe or Fink or Belgian. Anyway, I did this once in New York, upstate I mean. I'll be honest. I learned simply by doing it. I restored an old house."

Carter stared at him until he became nervous. Adrian shrugged and held his hands out. "I think you should restore the house."

"That'd cost more than building a new one."

"No, actually it wouldn't."

"You're saying that you would do this? Are you bonded?"

"Yeah, I would. And no, I'm not. Bonded I mean."

"What happens if you get hurt?"

"I won't get hurt."

"What do you charge for this kind of work?"

"Nothing. Just let us stay here for now."

"That doesn't make any sense."

"How much do you pay for an apartment?"

"I own mine."

"How much would I pay if I rented it?"

"Fifteen hundred, maybe more."

"A month is what? Twenty working days, let's say, for February at least. Into fifteen hundred is seventy-five dollars a day. That's nine something an hour—around nine thirty-five."

"And you have a calculator in your head." Carter paused. "So I come back here next week and I see something improved, right? What then?"

"That rates us staying another week."

"What about materials? Tools?"

"I'd try to get what I can. Then we'd have to talk about materials. I got tools."

"Is that wood-thing over there yours? Did you do that? You're an artist?"

"I carve wood and restore houses. Sorry, I mean house. Only one so far."

"Two now, right?"

"That's up to you."

"Why should I go for this— This offer?"

"Because this could be a nice, classic house if somebody took the trouble to restore it."

"And that's what you'd do."

"That's what I'd do."

Carter swept his eyes around the garage, then walked out onto the lawn. Adrian followed him. Carter looked up at the air vent at the end of the hip roof. "And you say there's a Belgian or a something or other thing—Pratt truss."

"That's just bullshit I came up with to try to convince you."

"What other bullshit do you have up your sleeve to tell me about? Drugs, right? Or you're hiding something I ought to know about."

"I can't read. It's dyslexia."

"Ohh," Carter said, nodding thoughtfully. "I've read about that."

"The other thing up my sleeve is that I have had a difficulty controlling a dependency on alcohol. Scotch, specifically. Drugs, no."

"Well, at least you're dependent on something *I* like."

"But I don't have as much of a difficulty with it since I met Tenley."

"I can understand that." He stared at the house and thought. Then he said, "So you had some kind of plan up your sleeve to convince me."

"Yes. I would make your hardwood floors gleam with the dark brilliance of a pool of oil. I would sand and varnish wainscoting, I would fill the termite holes in every board, replace any board that needed replacing. I would restore the elegance of a bygone time, when people lived with an expansiveness of design, even in a beach cottage, a time that will most likely never repeat itself because we've become too narrow and practical to see elegance and spatial magnificence. We prefer our large-screen TVs and our rolled-vinyl flooring and our Formica. Blah blah blah."

Carter laughed, shaking his head. "And you had this prepared. Why didn't you use it?"

"You looked too smart to use it on."

Carter's eyes widened. "Jesus Christ," he said, "that's the best con I've heard yet." He looked up at the roof again. "Son," he said, "what you do between now and next Saturday is up to you. If it looks good, we'll talk." He walked toward the house, then stopped. "And take the kayaks out anytime you want, okay?

The dusty blue one is a two-man, by the way. Stupid to have them just sit there."

"Thanks."

"You talked a good game, so now all you gotta do is show me something, okay?"

"'Kay, deal."

Neither Tenley nor her mother believed it at first. As long as they wanted, as long as he worked at restoring the house? Yup, although Mr. Fujimura might not like the idea. It might be too much of a disruption for him. When Jacob told Mr. Fujimura, the old man made a speech, later reported by Jacob: What, you tink I go ahsai an' wattah awchids an' trees and all dakine an' like seein' da house look like one fricken sinkeen ship? I live heah half dis century an' da house crumble down inna ground while I crumble down inna ground. So da boy feex um up? Guess what—feex me up too, ah? You watch. Make roofline shtraight, o' Fujimura's back go shtraight too.

But when Adrian was alone in his and Tenley's room, he felt a swoon of shame because he had blown the whistle on himself. It was a means of convincing Carter, and it may have even felt good at first, but it had cost him his secrets. Revealing those things took him back to the way he had felt at the group home. He felt a strange flippancy, as if the shame of those secrets coming out pushed him to not giving a shit about what anybody thought. But at least, he told himself, the scamming had had some positive effect.

He looked around the room. The logical thing would be to isolate one room, say this one, and work on it during the week. Then—

"Sst. We goeen beach," Tenley said from the doorway. "Jus' fo' hang. You like come?"

She came into the room. She wore the little green bathing suit, and his heart started to beat too fast. Feeling more scared than excited, he sat down on the bunk. "This is getting weird. I told Carter about the dyslexia and—"

She sat down next to him. "No mattahs," she said. "We have a place to stay. Mom can't believe it. But she keeps saying, 'I'm forty-four,' and I say, 'Mom, I think you told us that,' and she looks at me like she's scared of what this means. Now I'm the one who has to reassure her."

"Maybe I should come down and practice swimming."

At the beach, Tenley drifted off with Jacob. They walked along toward the woods at the edge of the neighborhood. Adrian found himself standing next to Denise, and he felt wary and a little anxious. He suspected a set-up, and he didn't understand what it might be about until she said, "Tenley told me the whole story."

"What story?"

Denise smiled. The warmth in her expression shocked Adrian. He saw how attractive she was and how much she resembled Tenley physically, or it would be the reverse, he supposed, Tenley resembling her mother.

"I had a hard time visualizing it," she said. "That business of burying your mother, and the braid."

He sighed. "All right, now you know the whole thing. What now?"

She looked briefly surprised. "What now? You don't understand. I was just amazed at what you did, and I think what you did was good."

"Really? I mean—"

"Technically it's illegal, but what's 'legal' anyway? I was thinking about what she told me, and wondered what would have happened if you'd gone to someplace park instead of A'ala Park. Then you guys'd never have met, and Tenley and I would never have—" She sighed and looked out at the ocean. "It makes me happy that this has happened. I know she told you everything about us, too. I mean, I know that when she tells a story, she leaves nothing out. About the canoe, about the University and its boiled-brains politics, and all that. I mean the basic idea of it is right, but the effect—" She shrugged. "I don't know. But she's hotheaded and so am I. We'll call each other all kinds of names, but we—" She was silent a moment. "We love each other."

"Yeah." He didn't know what else to say.

"It was awful how a bunch of petty ideas can mess you up. I thought a lot about that after she left. I fell for a professor's garbage, and it cost me my daughter." Denise paused, looking at the ocean. "And then the story about your father and that cane field thing. It's serious, that bullet coming through the window."

"Yeah, I don't understand it."

"Bodies in cane fields are nothing new here. I think this case was sort of famous because it was never solved. But if it's true, then this relative, this Junior Montross, won't let up. If he's a druggie or whatever, he'll go for weeks without thinking about you, then one day he'll wake up in the morning so full of hatred that he'll try again."

"I keep thinking that he doesn't even know me. But still he—"

"Your father is a haole, and he killed two local guys and got away with it. Somebody's gotta pay. You're the only one available. It doesn't matter how many years ago he did it. Sometimes race exaggerates it, sometimes it's something else."

"So if race exaggerates it, would Montross be Hawaiian? Or part?"

"Maybe. But it doesn't really matter. He's local. That's all he needs to be."

"My father is English and maybe ten percent French. It doesn't matter to him. I'm part Scottish, but bagpipes don't turn me on and I've never worn a whatchucall. Kilt."

"That's because France and England are thousands of miles away. Here, everyone's close to their blood roots. Everything that happens here happens only a few miles away." Tenley and Jacob were coming back along the shiny sand above the shorewash. Tenley's mother, her arms folded as she watched them, said, "It's always been that way."

They heard fire engines at around ten thirty. They had just watched the news, a regular part of Mr. Fujimura's schedule, and he wanted them all to sit around and talk about who was running for what office and so on. Nobody reacted to the sirens, except for Adrian, who went outside and listened. He could see orange light reflecting in flashes off a palm tree a few hundred yards to the south. He was about to go back in when he realized that the light seemed to be near their old house. "Nah," he whispered, and went back into Fujimura's house.

But sitting on the folding chair next to the couch where Tenley and Denise sat watching TV, he began wondering. Finally, he touched Tenley on the shoulder and then jerked his head toward the door. She followed him out. "The fire is down the street there," he said. "Right where the other house is."

They walked toward it. The reflection of flames no longer showed on the palm tree. The air held the odor of a doused wood fire, salty and acrid. It was not the house that had burned, they discovered, but the cottage out back. Adrian instantly envisioned all the planking, the window frames, the carefully constructed floor. There were two fire engines, one in front of the big house and one on the street that fronted the vacant lot behind the cottage. Before the house stood two policemen and John Murai's son and daughter. Tenley said, "Must have been a short circuit."

The daughter looked in their direction and said something to one of the policemen, who turned and ambled toward them.

"Hello," he said, "I'm officer Pang. Would you mind if I asked you a couple of questions?"

"No," Tenley said. "We just saw the smoke and came over."

"The young lady over there has suggested to me that you might have had something to do with the fire in the building behind that house. Is there a reason she'd say that?"

"She doesn't like us much," Tenley said. "We were at our house down the street," and she pointed behind her. "I know, I know, the address." She told him the street, but not the number, because she didn't know it, although, she said, he couldn't miss the house because of its age and condition. She then explained who was staying there and why. The "young lady" and her brother had evicted them. If Officer Pang wanted to go and talk to the other people at Fujimura's, they'd confirm that Tenley and Adrian had been at the house throughout the evening. Officer Pang looked at Adrian. He gave the policeman his name and pulled out his wallet to show him his New York State I.D. card. "Been here only a little while," he said.

"Well, thanks," Officer Pang said, studying the I.D. card, and then handing the wallet back. He nodded and left.

"Cops here are nice," Tenley said.

"It's that guy Montross, isn't it?" Adrian said. "I'll bet it's him."

She didn't say anything but seemed to be thinking about it as they walked back. She stopped and turned to Adrian. "Look," she said, "I could get a job, right? Temp or something. We can go live someplace else. And we don't really know if it's Montross."

He tried at first to convince himself that the fire could be a coincidence. But this was a kind of self-scam, he realized, to convince himself that there wasn't anybody after him.

In a cool breeze coming from the ocean, he crawled under the house to see about jacking it up where it had sagged. Tenley and

Mr. Fujimura were inside. Jacob followed Adrian, groaning as he worked along on his knees. "I get one screw jack. Can leef um. I done dis befoah."

Adrian looked around in the spider-webbed gloom of the crawl space. Strewn in the sand were oxidized beer cans, pieces of faded plastic toys, rotted paper plates, the skeleton of a golf bag, and a few hollow-tile bricks. A trench in the sand ran diagonally across the middle, indicating that water had once flowed under the house. Three of the footings were lower than the others by four or five inches. "Water erosion, see?" Adrian said, turning back to Jacob.

"'Ass it," the old man wheezed. Then he groaned, pulling himself into a sitting position, wiped dirt off his knees, and looked around. "You get da jack, 'kay? I stay."

"We need pieces of plywood or something. There's scrap in the carport. I'll go cut some squares and— Where's the jack?"

"Truck bed," Jacob said. "Inna little too' box."

Adrian went around and eyed the outer footings. Two more on the ocean side had sunk, making the house droop on the ancient carrier beam that bent in a subtle arc. The corner footings appeared to be plumb. At the back corner, he stood up from a footing and saw, through the window of their room, Tenley hanging a picture on the wall. She had also unpacked some boxes.

Adrian and Jacob stayed under the house all morning, Adrian struggling with the screw jack. The house snapped and groaned as it went up, a half inch at a time so that Adrian could slide the cut squares of plywood under the posts. They worked without a level, Adrian figuring that he could align it by eye, which seemed to work. Termite droppings stuck to their sweaty skin and got in their eyes. Inside, Tenley could feel the house going up. Each time Adrian turned the jack, she yelled down through the floor, "Yah, da cupboard closes!" and "Yah, da door to da back room closes!" and "Yah, no mo' walk downhill inna liveen room!" Mr. Fujimura positioned himself at the opening of the crawl space and sat on a low beach chair to watch. "Ho," he said, "why I no do dis? Can open windows, doors open an' close, teengs no slide onna kitchen countah."

When they were done and had crawled back out from under the house, Adrian went to the street to look at it. The roof wasn't right. It looked lumpy, as if some of the beams were in bad shape, but the bottom of the house was straight. He and Jacob and Mr. Fujimura went up the rickety steps, and Mr. Fujimura walked across the living room with his hands out, as if on ice. "Ho, faw down I no watch out," he said.

Jacob was staring at the floor. Then he laughed. "What?" Adrian asked. "Is the floor off?"

"Nah nah nah," he said. "My foot no work."

Tenley crossed the room. "Your foot doesn't work?"

"No work," he said. "I try fo' move um, an' it no work. Han' funny too."

Adrian thought he knew what it was, and he jerked his head to draw Tenley away. She followed him down the hall. "It might be a stroke," he said. "I saw this in one of my mother's books. He can't use his foot or his hand, which are symptoms. We gotta take him to a doctor or hospital."

"'Kay," she said.

They helped him to the truck. He seemed to find it funny that his leg and foot didn't work, and kept looking down and laughing.

Tenley drove, with Jacob in the middle. She explained to him that he might have had a stroke, but he shrugged it off. "Whatevahs. Cannot pay doctah bill but."

"Forget the doctor bill," she told him.

She drove past the small medical center in Waimānalo, figuring that Castle Hospital was the place they should go. "In fact," she said, "we probably should have called the ambulance."

"Ambulance?" Jacob said. "Nah nah nah. You call ambulance anytime any o' fut like me sneezes? Wase of money."

Once they arrived at the hospital, Adrian and Tenley helped him into the air-conditioned reception area. Adrian looked down at his dirty clothes. Jacob was filthy too, the termite droppings on his shoulders looking like reddish sand. Tenley was wearing her green bathing suit and a T-shirt with a logo on it that read "Roxy." But then, Adrian reasoned, you didn't stop to put good clothes on in an emergency. The receptionist, a large woman with gray hair, took over from there, and a nurse took Jacob away in a wheelchair.

Adrian and Tenley sat in a little anteroom that had a TV in it. She kept looking over toward the desk, biting her nails. Eventually, the receptionist came into the anteroom with a clipboard, which she handed to Adrian. "If you could, please fill out the information."

Tenley took it. "I'm his granddaughter," she said. "This is my friend."

"Does your grandfather have insurance?"

"No."

"Okay, we'll work that out later," she said, then went back to the desk.

On the TV, Steve McQueen and his soldier friends dug a tunnel under a prison camp to the sound of jaunty music. Charles Bronson apparently had problems with claustrophobia. Adrian would watch a while, hearing the ballpoint pen thumping on the board, and then his attention would drift to the activity in the reception area. Tenley took the clipboard to the desk and then came back. She stared into space, then turned to Adrian. "So what does he do now? He needs what? Rehab and stuff like that. I have to get a job. I mean if there are medical bills, I'd rather try to pay them, you know what I mean?"

"Yeah. I would too, I guess."

"Then what? I could be pregnant and not know it, right now."

"I know."

"Was it a bad idea?"

"No. You wanted to find a reason for doing something. I can understand that."

She stared at him. "Do you feel that way?"

"Yeah, I feel that way."

On TV, men standing in an open space inside the fence furtively unloaded dirt from their pant legs and then wandered away. Oblivious German guards with pockmarked faces watched from their towers.

"The second-most promising girl in my senior class married her high-school boyfriend," Tenley said. "He was handsome and cool. She was smart, bound for success. They got into drugs. He got paranoid or something. Finally, he shot her and then killed himself. All in two years."

"Sad," he said.

"And on TV, when they did the story, they showed their prom photos, she with a beautiful haku lei—that's a head lei—and him with a maile lei. I remember that when I saw it on TV, I kept saying, 'Why the hell would you use those pictures? Why?' Everything would have been kind of acceptable if they'd used something else, like mug shots from the police records or something. But they used their high-school pictures, and you can't believe how beautiful they looked."

"Leigh Donaldson was pretty too," he said.

"We're all pretty." She bit her nail. "And there's Donna too—remember the girl I told you about? I haven't thought about her in a while. But I'll bet she's half rotted away by now."

A man who introduced himself as Dr. Sakata came in, sat with them in the anteroom, and explained that Jacob would be kept overnight for observation. They were giving him the medication for what he called a brain stem stroke, which caused the lack of mobility in his leg and might cause problems with his left arm and hand. His speech might be affected too, although, the doctor said, he was quite lucid. The prognosis seemed positive. If anything, this event could be thought of as a warning to him to change his eating habits and pay more attention to his health. When it was time to take him home, they would be given a complete list of instructions on patient care and proper diet. They would also get prescriptions for his medication. At the moment, he was resting. Would they like to see him?

Jacob was in a ground-floor ward and smiled uncertainly at them as they approached. "Eh, I stuck hea ovanight."

"Oh Grandpa," Tenley said, "it's just to make sure you okay, 'kay?"

Adrian stood there while they talked. When Jacob looked up at him, he said, "Hey, we got the house leveled up. I'll take care of the rest."

On the drive home, Adrian could tell that Tenley was having second thoughts. He imagined her envisioning Hal's opulent apartment, martinis, nights out at expensive restaurants.

"I'm gonna look into a job," she said. "Subway. I worked there when I was in high school."

"I could too."

"No, we gotta have a place to stay," she said. "Jacob especially. You're working already. The more I think about this, the more I wonder. You gotta live somewhere, and you gotta pay to live there. Everybody has to go through this." She laughed, turning the corner into their street. "Is it any wonder people do drugs? I mean, it's all like, why bother?"

"I know."

"But you hafta bother. We can't just leave Jacob there with Mr. Fujimura. He hasn't got a cent. Neither do we. Even my mother. Here she's forty whatever and she's all, 'Shit, what am I gonna do now?' Boy did it ever sneak up on her. So what *do* we do?"

"What we're doing," he said. "And this Montross can fuck himself."

Tenley explained Jacob's condition to Mr. Fujimura while Adrian examined the floor and the wainscoting. By the time Tenley's mother came home, Adrian was scraping the wainscoting and taking off what appeared to be three or four layers of paint: dull yellow on top, dull blue, pink, and white. Tenley's mother kept saying "oh my" and "the poor man" as Tenley told her what had happened to Jacob.

At the rate the paint was coming off, Adrian began to wonder about doing the work by hand. He used a triangular file to dig the paint out of the seams, the dust making a bitter taste in his mouth. But he did it the way he had done it before: with the dogged attention of someone demented, oblivious to the voices behind him. But then the inflection of the voices began to change, and he slowed down, listening. "—can't be serious. Mom, are you crazy?"

The response was hushed. Fujimura was outside watering orchids. Then there was a derisive laugh from Tenley, and her mother saying, "I don't want to talk about it."

The wood file left the wainscoting somewhat rough, so Adrian worked on it with sandpaper. The idea would be to do one yard at a time so that Carter could see what a restoration would look like.

He heard Tenley and Denise in the hall. "Mom, I'm sorry," Tenley said. "I didn't really mean it."

Her mother came through the living room, went outside, and walked down toward the beach. Tenley followed her out the door. Adrian sanded. It was not his business. Wainscoting was his business.

After a while, he backed up and studied the wood. It still held the original stain, but looked clean, so he went out to the carport to look at Jacob's junk, hoping to find some varathane. He was going through a box of small paint cans when the tan Honda with the tinted windows went by, slowed down, and then disappeared around the corner. Adrian continued to look in the box, and he was beginning to feel a jaunty, aggressive resentment toward whoever was in the car. He walked out into the driveway to look at the corner where they had turned, but saw nothing. He started back to the carport and saw the tan Honda coming from the opposite direction, having gone around the block. The car made its way slowly toward him. He stood there with his hands on his hips and whispered, "Okay, here I am." The car stopped, backed into a driveway, and turned the other way, toward the highway. Adrian noted that the plate read FZU 308. He laughed, his heart beating fast. "Fuck you," he said. He went and found a screwdriver and scratched the license-plate letters and numbers on the side of one of the concrete footings of the carport.

After a while, Tenley and her mother came back from the beach, walking slowly. They seemed to have finished arguing. Adrian was putting the varathane on the last strip of tooled wainscoting board, and they both inspected the job. "Looks good," Tenley said, "but what about the walls and the floor?"

"You hafta have something to show him," Adrian said. "You can't show him bricks and jacks and stuff. The trick is to isolate one thing and do it right. So I'm gonna stick with this."

On Wednesday he rose from the wainscoting, his skin shining with sweat, and decided to take a break. Mr. Fujimura and Jacob were sitting on aluminum folding chairs outside in the shade of a little tree. Tenley was now employed at a Subway in a section of town called Enchanted Lake. Each day she went in with the squirt bottle so that she could take small hits when nobody was watching. She had mentioned to him that he could take the bus into Kailua and eat lunch with her, and she would be able to get a free sandwich. But he had no money for the bus and didn't want to ask Jacob, who seemed to have recovered from his stroke well enough to be able to sit and talk. He had his medicines, along with instructions to avoid strenuous activities, salty foods, and stress.

Adrian walked in the heavy late-morning heat, past the school and the supermarket, around a curve under Olomana Mountain, and up a hill toward Kailua. As he walked, wearing rubber slippers because his sneakers had all but rotted away and he didn't want to wear out the good Salvation Army ones, he looked down at the dark skin of his arms and feet. He had become used to sweat, to heat, to the sun, to the work, except for his hands, which were always sore. He was even used to the sensation of being a target, as if every car that came over that hill carried Montross or someone else who could easily put a gun out the window and kill him. But Adrian had developed a mantra for himself: fuck Montross. He repeated it over and over, even while he worked, his weary arms going up and down on the wainscoting with the sandpaper: "fuck Montross" as they went up; "fuck Montross" as they went down.

In the process of looking the house over, he had made a discovery. Underneath the house, he saw the termite-eaten planking of a tongue-and-groove floor. In the living room he saw the tongue-and-groove floor, but the planks ran from side to side, while underneath they ran from front to back. There were two layers of flooring, and if more than fifty percent of each was in good shape, he could cut and trim pieces until he had one solid floor.

"Naked," he said to himself as he made his way up the hill. He walked toward the road that turned right into the neighborhoods where, a long time ago it seemed, he had sold people sprouted coconuts. Once all the information on him was out, he could not escape the sensation of being naked. He looked down at his browned feet in slippers shooting out from under him step by step. Nobody in his right mind would wear these things, he thought, except here. In New York he would be laughed at. Without shoes, long pants, or a coat, he felt a nakedness that matched the nakedness of everyone knowing about him. Clothes were a kind of armor, but you almost didn't need them here. And at night, with light from the moon coming in through the window, Tenley would be there so that with hands and mouth and that other part of his body that seemed incapable of fatigue, he would go at it until they were glued together with their own sweat. It was as if they had liquefied into each other, the place of total immersion slick and hot, and he would go ahead and discharge himself in a spasm of exhilaration and horrible fright. He knew every square inch of skin and every mole and fissure of that compact, healthy body he had studied in the park, every soft, resilient cubic inch of her—as he supposed she knew everything about him. Before he came here, one of the necessities or even pleasures of life had been the list of secrets he was able to keep, but now there was no scam left to hide behind.

The walk took him past tract houses with different kinds of plants in the yards, past jogging women who nodded to him, and men working in yards who said, "Eh, howzit?" as he passed.

He found the Subway and crossed a hot parking lot to the door, and then looked down at himself. He had half-dried mud on his shirt and grime in the creases of his hands. He went in anyway, a blast of cold air making him shiver. Tenley was wrapping a sandwich and putting it in a bag. Then she removed a plastic glove and rang up the customer's purchase. The customer, a woman wearing what looked like a hospital uniform, walked past him and outside. He went to the high counter.

"How's Jacob?" Tenley asked.

"Okay," he said. She glanced at the wall clock, and then an older woman came out from the kitchen, smiled, and made a shooing motion toward her.

Tenley had ready one and a half sandwiches for the two of them. For him, a whole turkey sandwich, and for her, a half sandwich made of tuna salad. "You know the squirt bottle?" she asked. "I haven't used it yet. No real jonesing, leas' not daytime anyway. Maybe laters."

"Come to think of it, all I had today was a lot of water."

She ate, smiling at him as if she were holding something back. She looked around to where the other worker was ringing someone up at the register, then leaned closer to him over the yellow table. "I think I missed a period," she whispered.

"Really?" he said. "That's what you were after, right?"

"Yup." She took another bite, then squinted at him, chewing. "Don't worry, pard," she said. "I can see it written all over your face."

"What does that mean?"

She put down the sandwich and licked her fingers. "I'm just drawing the obvious conclusion."

"Nothin's obvious to me," he said. "And this doesn't change anything."

"You're sure? Because if you are, you sure have scammed yourself."

"That's true. I have."

"I scammed *my*self," she said. "But you know what? I'm sticking with it. It would be so easy to just go to some clinic and get this taken care of, but I was thinking, you know, making sandwiches and smiling and making change, that this feels okay to me. So I'm sticking with it."

"Well, it feels okay to me too," he said. "I thought we made a deal."

"Okay, okay," she said, then put her hand on her mouth. She turned and smiled at the other woman, and again leaned toward him. "It was just that your expression was a little strange. This means you're going to be a father, did you know that?"

"I guess I did. I don't really know what to think of it. I mean, shit, I'm nineteen."

"Is this stupid or what?" she asked brightly.

"It's insane. It's absolutely insane." He hesitated and then said, "Look, I saw that car again, and I'm thinking that I'd like to find out the rest, you know, about this Montross. I got his license-plate number. I want to find out where he lives and all that, and I want to call him up or something."

"Okay," she said, somewhat vaguely. "You're not planning anything dumb, are you?"

"I don't know," he said. That feeling of jaunty bravado surged like a low-level current through his flesh, and he was aware of the stupidity of it. "But I would like to know if it's really him."

"I looked the name up in the phone book, and there's one Montross. There's a chance that he's the guy, but I don't think you should do anything. You should leave it alone."

"All right, I'll leave it alone. By the way, I figured out how to do the floor."

She sat still, her expression strange. Then she said, "Well?"

Adrian figured that Frank Carter would show up on Saturday, so on Friday he worked on the living room. He cleaned off the vertical tongue-and-groove boards of the wall, then dug out all the termite damage, which was more cosmetic than structural, mixed some of Jacob's old Fix-All with water, and troweled the mixture into the holes. When that was dry after a few hours, he sandpapered it until he could feel no seam between the compound and the wood. Then he painted the walls a flat, quick-drying wheat yellow from a can he'd found in Jacob's boxes of junk. He was still at it when Denise and Tenley came home. They and the old men sat outside at the little picnic table while he worked. He finished before the sun was down.

As he cleaned the brushes in the carport, he heard Tenley call out, "Hui!" When he went to her, the old men were struggling up from the picnic table.

"We goeen walk onna beach," Jacob said.

"Are you allowed to?" Denise asked. "What did the doctor say?"

"He say, 'Go beach, no mattahs.'" They made their way slowly out to the street.

"Come," Tenley said to Adrian, "get manapuas, Bud, an' teriyaki chicken." The food was in oil-spotted bags and the beer sat in pools of condensation on the small table, and he had to pretzel himself in order to get his knees under it. He opened one of the Buds and started eating the chicken.

"Mom an' me get in one big dispute 'kay?" Tenley said. "An' we want you be referee."

Her mother laughed.

"I think she's crazy," Tenley said. "She thinks I'm crazy."

"That's because you are," Denise said.

"I feel so domestic," Tenley said. "I feel so domestic that I could puke. Mom, were you domestic when you were first like, you know, married and all that?"

"I was only eighteen. I worried about what laundry soap to use. I would stare at stuff, thinking about how to make our apartment more—well, you know, *Better Homes and Gardens* presentable."

"That's how I feel," Tenley said, laughing. "I told her I might be pregnant, and she thinks it's the stupidest thing I've ever done. But she had a kid when she was nineteen."

"I was married."

"We will be too," Tenley said. "I told you he asked me officially, right over there at the beach. This is not part of the— The con job we did on you. We just haven't gotten around to it."

"The question is why?" Denise said.

"You think we don't want it?"

"'We'?" Denise looked at Adrian, who shrugged amiably. "Now," she went on, "who's to say Mr. Branch here won't just up and split when it gets to be too much for him?"

"I won't," he said.

"Well," Tenley said, "who's to say Mr. Carter won't up and split when it gets to be too much for him?"

"When what gets too much for him?" Denise said.

Adrian realized what they had been arguing about: Carter.

"How do you know?" Tenley asked. "Maybe he's all, 'Hey, I'm with you guys and sovereignty and reparations because of a little—'" Then she held up two fingers, and with the index finger of her other hand, she poked repeatedly between them. Denise gasped.

"My God, that is crude," she said. "You little bitch."

Tenley laughed. "Mom, I'm trying to help you keep from becoming a slut."

"Look," Denise said, "I know a man who condemns everything haole here, complains about the thinning of blood and all that, and he has a wife with hair so blonde that it hurts your eyes. Politics and life differ sometimes. Frank's just a nice man whose generosity is sweet. Who wants to live alone anyway?"

Denise looked at Adrian. "I can't believe we're talking like this in front of you," she said.

"Well," he said, using a professorial voice, "I would say that this is healthy and frank, mutually supportive and psychologically uplifting. When one opens up to another, particularly in mother-daughter relationships, it is a process of giving and learning about each other that can only be reciprocally beneficial."

They both looked at him. "See?" Tenley said, "I tol' you he was smaht." She put her index finger partway into her mouth to indicate nausea and said, "But dat was corny."

"Don't you want to have fun before you start squirting out babies?" Denise asked.

"Everything is fun," Tenley said. "So what's different about Mr. Carter, the ultimate haole, and what's-his-name at the U?" Tenley turned to Adrian. "Wilmont, that was his name," she said, "but she never said if there was you-know-what between them."

"Snide, but cute," Denise said. "And I'm so pleased that you didn't do your nasty little finger thing again." Then she looked thoughtful. "Look, I listened to everything the professor said because I was attracted to him. I— What's the word you use? I scammed myself."

"Like with the canoe," Tenley said.

"Yes. And speaking of scams, something just occurred to me. What do you think Mr. Carter's going to say when you show him the improvements?"

Carter was impressed by the straight roofline and the restoration of the wainscoting, which he seemed most interested in. Five people watched, as if awaiting some carefully considered judgment. "I suppose they did it this way to keep furniture from scratching walls. But it looks good to me," he said. "What's this about the floor?"

"There are two floors," Adrian said, "the original underneath, badly damaged, and one on top, badly damaged. Both tongue and groove, about three-and-a-half-inch-wide boards. I take up both floors and put one back, and throw away the half that's damaged."

Carter looked at him. "How do you know it's two?"

"Underneath it goes front to back, and on top it goes across. Their answer to a termite-eaten floor was to put another floor on top, crossways."

"This is good work," Carter said. He pulled out his wallet and took bills out. "Here's—" He counted. "Here's a hundred fifty dollars." He handed it to Adrian. "Buy what you need, like stuff to finish it with, rent a sander or whatever you use to—"

"I can do it by hand. Makes a better job."

"Pupule, like I said," Jacob said.

"No," Adrian said, "I don't like power tools that much."

"Either way," Carter said. He looked at Denise. "Want to take the two-man out?"

"Love to," she said. Then she went to her room to put on a bathing suit. Meanwhile, Carter looked around, at the stained ceiling, at the windowsills that would have to be replaced. No, Adrian told him, the damage is surface damage. We fill that with Fix-All and sand it down and paint it. Denise came back out in a two-piece bathing suit, and Adrian could tell by Carter's expression that he had stopped worrying about the house. Adrian understood why: for someone her age, she looked good, like a slightly overweight calendar girl of the sort people called "ample."

After they'd left, Tenley gazed in mock bewilderment at the ceiling. A hundred fifty dollars. There wasn't even any order as to how to spend it. Tenley thought that it didn't matter, because he was making legitimate money, and bumbye he would get more. Maybe he would go into business as a house restorer. As for herself, she was sticking with the Subway job. "You know," she said when they were in their room taking a squirt apiece from the bottle, "the three of us working might make enough to live like any regular family."

"That's how it works, I guess," he said.

Everything would have been fine except that Adrian could not sleep. Weekends were times for creeps to do their thing, and the image of the old house aflame kept boring into his imagination. The next Saturday he went outside at three a.m. and sat in the cool night air at the little plastic picnic table, the cold edge of the table at his back, and waited for the shafts of headlights to appear bouncing above the street. He had to do something about Montross, and he knew that he could revert to the happy, mindless bravado he was so capable of. As much as he hated the idea, he could set a fire, too. He wanted to inform Montross of this, and considered different means by which to do so. The obvious one was to walk out into the street with his hand up the next time the guy came by in his little tinted-window car.

On Sunday afternoon, Tenley and Denise went food shopping in Kailua, Tenley first making sure that Denise would help out with dakine. If that was all Tenley was on for the moment, Denise said, then sure, as long as she didn't turn out to be a drunk. "Nah nah nah," she told her mother. "You think I would risk fetal alcohol syndrome?" Adrian told them that if it was all right with them, he would just as soon have a case of beer too because as Jacob said, he was on the thin edge of disappearing.

Later that day, he negotiated with Mr. Fujimura and Jacob for a way to tear up the floor in all the rooms in the older part of the house. He would do it in sections. First would be the living room, which meant that all the stuff from there would be moved to the other rooms. And then he would start at the front of the house and put back, say, eight feet of the floor, so they could carry stuff out the back of the house and around to the front. He didn't want anybody trying to carry furniture across the two-by-tens. "Eh," Fujimura said, "da soonah da bettah. Ho, dis nice, ah?" he said to Jacob. "Make one nice house, why I complain? "

But again, Adrian couldn't sleep. After Tenley crawled into bed, a gray specter in the filtered moonlight, she quickly fell asleep. He tried to, but the sound of surf in the distance, the dim yellow glow of reflected streetlights, the odd sounds that he could not identify, all kept him awake. Finally he dozed, but at five the sound of roosters crowing woke him up. He looked at the red block numbers displayed on Tenley's clock radio and cursed himself for his paranoia.

Jacob and Mr. Fujimura left early to fish, just after Denise went to work. Then Tenley left at about nine, and Adrian moved furniture and began work on the floor. He pulled a piece of rotted molding away from the corner and discovered a grit-filled space, the butt ends of the pieces of flooring misaligned, some of them eaten by termites. He pulled up molding from the ocean-facing wall and found that the tongues of the T-and-G floorboards were aimed at the ocean, which was good. He worked the first piece out. Four feet long, it had been fastened with cleats instead of nailed. The cleats came out easily, and the piece of board was scuffed only on the surface, so refinishing it would be easy. It appeared to be oak, the grain fine and distinct.

But he had to do something about Montross. The fact that Adrian was not his father was of no consequence to Montross. Vengeance worked that way. If Montross had it in his mind to exact vengeance and wanted to skip over the fact that he was a generation late, then so be it. Adrian had to convince the guy that he could match butchery with butchery, and the only question was who would strike first. The logic of it was simple. If someone was after you, you told that someone that you were after him, and you convinced that someone that you were more of a creep than he was and had far more developed perversions. You had to convince him that you loved to slit throats, torture people, burn them to death—no, maybe not that. The goal was to let Montross know that the seedy-looking guy he saw from his car was far more mentally bent out of shape than he could ever imagine, one who either would strike first or, if he survived Mr. Montross's strike, would retaliate in a way that was ten times worse. He was someone with a major screw loose, a type familiar to everyone. Do you remember those inmates at that prison in New Mexico who went around killing people with blowtorches to the face and reinforcing bars driven in one ear and out the other? Do you remember Jeffrey Dahmer? How about the Man with the Candy, who had all those bodies of boys buried under his house? Mr. Montross, do you have a girlfriend? If you do, I'm going to send you a box with her toes in it, those nails all painted. Or her eyelids, with those beautiful fans of lashes you loved so much. Montross had to lose sleep, too. Montross had to dream of someone who could be just outside his window with a gag, a pair of pliers, and a blowtorch—someone who wouldn't quit until every member of his family had died a gruesome and kinky death, infants included.

Adrian went into their room, found the scotch, and took a deep gulp, then another. Most likely, he would get some old lady if he called. After all, the guy might be employed. But if he didn't, he had to be ready to work on Montross.

When the buzz of the scotch began to alter his perception, he felt the warm roiling of an aggressive confidence. It occurred to him that if Montross were some early-twenties guy who loved to drink and do drugs, who loved to cruise with his buds late into the night, then he would be the type to have a job that allowed him to sleep late. It was now about nine thirty—the perfect time for slumbering creeps to be disturbed from their drunken sleep.

Adrian got out his card and went to the phone book. He ran his eyes down the columns of names beginning with M, then stopped to focus on the two and a half names that fit into the thin slot of the card, waiting for the little short that would make his brain flinch on letter combinations. In the section with the "Mon" prefix, he slowed down, then found the one with "tross" after it. There was a K. Montross at 636-4519. So. Adrian thought about ways to present himself. Tough would be wrong. Quiet, smoldering perversion would be the best, measured and unrelentingly pathological, a voice with a demented giggle put in here and there, and long pauses with the hint of eager breathing.

He punched out the number, his hand shaking a little, as if he were experiencing a fit of stage fright. On the fifth ring, someone picked it up. "Yah," the man said. Adrian didn't respond.

"Yah?"

"Is Mr. Montross there?" Adrian asked. "This is someone he needs to talk to."

"Kendrick, you fucka, dat you?"

"No, it's not Kendrick. It's Adrian Branch." There was a long pause. He waited, breathing evenly into the phone. Then he said, "I want to talk to Mr. Montross."

Another pause, and then he heard something muffled, as if the speaker had covered the mouthpiece of the phone. Then the muffled sound opened up. "Dis Kyle Montross, so?"

"You drive a tan Honda with tinted windows, right?"

"So?" he said, and then added, "nah nah, what da fuck is dis?"

"You like to cruise Waimānalo, right? Up one street, down another, right?" Now he felt fully in control of his voice. He concentrated on making it sound like the voice of someone who loved razors. "I know why you do that," he said, "and you know what? I know where you live."

"You shiteen me, right? Brah, fuck, what is dis?"

"After all, you're in the phone book. Kyle, why do you get all worried about something that happened so long ago? Besides, my old man is dead."

There was a little rumble, as if Kyle had touched the mouthpiece of the phone. Then he said, "What da fuck you talkeen about?"

He remembered something his mother had told him, about numbers and death and superstition. "Kyle, why did your parents give you a name with four letters?"

"Braddah, you get one screw loose."

Adrian laughed. "I know. I do. More than one. But why did your parents give you a name with four letters? Didn't they know what that meant?"

There was another pause, more muffling of the phone. He waited. When the phone sounded clear again, he said, "So who was it my father killed, Kyle? Was it your father? Your uncle?"

Silence. Apparently that had nailed Kyle Montross right in the middle of his little brain. Adrian was afraid the guy might hang up, so he said, "You can go ahead and hang up whenever you feel like it, but I just wanted to say that you may have stumbled across the wrong guy. My father's dead, like I said. Accidentally shot himself." There was a grunt, then more muffling of the phone. He waited. "Kyle, are you there? Kyle with a name that has four letters? What were your parents thinking? Doesn't it seem kind of inevitable that someday you'd stumble across the wrong guy? I love stuff like this. Can you see it? As if it was all preordained at our births? Stuff like this turns me on, man. I love it. I really get off on it."

"You fulla shit brah," Montross said. "You jus' plain fulla shit."

"I know. Kyle, who's that in the background you're talking to? Is it your girlfriend?"

"I not talkin' to anybody."

"What color eyes does she have? Do you have a sister?"

"You fucka. If you tink you—" Then there was silence, with no muffling of the phone.

Adrian thought that now there was little chance that Kyle would hang up. The tone of his voice had gone competitive, engaged, a mountain of outrage behind it.

"Kyle?" he said, "you've missed the boat two times now."

"Boat?" he said, "what boat? What da fuck is dis?"

"You fired and you missed, which means that the giddy rush you expected didn't happen, did it? What did you say? 'Shit, I missed.' You aimed and the bullet went past my head. You have no idea of the consequences of that. None. Stop and think about that. I'm still here and now I'm really stoked that we're doing this. It's fun. And what else? You torched the little house I was crashed in."

"Not. What you tryin' to pin on me, brah? I know nahteen about shit li'dat. I nevah even know it burn. You crazy."

"Ah, so when you say 'it,' that means you know which place I'm talking about."

"You crazy."

"You got that right. Boy, did you ever hit the nail on the head there. It's something I have learned to live with, and many people have done their best to try to help me out, make me normal again, but all to no avail. And Kyle? Every time you do something like this, the old me comes back. Torching the little house was beautiful in a way, and I stood there watching it burn, thinking, Kyle, but of course I didn't know your name then, thinking, whoever you are, you have set me back, taken me back to who I was before I was in the institution, and—"

"What institution? We no set fiah. Dat was not us, brah."

"Kyle, you don't need to lie to me. In any case I didn't tell the police anything about you. That would have ruined all of this. That would have been like taking the ball away from us so that we wouldn't be able to play. In fact, if you really didn't set it, then I'm disappointed, because I thought it was like a move in a game. I mean, gosh, if it's only shooting from the window of a car, that's only one move. I had all kinds of moves planned, and if you didn't set the fire, then I'm set back a little. Looking again at all my implements—"

Kyle Montross laughed hard, as if he had suddenly seen through the scam. Adrian flushed, realizing that the use of the word implements was stupid enough to have nearly invalidated his pitch. It was like something from a bad movie, a drooling actor with a death-white face and black, slick hair fawning over his polished leather case of razors and needles, scalpels, and other gleaming instruments of torture. Montross ended his laugh with a series of coughs.

"Well, Kyle, I guess you don't buy some of what I'm saying, do you?"

Montross said nothing.

"Do you, Kyle?"

"You assho. What, you tink I sked of you? Fuck you, you fucka."

"If anything happens to me, everybody I know knows where to go. Everybody."

"Hah! Who da fuck is everybody?"

"Oh, people. Friends. And then if something happens to you? Well, you'll already have told your friends. I know some friend told you, some guy who knew my parents, maybe named Vierra. But that doesn't matter. We're off the ground with this. Maybe soon I'll be in your neighborhood so that we can be closer."

"I kick yo' ass is what I do, brah."

"Why, Kyle? Is it because of your father or uncle or whatever, and my father? I know how that works here, you know, the unpaid balance of things. But like I said, my old man is dead. This cane-field thing happened when I was about seven. How old were you? About eight? How much do you remember? So you risk your life over shit like this? But I understand because I would do it too. It's a reason to get up in the morning."

Montross had no response to that. The phone was muffled again, and Adrian considered the effect of what he was saying. The phone sounded clear again. "Yah, is shit awright. Da ho ting shit. You fulla shit brah. I fed up wit' dis."

"I am too I guess," Adrian said. "So I'll hang up. But remember, I'm always nearby. I'm always ready to keep at it with you. I really get off on this. I really do."

"Go die somewheres," Montross said, and hung up.

Adrian stared at the phone. The earpiece was wet with sweat, and sweat had gathered in the crook of his arm. His hand hurt from gripping the receiver to his ear, and he could barely open his fingers to let go of it.

He went back to pulling boards up. As he worked, he carefully went over the conversation. Nothing in it indicated that Kyle Montross even knew anything about Adrian's father. Only the muffled pauses and Kyle's willingness to stay on the phone seemed to confirm the assumption that he did know. However, Montross wasn't thinking when Adrian had mentioned the Honda and had said, "So?" That was the main giveaway. And, Adrian thought, the use of the word "it" in reference to the fire meant that he knew of the little cottage, and the only place on the street that someone could see it was the stretch beyond the vacant lot, where the shot had come from.

As he worked, he felt better. Maybe the phone call had put Montross on the defensive, and Adrian began to think he might not see the car again. They had heard each other's voices, so the mystery of the other's identity was gone. Montross might now leave it alone. Adrian decided that it would be best not to mention the call to Tenley. No need to make her worry. Besides, the manner in which he had made the call now seemed childish and embarrassing.

He used the same technique on the floor that he had used with the wainscoting. When he started removing the top layer of the floor, he discovered that the planks underneath were all around six feet long, so he worked, his sweat dripping on the dusty wood, until he had removed eight feet of the top floor and taken it outside. Then he pulled up the original floor, which was more difficult because it was nailed to the two-by-tens and because the butt ends went to the base of the wall. The two-by-tens below had a lot of damage. He pulled away paper-thin sections of the damaged wood to reveal rounded-off termite runs and expanded areas that looked like a scale model of a desert with dunes and arroyos and alluvial fans. When he got to several live termites, he saw they were the size of off-white grains of rice. They had light-brown heads, and dark mandibles. Moving with a sluggish indecision, they searched for the darkness that was their atmosphere. He squashed them with his index finger and continued working.

Sometime late in the morning he heard Jacob and Mr. Fujimura come back from fishing. They did something in the kitchen, preparing lunch probably, and then they came to see what he was doing. "Need help?" "Nah, everything's fine." "We go back den." "Sure thing."

He found cold chicken in the refrigerator, ate, and went on with the work, receding into that half-mesmerized state he had experienced at the house in the woods, unaware of time passing, unaware that there even was time, a strange, almost blissful state of gape-mouthed single-mindedness, as if locked in the dopey awe of some mystical delusion.

He was brought out of it by the sound of tires crunching pebbles. Denise and Tenley had finished work at the same time, and Denise had offered Tenley a ride. Before they went into the house, Adrian stopped them and showed them the eighty square feet or so of new floor that he had installed and painted with polyurethane varnish, which was, as the can claimed, tough enough to skate on.

VII

On Saturday, Frank Carter showed up at nine in the morning while Adrian was pulling up more of the floor, having moved some of the furniture—the television set, three chairs, and a coffee table—back onto the new section. Carter stood there, observed by Denise from the doorway and by Tenley, Jacob, and Mr. Fujimura from the corner. He studied the gleaming tongue-and-groove wood, which was a light tan with a hint of red in it, merging with the repaired molding that finished the bottom of the darker wainscoting.

"What kind of wood is that?" he asked.

"Probably oak," Adrian said. "It's a hard wood, so there wasn't as much damage as I thought. There might be enough left over to use somewhere else. I can even make window frames out of it."

For some reason, Carter looked more perplexed than pleased. "It's really good work," he said. "What about termites? You said you saw termites."

"Dry wood," Jacob said. "Everybody get um. Bad ones, those groun' ones."

"I saw no mud, no wet stuff," Adrian said. "Jacob told me that ground termites transfer mud into the wood and can knock a house down in six months. But we saw no mud."

Carter reached for his wallet. He fumbled with it, thinking.

"I didn't use what you gave me last week," Adrian said.

"You didn't need to tell me that," he said. "Jesus, what kind of con artist are you?" Everyone laughed. "Okay, here's . . ." Fingering the bills, he seemed almost pained.

"It's all right," Adrian said.

"No no," he said, "that's not it. I was just thinking. Here. Here's three hundred."

"Okay," Adrian said, taking the money. "Thanks. I'll put most of it aside. There'll have to be new shingles on the roof, and there's gonna be damage up there."

Carter turned to Denise. "You ready?"

"Aye aye, cap'm," she said.

Tenley carefully observed them as they wheeled the kayak out the driveway. Then she turned to Adrian. "I do not believe this," she said. Jacob and Mr. Fujimura went out to the picnic table.

Adrian looked down at the money: two one-hundred-dollar bills and two fifties. Tenley looked at it, too. "Now you're really employed," she said.

"I guess," he said. He still felt uncertain about the doubtful expression on Carter's face. He looked at the floor. "I should probably go on with this," he said.

"We go beach laters," she said. "I gotta do clothes now."

He worked on, pulling up the floor and hearing the washing machine in the background. Jacob's and Mr. Fujimura's voices drifted to him from the picnic table. Three hundred dollars times four would be twelve, times twelve would be fourteen thousand four hundred in a year, assuming that he could restore houses all year, which of course he could not.

By the time Tenley was hanging the wash out on the line, Adrian had the rest of the first layer of oak flooring outside in a pile. He stood at the window and watched her as she raised one article after another and clipped each one on the line, her hair bound up in a blue kerchief, her brown shoulders flexing as she worked, and each time she reached, standing on tiptoes, her buttocks flexed under the green bathing-suit bottom. He remembered burying the braid and her telling him what she wanted there on the beach at Mālaekahana. It amazed him how far she had come from that night at A'ala Park. He had lost count of the number of days or weeks since that night, and watching her as she put the clothes on the line, her shoulders dimpling each time she raised something up, he had the feeling that his mother had somehow known this would happen.

Later Tenley was out on the front lawn, next to the dirt driveway, watching him as he sanded the boards, then sanding some herself. He gradually slid his work on the grass, following a small patch of shade created by the top of a palm tree in the yard next door. Despite the shade, he dripped sweat, and she twice brought out water. Back inside the house, Adrian continued pulling up the old floor and checking on the condition of the beams underneath. The phone rang.

"Hmm," she said, "should I pick that up?"

"I guess. Fujimura's right out there, but it's gonna take him a while to get here."

She picked up the phone, then stared at the wainscoting with a scowl while she listened. "Get who? Who the hell you talking about? Adrian what? What kind of a name is that? Get me too? How you gonna do dat? Listen, you—you zip-locked bag of shit, the only thing you gonna get is your right hand." Pausing, she listened. "Which hand do you use then? Are you left handed? Do you whack off with your left hand? Lucky for the assholes who shake hands with you." She listened, scowling. "Well, all I have to say is fuck you. Yeah, yeah, sure. Fuck you. Thank you. Mahalo and aloha." She put the phone in its cradle and stared at it.

"'Zip-locked bag of shit?'"

"I couldn't think of anything else."

"Listen, there's something I didn't tell you."

He described the phone call to Kyle Montross, going over it carefully, in places recreating the tone of voice he had used: "and many people have tried to help me out." He told her he had tricked Montross into admitting that he owned the Honda, then tricked him into admitting that he knew of the cottage behind the other house. Imitating the voice, he said, "We no burn no fahkeen cottage, brah."

Tenley laughed. "*God*, that's a bad imitation of pidgin."

"I know."

"But this guy didn't really have that much of a pidgin accent," she said.

Adrian thought about that. "Montross has a thick accent. Maybe this was one of his friends."

She snorted, then dismissed the problem by waving both hands. "This is just talk. The whole thing is a lot of talk. As long as people talk, they don't shoot." She paused. "At least maybe not a second time."

"That's what I thought. But how did they get the phone number?"

She pointed at the front window. "Fujimura's name is written on the mailbox. All it takes is going through the fifty thousand Fujimuras in the book and finding the right street." She shook her head and laughed. "I think of high school. 'I keel you, I tawch yoa house at night you, fuckah,' and 'I ketch you alone, I lop yoa head off.' I heard plenty of that by the time I was in ninth grade."

"Okay, then all I can say is fuck Kyle Montross. Maybe he'll think about what I said. I mean not the pathological shit, but the idea that it's stupid to do this because of something that happened so long ago." Adrian put the hammer claws under the edge of a board and popped it up, revealing an opening through the original floor. A breeze wafted up to his face. Then he added, "Whether it's in people's blood here or not."

By mid-morning on Tuesday, he'd reached the other side of the living room, having moved all of the furniture onto the new floor. It looked so good that he was becoming aggravated by the grubby look of the windowsills. That would have to be next. He would fill the holes in the wood, then ripsaw and laminate on a layer of floorboard pieces. After that, he would pull up the flooring in the bedrooms, which meant that he would have to try to get the room done in a single day. The prospect of this sent a surge of exhilaration through him. Take a look at the floor when you go off to work, then again when you come back. He would start right after—

Mr. Fujimura came into the driveway walking fast, stooped over and pumping his fists. He came to the front door, pulled himself up the wooden steps, and came into the front room. "Onna beach. Jacob wen' pass out. I call ambulance."

Adrian ran down the street and the right-of-way to the beach and saw Jacob lying under an umbrella, which rose up in the wind and bounced off down the beach. Adrian ran after it and caught it, then ran back toward Jacob, holding it out in front of him, bulling his way through the wind. When he got to Jacob, he jammed the umbrella into the sand and twisted it so that it spun, the aluminum screw at the bottom of the pole disappearing into the sand. When it was secure, he stooped down. Jacob appeared to be half-awake, and his left eye was running. "Jacob?"

He waved his hand at Adrian. He opened his mouth to speak. "One dizzy spell. I see funny."

"What do you see?"

"One eye get—"

When he didn't continue, Adrian said, "One eye get?"

Jacob blinked, looking to his left. Then he relaxed and stared at the ocean. The wind picked up, and Adrian held onto the shaft of the umbrella. There was nothing else he could do but wait, leaning the umbrella into the wind. Then he heard the wail of the siren in the distance.

Adrian sat in the waiting room throughout the afternoon, first watching people walk by and then watching Charlton Heston gradually prove to his monkey captors that he could speak English and was not to be messed with. He had driven Mr. Fujimura's old Toyota, following the ambulance at a distance so as not to attract any police. Then Tenley and Denise showed up, Tenley still in her Subway uniform, and he told them what had happened. He told them that he had received no reports yet on Jacob who was in intensive care.

Denise sat down, and Tenley sat in the chair next to her. Tenley put her hands to her face and tried to remain calm, but each time she looked up at the door that led to the intensive-care wing, her expression turned to one of fright and devastation. Finally she whispered, "I'm scared."

Denise looked at her. "I am too."

Dr. Hallstrom, a man in his sixties with a deep tan and hair combed in thin strings over a sunburned bald spot, identified the stroke as a "cerebrovascular accident." His belief was that, because he had numbness in his left leg and some impaired sensory functions, Jacob had experienced an event in the anterior cerebral artery. The doctors would now look for other symptoms, such as incontinence and modified behavior, or behavior that did not seem true to someone as amiable as Jacob. The fact that he complained of vision problems confused this diagnosis because that symptom occurred more frequently with posterior cerebral arteries. They would continue to do testing, which would include an EEG, a brain scan, and an angiograph, which should locate the site of the occlusion. The doctor's feeling was that Jacob should recover. For the present, he would stay in the hospital, and when his condition improved, he could go home and begin physical therapy.

As for his medications, they were giving him corticosteroids to minimize edema. When the time was right, they would determine the nature of the therapy. The help of his family would be essential, because when he was able to return home, there would have to be careful observation of his progress. He would be prescribed stool softeners so as to avoid straining at the bowel, which causes intracranial pressure. The family would have to keep watch on his mouth, noting any problems there, and on his left eye. "You must make sure that he can completely close it. If not, then he'll need a patch," he said. "But I'm summarizing this too much. We'll keep him here, and you folks should go home and return during visiting hours tomorrow. Whatever you do, don't worry. The signs, at the present time, are good. With your help, he should make an excellent recovery."

They followed Denise's car back, Tenley driving the truck. Adrian described to her the scene at the beach, with the guys trundling Jacob off to the ambulance, and what had happened at the hospital before she arrived. "I had a funny feeling at work," she said. "Like I knew something wasn't right."

Back at Mr. Fujimura's, they sat around the living room, their bare feet resting on the varnished oak floor, their images mirrored faintly in the surface.

Denise shook her head. "The poor man," she said. "I don't see how we can do all those things Dr. Hallstrom talked about. He needs professional care."

"He said the family could do it," Tenley said. "At least he implied that."

"Honestly," Denise said, "try to picture yourself holding down a job and taking on this responsibility. Really."

Tenley's face flushed, and her expression bordered on anger. Mr. Fujimura must have seen it too because he struggled up out of his chair and said, "Ho, gotta wattah da plants."

Adrian looked at Denise and then at Tenley, and he got up too.

"You should stay, I think," Denise said to Adrian.

He sat down.

"What the doctor said seemed fairly simple to me," Tenley said in a flat, level voice.

"Ten, this is very noble of you," Denise said, "but do you know what you're getting into?"

"I know what I'm getting into."

"No, you don't. For the life of me I can't figure you out. You talk about wanting a baby, you get a job, and then you want to take on the care of a stroke victim—all the while expecting nothing to go wrong. Are you crazy?"

"Mom, you're pissing me off, really," Tenley said. She had reddened more than before, apparently on the edge of blowing up. Denise seemed surprised at this reaction. Adrian was, too, but he knew right away that he would side with Tenley.

"So what about you?" Denise asked, looking at Adrian.

"I've taken care of a sick person before," he said. "I know how."

"I think you should just look into what the state has to—"

"The state is *not* taking care of him," Tenley said, wiping her eyes. "I am."

"My God," Denise said, shaking her head slowly, "you are children!" She threw her hands up in front of her. "What happens if he has another stroke when you're not around?"

"We'll be around," Tenley said.

"What? Changing diapers? You're not even in your own place."

"He goes with us."

"Where? A'ala Park?" She leaned forward and pointed at Tenley. "Sistah, *think*."

"I am thinking. I've done a lot of thinking."

"What you're doing may seem right to you, but it's not very smart."

"Fuck you."

Denise sighed. "All right," she said. "We've made our way to this in about, what, five minutes." She looked at Adrian. "This isn't unusual with us," she said, "so don't worry about it. I don't take offense at all, but let me just inform you that this house is not any kind of sure thing. Frank's got money, but the way he keeps it is by using the property he owns."

"So he's going to kick us out," Tenley said.

"No, he's not. But the other day out on the kayak, he muttered something about the work being really good." Adrian nodded. "At first it was just, hey, why not, the folks need a place to stay. But now he sees the work, and he keeps grabbing his lower lip the way he does when he thinks. 'What happens when it comes time to sell?' he's thinking. 'If it's fully restored, what do I owe the kid? Can I even think about selling it while it's being restored?' Stuff like that."

"We can get our own place and take Jacob with us," Tenley said. "That's how it's gonna be."

"Look, Frank's a wonderful guy, believe me. I'm just letting you know, that's all."

"I know," Tenley said, perking up. "You're moving in with him."

"I was thinking about it."

"That's why you suggested looking into what the state has to offer. Warehousing, right?"

"No, that's not why I suggested it. But we have to be realistic."

"Well I'm being realistic," Tenley said.

"And I suppose you are too," Denise said to Adrian.

"Well, as I said, I've taken care of a sick person before. And whatever Mr. Carter there has in mind for this place is up to him. I'm doing this work on it. That's all I know right now."

Denise went out with Carter each night following Jacob's hospitalization, and Tenley seemed to settle into a strange, almost mulish domesticity. She would become disgusted with, say, the grime-infused fabric on the old couch and then drive off to Kailua to buy a can of something that lifted it out and made the couch look much better. Cleaning a dirty window seemed as important to her as a perfectly varnished windowsill was to him.

More stuff appeared in their room: pictures, a little bookcase with some of her college books, clothes, and a glass case with enameled gold, silver, and bronze paddling medals in it. As for the question of her being pregnant or not, she said no more about it, and Adrian accepted that. Now that Adrian had seen that perplexed expression on Carter's face and had its meaning explained by Denise, their having to leave seemed just around the corner. It might be a relief. When Denise stayed overnight at Carter's apartment, Adrian felt strange about him and Tenley being alone with Mr. Fujimura, because Denise and Jacob's absence seemed to make their stay even more of an imposition.

However, Mr. Fujimura said, more than once, that everything would return to normal when Jacob got home. The fact that he used the word home seemed to show that he had not changed his mind. He went with Tenley and Adrian, and with Denise when she was around, to visit Jacob. At first, Jacob was sitting up in a bed, and after three days he was sitting in a chair next to the bed. He was amiable and passive, sometimes fatigued. Adrian could not tell how he was affected by the stroke except for a tendency his left eye had to turn reddish, the lid drooping and swollen. But he could blink. He also used his left hand far less than his right, and although he could move his fingers, his hand seemed to rest in a cupped position in his lap most of the time. He was lucid and his memory was still good, though during the third visit, Tenley discovered something strange: he could not read the wall clock. Tenley had been sitting next to him, had said, "Time to go," and had risen from a chair. "What time is it?" he'd asked, looking at the clock. She read it off to him, and then stopped and asked, "Can you tell what time it is?" at which he laughed and said, "Nah. Cannot. I try fo' figgah dat out befoa. Strange."

She asked Dr. Hallstrom about it, and he told her that it wasn't unusual for stroke victims. Jacob would have to re-learn how to read a clock.

One day when Mr. Fujimura was out watering his plants and Adrian was working inside, the phone rang. Adrian picked it up and heard static, then a faint hissing sound. When he said, "Yeah?" there was no response. He wanted to ask if it was Kyle, but did not. After a long pause, he heard a click. Maybe it wasn't Kyle. In any case, he thought, fuck Kyle. Then he stopped and stared at the phone. Why the static? He wondered if the call was long distance, and this made him wonder if it was his father on the line. But why would his father call him? How could he even know where Adrian was? Nah, he thought. And then he whispered, "Fuck him too."

Jacob came home after a little more than a week and seemed to feel comfortable right away. It was Denise who was uncomfortable. She tiptoed around Jacob and did not seem to know how to speak to him. The first night, she was standing by the window near where he was sitting. She was waiting for Carter to pick her up. "How do you feel?" she asked loudly. Then Tenley came in the room, and she said to her, "Do you think he's all right?"

Tenley drew her mother back down the hall, where Adrian was sanding oak planks for Mr. Fujimura's floor. She stood before her mother with her arms folded and said, "Mom, he's had a stroke. He's not deaf. You're not supposed to talk about him as if he's not there, 'kay?"

Her mother looked embarrassed by her mistake. "Sorry," she said.

"You would have known if you were there for the instructions."

"I know," Denise said. "I felt so helpless when Grandma was sick. I'm no good at this."

"Who is?" Tenley said, and then shook her head.

Tenley took over the care of Jacob as if he and his illness were her possession. No one needed to help her, at least when she was there. When she was at work, she left specific instructions for

Adrian. "You have to toilet him at ten a.m. and make sure that the stool softener worked, then help him brush his teeth. Keep an eye on his eye. Give him forty-five minutes of squeezing the rubber ball with his left hand, and make sure he does it." She would come home from work and immediately resume taking care of Jacob. Adrian was impressed. He'd been glaringly neglectful, he realized, when he took care of his mother. Had Tenley been there, she would have made sure the sheets were clean. As for "toileting," Jacob seemed able to take care of himself, so there was nothing Adrian had to do during the day that would embarrass him or Jacob.

The roof was a complicated problem. Adrian could not simply tear the whole thing off and put another one on, and Mr. Fujimura told him that it would cost money just to dispose of the old one. He was going to have to do it the way he did everything else: bit by bit, bag by bag of shingles. The transfer station was on Hīhīmanu Street in Waimānalo, and he could put old shingles in garbage bags along with hedge clippings. Mr. Fujimura borrowed a ladder from a neighbor, and it was a good one, Adrian thought, an aluminum thing with red plastic feet and an extension.

He discovered why the roof of the house didn't look right. He'd started by pulling the old roof off—ten feet of it from the street side up to the hip on the driveway side—and found that some of the planks nailed to two-by-fours on the ridge were termite eaten. When he pulled one bad plank up, he was hit by a blast of hot, dry air swirling with dust. The two-by-fours were in good shape, though, as if termites liked the planking but not the wood that supported it. He peered into the dark space and saw that it was not really a six-panel Pratt truss system but one of the others: boards installed like huge Xs in a line from the front of the house to the back. To replace the planks, he used leftover floor and shimmed it to the right thickness with other scraps. Where two or three planks were damaged, he used industrial ply.

After Tenley had come home and tended to Jacob, she came out to look up the ladder. "What's it like?" she asked.

"Not bad. I gotta buy shingles, and then paint for the house."

"Green with white trim," she said. "We get shingles an' I show you an example of the classic local house."

The house was a pretty cottage in a place called Maunawili. It was set back from the road and was painted a deep green. "I always wanted a house that looked like that," Tenley said. "You know," she said, turning to look at him as she drove, "I took the test. I'm hāpai."

"I know what that means," he said. "I sure do know what that means."

He looked out the window. A strange shudder ran through him, a sweeping sensation of exultation mixed with a creeping fright. It was insane, the whole thing, and they were going through with it. He had felt the same way when he held the Enfield, and speculated on blowing the back of his head off. Why this was so, he didn't understand.

"For shingles," she said, "you use light green."

The hardware store in Kailua did not sell them, so they drove over to Kāne'ohe. They found the shingles at a building-supply store for fifteen dollars a bundle, each bundle capable of covering forty square feet. He bought three bundles, a roll of tarpaper, and a bag of roofing nails. He studied Tenley as they spoke with the salesperson. There she stood assessing the color of a sample shingle while inside her a series of complicated things was taking place: cells were dividing, rudimentary shapes were undergoing their expansive metamorphosis, miniscule tubes were forming and hitching to the marble-sized sack holding that mysterious protoplasm. Denise was probably right. The idiocy of it was such that you had only one option. To go ahead with it. They left with their roofing materials and two gallons of green paint, which, Tenley said, she would begin slapping on the house on the weekend.

Frank Carter stood on the street and looked at the roof. By the weekend, Adrian had covered around two hundred and forty square feet, all on the driveway side of the house, and put a blue tarp over the opening at the top in case it rained. The part redone was as plumb as the roof of a new house. "You can't see a lump," Carter said. "Not a one." And then he looked at Denise, she nodded, and they were gone.

Tenley's schedule changed so that on three weekdays she worked at night, from five to ten p.m. That was fine with her because she wanted to start scraping the house and painting and because she felt better being around during the day to take care of Jacob.

According to Tenley's instructions, if Jacob wanted to watch TV and eat snacks, they had to be salt free. "Chips," Jacob would say, and Adrian would say, "Nope, unless it's those Mexican chips with no salt, okay?"

"'Kay 'kay. Go 7-Eleven an' get um. An' get dakine too, whatchucall. Salsa. 'Ass salt free, yah?" Adrian would walk up the road to the two-lane highway, turn left, and head for the 7-Eleven. He would go over in his mind everything he should not worry about: the baby, the house that did not belong to him, and figuring out where to live after they were kicked out.

One night, Jacob wanted ice cream. "Okay, what kind?" "Neapolitan," he said. "Okay, Neapolitan it is, and you can bet your ass there's no salt in that, huh?" "'Ass right, brah. Go get um."

A hundred yards from the highway Adrian became aware of the hum of a motor behind him. He turned because he saw no headlight shafts, and was knocked off his feet. His head hit the pavement with a sickening silver flash, and he sat up, thinking,

All right, so I was in the middle of the road. My fault. But you didn't have your lights on so— Someone helped him up, and he lost his balance, and then someone pushed him so that his forehead hit the top door sill of the car. He found that he could not bring his hands around to his front, but he was so dizzy that he assumed he was being helped by the person. He felt motion and smelled leather. He was on a leather seat in the back of a car. Then he heard someone say, "No blood!" He bowed his head a little, dizzying flashes of light pounding in his eyes. He did not want to bleed on the man's car seats while they took him to a clinic. The car moved fast, and the engine made almost no sound. Then he heard laughter right next to him, and he tried to turn to see who it was. But he saw only a silhouette of a head, and then his own head drooped again, and as it did, he caught the flickering image of two heads in the front seats. He tried to move his hands, but they were jammed behind his back. He smelled cigarette smoke and then realized that he'd lost his slippers.

Something struck his shoulder hard. "Goddammit, no blood, I said!" Then the cab of the car was filled with laughter from two people. He'd thought that they might be taking him to a hospital or clinic, but he saw only brush, trees, and houses sweeping by. "Fuckeen idiot," the voice from the front said. "Can get thousand dollahs fo' leather seats, an' you fucka, you get blood on um. No blood, I said!"

"Fuck, no blood he says. What, we gotta wait. Cannot cut his balls off now, ah?"

That voice he recognized, but he could not assign a name to it. His head felt so swollen that he had pressure in his sinuses and a bleary pain whenever his eyes registered anything. When he closed them, there was again motion and laughter, and then he lapsed into a strange, dizzy half sleep, unable to tell how much time was passing. Slowly he became aware of a smell. Marijuana, he thought. Yes, the thick, sweet smell of marijuana. The smoke haloed the silhouette of the head.

An arm came over the seat, at the end of it a little orange point, and the man next to him took the joint and puffed it. "Need someteen shtrongah, brah. Need crystal."

"Laters," the driver said. "Shit, you stupit fuck, watch out. When we pass cops, you stay quiet, 'kay? We stoke crystal laters."

"Fuck da cops. Dey no have any clue dis rig even been taken, ah?"

"Until the owner comes back from where? Paree?"

More laughter. Adrian realized that it was cold in the car. Air conditioning.

The dizziness faded, replaced by a sense of dread. This had nothing to do with a clinic. Kyle Montross, he thought. It was Kyle Montross.

"What car is this?" he said.

The one next to him laughed. "Mercedes, assho. We shtreep um. Big bucks. But shtreep um laters, brah, aftah we roas' marshmello." There was more laughter, and then the man next to him picked something off the floor. He held a pale rectangular can before Adrian's face and then squeezed repeatedly, producing a series of flat, metallic popping sounds. Lighter fluid.

The man in front of Adrian held something up. A video camera.

Adrian shrunk against the door and tried to pull his hands in front of him, but they were tied with a long piece of rope. He could almost get his fists to his hips. When he understood what they were planning, his mind emptied into a hollow vacuum that made speech impossible. Whatever pain he had felt in the back of his head vanished, and he trembled, his heart banging rapidly in his chest.

"Saw dis on TV 'kay?" the man next to him said. Kyle.

"'Kay?" one of the two in front said.

"Was da Philippines, 'kay? Dese bandit guys wen' take one village girl and do dakine to her. Get da peoples so mad dat da men beat da shit outta da bandit guys, and dey layin' onna ground like in da middle of one fiel'? Groggy an' beat up."

"'Kay."

"Dis on TV, 'kay? Guy comes up an' dumps one can fulla gas on da tchree guys and drops one match on um. Ho, you shoulda seen um jump. All rolling aroun' on fiah. Was cool, man. Was so ugly. Da guys, da women too, standeen back watchin' while da fuckeen guys die. Ho, was cool." They passed under powerful orange lights mounted high on poles on a wide highway. Adrian could see, as they went under the lights, the faces of the three men in the car. The one in front of him and Kyle, next to him, looked excited and flushed—from the marijuana, he guessed—and the driver, his face set in contemplative anger, looked ahead at the road, his jaw working as if he were grinding his teeth. All three had short black hair and dark skin.

Adrian couldn't control the trembling, and his breath became short and jerky. He inhaled and then let it out, fixing in his mind what was happening. They were going to kill him. He looked out the window. He did not know where they were. The car swept along smoothly, making almost no noise, and he tried to concentrate on what he was seeing: a brushy bank, then the bank going downward to a little shopping mall. Then the car slipped into darkness again, floating along with the brushy roadside going by and houselights up on a hill.

The one in front lit up another joint. They passed it back and forth. "Marshmello," the one in front said, and they both cackled with laughter, making the silent, angry one driving look to his side and laugh too, but only briefly. Then he focused on the road.

"I told you my father was dead," Adrian said.

Kyle laughed and punched him on the shoulder. "Fuck you," he said. "You gotta pay."

"He died because he tried to defend my mother," Adrian said. "My mother is part Hawaiian." They cackled again. "This was in New York," Adrian said.

"My kind of town," the one in front sang.

"'Ass Chicago, you babooze," Kyle said.

"My mother was going to church in our town in upstate New York," Adrian said. "There was a haole guy who didn't want her to go."

"Ho, one whatchucall, revelation, brah. Get haoles in New York?"

"Well, all of them are. She went into the church, and this guy got up, came to the back, and asked her to leave."

The car raced along toward a darker area, down under huge trees. Adrian thought he recognized it. "My father was there," he went on, "and he said, 'You lay one hand on her and I'll kill you.'"

The two smoking the marijuana laughed until they coughed. Adrian recognized a cough from his phone call to Kyle. The driver had his head partway turned. "An' den?" he said.

"In the parking lot, she tried to say it was her right to go to their church, and the man just reached out and sort of pushed her toward our car. My father reached into the car and pulled out a .357 Magnum and shot him, but it was strange because he shot the front of his face off. I mean there were people out there who saw the jaw flip away from him and land on the blacktop of the parking lot, and people screamed and looked at it, all the teeth on the bottom still perfect, and you could see the fillings and everything. A big piece of tongue went in another direction. The guy's nose had flipped and was lying there. The other parts went this way and that, some of them landing on the ladies' dresses, and they looked down at the bits of teeth and tongue and stuff and screamed. He was on the ground dead, his forehead protruding way out and his face gone. My father got us into the car and we went home."

Silence. The car swept along. He began to see sky opening up and then, ahead of them on the left, mountains. He knew where they were. They were driving toward the North Shore.

"An' den?" the driver said.

"When we got home, my father realized that the cops would be coming for him, so he packed up some camping stuff and walked into the woods. He had the .357 with him, tucked in his belt. He's a survivalist, so he figured he'd just hide and then make his way out of the area."

Ocean. They were now passing ocean. Adrian could see the white breakers far out and, along the shoreline, openings here and there to the beach, and a few houses, and boulders by the side of the road. "I know you hate my father," he said to Kyle, "but I'll tell you the rest. He went into the woods. He had a cell phone, food, and the .357. Within about ten minutes, the men of the town were at our house, and then the cops. The place was crawling with cops, and they looked in the barn, all around the house. I told them they'd never find him. 'Which way did he go?' they asked. I pointed in the opposite direction."

"Oh, dis geteen dramatic, brah," Kyle said. He picked the lighter fluid up and popped it a couple more times.

The man in the front passenger seat laughed uncontrollably, maniacally, then wiped his eyes.

"It was near winter when this happened," Adrian said. He shifted to make his arms more comfortable and realized that he was sitting on the connecting rope. "They couldn't find him. He called home once, then we heard no more from him. I was there when they found him. Kind of a strange coincidence, but we were in the woods with some friends of my father's, to try to convince him to come out, because the folks in the town had discovered that the man who didn't want my mother in the church had been abusing little girls and videotaping them. After my father shot him, one of the girls had said that she was glad he was gone, and then when her mother asked why, the girl told her about the abuse. And it was corroborated by a doctor."

"'Corroborated?'" Kyle said. "You fucka, you talk so haole. I'm gonna poa dis shit in yoa mout' an' light um."

"In the meantime, my mother got sick. Cancer. I wanted to tell my father about it because she was dying."

The laughter that followed this was so loud and demented that Adrian shrunk against the door. These people were crazy. They would experiment first—slice him up, poke out his eyes, cut his limbs off—before they squirted him with the fluid and lit the match. He tried to remain calm, working over the story. "So we went into the woods, looking for him. A friend of mine is good at tracking, and—"

That set them off again. They writhed with laughter, unable to control themselves, except for the driver, who remained as angry and as cautious about his driving as he had been at first. It was as if he simply wanted to get the killing over with and the talk was getting in the way.

"By this time, people were saying, We gotta find the guy who shot that son of a bitch Cliff Parker. More girls had come forward to, like, testify about what he had done. It was fifteen of them in all. He had videotaped all these rapes and now the people were all thinking they wished *they'd* been the ones to shoot him. Anyway, I remember finding my father sitting against a tree, frozen solid. It turned out that he had been climbing in a gulley and the .357 had gone off and shot him in the groin, messed him up bad. We found him with his cell phone, a pack of cigarettes, and a lighter that had no fluid in it."

More laughter, and the can came up again, Kyle popping it before his face.

Adrian leaned toward the window, his forehead on the cold glass. Then Kyle punched him in the ribs hard, and the driver said, "I tol' you, no blood, goddammit! Stop movin' onna seats!"

"Yah, yah, 'kay, no blood. Jus' because of fuckin' seats. Fuck you. I like cut 'im up now."

The driver's jaw worked, his hands tight on the wheel. The man in the front turned and aimed his camera at Adrian. "Shithead," he said, "get anyting fo' say before you die?" Then he laughed, turned back, and began rolling another joint.

"Fuckin' cah seats," Kyle said. "Cannot hit da guy. Shit, it burns me up."

They cackled insanely again, and then the joint came over the top of the car seat.

Adrian slumped against the window, his ribs hurting, the soft vibration of the car buzzing the skin of his forehead. His throat stiffened, and he closed his eyes. He saw only one thing: Tenley hanging wash, her shoulders dimpling. Tenley in the green bathing suit, reaching up to hang wash, her shadow elongating on the grass. The car went over a bump, and he opened his eyes. Ahead he saw more water, a stretch where it came close to the road, and he could see more open space ahead. He felt the lump in his throat recede. He held his breath, understanding what he had to do. There wasn't any other choice. He was going to have to throw himself out of the car.

The man next to him was drawing on the joint. Adrian wormed his fists along his hips until he felt the rope under his thighs, and experimentally he drew his right knee up and tried to get his foot over the rope. Just when he thought his leg would cramp from being folded, he felt the rope go under. He raised the other knee, remaining hunched against the door, his head on the window. When that foot went through without anyone's noticing, he said, "I'm gonna be sick."

"Get sick den, assho," Kyle said.

The driver turned his head around to look at Adrian and slowed the car down.

"I'm gonna throw up," Adrian said. He jammed his fists against his sides, the rope across his lap. Kyle didn't notice anything. "I swear, I'm gonna puke. Another few seconds." Ahead he could see the roadside, then rocks, a tree down below them, and the water.

"Open da window," the man in the front said. "Open um. No wan' da seats fucked up, brah. Open da goddam window, ah?"

A car sped past, going the other way.

The window slid down, sending a blast of salty, humid air into Adrian's face. He put his head out, his fists still at his sides, looked ahead, and then gagged as loud as he could. Signpost, rocks, then an open area where the car could pull off. The car slowed, the driver probably thinking that speed and vomit didn't mix. Adrian's heart was slamming, his body trembling, almost numb, because he realized he could not do it. The open area was passing and he couldn't do it. If they set him on fire, he had no say in it, but this—

He grabbed the door sill and pulled himself out, his knees banging the padded part under the window so that he went over in the air and came down on his buttocks and the heels of his hands, the air blasted from his lungs, and he tumbled again, the hard dirt scraping his spine, his hip, and right shoulder. He slid into tufts of grass and down onto sand. He tried to make himself move, but he was numb, his legs refusing to obey him, and he breathed deeply, aware of the sound of the car spinning its wheels, pebbles hitting fenders. Then he heard other sounds that he realized were his own moans. He pulled himself down the sand, feeling his legs waking up, and then his hands felt water and stung. He kept crawling into the water and then was afloat, his knees hitting rocks on the bottom. He felt the sting of the salt all over his body. When he turned to look back, he saw the profile of the car on the bank and the three men coming down to the sand. He tried to move further away, but something caught the rope between his wrists and he could not get it off. He simply floated there, keeping his head out of the water. He felt too tired to do anything else. Then he laughed, because they couldn't set him on fire.

The men were yelling at each other on the sand, but Adrian couldn't understand what they were saying. They were not yelling at him, and they were not coming into the water. "I sick of dis shit!" someone yelled. "Now look what happened, you fucka!"

"Leave 'im den. Fuck 'im."

"No!"

"You fucken chicken. You fag. You no can do um, ah? Like you no like do anyting else, ah? I sick of you, 'ass what. Go die."

"Fuck you!"

"Pussy. I kick yoa ass."

Then they were fighting. Two appeared to be punching a third, and then the third fell back and onto the sand. "Yeah," one said, "you stay hea, you bum, you fuckin' bum." Then the two others went up the bank, got in the Mercedes, and pulled onto the road, spinning tires in the dirt. The man left behind stood up and threw a handful of sand after them. "Goddamn stoopit! Stoopit!" He threw more sand. "I hate dis! I hate it!" Then he roared, facing the street and the mountains.

Adrian felt under water to see if he could find where the rope was caught. It was caught on a hook attached to a hollow tile brick. He eased the rope out of the hook and turned to work his way farther out. He heard splashing behind him as if someone were wading through the shallow water. Then he felt hands on his shoulders.

"Hol' um," the voice said. "Hang on, brah."

Adrian was too tired to struggle. The pain in his shoulder, back, knees, and hands was so great that it now hurt to move.

"C'mon, come back. Wait, lemme get da rope." Sitting in the water up to his chest, Adrian held his fists out, and the guy began fiddling with the knots. Adrian shivered, the breeze off the ocean cooling his shirt.

"Who are you? You were driving. Who are you?"

"Kyle."

"I thought the guy next to me was Kyle."

"No, 'ass Derek. Wait." He kept fiddling with the rope, and Adrian felt his left wrist go free, then the right. Kyle threw the rope up toward the beach so that it pinwheeled in the air, the light from a streetlamp briefly making the drops look like tiny shooting stars.

"Come up da beach," Kyle said. "You bleedeen."

"I don't know if I got any broken bones." He tried standing up. "Maybe not," he said. He walked slowly, the resistance of the water on his lower legs reassuring.

"Easy," Kyle said. "No step on rocks. I help you." Kyle supported him. "We go up by da light an' see. I tink you ripped up."

Adrian walked up on the sand, his knees and left hip stinging and the heels of his hands feeling strange, as if hunks of flesh had detached from them. He saw that his left hand had lost a layer of skin, and the other had thin lines, like slits, across the base of the thumb and the heel. He made his way up the bank to the gritty roadside, trembling from the cold, his shirt plastered to his skin, his feet hurting from pebbles. Kyle was already up, looking one way down the road, then the other. "I wonda if dose fuckas come back," he said. Then he put his hand on his face. "Ho, sore jaw tomorrow."

Adrian was still shaking. The spots on his body that hurt seemed to be tightening up, and his breath halted in his throat. He felt sick to his stomach and fought off a wave of nausea.

"'Kay," Kyle said, "one light up da shtreet. We go an' I look at dat, 'kay?"

Adrian followed Kyle, walking gingerly along the roadside, the pebbles digging into the bottoms of his bare feet. He had to call Tenley. She would think that he had decided to leave and had chosen the time he was supposed to be watching Jacob. Ahead, the streetlamp threw a large circle of light on the road and illuminated high weeds at the edge of a field. Directly under the light sat a sparse hedge fronting a house with no lights on. Kyle walked around behind Adrian and pulled the shirt away from his shoulder. "Shit," Kyle said, "'ass bad. Dat gotta be sewed up."

"I should go home. I gotta call someone."

"No, 'ass gotta be sewed up. One big flap skin. Look ugly. We wait. Somebody come by, we go Kahuku. Got one hospital."

"Okay." Adrian stood there, still shaking a little, but his stomach felt better now. "What happened?"

Kyle walked around in front of him, scowling. In the better light, Adrian got his first clear look at him. He was Adrian's height and had black hair parted in the middle. He was what Tenley would call hapa. "Is all booshit," he said. "Derek— Shit, I don't know."

"He was the one I talked to on the phone."

"Yah, I was inna room too. He kept looking at me, waving his hands around, and I was like, What the hell you want? So what if it's him? Say what you want. And he keeps talking, den hangs up and tells what you said."

Headlight beams bounced above the road, coming from the east. Kyle stepped closer to the edge and waited until the cars, three of them, went by, ignoring his waving hand. "'Kay," he called, "mahalos to you too, brah."

Then he walked back to Adrian. "Anyway," he said, "it was one of those things. We sit around and drink beer, we talk, Derek keeps saying, 'His dad wen' kill yoa dad,' over and over. Was about drugs. Then we take some drugs, you know, stoke up the pipe. I hated it. At that time I was off that shit for almos' a year. But Derek, he pushes and pushes. So I'm sitting there and I try to remember my dad. Then Derek keeps saying, Fucken haole—you gotta pay back, man, and I'm sitting and it comes slow like, I gotta pay back. We get Doug Vierra too. His faddah have all kine troubles because of this thing with Ray Branch. I never want to, but I keep it up with the pipe until I say, Yeah, we kill dat fuckah, and then Derek is repeating me all you said and how you said it, and he says, Da guy not right. He's not right—I'd watch my ass if I was you. Get him before he gets you. Give me da creeps—dis self-defense, brah. So it was the self-defense that turned it. At least until I saw you in the car. I shoulda known. Den I'm thinkin' maybe dis one joke. We jus' scare you is all. But Derek—" He shook his head. "These guys are creeps and I don't know why I hang around with them. Derek thought that killing you would be cool, like he's all, 'Hey, someteen we no do yet. What goes around comes around,' and all like that. 'This is legal, brah. We can do um an' settle the score.' At first I tried to tell him I didn't want to kill nobody. But he calls me pussy an' all like that. The dope takes over too. After a while I'm thinking, Yeah, let's go kill da fucka. And then we're driving by, an' Derek, dat stupid asshole, pokes the .22 out the window and lets off." Kyle looked at Adrian with a baffled expression. "But why? We used to beat up haole boys at school, we break in houses, we do all kine shit, even do what we did wit' you—kidnap um, beat um up. But I *finished* with that. What the hell do I care who killed my father? The guy was a prick as far as I know. All it takes is some dope, and you can do stuff you hate yourself for. It's stupid. The whole thing is bullshit."

"That story I told you about my father was bullshit too," Adrian said. "He's still alive. My mother's dead."

"You made that up? That jaw thing?"

"Yeah. The call was made up too. It was just to scare you, I guess. So Doug Vierra is related to a guy I talked to a while ago, an old man who lives with Mildred Vierra."

"Uncle. His faddah dead now couple years. Millie dead too, las' year."

"She's dead? Why didn't he tell me that?"

Kyle shrugged.

In the distance, Adrian saw the blue point of a police car light. They watched it approach, the beams faintly illuminating the weeds on the other side of the road. When it got closer, he said, "Let's just fade back by this hedge."

Kyle moved back to the hedge. Adrian followed, hobbling on his bare feet. They both moved around behind the hedge, and the car went by. Then they moved back out under the light again. "Brah, that was dumb," Kyle said. "They'd've taken you to the clinic."

"Maybe it would be better if we didn't involve them."

Kyle looked at the red pinpoints under the blue speck in the distance. "Yeah, maybe we should have a story."

"I fell off a truck."

"'Kay."

"I mean, these guys gave me a ride on like a flatbed truck, right? So I told them I'd just jump off at a stop sign or something. The little window in the back of the cab was blocked by a— Was blocked by a refrigerator tied there. We went over some kind of a bump and I fell off."

"'Kay."

"They never knew I fell off. They probably figured I jumped off when they slowed down somewhere. You came along. You were, uh, jogging?"

"Jog? I don't jog, but 'kay." Kyle laughed. "Air tight," he said. "But I still fucked it up." He shook his head, looking up the road. "Almost get there and den I fuck it up. Shit, you shoulda seen me the night Derek shot the .22. I was watching television all in a sweat, waiting for them to come on and say somebody is shot. One drive-by shooting in Waimānalo. Later—day, two days, whatevers—I drive over and look to see if you're still there. No. I go again, an' again I no see you. Den I saw you, an' shit did I ever heave what they call one huge sigh of relief."

"Did you steal the car?"

"Nah, Derek an' Doug. Dey pick me up, tol' me nobody home, so nobody knows the car gone. Dey come over, give me some crystal. I hate it, but I do it anyway, promise myself I'll never do it again, but I'm already a little high, an' I think, the seats are worth fifteen hundred dollars. Maybe just this one last time I cash in. So stupid. Firs' time I'm doing something real, you know? An' then all this."

"Did you guys set the fire?"

"No, that had to be one what? Short circuit or something."

"What are you doing that's real?"

"Golf."

"Really?"

"Yeah, play golf, get one good job at a pro shop, and now they're gonna let me teach. Kids first, and then adults. Big bucks. Yeah, I play golf. Good, too."

Another car came from the east. Kyle stood out on the edge of the road and waited until it was close, and then he waved. It was a small pick-up truck, a slightly better version of Fujimura's. The truck pulled off the road, and the doors opened. The men who got out looked to Adrian as menacing as anyone could look: large, beefy men who had brush cuts and wore slippers, shorts, and tank tops stretching over their huge trunks. Kyle talked to them, and they walked over to Adrian. Both were local—Hawaiian, Adrian guessed.

"Eh," the bigger of the two said and walked around behind Adrian. "Lemme see," he said, and Adrian felt the shirt being pulled. "Ho, wide open brah. But is not detached. Get all kine shit eensai. 'Kay, we take you Kahuku so you can get help, 'kay? You fell off one truck?"

"Yeah, I don't think the guys even know."

"What, you from mainlan'?"

"Yeah, upstate New York."

"No being nosy," the other guy said, "but what is one touris' from New York doeen falleen off one truck way da hell out hea?"

"You got me," Adrian said.

"You was onna wrong tour, ah?"

"I think so."

The bigger of the two went to the truck and came back with a plastic bottle of water and a towel. "Brah, I squirt wattah on dat hole an' wrap um inna towel, 'kay? Gonna sting."

"The towel'll get blood on it," Adrian said.

"You want flies an' shit on dat? Get pebbles an' dirt. Come, on'y one towel, you know."

He turned Adrian around, and the water hit the wound,

feeling cold and abrasive and making him shiver. Then it ran down into his shorts. The man pressed on the wound with the towel, draped one end over his shoulder, passed part of it out at Adrian's waist, and put the other end over his shoulder. "Hol' um tight, 'kay? Come, we go clinic."

They made him sit in the cab. The bigger of the two men sat in the bed of the truck with Kyle and some spackling-crusted buckets and fishing rods. The driver told Adrian to lean forward—"da seat filthy 'ass why,"—and when he pulled out onto the two-lane highway, the little bumps the truck went over shot a deep, heavy pain into Adrian's hip.

Then the man said, "In New York, you guys feesh?"

"Yeah, people do. Trout."

"Trout ono. We buy um Safeway."

"There are streams up there, and you can see them in the water, you know, black on top and silver on the sides." The truck went over a bump, and Adrian gritted his teeth.

"Sorry," the man said. "But anyway, 'ass like ulua. Look black from above, silver like one blazing light from da side. Āholehole too."

"And we have bass-type fish in lakes. I never ate one of those. Mostly we hunted up there."

"We hunt wild peeg."

"Really?"

"Yah, dakine wit' da tusk?"

"Somebody told me they were here. They still are?"

"Yah, plenny. Waimānalo, da Ko'olaus, odda range too. Meat tase shtrong but."

The conversation went this way: "How do you hunt pigs?" "What do you mean 'he'e'?" "'Ass octopus? Ho, tase ono. Try do poke an' mix um wit' kimchee sauce." "What's that?" "Da sauce in kimchee. What house you fixing up? Waimānalo you said? Chee, sound like Chip Soares. Dat name ring one bell?" "No, this man's name is Fujimura." "Oh, mus' be anodda house den, but if you like fix house, try Chip Soares. He cannot because get haht problems and li'dat."

The men dropped Adrian and Kyle off at the entry of the hospital's emergency room. Before leaving, they shook hands, the two of them very gently with Adrian, and the driver of the truck said, "You take care, 'kay?"

"Stay offa trucks, 'kay?" the other said. "Take da bus."

Sitting in the waiting room, Adrian admitted to Kyle that he had a problem with reading and writing, and Kyle helped him fill out the form. After that, he got some loose change from Kyle and tried calling Tenley, but the line was busy. While they waited, Adrian had a weird swoon and then found himself giggling, and then laughing. Kyle leaned out from his chair and looked at him. "What, you goeen pupule on me?"

"No," he said. "I just can't understand this. You were supposed to want to kill me, and you don't. Two of the meanest guys I ever saw come up the road in a truck and turn out to be two of the nicest guys I ever met. I went out a car window." He lowered his voice. "Now I'm sitting here with you, and those two guys you were with—they're out in a Mercedes."

"Fuck um," Kyle said. "We leaving guys like dat behind. I finished wit dem. They can blow their brains out with drugs, fuck demselves up all dey want. I won't be seeing um for a while. Maybe never. 'Ass why it good you tell that story about falling off the truck. You save my ass. Now I back at the beginning. They let me do lessons, an' 'ass the first step."

"Me too. I'm on my first step."

They sat. After a while, Adrian said, "You know, you don't hafta stay here. I'll figure out how to get back."

"I go work tomorrow," Kyle said uncertainly, as if apologizing.

"You got a way home?"

"I call my braddah. Find out if you okay, den call. He get work tomorrow too, so he stay home now, no problem. I wait till dis finished, an' he can take us both home, 'kay?"

They sat. Then Kyle said, "What's dis first step you're on?"

Restoring houses, Adrian said. He explained what he was doing at Fujimura's, then described the house in the woods back in New York. Kyle sat there frowning, as if he wasn't sure what the value of this step was, but after a while, he began nodding, "Yah, I get dat, I get dat. You mean like why pay for one new house when you can fix up an ol' one so it look new? Make sense." Then Adrian explained the carving of the fist and paddle, and Kyle nodded through that, too, and when he was done, Kyle said, "So I look for dat big fist in one bank, ah? When I go cash my check from doing golf lessons."

"You got it."

Adrian was in the doctor's small examining room for forty-five minutes, lying on his stomach while the doctor cleaned out the wound on the back of his shoulder and then sitting up so that he could look at the others. "How you did not break a bone falling off this truck is a miracle," he said. "This contusion on your okole is deep, but aside from having a little trouble sitting down for a while, you'll be okay. The heel pads of your hands aren't seriously injured, though the left one isn't going to feel good for a while because the injury is effectively like a deep blister, which will heal itself. Your knees aren't bad, considering. The back of your head is all right now that I got the pebble out. You'll need no more than a tetanus shot, and I have samples I can give you of a one-a-day antibiotic, but you have to remember to take all of the tablets. I can also prescribe painkillers." "I don't need painkillers," Adrian told him. "I feel all right. How do I pay for this?" The doctor said that the address written on the form would receive a complete bill. "Just get a follow-up appointment for, let's see, four days from now."

Adrian left the small room with his right palm bandaged and with what felt like a small pillow taped to his shoulder. The receptionist wrote down the appointment on a card and gave it to him. "To remove the stitches and check on the wound," she said.

Kyle's brother was named Chris, and if there were any strange feelings about giving a ride to the son of the murderer of his father, Adrian couldn't find evidence of them. If anything, Chris Montross seemed very much in control of his life, and accepted the inconvenience of giving his brother a ride without any irritation at all. Adrian sat in the back and watched the dark trees and houses sweep by. The conversation seemed more like one between father and son, Chris asking Kyle what had happened and Kyle telling his brother the whole story. "So he told the doctor the story about falling off the truck, then," Chris said. "Yah yah yah," Kyle said. Chris turned in the seat as he drove and said to Adrian, "Eh, thanks for getting my babooze of a brother off the hook." Then he said to Kyle, "'Kay, you hanging with them tomorrow?" "No, no chance—really, I swear." "You made one fricken gem of a mistake you know." "I know I know I know." "How you going get one titanium golf set?" "I know I know I know. I work for um. I know. I know that."

The brothers dropped Adrian off in Fujimura's driveway. Kyle leaned out and said, "'Kay, when I need my house fixed up, I come get you."

"Okay, when I want golf lessons . . ."

"Same same," Kyle said. "Take care. I sorry about the whole thing, really."

"Don't worry about it. It ended up being kind of fun."

"Anyting, you know. You got my number."

"Thanks."

Then they were gone. Adrian stood there and watched the car go around the corner. Then he turned and walked toward the house. He was halfway down the driveway when Tenley came out.

Adrian spent the next half hour explaining everything to her. The story shook her more than he had thought it would. What would have happened if he had broken his neck, or if he hadn't jumped from the car? Would they have burned him? He thought maybe not, because of Kyle. He told her that Kyle was one of those people trying to make their way over the line, just the way he and Tenley were, for no other reason than that it was time to do it. But the story scared her. He could tell that she had been crying and asked her why. She said she thought that he had decided to bag the whole thing and that she had been scammed after all. She checked all his wounds, looked at the bruise high on his buttock, tried peeking under the wad of bandages on his shoulder.

"So all I am is sore," he said. "I mean, after all that, all I am is sore. We're okay now. So we just keep going where we left off."

She thought a moment, then shook her head. "Well, not here," she said. "My mom's moving in with Mr. Carter, and he's decided to sell this place."

"All right," Adrian said. "So he's selling. We just keep going where we left off." He felt a peculiar, airy sensation, almost like exultation.

"We have to get some other place," she said. "Where we can take Jacob. Mr. Fujimura has relatives, kids, and grandkids. We have to take care of Jacob."

"All right, so we will, and we keep going where we left off."

That night, Adrian lay in bed on his stomach, and the contact of his knees on the sheet kept him awake. From time to time he dozed, aware of the warmth of Tenley's body next to his. Then he woke up. It didn't matter that Carter was selling the house. He would continue working on it anyway. It would increase the value of the house, and he didn't care if Carter paid him any extra. He also decided to get back to the fist and paddle. If he couldn't work on the house once it was sold, then he would finish the fist and sell it. He tried to pull himself into a sitting position. "Oh boy," he whispered. The pain and stiffness were so bad that he could barely move.

In the morning, he sat outside at the picnic table with Tenley. Mr. Fujimura and Jacob were in the house watching television. Tenley had told them the story. Adrian was sore, his left hip flashing with pain with each step, and the heels of his hands were so tender that he couldn't hold anything heavier than a cup of coffee. Tenley scanned through the ad section of the newspaper, looking for rentals. "Nope, no, no to dat too. Too much."

"What about some remote place, you know, where they'd be cheaper?"

"I like dis remote place," she said, not looking up from the paper. "I can borrow money from Mom maybe, at least for the first month. You gotta pay a whole month down on these."

"I can get a job, too."

"No, you do your art thing. You restore houses. That's your thing."

He thought, Okay, if that's what my thing is, then I'll do that.

A black Thunderbird with a blue light on top drove down the street, followed by a blue-and-white police car. Tenley looked up from the paper, then back down. Adrian felt a familiar agitation at seeing the police and then remembered that he had done nothing wrong for a long time. But the cars pulled off the street and stopped in front of the house. "What's this?" Adrian asked.

"I don't know," Tenley said.

"Look," he said, "if they ask about a Mercedes or about Kyle Montross, or any of that, you don't know and I don't know. I fell off a truck, okay?"

"Right," she said. "What about the rip-off of the bag? At the hotel that night."

The driver's door of the Thunderbird opened and a man in civilian clothes got out. A uniformed policeman got out of the other side. The policewoman in the blue-and-white stayed in her car. The men consulted a piece of paper on a clipboard and then walked into the driveway. When they saw Tenley and Adrian, they nodded, and the one in uniform said, "Hello there."

"Hi," Tenley said.

"I'm Officer Park," he said. "This is Officer Martin. We're looking for an Adrian Branch."

Adrian raised his bandaged hand. The policemen looked at him for a few seconds, and the uniformed one said, "You've been in an accident?"

"Yeah," he said, "I fell off a truck."

The men nodded, and Officer Martin squinted at the piece of paper on the clipboard, which reflected sunlight onto his face. "Come in the shade," Tenley said. Officer Martin continued standing, and Officer Park sat at the table across from Adrian. "Mr. Branch," he said, "we're here to try to verify the manner of a death."

Adrian suddenly felt weak. So those idiots had done something with the car. Tenley looked at him in confusion, then said, "What death?"

"Could we speak to you alone?" Officer Martin said.

"Is it all right if she stays?" Adrian asked.

The two policemen glanced at each other. "Well, I think that would be all right," Officer Martin said. He looked again at the paper on the clipboard. "This involves the death of a Rose M. Branch."

"She did die," Adrian said, "about two months ago."

"It's the manner of death we're here to verify," he said. He looked up at Officer Park, his expression perplexed and doubtful, as if he did not like what he was doing. "We have a report here, actually an inquiry, from Utica, New York."

"No," Adrian said. "Something happened. My father? What happened?"

The man sighed. "The report says that a body was discovered."

"Whose body?"

"A Rose M. Branch. You are her son?"

"Yes."

He looked up at Officer Park, who nodded.

"Would you like to know the circumstances?" Officer Martin asked.

"Yes, I would."

He sighed and looked at the report. "A man with a sick dog found a human finger in the—the dog's vomit. He took his dogs out, followed them, and discovered that they had dug down to a human body and had been—had been more or less feeding on it."

Adrian stared. He couldn't speak. He began to shake, then felt Tenley's hand on his upper thigh. "I know the dogs," he said. "I know the dogs."

"The authorities in Utica are looking into these circumstances," Officer Martin said. "The body was removed and an autopsy was performed, and the results were that Mrs. Branch had died from her illness. Utica wanted to determine if there was any foul play, and they came to the conclusion that there was not. At this time, they're looking into what other questions need to be addressed in connection with the disposal of the body, that is, the particular manner of its disposal and the question of the law."

"I buried her," Adrian said. "She asked me to. She told me to take the braid—"

"Braid?"

Adrian looked at Tenley. She turned to the two policemen. "There was nothing wrong with what he did," she said. "Nothing. It's a long story and you ought to hear him out, because there's absolutely nothing wrong with what he did. If you do anything—" She stopped.

Officer Martin was shaking his head, one hand up. "The report we have recommends nothing more than that we verify the manner of death," he said. "We're not here to take anybody away or do anything, okay?"

"Somebody'll come up with something, right?" Tenley said. Then she waved her hands at them. "I'm sorry, I didn't really mean that. You should hear him out."

And so they listened. It took Adrian around fifteen minutes to give them a detailed description of what happened so that they appeared satisfied. At the end of his explanation, Tenley said, "The braid is buried in a secret place. No one is to ever find out where it's buried. I won't tell you, he won't tell you, nobody'll ever tell anybody. Nobody."

"Miss," Officer Park said, "we won't even ask. We know why it's where it is."

"Do you *really* know?"

"I do," he said. "We both grew up here. We know."

Officer Martin said, "There's the question of what to do with the remains of the deceased."

"I think cremation," Adrian said.

"There's a Raymond Branch, her husband. He would be the one to decide."

"If you can find him," Adrian said. "I don't know where he is, but I'll sign anything or do anything that makes it legal to cremate her."

"Well, we'll wait for word from Utica," he said. "There may need to be no more than an interview. Maybe this morning will do. It depends."

"When you said that the dog had been, you know, feeding on her," Adrian said, "did they say what part— I mean, did—"

"There weren't details about the condition of the body," the man said.

"You don't need to know," Tenley said. "She's not there anyway. She's here."

"She's here," Adrian said. He pictured her wrapped in the sheet, and then pictured the black coil of the braid in the hole in Mālaekahana, the seeping water under it. "She said she wanted to be here," he said.

"Is there a phone number where we can reach you?" Officer Park asked.

"Call the Subway in Enchanted Lake," Tenley said. "I work there. You can leave a message. We have to leave this place soon, but if you need Adrian, I'll pass the message on."

"All right," Officer Martin said. Then he thought a moment. "About this braid," he said. "I'm just curious. Would you have come out here if she—I mean, was the reason for coming here only to bury it?"

"Yeah. Otherwise I would have stayed." Officer Martin looked toward the ocean, then nodded.

After they left, Adrian and Tenley sat in silence for a few moments, Adrian staring at the table. He felt numb, as if the information the police had brought to him had placed him alone in some arid, vacant place, and he had no idea what to do next. Tenley looked at him, then said, "I can bag work today."

"No, that's all right."

"I don't think you should worry about it."

"I won't. I'll try to ignore it."

"And I gotta pack up my junk."

He was in the back room, helping her, rolling the glass case of paddling medals in an old shirt, putting stuff in boxes, when she opened a box that had dried-up tape on it. From the box she drew out a Polaroid camera. "From high school," she said. She fiddled with it and looked at the lens, and it flashed. "Holy shit," she said. Then she stared at the camera, blinking, as it began to grind away, the picture coming out of the bottom like a pale tongue. "Wait a minute," she said, studying the fuzzy, inverted picture of her own face as it slowly materialized. "I've got an idea."

VIII

"You put these in the mailboxes of houses," she told him. "You wanna get one job, you advertise, 'kay?" The flyer was done in color and had a picture of Mr. Fujimura's house that was taken from the best angle and that showed a clean, nearly finished roof, the old section in the back lumpy and faded. The wall along the driveway was green and had white window frames, orchids lining the lattice of the crawl space. She had taken the picture with her Polaroid and had the flyer made in Kailua. At the top were large block letters that said, "Low Cost Restoration – Don't Tear Um Down, Fix Um Up."

"All it'll take," she said, "is cruising Kailua in Mr. Fujimura's truck and looking for the most beat-up houses, assuming that some of them are owner-occupied. In the meantime, you work on the fist and paddle." And so that's what he did, working in little bits, his hands still not healed. "I'll make calls to see if any of the canoe clubs like buy," she said. "How much?" he asked. "Say, two thousand dollars, maybe more." He shrugged and went on with the work, not believing that anyone would pay that much for it.

It was true that Mr. Fujimura had relatives, but he was able to conclude, after letting them know of his situation, that help would not be coming from them. Tenley found an unfurnished three-bedroom, one-bath house in Kailua for a thousand a month, utilities not included. She had to borrow five hundred dollars from her mother, who came over to see the new house. Things were okay between her and Frank Carter. In fact, she said, they were going to Las Vegas for a while, and she and Frank had hosted a meeting of Ku I Ka Niʻo at their apartment. Frank, she told Tenley, was a little more receptive than any of them had assumed.

Mr. Fujimura had a small income as did Jacob, and they pooled their money along with a large part of Tenley's salary and came up with enough for the rent. "See?" she said to Adrian, "dis how people live." The two old men spent much of their time under a mango tree in the yard, sitting at the picnic table. Mr. Fujimura had all the instructions on what to do if Jacob showed any signs of a relapse.

So Adrian worked on the fist and paddle-handle while Tenley worked at Subway, and when she came home, smelling of bread and salami and vinegar, they would get in the truck and go to all the places they had left flyers, knocking on doors and inquiring if the occupants were interested in restoration.

After a week and a half of this, Adrian told her that it wasn't going to work. They'd been turned down by the fifteenth house.

"Yes, it is," she said. "No worry."

But after two weeks, even her optimism began to fade. The fist was nearly done, and Adrian had completed all sorts of work on their rental simply because it needed it. "Selling coconuts worked better than this," he said, after being turned down again.

"You wanna sell coconuts?" she asked. The tone of her voice was flat, almost angry, and he flushed and shook his head. "Go sell coconuts den," she said, pulling the old truck off the street.

"All right," he said, "no coconuts."

Four weeks. They cruised the streets again, having planted more flyers. "Dis one," she said.

"Did we put a flyer here? I don't remember putting a flyer here."

"Trus' me," she said.

The place was a mess. The canopy of a large tree created open areas of bare dirt, littered with grimy, sun-bleached windsurfing equipment and the fenders of old cars. In the carport was a partly reconstructed two-seater MG and, beyond that, another car. The walls of the house were an odd tannish-brown color, as if it were covered with oil or some bad shellac. Everything was stained with grime and mildew.

Tenley knocked on the screen door, and a fat Caucasian man answered, remaining inside the house. Adrian heard sounds of a TV game show and the squawks of birds.

"What?" he asked.

Tenley launched into her speech: "We left a flyer describing our service and came to discuss your situation, the walls of the house"—she leaned away to look—"covered with some odd material that does nothing to enhance the beauty of your home. Are you the homeowner?"

The man's wife, an Oriental woman with what looked like twice as much hair as was natural, appeared behind him. "Yes, we're the homeowner," she said.

Her husband shook his head and muttered something. He cleared his throat. "We don't need anything done right now," he said.

"The fuck we don't," his wife said. "I tol' you get dat fucken siding up lashyear."

Adrian cleared his throat.

"My back doesn't permit me to put the fucking siding up," the man said, carefully enunciating each word. Then he smiled at Adrian. "That is what the problem is," he said amiably.

"We can do it for you," Tenley said. The woman looked at Tenley, opened the door, and came out. "You no goin' up any laddah, sistah," she said.

Tenley put her hand on her stomach. "He does that," she said, pointing at Adrian. "I— How can you tell?"

"I can tell," the lady said, walking toward the corner of the house. "Come."

"We don't need work done!" the man called out. His wife turned and held her middle finger up at him.

Along the side of the house was a huge pile of white vinyl siding, blackened by mildew and toppled on the dirt, one end of the pile fanning away into mud. There were also corner caps, mounting strips, bent aluminum flashing, and rusted cans of paint. The woman's husband came around the corner. She said to him, "You put dis onna walls, nail heah, nail o'dea. That's the problem, right?"

"It's not that simple," the man said.

"How much you cost?" the woman asked.

"That depends," Tenley said.

"So that stuff on the wall is the preparation, right?" Adrian asked. He touched it, and it felt vaguely sticky. It was plastered with dead leaves and feathers.

"Yah, is butt-ugly too, yah?" the woman said.

"So all you need done is the siding," Adrian said.

"That's seventeen fifty an hour," Tenley said.

"What?" the man said. "Why that? Why not seventeen, or eighteen?"

"I don't know," Tenley said.

"You do um fifteen," the woman said. "'Kay?"

"Okay," Adrian said.

"So there's a contract, right? And taxes? Excise tax?" the man said.

"Uh, we don't mess with taxes," Tenley said.

The woman looked at her husband. "Hah, fo' once we no geev da fuckas dat, ah?"

The man's head wobbled if he were dizzy. "I suppose," he said. "For once."

"You goeen breas' feed?" the woman asked Tenley.

"I don't know." Then she thought. "Well, maybe I will."

"You mus' breas' feed," the woman said. "I get a shitload of stoffs eensai tell you how fo' breas' feed. An' plus, breas' fed babies-get higher IQs."

"For real?" Tenley said.

"Garans," she said. "They did one study."

"Who did the study?" the husband asked.

"Who da fuck care who did da study? *They! They* did one study. I seen um TV."

"Very well," he said dryly.

"An' I wan' dat fricken tree out too," she went on. "You do tree trim too?"

"Yup," Adrian said. "Which tree?"

"You will notice we are standing on dirt, in the shade," the man said carefully. "It would follow that it is the tree we are under. Do you see the connection?"

The tree's canopy covered the house and most of the yard. The trunk was five feet in diameter, with massive, perfectly tubular branches going out from about twelve feet up. "Is one monkey pod," the woman said. "I like grass, I wan' one lawn, like aftah twenny-five fricken years."

"That is expensive," the man said.

"Fifteen an hour," Tenley said.

"Hauling fees make it more, I assume."

"No, 'ass free," Tenley said.

It dawned on Adrian that they could keep the wood. And he thought, Holy shit. There's enough there for half a lifetime's work.

"So how do we pay?" the man asked. "When?"

"I'll come tomorrow at, say, nine and work eight hours. That's a hundred twenty dollars at fifteen an hour. If you like what's done by the time the day's over, then you can give me the money. If you don't like what's done, then you can fire me at . . . let's see. Well, make it at no cost, okay?"

"Ho, 'ass one deal," the woman said. Then she turned to Tenley. "Come, I show you breas'-feeding stuffs an' you can meet my birds, 'kay? Also get pitchas my kids too. Dey in college mainlan'." Then she stopped, gasped, and slapped her forehead. "Ho, serious mento problem. I get one playpen! An one crib! I give you dat too, 'kay?"

"That would be great," Tenley said, and they went into the house.

Adrian was left standing with the man. After an awkward silence, Adrian said, "You restore cars."

"I restore cars."

After another silence, Adrian said, "So all this is okay with you," and he waved at the pile of siding. "I mean, it's all right."

The man snorted.

"You know, the siding will create an air space," Adrian said. "It'll make your house cooler."

The man nodded, looking at the pile of siding.

"Look nicer too, I guess," Adrian said.

After a long silence, the man said, "I guess."

Tenley wanted to distribute flyers in Waimānalo. And there was the man that the guy in the truck had mentioned to Adrian on the way to Kahuku. "What was that name? I think it was Chip something," Adrian said. Tenley drove past the polo field into the beach section of Waimānalo and turned into Mr. Fujimura's street. "We might put one in the mailbox of the old house, yeah?" she said. "I can write a note saying we can finish the job cheap."

"I can't get to it until I finish the siding and do the tree," he said.

"Whatevahs," she said. "We advertise anyway, 'kay?" She looked ahead toward the corner, where there were trucks parked in front of Fujimura's driveway. "You schedule times for the work, 'kay, and you—"

Fujimura's house was not there. Tenley pulled off to the side of the street, almost as if made dizzy by what they saw: a massive pink house built in the manner of a Mediterranean villa, or maybe a small castle, two stories high, with a third, smaller floor perched on top, above the driveway. In the center of the second floor, there was a half circle of glass bricks twenty feet across. The driveway was made with huge flagstones, bordered by immense, bullet-shaped concrete posts, and the workers were encircling the entire yard with a six-foot-high wall made of wood framing and chicken-wire covered with concrete that they were troweling on. There were smaller, bullet-shaped posts every twenty feet. The second-floor roof was encircled by a veranda with large, concrete urns decorated with reliefs of grapes and running maidens. The roof was blue tile. The front door was more than ten feet high and made of heavy wood with ornate brass fittings. Adrian stared at it, and the only thing he could think of to say was, "What did they do with the house?"

"The cannons and the guards go on the second floor," Tenley said, staring too. "But where does the papaya tree go?"

Adrian laughed. "Yeah, where does the papaya tree go?"

"'Kayden," she said. "Let's bag this. We gotta go get a chainsaw."

"What for?"

She stared at the house, then turned to him. "What, you think you can cut a monkey pod tree with a hand saw? Get real."

Adrian sat up in the cool, humid darkness. He thought there had been some sound in their room, a furtive, whispering movement, and he sat very still, listening. It was as if someone were in there, moving around, and had stopped once he'd sat up, a presence that was secretive and even mischievous, waiting for him to put his head back down. He had been dreaming, he remembered, of feeding chunks of wood into a fire, and then the sound had awakened him. He listened because he could not convince himself that he had been mistaken. He decided that whatever was in the room posed no threat. He flexed his fingers because they were sore and thick, the skin calloused and partly numb, the joints tight and stiff. A rooster crowed, the tail end of its call truncated by a grinding squawk, and he looked at the clock radio, which read three fifteen. He listened to the silence. Tenley asked a garbled, high-pitched question in her sleep and answered herself in an equally nonsensical way. Then the rooster crowed again.